ENGAÑO

A DEWITT AGENCY ADVENTURE

A NOVEL BY
LANCE CHARNES

WOMBAT GROUP MEDIA — ORANGE, CALIFORNIA

Wombat Group Media
Post Office Box 4908
Orange, CA 92863
https://www.wombatgroup.com/

First Printing September 2021

ISBN 978-1-7333989-3-0

For Betty

Who often wonders what I'm

up to when I'm writing

Engaño Cast of Characters

The DeWitt Agency

- Carson / Tarasenko / Lara / Larochka: *Former Toronto Police Service detective sergeant; associate #126 at the DeWitt Agency*
  - Lisa Carson: *One of Carson's cover identities*
  - Ron Carson: *Carson's ex-husband, a TPS inspector*

- Allyson DeWitt: *Carson's employer; "fills needs" for wealthy/powerful clients*
- Olivia: *Allyson's major domo and fixer; a voice on the phone*

Assisting Carson

- Genadiy Rodievsky: Pakhan *of the Solntsevskaya Bratva in Vienna; Carson's sometime employer*
- Brianna McMurphy: *Carson's best friend; another former TPS officer*
- Edik Rogozhkin: *Retired Russian Army spetsnaz officer; now caretaker of a seaside estate in Cyprus*
- Denis Vlasenko: *Russian mini-oligarch; owns the mansion Rogozhkin cares for in Cyprus*

"Project Karma"

- Viktoriya (Vicki) Baranova: *Independent daughter of Oleg Baranov, Russian Minister of Internal Affairs*
- Iris Vernon: *American daughter of a long-time Newport RI family; Viktoriya's right-hand woman*
- Dareh Abbasi: *Son of a ranking Islamic Revolutionary Guard Corps officer*
- Celeste Aguenier: *Daughter of French government officials; musical prodigy; possibly autistic*

- Sebastian Counihan: *Son of an Irish banking executive*
- Tamara Gómez-Acebo: *Niece of the King of Spain; aspiring chef*
- Karl Greininger: *German son of a senior Volkswagen engineer*
- Amabelle Maniraguha: *Daughter of a Francophone Rwandan business tycoon*

Zapadneft (third-largest oil company in Russia)

- Damir Severinov: *Chief Security Officer for Zapadneft*
- Yuri Grebnev: *Director of Physical Security under Severinov*
- Konstantin Brusin: *Money launderer; services Zapadneft executives, various organized crime groups in southern Spain. Based in Malaga*
- Karik: *Commander of a tactical squad Severinov hired from a Russian private security contractor*

Grupo Sabadell (Catalan narcotics-trafficking organization)

- Ferran Balaguer-Noguera: *Grupo Sabadell's capo-equivalent*
- Håkan Kallström: *Balaguer's Swedish security chief and enforcer*
- Anders: *Kallström's closest friend from their outlaw motorcycle gang*

All action takes place August-October 2016.

For bonus chapters from **Engaño**, a downloadable cast list, reading group questions, and an interview with the author, check out https://www.wombatgroup.com/dewitt-adventures/engano/bonus-material/

ENGAÑO

A DeWitt Agency Adventure

Chapter 1

BRATISLAVA, SLOVAKIA

West of the warehouse, a black Audi SUV pokes its nose around the street corner, then backs out of sight like a cat waiting for the mouse to get closer.

Carson kicks the roll-up door's jamb. *Shit, they're here already.* She digs in her pocket for the key to her rented VW Tiguan, parked a few steps away.

The remote fob comes out in pieces, thanks to Pawel, the big moose slumped on the metal flatbed cart next to the SUV.

She fumbles the key into the driver's door lock. It's stiff— nobody ever uses the physical key. Eventually she gets the engine started and the back doors open. On her way into the warehouse, she stops by the cart. Pawel's been a pain in the ass and tried to break her spine, but the poor dumb bastard was only doing what he was told. If she leaves him, the opposition will kill him, probably after torturing him for info he's too dense to have.

Leave him.

Can't. It's like leaving a dog to be kicked to death. She kicks Pawel's leg. "Wanna live? Get in the back and lie down. Now."

Carson gimps back to the small safe. She needs to slow down the opposition so she and Pawel can get away. Those assholes followed her all over Bratislava; there's no doubt in her mind what they'll do to her if they catch her. They've already killed two people she talked to about the red-and-white Sparta Prague thumb drive now hiding in the duffel slung over her shoulder. They'll probably want the €20,000 in cash and the bottle of good whisky she took from the safe, too.

After a few moments of scheming, she pulls the pin on an old Russian hand grenade in the safe, sets the nearby baggie of coke on the grenade's spoon, then almost closes the door.

She hobbles as fast as she can to the SUV. Pawel's collapsed on the back seat with his feet poking out the open door. She slams the door, climbs behind the wheel, then stomps the gas.

Three black Audi SUVs race out to block the road ahead of her.

"Grab and hang on, Pawel."

The Tiguan goes backward surprisingly fast. To her left, the rusted river barges choking the industrial marina blur by. Carson jams on the brakes an instant before the SUV reaches the warehouse complex's far end. The Audis charge toward her in a file. *Get greedy, assholes. Stop for the safe.*

The front two SUVs swerve into Pawel's warehouse. The third one races toward her.

She shifts into first gear and floors it. The Tiguan leaps forward. The distance between her and the Audi shrinks crazy fast. *If this doesn't work, I hope the airbags do.*

At the last possible moment, the Audi swerves and crashes into a rusted shipping container. Its airbags work fine.

Carson tears her eyes away from the rear-view mirror so she can concentrate on avoiding the potholes and derelict cars.

"One-Two-Six? Are you there?" Olivia's creamy Oxbridge voice cocoons in her ear through the open phone connection. She keeps track of DeWitt Agency associates in the field, helps get them what they need for their projects, and makes sure they're paid.

"A little busy."

"The client will take charge of your man. I'll text the rendezvous point. Are you well?"

Carson glances in the mirror. Her face looks like bad Halloween makeup. Every part of her body aches from Pawel—now groaning in the back seat—trying to smash her bones into dust. *Crawled through the armpit of Bratislava to find the fucking drive. Ate bad food. Got the shit kicked out of me. Feel like a truck hit me. I hate this fucking job.*

She sighs. "About average."

Chapter 2

Carson scowls across the two-top table at Brianna, the best of her very few female friends. "I didn't forget my birthday. I'm ignoring it."

Brianna almost snorts beer out her nose. "So it'll go away? They're not like stray dogs, you know. More like horny guys. The more you ignore 'em, the more they think it's a come-on."

"When I hit forty, I'll start going backward."

"Why wait that long? Why not start now? Let me know when you're nineteen again. You were a helluva lot more fun then."

Carson sighs. "I know." She bites off another mouthful of Downtown Brown Ale and watches the black-and-white Hanlan's Point ferry churn across Toronto's Inner Harbor. It's a perfect Ontario summer day: 25° Celsius, a huge blue sky smeared with wispy clouds, only fifty percent humidity, no wind worth mentioning. Two and a half more hours of daylight and a jaunty crescent moon hanging in the west over Brianna's head. The harbor and Lake Ontario stretch flat and blue off to the horizon. These are the days she likes to remember when it's January and -15° with the lake wind blasting snow sideways through the streets.

As usual for a summer evening, the red-brick Amsterdam Brewhouse is busy, its harborside top deck full. How Brianna scored a prime table like this is beyond Carson, though she's glad for it. One of her favorite places in the GTA, with one of her favorite people. Too bad about the birthday part.

Brianna sets down her glass of Boneshaker IPA and pats Carson's hand. "You okay? Still hurt from that last job?"

"Bratislava? Sorta. Bruises are gone, lip's almost healed. Back's still sore." Almost three weeks. It's taking longer to mend these days. "I just feel old."

"You can't be old. We're the same age, and I'm sure as hell not old.”

“It's mileage, not years.”

Brianna shakes her head, then takes another swipe from her beer. “So, where's your next trip to?”

“Don't have one yet. Know how you want something to happen because now sucks, but you don't want it because you know the new thing will suck worse? That's where I'm at.”

“At least you get to go somewhere. All I do is sit behind a radio and push fire engines around. I swear my butt gets wider every day.”

“I go to shitholes—”

“Like Milan?”

“—and get the shit beat out of me. Careful what you wish for.”

Brianna knows all about Carson's two jobs. She's the only civilian who does. Anything she tells Bri will stay between them; she knows enough of Bri's secrets to put her in jail, while Bri knows enough to get Carson killed. Being able to unload to someone she trusts completely is a luxury Carson knows not a lot of people have. But sometimes she simply doesn't want to talk about it.

“How's Jason?” Bri's mostly-steady boyfriend, an EMT with the Toronto Fire Services.

Brianna puts on that goofy smile she always wears when she talks about Jason. “He's good. We're waiting for the results from his captain's test.” She holds up crossed fingers. “It's his second try. He says if he makes it, he'll make an honest woman out of me.”

“What, he's a magician now?”

Brianna sticks out the tip of her tongue. “How's *your* guy?”

“What guy?” Knowing perfectly well who Bri means.

“The Russian guy? The one who keeps calling you. What's his name? Ro…something?”

“Rogozhkin. He's not ‘my guy.’ He's a guy I met in Ukraine.”

“Who keeps calling you. You gonna go see him?”

“Well…” Carson had wanted to skip telling Bri until afterwards. Now that Bri's asked, that's not an option. The one rule they have is that they never lie to each other. “Um, yeah. Sunday.”

Bri's eyes light up like there's a nuclear reactor behind them. “Sunday? Like, six days from now?” She whoops, drawing looks from nearby tables. “That's *awesome!* Is he stoked? Are *you* stoked? How long are you staying? He's living in that mansion, right?

What—"

Carson holds up a "stop" hand. "Cool your jets. Breathe." This is why she didn't want to tell Bri until after the trip. "Yeah, he's jazzed. He keeps coming up with stuff he wants to do and things he wants to show me and I keep saying, 'Chill. I wanna relax. I wanna talk.' There's a lot we need to talk about. The kind of stuff you don't want to go over on the phone."

"That's what you do after sex, right?"

"Bri…" Carson growls, then brings up yesterday's Rogozhkin text and lays her phone in front of Brianna. "Here's the latest."

Bri picks up the phone and scrolls with her thumb. Her eyebrow arches. "It's in Russian."

"Oh. Sorry." Carson pushes down the phone's top edge so she can see the screen. Rogozhkin sent her two photos. She points at the first, a shot of a wooden sunbed in full sunshine. "This one says, 'Your place.'" The next picture shows the edge of an infinity pool that almost matches the Mediterranean behind it. "That one says, 'Your view.'"

"Awww. That's so sweet!" She drops the phone on Carson's paper placemat. "He's into you! Why aren't you excited about this? What's wrong?"

Bri's right—it's awfully sweet coming from a retired Russian special-ops officer. "Remember the part about he's fifteen years older than me?"

"So? You were just bitching about how old you feel. Maybe you're the same age mentally."

"Nice. I don't wanna build up a lot of expectations." Carson's looking forward to the trip. The man she's gotten to know over the phone seems a lot steadier than most of the men she's been with. Still, her history doesn't give her a lot of reason for optimism. She slams the rest of her beer. "What's the point? It won't—"

Before Carson can finish, her phone starts playing Bowie's "Strangers When We Meet," her ringtone for a caller who's not in her contacts. She doesn't recognize the number, but it starts with "+43" and it's twelve digits long. Vienna.

She knows exactly who's calling. Damn it.

◎

Once she gets to a solitary place on the walkway by the marina, Carson unmutes her phone and growls, "*Shto?*" Russian for *what?*

"Larochka." A familiar deep, rough Russian voice that's covered a lot of road. Rodievsky, the only man who can get away with using that little-girl diminutive of her name. "You are always so abrupt when I ring. Do I interrupt something?"

"Dinner with a friend."

"For your birthday? My best wishes to you. A man friend, perhaps?"

Why's everybody so hot to hook me up? "None of your business. You're up late."

"When you are as old as I am, you sleep less. Also, a very good friend woke me with an urgent request. Tell me—Miss DeWitt has no plans for you in the near future?"

"Not that she's told me." Not that it would matter. Rodievsky gets first dibs on her.

"Very good. Do you know the name Oleg Germanovich Baranov?"

Carson paces along the railing that separates the concrete pavers from the water. "No. Should I?"

"You should. He is the Russian Minister of Internal Affairs." Otherwise known as the MVD. "I always make certain I am good friends with the minister, whoever he is. It is very good for my business."

His business is being the *pakhan*—godfather—of the Solntsevskaya Bratva organization in Vienna. The Solntsevo gang is one of the Russian *mafiya's* largest offshoots. Carson's tied to Rodievsky now because her father was incredibly stupid about whom he borrowed money from to start a security company that failed.

"Glad you got a social life," Carson grumbles. "I care…why?"

"Larochka." She hates that nickname. "Please. Oleg Germanovich has a number of business interests that happen to coincide with my own. Also, he controls the *politsiya*, the Main Office for Drug Enforcement, and the Main Office for Migration. You can imagine how this interests the *Bratva*. So when my good friend Oleg Germanovich rings after midnight, I do answer the phone and listen carefully. Just as when I ring you, you answer and listen carefully, yes?"

Carson does, but wouldn't admit it under torture. "What does your good friend want in the middle of the night?"

Rodievsky clears his throat. "He has a daughter, Viktoriya Olegovna. A lovely girl, and very intelligent. She graduated with honors from Cambridge University two years ago. She is also very willful and independent, much as I imagine you were at her age."

"I was a cop at her age."

"I know. Still, I like to think you were as hard-headed and rebellious then as you are now. I say that with great affection. I have three sons, and each is a perfect *apparatchik*. They bore me."

Carson's always uncomfortable with these late-night (for him) calls. Rodievsky tells her things she'd rather not know about him. He also takes a long time to get to where he's going. She doesn't want to be his surrogate daughter or confidant or whatever he thinks she is. They have a business arrangement that works completely in his favor, that's all. "Let me guess—Viktoriya doesn't want to come home and marry some nice Russian oligarch and start calving."

"Calving?" He sighs. "You spent too much time on farms in your younger days. No, Viktoriya has been running wild around the Mediterranean for the past two years. She goes to parties and nightclubs and consorts with inappropriate men and spends her money foolishly. Oleg Germanovich has indulged her until now. He wants her to come home to Moscow so she can start learning his businesses. He wants her to take over when he retires."

"Isn't that usually the son's job?"

"Yes, if there are sons. Baranov has none, only two daughters. The younger one, Valeriya, is also very pretty but not nearly as intelligent as her sister. She will be the one who marries the oligarch and calves. That is not the point. Her father has been trying for six months to bring Viktoriya home. He has sent several of his men to fetch her. She always gets the better of them and escapes. So Oleg Germanovich calls his good friend for help. Can I use my resources to bring his older daughter, the apple of his eye and dagger in his heart, back to her home and family? And of course, I say yes."

"Of course." Carson knows what's next. "How many *boyeviki* work for you?"

"There is no reason to think *Bratva* muscle can reach Viktoriya if MVD muscle cannot. I want to try something different. Send a woman. Someone who can speak her language, maybe who is or was like her. Reason with her. Convince her that playtime is over and it is time to become an adult."

"You're fucking kidding me."

"I am not." Rodievsky's voice hardens. "I am very serious. Oleg Germanovich is anxious to bring her home before she ruins her future. You—"

"By getting knocked up?"

"That can be managed. Drugs, arrests, diseases, inconvenient politics…those are bigger worries. You will find her, talk to her, get control of her, and make her go home. I have promised her father I will do this, so it is now a matter of honor. Do you understand what that means?"

"Yeah." It means if she fails, he'll consider it a personal insult. That's how sudden deaths happen. *Shit.* "How do I find her?"

"She makes it easy. Do you know Instagram?"

"Yeah."

"She has an account. I understand it is very popular with a certain audience. I will send the address to you now." He sighs again, then lowers his voice. "Larochka. This should be pleasant for you. No violence, no danger. Warm, pretty places with clean water and soft bedsheets. When you succeed, I will reduce your debt to me by fifty thousand, plus whatever reasonable expenses you incur. This is my birthday gift to you."

Good thing she took that €20,000 in Bratislava to stake herself. She has to pay all her own expenses on Rodievsky's jobs. Luckily, she usually spends less than he knocks off her father's debt. "Euros or Canadian?"

"Euros, of course. Although I am still very fond of your coins with the little birds on them. You will start immediately. Please keep me informed of your progress. Have a good evening, Larochka."

Carson's thumb stabs her phone's "disconnect" icon hard enough that it should crack the glass. Babysitting and life coaching—two of her least-favorite things. This will also blow up her visit with Rogozhkin. Despite what she told Bri, she really does want to see him. Figure out whether there's anything they can build together, or maybe just have some fun.

She checks the new email in her inbox and finds an Instagram link. Dreading what she's about to see, she punches the link.

Oh. *Fuck*. No.

"God, I want her hair."

Carson's gnawing on a smoked rib. She frowns at Brianna. "Why? You're already blond."

"Yeah, but this…this is *movie star* hair. This is red carpet hair."

"You need that with your radio headset."

"Liss! Jeez. Lighten up." Brianna scrolls through more pictures of Viktoriya playing on the south coast of Spain. "I have twenty-two Insta followers and they're all related to me. She has a hundred sixteen *thousand*. Can you imagine that many people caring about what you do?"

Carson thinks about it for a couple of seconds, then shudders. "Sounds like a kind of hell."

Brianna tsks. "While I'm at it, I'll take her face, too."

"You're already pretty."

"No, I'm 'cute.' I've always been 'cute.' You know what that's like?"

Carson glares at her. "No. I don't. Never been accused of it."

"Oh, come on. You look fine. You got that great skin. You're gonna look the same when you're seventy—"

"Oh, thanks."

"I didn't mean it that way—"

"Thanks anyway."

Brianna growls, then scrolls. "She looks like she's doing fine to me. What do you think?"

"She's a waste of space." Carson sets down her de-fleshed bone and moves on to the next rib. "I mean, all that money and all that education, and she blows it on Champagne and clothes she wears once."

"She's having fun. Remember that?" Sigh. "I wish I could've done this when I was her age. It took every loonie I had to get off the farm and come down here." Bri picks at her lemon chicken schnitzel with one hand while she scrolls with the other. "Remember how poor I was when we met, back at cadet training?

You had to buy me toilet paper?"

Carson chuckles at the memory. "Had to feed you more than once, too. Surprised you survived my cooking." She nods at the phone. "Rodievsky wants me to talk to her. Reason with her. How do I do that? I look at her and see a spoiled rich bitch burning daddy's money. Do we even speak the same language?"

Bri turns off the phone and sets it in front of Carson's plate. "You sound like my mother."

"Told you I feel old."

"What about your trip to see your Russian guy? Can you do that first?"

"You don't tell Rodievsky 'later' or 'no.'" Carson shakes her head. "He's never gonna let me go."

"Even after you pay off your dad's debt?"

"He'll make sure I never do. I'm too useful to him, and too cheap."

Brianna digests this for a few seconds. "Okay, go. But make it a vacation. I mean, the Costa del Sol. Gorgeous beaches, great weather, warm water. Hot Spanish guys."

"Now you sound like Rodievsky. 'Clean water and soft sheets.'"

"You've done worse. Don't look for Viktoriya too hard. Get a tan. Swim. Drink umbrella drinks. Get laid. Adjust your attitude. Then you'll be all tan and relaxed when you see your guy. And maybe you'll be in a better mood when you find this Viktoriya chick."

Carson snorts. "If I have to keep looking at that shit, I'll wanna wring her neck."

Brianna sighs and sets down her fork. Her mouth and shoulders sag.

Carson knows this look: Bri's hurt or discouraged. *Have I been that bad? Yeah.*

"Give me your hand." Bri holds out her right hand, palm up. "Come on." Carson does; Brianna folds it in both her hands. "You know I love you, right? You're my sister—"

"—from another mister. Yeah." Carson looks through the Plexiglas next to her at the harbor. "And...I..."

"I know." Brianna squeezes. "I know it's been hard for you, these past five years."

"Longer than that."

"Yeah. I get it—you don't want to hurt anymore. I've been there too. But because I love you, I can say stuff like this to you: Let yourself live. Let yourself *feel*. Stop trying to control everything. The best things that happen in life are the things you never planned. So let things happen and enjoy them. I want my best friend back. I really, *really* miss her. And I worry about her. Okay?"

Carson doesn't dare look at Bri, not when she's having trouble with the hitch in her throat. She's been a shitty friend lately. Her bad mood's become semi-permanent, and even she doesn't want to be around herself. Finally, she nods, because she doesn't trust herself to say a word.

Chapter 3

MÁLAGA, SPAIN

Yuri Grebnev follows a servant through a quiet, arcaded courtyard in the center of the stately, whitewashed Mediterranean villa. The sun isn't high enough yet to reach the courtyard's terracotta floor, leaving the space cool and still. They skirt the obligatory tiled fountain on their way to three graceful arches that appear to open onto thin air.

Grebnev can't tell exactly what function the person he's following fills here. The plain black slacks and long-sleeved, white button-down shirt don't give away any clues. Housekeeper? Server? He's finally figured out she's female; her unisex face and hair could go either way.

The arches lead to three broad steps down, then to a terrace overlooking a swimming pool as blue and nearly as large as the summer sky. The heat hits him immediately: nine-thirty in the morning and it's already over 30° C. Despite the two large patio umbrellas and the misters, Grebnev deeply regrets the slate-gray wool suit that's now slowly broiling him.

A black wrought-iron patio table sits dead-center on the carved-stone railing, flanked by matching chairs. An elaborate breakfast covers the white tablecloth. A man draped in a knee-length, embroidered dressing gown lounges on the chair to Grebnev's right, scrolling through a tablet's screen.

He grins. "My dear Grebnev! Welcome." His Russian comes from south and west of Moscow—Belarus, Ukraine, that area. He stands to shake hands. "Now that I see you, I recall that we met in Rublyevskoye two years ago. Your CEO's dacha. Ex-CEO, I should say."

Grebnev's reasonably sure he's never seen Konstantin Brusin in his life, though he's heard plenty about the man. He sits in the unoccupied chair and glances out on the cascade of red tile roofs spilling down the hill to a broad beach and blue sea. "Lovely view."

"It is, isn't it?" Brusin settles into his chair and waves a hand over the table. "Join me for breakfast? My chef is a miracle."

"No, thank you. I already ate." At six, his usual time. Grebnev's not sure he could stomach breakfast this late in the morning. "Coffee is fine."

Brusin aims a stream of Spanish at the housekeeper, who leaves with a little bow. Then he turns to smile again at Grebnev. "To what do I owe the honor of this visit?"

"Mr. Severinov didn't tell you?"

"He told me to expect you, not why you're here. I assume it has something to do with security since, well, Severinov."

The Chief Security Officer for Zapadneft, Russia's third-largest oil company, and Grebnev's immediate superior. "It does. We have a…situation. We're hoping you can use some of your contacts to help us resolve it."

"Of course. Anything I can do for a valued client."

Splashing water and laughing distracts Grebnev. A good-looking young man and a pretty young brunette are playing in the pool. Both are quite nude and apparently know each other extremely well. Grebnev clears his throat and returns to Brusin. "Am I interrupting a party?"

Brusin glances toward the pool, smiles and waves, then chuckles. "No, no. The party was last night. And this morning, too, I suppose. I love high season on the Costa del Sol. Please, continue with your situation."

"Right. It appears we've been hacked. Someone managed to break into our financial system and created more black accounts."

"Like the ones for your executives."

"Yes. The funds disappear into numbered accounts all over the world and that's the last we see of them. I'm told they were quite skillful about it. That may be why we hadn't noticed it until recently."

The housekeeper sets a chrome-handled glass mug in front of Grebnev. The top half is dark coffee; the bottom half is something creamy white.

Brusin notices Grebnev's puzzlement. "It's a café bombón, from Valencia. Espresso poured over condensed milk. Live a little."

"Of course." Grebnev doesn't usually have much tolerance for experimenting with coffee, but he needs to be as gracious a guest as possible. He sips the espresso, then glances at the hovering housekeeper.

Brusin says, "Go on. She doesn't speak Russian."

"How do you know?"

Brusin laughs. "You got me there." He dismisses the woman. "Have any accounts I process been affected?"

Process. An interesting euphemism for *launder.* "No, they're all fine. The people in Finance and IT who were asleep at the wheel have been dealt with. But we're left with accounts we can't, ehm, *account* for, if you will. Also, IT has yet to discover how the hackers pulled off the exploit. We're leaving the accounts alone for now to see if the people who created them come back to tweak them."

"Oh, Connie, darling!" A woman's voice with an English accent pulls Grebnev's attention to the pool again. A striking young blonde with a scarlet streak in her jaw-length hair stands next to the pool in a frilly white robe. Her fists are planted on her hips. "Are you coming? It's too hot to stay out here for long."

Brusin stands and leans his palms on the balustrade. "Of course, my dear," he calls in lightly accented English. "In a few minutes. I have business."

"You always have business. Don't take too long." She flings off her kimono—she's also quite nude—and paddles to the young couple. She appears to know them both extremely well. Grebnev watches for a few moments, both fascinated and a bit embarrassed. Things like this never happened in the army.

Brusin thumps into his seat, chuckling. "Mixed doubles, my dear Grebnev. When in Rome and all that. If I may ask, how much have they taken you for?"

"Six and a half million euros, more or less. Small compared to our revenues, but it's the principle of the thing." He watches Brusin butter a roll. "For a while, we thought it was you."

Brusin's head shoots up. "I would never. I don't need to. Between the corporate accounts I process and the black ones for your executives, I have more than enough business from you." He takes a generous bite from the roll and sighs. "Tastes like a cloud. So, what do you need from me?"

The splashing and laughing and short, sharp cries keep tempting Grebnev to watch the pool action, but he resists. He's never been part of this kind of scene, and he doesn't need to waste brainspace wondering what he'd say if Brusin (or the striking blonde) asked him to join them. "Our cybersecurity team traced the hacking activity's origin to this area. It apparently moves from time to time. Several other firms in our commercial space have noticed the same kinds of intrusions. Normally, we'd deal with the problem ourselves, but...well, I'm sure you saw the news reports about that disaster in Riga last year."

"I did. I was embarrassed for you all, truly." Brusin sets down his fork, leans back in his chair, and folds his hands in his lap. "Were you...part of it?"

Grebnev hesitates. "I was there. I wasn't in command." That was Ivlev, then the company's Director for Physical Security. The stupid bastard who Grebnev replaced after the purges ended. That inescapable news photo of the two dead women shielding the dead baby under their bodies still haunts him.

"Well done." Brusin spreads his hands. "I don't have an army like Zapadneft does. What use can I be in this?"

"Someone in the hacker group going by the name 'Sonia' is engaged in some low-rent drug dealing on the side. It's surely an alias. We know that some of your clients also operate in that space. We'd appreciate it if you could convince one to eliminate the competition." He finishes the espresso in his drink, leaving the condensed milk mostly untouched. "It should be easy. Hackers aren't usually hard targets in the physical world. Your client would benefit from it in market terms, of course. One less rival in a crowded field. That may lead to more money for them and larger fees for you."

Brusin chuckles. "And Zapadneft comes out ahead. You have your hacker problem solved for you without getting your hands dirty. Clever." He sips from a tall tumbler of intensely red liquid. "As it happens, I have clients who may be just the thing for your scheme. An up-and-coming Catalan group trying to expand into the Costa del Sol. They're certainly not afraid to break eggs to get what they want." He raises his glass to Grebnev in a mock toast. "This could be very interesting for us all, yes?"

Chapter 4

MARBELLA, SPAIN

Carson arrives in Marbella after ten and a half hours overnight on Lufthansa via Frankfurt, then over an hour driving from Málaga. It's well past one in the afternoon by the time she checks into the beachside Hotel Fuerte Marbella. She staggers onto her private ocean-view balcony on the fourth floor, still buzzing from the lack of sleep and traffic she hadn't expected.

She closes her eyes, lets her head fall back, and takes three deep, slow breaths. At least it doesn't smell like rotting kelp or an oil spill. *Finally here. This* will *be fun.* She doesn't believe it, but she hopes that thought borrowed from Brianna will come true.

Three days ago, Bri made her promise to not look for Viktoriya for the first day after she arrives. Because she promised and takes promises seriously even when they suck, Carson doesn't take her phone off airplane mode. No calls from Rodievsky; no Insta posts from Viktoriya. After a quick shower and change of clothes, she goes out to recon the area.

Marbella is like two different cities. Above the four-lane Avenida Ramon y Cajal, the main east-west road running through town, is the Spanish city she'd expected—narrow, twisting streets, tiled walkways, whitewash, wrought iron, pastels. Every other door leads into a boutique with a name like "Bily Bily Baby"; every fourth door fronts a small hotel or restaurant. Unexpected courtyards pop up randomly. There's not a single feral dog, trash-barrel fire, or burned-out car to be seen. Trees, pretty flowers, fountains, sunny, 25° C; it would be a pleasant walk if it wasn't jammed with tourists.

An unexpectedly leisurely lunch at a café on the Plaza de los Naranjos—a lush courtyard surrounded by orange trees—gives Carson a chance to confirm that the tap water's drinkable. At the next table over, a young guy in flashy clothes and neck tattoos has three cell phones lined up next to his plateful of animal protein while he mutters some Balkan language into a fourth. She knows his type: a drug dealer or low-level distributor. *Huh—right in front of City Hall.* Bri didn't tell her about this part of Marbella.

Afterwards, she heads below the main drag into high-rise hell: hotels, condos, and office buildings smashed shoulder-to-shoulder, blocking any view of the Mediterranean until she reaches Avenida Duque de Ahumada, the pedestrianized beachside street that stretches the length of Marbella.

And more tourists.

The beach is jammed with hundreds—no, thousands—of sunbeds and umbrellas. Bodies as far as she can see. The people who aren't roasting themselves on the sand are in front of her on the *paseo*, shuffling along slower than crippled snails. Outfits range from caftans to nearly nonexistent swimsuits; bodies run the gamut from magazine-spread ready to please-God-strike-me-blind. She hears far more British English than Spanish.

The way Brianna had talked about this place, Carson expected nonstop beautiful people cruising quiet streets in their Rolls-Royces. Because she rarely goes to tourist spots when she works for Rodievsky or the DeWitt Agency, she didn't realize that when northern Europe shuts down in August, it's because those people are all down here. In a way, she's glad. She's in the middle of the pack as far as physical attractiveness goes, and her brand-new navy-blue shorts and blue-and-green floral sleeveless top fall about midway on the local fashion spectrum.

She steps down to a beach, pulls off her runners, then walks into the water up to her ankles. The Med is like a once-hot bath left to sit for a while, still warmish but not what she'd choose for a shower. Still, she walked on a beach and got in the water. Brianna will be proud of her.

By the time Viktoriya drops her first Insta post of Friday morning, Carson's already had breakfast and finished a truncated version of her usual three-hour workout in the hotel's gym and the larger of the two swimming pools.

Viktoriya's draped over a sunbed, wearing a sheer white cover-up open over a gold-belted, one-piece white swimsuit with a plunging neckline. Gold drips from her ears and neck. She looks amazing (the bitch). She's holding a half-full Champagne flute next to her face. Below is a caption:

```
Marbs brekkie @ noon where
better? #purobeachmarbs
#virginiamacari
#queen_of_queens_marbella
#beachlife #beauty #summer
#marbella #spain #españa #fashion
#fashionista #looksoftheday #glam
#look #style #marbella2016
#beachwear #outfit #outfitoftheday
#collection #styleoftheday
#myoutfit
```

Carson had to read dozens of these before she could decode the hashtags. Viktoriya always leads with where she is (Purobeach Marbella, a beach club about twenty klicks west of the hotel), then follows with what she's wearing (Virginia Macari swimsuit, Queen of Queens robe). The rest is fluff.

While she was locked in German airliners, Carson paid the exorbitant fee for the in-flight Wi-Fi so she could drag through a year's worth of Viktoriya's drivel and try to establish patterns for her. She posts most everywhere she goes, including the washroom (at least four bathtub shots, extra bubblebath). She makes the rounds of all the hotspots in the western Med: Lagos and Faro in Portugal; Marbella, Málaga, Alicante, Valencia, Barcelona, Ibiza, and Mallorca in Spain; Marseille, Cap d'Antibes, and Cannes in France; and some places in Morocco Carson's never heard of. It's a regular cycle. She showed up at ski resorts a few times last winter, then always fled to #beachlife again. Clubs, shops, bars, restaurants, beaches, mansions, boats, pools, gyms (full makeup on the Peloton, of course). She guzzles Champagne by the barrel. She works off the fancy lunches and dinners with sailboarding, swimming, hiking, snowboarding, and roller skating. About half the photos are selfies (like this latest); the other half are clearly assisted, though she never mentions who's pushing the button.

Carson hates her guts. She'd bet Rodievsky's fifty grand that

Viktoriya's never been to Bratislava, far less the Donbass, and probably wouldn't survive her first day in either.

Anyway, Carson has to get to Purobeach Marbella to interrupt Viktoriya's brekkie.

Except Viktoriya's not there.

Carson pays €45 for a pool sunbed and tries to cover the entire pool area without race-walking. Despite what the YouTube videos implied, not everybody is young, pretty, and tan…just most everybody. Carson's very aware of her pasty Canadian winter skin and how her tank swimsuit could belong to the mothers of some of the young women decorating the sunbeds. At least it's black. She also appears to be the only woman wearing deck shoes—espadrilles with improbable wedge soles are popular, as are gladiator sandals.

Since it's almost two and still far too early for people to be eating lunch, Carson scores a table under an umbrella without a fight. The chillout house music brings Carson's blood pressure down. A couple of beers help.

Where the fuck is Viktoriya?

Her last post arrived as Carson ordered lunch; she should still be here. Carson even found where Viktoriya shot the picture, with Morocco's Atlas Mountains drifting far in the background. But she's gone. *How did I miss her?*

So Carson has lunch and waits for the next Insta bomb to fall. The Spanish-Asian fusion food is actually good. The waiter—a youngish guy who could be Chadwick Bozeman's more handsome brother—isn't bad to look at, either.

Viktoriya's next post happens at three-thirty.

```
Watching cute guys with big
sticks play games. #santamariapolo
```

By four-fifteen, Carson's parked her SEAT two-seater between a Bentley and a Range Rover and is combing the sidelines of the Santa Maria Polo Club in Sotogrande, about fifteen klicks southwest of Purobeach. She works her way around the field—the size of nine football pitches—trying to find Viktoriya's loose, white-lace dress and her colorful folk-art bracelets. It's not the flesh market that Purobeach was; comfortable-looking men in khaki and golf shirts sit with well-kept women in respectable resort wear.

Once again, Carson finds where the photo was taken, but

Viktoriya's not there. If she is, she's doing a helluva job hiding. Then she notices something. A polo player was riding behind Viktoriya when she snapped her photo. He wore a green shirt with white stripes.

The players on the field now wear either navy-blue or yellow shirts.

And the match started at four, not three-thirty.

What the fuck?

Chapter 5

Ferran Balaguer-Noguera stands at the *Campió's* aft rail, gazing across the flat, black water toward shore as he sips his *jerez fino* sherry. The lights of Puerto Banús shimmer in the distance. If he concentrates and the light breeze comes offshore, he can hear the distant bass thumping from one club or another.

It's certainly more restful than listening to the sounds of the women servicing Alonzo on the banquette behind him.

Campió—his yacht, his favorite toy, his usual home-away-from-Barcelona—rides easy on the low, lazy swell. He loves it out here, three kilometers or so offshore, close enough to see land but far enough away to not have to deal with it. Should the state police boats decide to take an interest in him, a short run out to sea takes him past the three-nautical-mile limit of their jurisdiction. By the time the *Guardia Civil's* ships reach the area, he'll be tucked away safely in Moroccan waters.

Not that he expects that tonight. The *Servicio Marítimo's* usually too busy around Gibraltar and Ceuta to bother the nice, upstanding yacht owners of Marbella.

Alonzo reaches his destination with the usual grunting and devotions to God.

Ferran finishes his sherry while he waits for things to settle down back there. After two bottles of Champagne, three lines of Ferran's best cocaine, almost a hundred grams of caviar, and two blowjobs, the owner of Marbella's Club Tangier should be just about ready to talk business.

The heavy breathing finally gives way to murmuring and giggles. Ferran pastes on his warmest host's smile and returns to the banquette and deck chairs arrayed around the electric firepit at *Campió's* stern. Alonzo—early thirties, fashionable black stubble, wearing the latest clubwear though minus his trousers—sprawls between Iniga (a sleek Italian like *Campió*, miraculously a natural blond) and Mihaela (a Romanian chemical redhead with inspirational breasts). Both women are naked except for their astoundingly tall stiletto heels. Iniga's draped over Alonzo, while Mihaela's absorbed by her phone. Alonzo looks dazed, as well he should be.

Ferran sets down his glass. "Are you enjoying yourself, my friend?" he asks in Spanish.

The young man blinks slowly a few times. "Yeah, bro. It's lit. You know how to party." His voice wanders, the words bumping into each other.

"Excellent. I like to show my guests a good time." Ferran claps his hands once. "Ladies, if you don't mind, Alonzo and I need to discuss some business."

The women saunter into the after lounge. Alonzo stares as they go, his mouth hanging open. "Where'd you get them? They're smokin'."

Ferran shrugs. "Oh, just a couple of ladies I know who like to have fun." Not quite: they're dancers at Paraíso, the gentlemen's club Ferran owns in Puerto Banús not too far from Alonzo's nightclub. "You see, I like to treat my business partners—my *friends*—well. I want you to see this so you have an idea what it'll be like to do business with me. Impressed?"

"Defs." Alonzo waves a crooked line. "Love this boat. The all-black thing. It's, like…savage."

As well as changing the name, Ferran had *Campió's* upper works painted metallic black so he could get this kind of reaction. It also helps on those night runs to and from North Africa. "If we can come to an agreement, you can spend a lot of time on her partying with me and my other friends. And…" he gestures toward the lounge "…ladies, of course. But first, we need to settle our business." Ferran leans his elbows on his knees. "You screen your patrons for contraband before you let them in your club. That's smart. But what do they do once they're inside? Have you provided for their needs?"

"You mean, like…a house dealer?"

"Exactly. If you have one, we haven't found him. Or her. And that's a lost profit opportunity. You know your competitors offer their patrons full service. Why shouldn't you? Tangier's one of

Marbella's top clubs. But if your patrons can't party the way they want…"

"No, no, totally." Alonzo grabs a Champagne flute from the low glass-and-chrome table at his knees. It's empty, but it takes him a few moments to figure that out. "I get what you're saying. It's just, well…" He sets down the glass, barely avoiding missing the table's edge. "There's a lot of agita between you and the other guys, you know? Don't wanna drag my club into some turf war or anything. Right?"

Ferran empties the Champagne bottle's dregs into the flute and hands it to Alonzo. "Of course. My organization—Grupo Sabadell—is consolidating the coastal market now. We're trying to lock in the club concession all up and down the Costa del Sol and into the Balearics. No more of this foolish specialization, where you have to go to one seller for blow, another for *roca*, another for Molly. No. One venue, one vendor, anything you need. You get ten percent—a franchise fee, if you will. And we make certain there's no trouble in your club. It's as simple as that, my friend." He senses a large presence to his right. "Alonzo, I'd like you to meet my associate, Håkan."

Håkan Kallström—Ferran's chief of security—leans across the table to shake Alonzo's hand. For a trained gorilla, he looks quite respectable tonight in his tailored gray dress slacks and pristine, collarless, fitted white button-front shirt. Ferran's coaching may be finally rubbing off. *If only he'd do something with his hair…*

Alonzo squints at him. "What kinda name is Håkan?"

Kallström says, "Swedish." Like the accent he loads on his Spanish. He settles on the banquette within arm's reach of Alonzo.

"Whoa." Alonzo nods a few times. "A long way from home, bro."

"Our business is global."

Ferran clears his throat— Kallström's cue to stop talking before he kills the mood—and smiles at Alonzo. "We can start immediately. Our salesforce will look like any of your patrons. I insist that they fit in. No gangsters or motorcycle toughs." He glances at Kallström, who still belongs to a Swedish motorcycle gang in Andalusia. The Swede gives him a look that could be indigestion, but isn't. "Do we have a deal, my friend?"

Alonzo tries to blink his eyes clear. "Wow, um…you know, one source for flake and ice would be solid. Cancel the slags we got there now. But we're good for Molly, bro. Have been over a year. Good product, reliable. But it's chill, no worries."

Kallström's intense blue eyes turn even steelier. Ferran knows the Swede hears resistance, which he likes to think is futile.

Ferran's not ready yet to turn the wolf loose on Alonzo. "My friend, leaving another dealer in place doesn't suit our purposes or yours. There's too much room for…misunderstandings. Conflicts. I'm sure you understand. When you work with us, we take care of everything."

The club owner shrinks a bit. He may have finally realized that none of this was framed as a proposal or a request. He looks from Ferran to Kallström and back with eyes that get larger every time they change focus. "I…I made a deal with Sonia—"

Sonia. Not her again.

"—she's been primo, great to work with. I gave her my word, two years to start. I…"

"Do you have a picture of this Sonia? I want to make certain we're talking about the same person other club owners have told us about."

"Yeah. Yeah, for sure." Alonzo reaches for the phone in his back pocket, then realizes he's not wearing any pants. He fumbles for his trousers—in a puddle of Champagne on the deck, under the table—wrestles his phone loose, then frantically scrolls through his Instagram feed. He finally brings up a photo of himself between two women, his arms around their waists. He points to the one on his left, who's kissing his cheek. "That's her. That's Sonia."

Ferran takes a good look, then passes it to Kallström. The Swede makes a disgusted noise. It's definitely Sonia.

Kallström tosses the phone on the table and leans toward Alonzo. "You are fucking her?"

"No. No, man. I mean, I wouldn't mind. She's kinda hot. But—"

Ferran sighs and shakes his head. He knows what's next.

"You come to our boat." Kallström drills his index finger into the thin skin under Alonzo's collarbone. "You drink our Champagne. You use our cocaine. You play with our girls. You think you say 'no' now?"

"But…" Alonzo looks to be sobering up quickly. His eyes blink enough to be sending Morse code. "I thought this was, like, a proposal. Just talking. There's—"

"I'm sorry I was unclear about the situation here." Ferran gives him an empty smile. "Håkan's not always…let's say, as *delicate* about these matters as he could be. We're very generous with our friends. Our business partners. We'd rather that you be our friend since we'll be a regular fixture in your club from now on. I'd hoped we could come to a mutually beneficial arrangement. But…" He shrugs. "Perhaps not."

Alonzo's hands start to shake. "I need some time, bro. Talk to people. Square things."

"I'm sure."

Kallström clamps his big right hand around the back of Alonzo's neck. The club owner's eyes get even larger. "You remember Isidro at Le Fénix?"

"Yeah. That club up in the hills. He ran it." Alonzo's eyebrows touch. "Wait. He was in it when it burned…"

"Yes. Terrible thing." Ferran taps the glass tabletop to get Alonzo's attention. "Now do we have a deal…my friend?"

Chapter 6

MARBELLA

Once Carson figures out that Viktoriya is scheduling her Insta posts, she sets herself up on her hotel balcony and starts analyzing Viktoriya's past movements so she can make a new plan.

First, she looks at photos from the polo matches—apparently some kind of international tournament—to find players wearing green-and-white shirts. The team she'd seen in navy-blue shirts with silver Xs on their chests was Ayala, a home team; the guys in yellow were from Brunei.

The only team she can find in the Santa Maria tournament pictures with green-and-white striped shirts is from Dubai. They played on Wednesday.

Carson checks Viktoriya's posts from Wednesday. Stores and dinner; no event to hang a date on.

Her first Marbella posts after southern Portugal's Algarve dropped on Tuesday: Ocean Club, "Timeless" with DJ Tom Novy.

"Timeless" happened on Sunday.

She's delaying her posts by two days. She arrived in Marbella no later than Sunday.

Viktoriya usually stays in one place for two to three weeks. She was in the Algarve for twenty days, or at least was posting photos from there for that long. But she normally posts four to six times a day, and for her last seven days in the Algarve, she posted only once a day. Was she really there, or was she covering for being somewhere else?

Carson assumes Viktoriya was covering. She left the Algarve after thirteen days and has been in Marbella for six. That leaves her another seven or eight days here.

Viktoriya does certain things every time she goes to a particular place, and almost always does one or two completely new things. Some she does early in a stay; others she leaves until the end.

Carson looks at the last two times Viktoriya was in Marbella and checks items off the list. She didn't go to "Timeless" last time, in February, but it's a summer event and she attended last July. Purobeach, check; polo, check.

It's getting dark on the balcony, though it's still warm. Time passed faster and more painlessly than she expected. Burying her nose in this dumbshit girl's business should've been excruciating. Instead, it's like being a detective again. She's always loved putting the clues together to solve the puzzle; this is simply another version of it. A version where, instead of staring at hundreds of CCTV stills of ugly biker toughs or Russian leg-breakers to put together a pattern of behavior, she has to look at pretty clothes and pretty places. It could be worse.

Carson surveys the work she's done. *Nice, but, how's this help?*

She knows she doesn't have to chase the Insta feed because it's about the past. The longer Viktoriya's here, the shorter her to-do list, and the easier it'll be to predict where she'll go. But what does Carson do in the meantime?

She leans back in her patio chair, nursing what's left of the minibar San Miguel beer. Watching polo today was fun. She'd seen cowboy polo when she was growing up in Alberta—a pack of guys (sometimes some girls) on cow ponies, whacking a medicine ball around a rodeo arena—but she'd never seen a real polo match in person until today. It's a pretty game, with beautiful, fast horses running like hell across a huge, grassy field.

Even Purobeach was nice after she got over her irritation at missing Viktoriya. The food was fine, it was a nice day, and there was good people-watching, something she usually has to go to a street fair or flea market for.

Carson knows where Viktoriya tends to go in the middle of her stays here. Maybe she can drop by at the times Viktoriya posted before, check things out. Maybe get lucky and see her.

While she's at it, Carson can see how the other one percent lives here. Maybe work on her tan, too.

So that's what Carson does.

Friday night before dinner, she grabs a less-over-the-top photo from Viktoriya's Insta feed and puts it in her phone's photo gallery.

Over the weekend, she goes to shops and restaurants and beach clubs and nightclubs. She tries to fit in, though she doesn't have the wardrobe for it. She's not one of those effortlessly lovely women who sweep by in their weightless summer dresses or wraps, their hair wind-blown just enough to be sexy as they air-kiss their friends and drink their mimosas. Then again, she's also not one of the many loud, obnoxious tourist women, drunk at eleven in the morning, abusing the staff, with purple-streaked hair, nose rings, and "Spoiled Rotten" tees. Somewhere in the middle seems to be the sweet spot. The sales clerks are polite to her even though they probably know she won't buy anything, the waitstaff doesn't ignore her excessively, and the bouncers and doormen check out her legs but don't fawn over her or turn her away.

Everywhere she goes, she shows her Viktoriya photo to the clerks and waiters and asks, "Have you seen my friend? I was supposed to meet her here…" A few times she gets, "She looks familiar, but not from today." But no Viktoriya sightings.

The stores are a revelation. Carson normally shops at places like Hudson's Bay, Winners, and Marshalls. Nordstrom is a splurge. When she walks into Tamara Comolli—Viktoriya's favorite high-end jeweler—in the Marbella Club hotel, she thinks she's wandered into a small museum; it's all sleek white surfaces and a few pieces of downlit, gorgeous statement jewelry. The Queen of Queens shop that Viktoriya's mentioned several times is full of very pretty, very expensive resort clothes (€300 bikinis!) Carson would never dare wear. But for some reason, she feels special just walking into these places.

But still no Viktoriya. Carson's running out of time. She needs to get this right.

Late Saturday morning, Carson discovers she has a shadow.

She's not exactly looking for tails. Her cop radar's been on since she got here, though, and it's been working overtime. The tourist part of Marbella is mostly confined to the beach strip, the old town, and Puerto Banús a few klicks down the road, and those areas are flooded with vacationing northern Europeans. Crowds this size add up to a lot of sketchy activity. A pickpocket lifts a mark's wallet. An addict huddles behind a dumpster. A man holds his woman's arm too tight and yanks her around too hard. A toke taken not covertly enough. A pair of rough-looking men shadows a group of three young women. A store clerk chases a shoplifter. A dime bag of coke changes hands. A flock of Roma kids surrounds a tourist woman, trying to snatch her purse or jewelry.

Everywhere she looks, Carson sees indictable or super-summary offenses happening or about to happen. It's become visual noise. *Gotta stop looking at this shit*, she tells herself. *Gotta focus on finding Viktoriya.*

Because her filter's up, she almost missed the shadow.

She's not sure if it's a tail. She's covered enough territory by now to recognize several people who repeatedly cross her path, but this isn't one of them. There's no reason she can think of to have a tail; Rodievsky didn't mention opposition. One other thing that doesn't add up: the shadow is a young woman. Carson's never been followed by a woman before…that she knows of.

The streets in the old town are narrow and busy. Carson stops to look in the window of yet another boutique selling the peasant crop-tops and miniskirts that seem to be this week's must-haves among the tourist girls. In the window reflection, she sees the maybe-shadow peer into a shop window maybe twenty meters away across the street. A triangular face with a long, thin nose and prominent cheekbones, slender going on skinny, and long, bare legs. A thick braid of tarnished-copper hair dangles between the woman's shoulder blades. Mid-twenties? Whoever she is, it's not too likely she's as fascinated by artisanal olive oil—the shop's specialty—as she wants people to think.

Hmm.

Carson turns right at the next corner, stops abruptly, then turns to face the street she just left. She rolls back the video loop in her head. She first remembers seeing the shadow about half an hour before, window-shopping the route Carson's been taking to reach a leather-goods store Viktoriya seems fond of. She didn't think much of it at first; a pair of gray-haired German women had also been following her wake until they disappeared into a shop a few minutes ago.

Gonna feel stupid if the redhead shows up with a bagful of olive oil.

The redhead turns the corner and screeches to a halt a meter from Carson. No bag of olive oil. Her eyes get huge.

Carson gives her a once-over. Flimsy tank top, booty shorts, no bra. In her platform sneakers, she's taller than Carson. "You following me?"

The redhead works her mouth for a few moments before she lets out an embarrassed smile full of nearly-perfect teeth. "Um…hi."

"Answer?"

"Um…yeah, I guess I am." American accent. She nibbles on her upper lip.

"Why?"

"Because…you're cute?"

"Bullshit. Try again."

The redhead sighs hard enough to sag her shoulders. She runs her left hand over the intricate, full-color tattoo of tangled vines and tiny flowers that winds down her right shoulder and bicep. "Okay. You wear shorts better than, like, ninety percent of the women I've seen today. I think you're hot. And I've got this thing for really fit women." She shrugs. "So sue me."

It's Carson's turn to sigh. One of the many drawbacks to being a "really fit woman" with muscles is that both men and women think she's a lesbian. She expects men to be stupid, but it always disappoints her when another woman can't see past the stereotype. "You're trying to pick me up."

"Well…I'd like to. You're by yourself, I'm by myself. We could have a lot of fun." Confidence is creeping back into her voice. She's done this before.

"You're not my type."

"What's your type? Short? Blond?"

"Male."

The redhead's face collapses. "For reals? Jeez, my gaydar's all dorked up." She cocks a well-plucked eyebrow. "You're sure?"

"Real sure." Carson's a little embarrassed herself. She usually doesn't misread cues this badly. Looking back, she should've seen that this woman was too amateurish to be a serious tail. *Score one for my paranoia.*

The redhead stammers out an apology and hurries down the street, not looking back. Carson waits for her to disappear before she moves on to the leather store.

Maybe Rodievsky was right. No danger here. Just tourists out to score.

Chapter 7

L'HOSPITALET DE LLOBREGAT, BARCELONA

Ferran stares at the large windows across the office's back wall. "Is it secure in here?"

Konstantin Brusin smiles and spreads his hands. "Of course it is, my dear Balaguer," he says in English. "This is my office away from home. It's scanned daily for eavesdroppers. The windows are mirrored. Vibrators shake the glass so the police can't use their tech toys against them. Please, sit." He sweeps his hand toward two ornate armchairs set in front of a massive carved-walnut desk the size of a small freighter.

With one last sour look at the glass, Ferran settles on the chair to the left. It's as uncomfortable as he expected for something that looks more like a throne than twenty-first century office furniture. Kallström unbuttons his suit jacket and sits in the other seat, then fidgets like a boy trying to find the soft spot.

"Drinks?" Brusin's moved to a well-stocked bar cabinet and sink. He's wearing a particularly florid golf shirt and casual slacks that are probably supposed to be tan but look slightly pink in the light.

"Mineral water, please." It's a business meeting; Ferran needs to keep his head clear.

"Mr. Kallström?"

"Beer." Ferran shoots him a look. "Water."

Drinks distributed, Brusin backs into the large oxblood leather swivel chair behind his desk. After a sip of his *tinto de verano*, Brusin says, "Thank you, gentlemen, for meeting with me today. I have an opportunity for you. Once you hear it, you will know why I didn't want to speak of it on the phone." He swivels to face Ferran. "Your expansion into the Costa del Sol is still doing well?"

"Yes. Thank you for asking." Ferran would rather speak Spanish or Catalan, but Brusin prefers English, and this is his meeting.

"Have you met with any opposition?"

"None that we can't deal with."

"I see." Brusin flips open a yellow file folder, then slides a photograph to the front edge of his desk in front of Ferran. "Have you seen this woman?"

Ferran picks up the photo. It's a surveillance shot, but clear enough. He nods, then shows it to Kallström, who snorts. Ferran says, "Sonia. That is the name she uses when she is dealing with the club owners. We have pushed her away from several venues in the three months past."

Kallström says, "No opposition. What you say…road hump."

Brusin nods once. "Right, then. Your Sonia works with other people. This group has become inconvenient to especially important people in Moscow. These important people would be extremely pleased if you eliminate Sonia and her gang. Of course, that also makes your competitive position much better. Will you do this?"

Ferran considers this before he says anything. Getting rid of a competitor has its attractions; it's how Grupo Sabadell grew so quickly, and how Ferran got *Campió*. However… "She isn't so big a problem to be worth the attention we would draw by killing her."

"You've killed before."

"Yes, but the stakes were higher. The benefits were worth the risk. Here?" Ferran shrugs. "Why don't your important people do their own killing? It seems that Russia has no problem eliminating inconvenient people."

"Russians are sloppy." Kallström gives Brusin his jackal smile. "Always they are caught. Get in big trouble."

Brusin puts a lot of concentration into finishing his drink. "My people in Moscow would rather this be a case of locals fighting locals. Let's leave it at that. While they don't want to be operationally involved, they're happy to give surveillance and intelligence support. That photo, for instance, is only four days old." He leans forward to fold his hands on his desk blotter. "Will you do this?"

Ferran switches his focus to the windows again while he thinks. It would probably be easy to get rid of whatever organization Sonia has. She hasn't pushed back after losing turf; she may not be able to. Then again, Brusin doesn't need to know that. "There is some risk to us in this. If we succeed, what will it be worth to your special Moscow people?"

Brusin chuckles. "Of course. That question is always there, isn't it? I expect that some type of reward can be decided on. It will depend on how quickly and quietly you do your work. I can tell you what will happen if you *don't* succeed: the people I work for wouldn't want me to continue processing cash for unreliable clients. Their decision would be completely out of my control. Of course, your decision is entirely up to you."

Ferran and Kallström exchange a quick, worried glance. The man's right; they'd be buried in unspendable money within a week or so. It sounds like the kind of problem everyone would want, but Grupo Sabadell already handles vanfuls of euros every week.

What Brusin isn't saying is that Ferran doesn't have a choice.

From his parked white Transit van across the street from Brusin's office, Grebnev listens to Balaguer drag out saying "yes" to Brusin's ultimatum, courtesy of the Zapadneft cybersecurity division's hack of Brusin's phone.

The reluctance sets him on edge. He would've preferred that Brusin not have to strong-arm this Grupo Sabadell; they'd be more zealous if they volunteer.

He'll have to keep a closer eye on Balaguer than he'd planned. He may need to provide more direct support, or push them aside if they're out of their depth.

Then again, a woman and some hackers? How hard a target can they really be? It's not like going up against a military target, where everyone's trained in the arts of violence.

Still, when Balaguer's black Mercedes Gelandewagen exits the sliding gate across Brusin's warehouse driveway, Grebnev notes the registration plate number.

Chapter 8

MARBELLA

Three-forty a.m. Tuesday morning.

Carson's at Olivia Valere, a nightclub on the western fringe of Marbella. The outside looks like a deli-mustard-yellow fortress; the inside is an Arabian Nights fever dream. It's dark, hazy from shisha smoke, and packed. Between the pulsing red-and-purple lights and the heavy bass backbeat, it's like being inside a heart that's working way too hard.

The last time Viktoriya was here, she sat in the VIP section facing the DJ's podium across the dance floor. Table rental in that section is €3500 for up to twelve people. Carson hopes they get at least a free drink each for that. The €70 she forked over at the door also got her a Manhattan, which she's been nursing for the past forty minutes.

This is the third night in a row that she's worn her one-and-only club dress: a mid-thigh, backless, sky-blue jersey sheath with a choker collar. She bought it in to wear to a Milan World Expo opening party during a DeWitt Agency project. It's not her favorite. It looks like it's painted on and makes her go braless, something she dislikes (the girls need discipline). Matt, her partner on the project, looked like she'd hit him with her baton the first time he saw her in it. It's about right for the women's outfits here. Her strappy, mid-heeled black sandals aren't nearly as tall as the stilettos some women here are tottering around on, but she's already tall and hers are dance shoes with steel shanks and reinforced heels.

Carson's stationed herself near the bar. She has a decent view of the VIP tables and the route from them to the dance floor. As crowded and dark as it is, though, it's possible Viktoriya could walk right past her and Carson wouldn't see her. She swept the place at three a.m., checking out the VIP tables in front of her and also behind the DJ podium, the Le Prive Lounge, and Karen Valere's Lounge. It took her twenty minutes. Men grabbed her ass at least half a dozen times along the way, and a woman (!) groped her right breast. She won't try that again for a while.

What do I do if I can't find her?

Viktoriya's been careful to not say where she's staying. She's put up a couple of posts featuring the pool at "Bruno's crib," wherever that is. Without a home base, finding her is all about luck. That's not the kind of plan Carson likes.

A hand lands lightly on the small of her bare back. Before Carson can pivot away, a woman's voice purrs in her ear. "Hi. You're looking for someone. Me, maybe?"

The voice belongs to the redhead stalker from Saturday. *What the fuck?* Carson's learned that coincidences do happen sometimes, but this is a bit much. "Did you follow me here?"

A momentary flash of white light shows copper hair piled on the woman's head, surrounded by two gold metallic bands. Carson's five-nine barefoot and five-eleven in tonight's heels, but she still has to look up slightly to find the redhead's eyes.

"What? No. Just lucky. I love this place. This is my second time here this week."

She's either a great actress or she's telling the truth. Either way, Carson will pretend she believes the story—for now. "Why do you think I'm looking for somebody?"

"You've been staring at the VIP section for ages." The woman has to put some wind into her voice so Carson can hear her above the electronic dance music. "A guy?"

After their Saturday morning encounter, Carson saw the woman two or three more times before now. In each case, they were heading in opposite directions. The redhead would always smile and wave. Now she's here. Deliberate?

Carson picks through a list of possible answers until she settles on, "A woman."

"Ooh, that sounds promising. Changed your mind about types?" She pushes tighter against Carson, who's stuck between her and a group of guys standing almost on top of her.

"A friend. Her name's Viktoriya."

"Got a picture?"

Carson fishes her phone out of her pleated black-satin clutch and shows the redhead the photo. The woman arches a thin eyebrow. "I know her."

You know her? It's either bullshit, or Saturday wasn't a coincidence. *Did Viktoriya put her on me? How did she know?*

The redhead goes on, "She's not in the VIP section, though, not yet. You know you can just go look, right? There's no rope."

"How do you know her?"

"Oh, you know." The redhead waves vaguely. "It's a small town. Have you known her long?"

"Not long." *If she knows Viktoriya, she already knows that answer. Or is this just a come-on?* The silk-covered nipple rubbing her bicep might be a clue.

"Maybe I can help you look. I'm Iris. What's your name?"

Names aren't always straightforward for Carson. She has several to choose from, occasionally including her real one. On this trip, she can go for the one on the passport she's traveling under, a sort-of Anglicized version of the name her Ukrainian parents gave her. "Lisa. I'd shake, but I'm out of hands."

"Oh, we don't shake." Iris suppresses a smile badly. "Here, it's *dos besos*. We kiss." She maneuvers to face Carson, then leans in. "Turn your head to your left." Soft lips brush Carson's right cheek. "Now to your right." Another brush on her left cheek. "And if we want to get to know each other better, we do this." Iris lays fingertips against the right side of Carson's chin, then kisses her lips.

Carson breaks the kiss, drops her clutch, and wraps her hand over Iris's mouth. "Still not gay."

Iris shakes free. She tries a smile that doesn't quite come off. "Just checking." She closes in gingerly. "Are we still friends?"

Carson suppresses an eye roll. "To be 'still friends,' we'd have to have *been* friends."

"Good point. First things first, and all that. Let's go up there." She points toward the back of the VIP section. "We can still look for Viktoriya, and we'll be out of the way."

Out of the way sounds fine to Carson. She scoops up her clutch and follows. Iris is wearing a drapey, shimmery lime-green thing that covers her left arm and shoulder and ends a smidgen below her ass. She has very long legs.

"This is better." Iris winds an arm around Carson and pulls her in tighter. "Comfy?"

All the physical contact is making Carson's teeth itch. If Iris hadn't said *I know her* when she saw Viktoriya's picture, Carson would've chased her off by now. She'll have to put up with Iris until she gets whatever information the woman has, if any. "How do you know Viktoriya?"

"I'm around, she's around." She shrugs. "Are you American?"

"Canadian."

"I *love* Canadians! You guys are so nice."

"Never played hockey, have you?"

"No, 'fraid not. You've probably guessed I'm American. Can't help it. So, is tonight just you and her hanging out, or is there a plan?"

Warning buzzers go off in Carson's head. "Why do you care so much?"

"Because I'm a horrible snoop, and I need something to entertain me since I'm here all by my lonesome." She gives Carson a squeeze. "C'mon, hon. Help a girl out."

Carson doesn't believe it's only idle curiosity. Iris has an agenda involving Viktoriya. Is she being territorial, or is it something else? "I need to talk to her."

"Ohhhhh. Well, why don't you talk to me while we wait for her? I know I'm a poor substitute—you must already know how charming she is—but it's better than standing here alone and having guys pinch your butt."

"Been there, done that."

"You see? We'll have fun. Not the kind I was hoping for when I first saw you, but I'll cope. Ask me anything."

Carson needs to see if Iris really knows something. Getting her used to answering questions could be useful. She points toward the two VIP tables in front of them. "What makes sitting there worth over three grand?"

Iris giggles. "It's kind of silly, isn't it? Let Auntie Iris explain. When you reserve your table, you promise to spend at least X euros on drinks. The better the table, the more you have to spend. The table itself is free."

"That's a shit-ton of booze."

"Not really. See the Patron Silver that caveman down there is guzzling? That's a €450 bottle of tequila. It adds up, especially when you spill half of it, like he is."

"That's fucking insane."

"Uh-huh. But it looks great for your buds on Insta or Twitter. Plus, you might end up sitting near someone famous. See the two guys at the end of the table on the right?"

"The ones necking with two girls each?"

"The very ones. They play for Granada's pro soccer team. Do you guys say 'soccer' or 'football'?"

"Soccer. We have football, too."

"Gotcha. Anyway, I guess if you're totes into soccer, sitting across from those two would be a big deal." Iris leans her lips to Carson's ear. "They're not even that good a team. Imagine how many girls those guys would have if they actually *won*."

Carson almost spits the last mouthful of her drink.

Iris beams. "My turn to ask." She points at Carson's chest. "Are those real?"

"Yes."

"Can I check?"

"No."

"Well, phooey. You can't blame a girl for trying, right? Your turn."

"What do you like so much about this place?"

"Over-the-top makes me feel warm all over. Too much is not enough and all that. My turn. Have you ever kissed a girl before me?"

Really? "Grade seven. We were practicing so we knew what to do with boys. My turn." This one might scare her off, but it's worth the risk. "Viktoriya's not coming tonight, is she?"

Iris's smile is a bit strained. "Now, how would I know that?"

"Because this works one of two ways. One: you don't know her at all, but you said you do to keep hitting on me. Two: you know her a lot better than you said, and you're screening me or something. Which is it?"

Iris looks toward the dance floor as she absently strokes Carson's flank. After a moment, she grows a grin. "Okay, you caught me. You have amazing legs, and I want you to wrap them around me."

"Fuck off." *Should've known.* Carson peels off Iris's hand and throws it back to her. "That means 'get lost.'"

Iris's mouth droops almost as much as her shoulders. She sighs, then drifts down the steps toward the dance floor.

Carson's rational voice chimes in before Iris gets four steps away: *What if she really does know Viktoriya?*

You heard her. She wants to get laid.

Maybe she's testing you. See how bad you want to meet Viktoriya.

Still not fucking her.

No…but you can be nice to her. Everybody likes that. And you might get what you need.

Carson hates it when her rational voice says sensible things. The sooner she finds Viktoriya, the sooner she can get this over with. If Iris can truly help with that… "Hey, Iris."

Iris stops. Her shoulders heave up, then fall again. She slowly turns around. Her lower lip is pushed out a skosh. "You told me to get lost."

"Yeah." Carson closes half the distance between them. "Look, I'm tired of explaining to people that I'm straight. Pisses me off. So…"

"I get it." She takes a tentative step toward Carson. "Everyone has this picture of what a lesbian's supposed to look like. It's you, not me. It's not fair, and it's frustrating for us both, I'm sure." Iris stands still, one knee cocked, carefully watching Carson.

Say the words… "Sorry I barked. You really know Viktoriya?"

Iris checks the carpet for spills for a while, then gives Carson a sad-accepting look. "Well enough to text her. Maybe…*maybe* I can set up a meeting between you two. But you have to tell me what you want to talk to her about. She'll ask."

Carson watches her for a few moments, waiting for the tell that says *I'm lying.* It doesn't come. "Her family's worried about her. I guess they don't talk. They want me to get a read on how she's doing."

"Why you?"

"Guess they think she'll talk to another woman."

Iris nods. "Maybe they're right." She props her chin on her upraised fist while she considers Carson, her lips pursed. "I'll make you a deal. I'll set up a meeting between you and Viktoriya—if she'll do it, I can't guarantee that—if you dance with me."

"What?" *Unbelievable.* "I told you, I'm—"

"Not gay, I know, I know. But we're here, and that"—she

points to the jammed dance floor—"looks like fun, and I'd feel like a dork out there all by my lonesome. So, dance with me. I *swear* I'll behave." She actually crosses her heart. "I won't touch you unless you want me to."

"When do you send the text?"

"When we're done. You can watch me. Correct my spelling. If I don't do it, well…you can hurt me. Spank me. Say, that sounds like fun, too." Carson's glare shrinks her a bit. "Kidding! Just kidding. I double pinkie-swear promise I'll do it." Iris holds out her hand. "C'mon. Let's dance."

For fuck's sake. Carson hasn't danced with another female since grade seven. But she can put up with it to short-circuit her search and get on with her job. If Iris gets grabby, Carson can deal with that quickly and in ways the bruises won't show.

She loops her clutch's silver chain over her neck and right shoulder, sets her highball glass on a ledge, and takes Iris's hand.

Chapter 9

MARBELLA

Carson pries open her eyes enough to see the time on her phone. The numbers are blurry, but they may start with a ten. *That's not right.* She grinds the crap out of her eyes and tries again. Ten-eighteen a.m. No wonder it's so light outside.

She flops onto her back. Her ears still ring from the full-throttle dance music last night. This morning. Whatever.

She didn't leave the club until almost six, when the eastern sky was turning lilac. The streetsweepers and garbage trucks were already out as the BlaBlaCar—Europe's answer to Uber—drove her to the hotel. Her dress was soaked with sweat and spilled booze, and her feet and calves ached from dancing.

Iris was good company after she stopped trying to pick up Carson. When they took breaks from dancing, Iris told her funny stories about things she'd seen at other clubs and catted on people in the dance-floor scrum. They fell into easy high school-level mutual-insult humor like they'd been at it for ages. Carson laughed a lot at the silliest things.

It was fun. She had *fun.* The way she and Brianna used to when they were young and single and still believed they could do anything.

Carson finally heaves herself upright, then lets the whirlies pass. She's over four hours past her normal feeding time, and her fasting hypoglycemia has riled up both her gut and her head. She staggers into the washroom, splashes water on her face and bedhead, pulls on her workout clothes, then searches for her phone. It's in her clutch, dropped on the floor next to the crumpled heap of her dress. Two texts from Iris wait for her.

Meet V @ Pangea banus 11p tonite. Dress 2 party!

U animal.

While Carson puts herself together to meet Viktoriya, Rogozhkin calls. It's a relief; he'd been disappointed when she told him she had to postpone her visit and she'd wondered if he'd call again. He asks "Did I catch you in the middle of something?" with a hopeful tone.

"Getting ready to go to dinner."

"What are you wearing?"

As it happens, she's fresh out of the shower. *Play along? Sure.* "Water."

"Hmm. Should we turn this into a video call?"

"Use your imagination."

"Oh, I am." He chuckles. "Tell me about Marbella."

She does as she towel-dries her hair and pulls on her blue party dress. Good thing the hotel laundry turns around cleaning orders in only four hours. They get a good laugh out of Iris making a pass at her. Carson asks, "What are you doing up this late? There's music behind you."

"I'm at my favorite *taverna*, imagining you sitting next to me. What do you drink?"

"Single-malt whisky."

"A woman after my own heart. I'll have some waiting when you visit. Which I hope will be soon?"

When they finally stop flirting and say "good night," Carson catches herself in the washroom mirror wearing a silly grin.

Puerto Banús is a development seven klicks west of Marbella. It's mostly hotels, condos, and an enormous shopping mall. The centerpiece—where Carson is now—is a shopping and entertainment complex next to a large marina. The buildings are white and geometric, reminding her of pictures she's seen of Spanish or Greek villages. Even Carson could recognize the names on the stores. The boats get larger the farther west they're parked in the marina.

The area's crowded at almost ten at night. Strolling couples and drifting shoals of hen and stag parties fill the streets and sidewalks, dodging a line of Aston-Martins, Ferraris, and Lamborghinis prowling for waterfront parking. By now, Carson knows this is about people on their way to dinner, or the after-dinner crowd looking for a bar to burn time in until the nightclubs open.

Carson sits in Mumtaz, an Indian restaurant next to the Dolce & Gabbana building where Pangea's located. The restaurant's finally starting to fill up. There are only three ways someone can get to Pangea, and she can see all three of them from her table. She's been slow-rolling her excellent *karahi murg* and *bengan bhaji* for one reason—she wants to see Viktoriya on her way into Pangea. Does she travel alone? Does she have an entourage? How many people? Bodyguards?

Carson doubts Viktoriya will go back to Moscow quietly. She's had more than enough opportunity already. So Carson has to plan for a rendition—not her favorite choice, but she has to at least consider it. If Viktoriya has a posse, a rendition gets even messier.

She finally surrenders her used dishes to the busboy at a shade before ten-thirty without having seen Viktoriya yet. Do insiders know some back way into the bar? Is she going to show at all?

That's when Carson sees a man throw a woman against a car.

He's one of the gangster boys Carson's been seeing around—shiny shirt with brand logos, neck and hand tattoos, a fade. Probably strapped. She's one of the party girls Carson's usually seen hanging around the gangsters in the clubs—ultra-short shrink-wrap dress, push-up bra, heels that make her walk on her toes. She bounces off the passenger's-side rear door of the chrome-yellow Mercedes-AMG GT across the street from Carson's nearest window. When she sprawls on the pavement, she flashes her G-string to everyone in the restaurant.

Carson can't stop the anger burning its way up her esophagus. No woman deserves that shit, no matter how many bad choices she's made.

The couple leaps into a screaming match. The restaurant's windows erase the sound, but the hand gestures and twisted faces make clear there's no happy ending in the cards for these two.

Diners around Carson murmur alarm and *tsk* at the scene. A nearby woman stage-whispers to her man, "Should we call the police?"

Party Girl tries to stand. Gangster Boy wallops her, a wide-swing slap with big follow-through. She caroms off the Benz again, her mouth spraying blood across a yellow door.

Carson stands. She's seen enough. She grabs—literally—the nearest waiter and snarls, "Call the cops *now*. I'll be back in a minute. Have my check ready." Then she stalks through the tables toward the front door.

A group of young people passes the glass door just before she pushes through. Carson slams on her brakes. There's five of them, four women and a guy, but the only one she pays attention to is the one in the middle.

It's Viktoriya.

Carson recognizes her immediately—she's been staring at pictures of the woman for days. Streetlights make Viktoriya's white, mid-thigh, sleeveless dress radiate. She raises a hand to stop her posse, and all five watch, horrified, as the now-crying Party Girl tries to swat Gangster Boy's fingers out of her hair before he hauls her off the pavement with it.

Carson sorts through her options. She doesn't want Viktoriya's first sight of her to be Carson beating the ever-loving shit out of Gangster Boy; it may be an accurate first impression, but it'd be a bad one. But she can't let that asshole put Party Girl in a hospital or the morgue.

Before Carson can decide, Viktoriya hands something to Iris, taps the guy on the shoulder and points north along the street, then marches fast toward the fighting couple.

What the fuck…?

The guy sprints up the street, going who-knows-where. Iris flanks Viktoriya about two meters to her right. They neatly bracket the combatants when they reach the yellow Benz, Viktoriya closest to Party Girl, Iris just behind and to Gangster Boy's left side. He tosses Party Girl against the Benz again, then swivels toward Iris.

They act like they've got a plan. Carson pulls her small collapsible baton from her black-satin clutch. *Can't see what it is, though.* If Gangster Boy decides to push back, Carson might be sending Viktoriya home in a casket.

Gangster Boy's arguing with Iris, using the same slashing arm movements as he had with Party Girl. Viktoriya takes advantage of Iris's distraction to gather the sobbing Party Girl in her arms and quick-walks her away from the Benz. *Nicely done.*

But Iris is stuck in place. She's not exactly an imposing figure. Carson tries to game out how Iris gets unstuck without having Gangster Boy take up with her where he left off with his now ex-date. Everything she thinks of ends up with Iris in a bloody heap on the ground.

Iris is talking a lot—no surprise there—with both her mouth and right hand. Her left hand clutches something small behind her back. She thumbs over her shoulder at the restaurant, probably pointing out all the potential witnesses. She points north up the street toward…flashing blue lights.

Cops. That's her escape plan.

Gangster Boy jerks up his right hand like he's about to hit Iris. She doesn't flinch, which surprises the hell out of Carson. Then he dives into the Benz, screeches out of the parking space, and growls up the street.

A white Renault with blue-and-white checkerboard stripes along the sides stops near Iris and disgorges two cops and Viktoriya's posse guy. Viktoriya—who's been comforting Party Girl along with the other two women in her posse—guides her patient to the nearest cop.

Two minutes later, Viktoriya and her friends stroll down the street toward Pangea like it's a normal evening out.

Carson stands by the restaurant door, trying to sort out what she just saw. If Viktoriya and Company spend as much time here as Instagram says they do, they should've known what Gangster Boy was. Approaching that fight was either incredibly stupid or ballsy as hell. But Carson didn't see a moment of fright or panic or disorganization. Viktoriya directed her people quickly and crisply, and they obeyed without hesitation. They defused the situation without force or violence. Only Gangster Boy's ego got bruised.

Whatever Carson saw, it wasn't the work of a self-absorbed airhead.

She's gotta meet this woman.

Chapter 10

PANGEA, PUERTO BANÚS

Carson follows Iris through throngs of partiers on their way to Pangea's roof deck. Iris thoroughly searched Carson's handbag—for bugs or trackers, she claimed—when they met at eleven by the base of the old stone watchtower next door to the bar. The lights sparkle off Iris's alarmingly short cocktail dress encrusted with blue, green, and black beads in a zebra pattern. The spaghetti straps show off her shoulder tattoo.

As much as Carson wants to, she hasn't asked Iris about her performance with Gangster Boy. The more Carson thinks about it, the more she's convinced that the hapless would-be stalker act Iris put on when they first met on Saturday was just that—an act. Which leads to Carson's next question: who is Iris really?

The crowd on the tiled roof deck is largely but not exclusively young. White dresses on the women, white shirts on the men. The lighting leans heavily toward blue and magenta. To Carson's right, the old stone tower is uplit against the night sky with "Pangea" in fake Hindi script projected across the top. A DJ spins R&B and hip-hop from a podium near the tower. Iris drags Carson by the hand through the knots of drinkers toward an open pavilion with a conical thatched roof held up by what look like thick bamboo poles. When they approach one of the freeform benches surrounding it, Viktoriya stands to face them.

A downlight on the canopy makes her glow in the semi-darkness. The pavilion's surrounded by people, but it's like Viktoriya's in the eye of a hurricane: calm in the center, noise and chaos all around.

Don't know what you're dealing with, Carson tells herself. *Let her make the first move.*

When Carson and Iris break through the eyewall, Viktoriya gives her a brilliant smile. "You must be Lisa. Iris has told me all about you.”

Carson expected a loud, bored, little-Russian-girl voice. She wasn't prepared for a buttery English accent spoken so softly that Carson has to lean in to hear. “That's me.”

“So very happy to meet you.” Viktoriya exchanges *dos besos* with Carson. She pulls back and tilts her head as Iris whispers in her ear. After a moment, Viktoriya shoots a surprised look at her, then turns to Carson, frowning. “Iris tells me you have a weapon. Is that true?”

Here we go. “A baton. I usually have one.”

“I see.” Viktoriya's eyes search her face for a long few beats. “She says you also have something for tying up people. Will you try to use these things against me?”

Zip ties. A hundred and one uses. “Wasn't planning on it.” What Carson doesn't say is, *I won't need to.* They can look each other straight in the eye, but only because Viktoriya's heels are twice as tall as Carson's. Carson has at least fifteen kilos on her. It wouldn't be much of a fight. “Iris seems interested in getting tied up.”

Viktoriya hides a giggle behind her fingers. “That sounds right.” She smiles, then turns to Iris. “I'll be fine. Can you find Celeste for me? The noise may be a bit much for her.”

“All right.” Iris strokes Viktoriya's arm. “Sure you'll be okay? I can stay.”

“Thank you, but I'm not worried.”

“Okay. I'll be close.”

“I know.”

Iris disappears into the crowd outside the pavilion. Viktoriya takes Carson's hand in both of hers. “Sit with me.” They sink onto the same black-vinyl cushion, touching knees. “Are you tired of Champagne yet?”

“Had enough for now.”

“So have I.” That's news; she's usually hoisting a half-full flute on Insta. “What do you drink?”

“Ale. Stout.”

“No, liquor.”

“Single-malt whisky.”

“Ah. I gained a taste for that when I lived in England.” She flicks her right hand to head height. A young man all in black appears within seconds. "Please bring us a bottle of J&B Rare."

Once the waiter vanishes, Carson asks, "Why aren't all those people out there in here?"

"Because this is the VIP section." Viktoriya sweeps a hand along the bench she and Carson have to themselves. "My friends and I have this part of it. You'll meet some of them tonight." She collects Carson's hand again. "Father sent you to find me?"

Carson's pleasantly surprised; she'd expected endless empty chat before they got to work. "Not directly. He called a friend. The friend sent me."

"Ah. Was this one of his FSB friends?"

"No." It's time for Carson to let her know what kind of trouble she's in. "One of his Bratva friends."

One of Viktoriya's perfectly plucked eyebrows arches. "Which sort?"

Props to her; she knows there's more than one kind of Russian mobster. "Solntsevskaya."

The other eyebrow levitates. Viktoriya's eyes grow wider. "I see." She watches her fingertips smooth over the back of Carson's hand.

The cylindrical cocktail table's illuminated base washes Viktoriya with a pale yellow light. Her dress looks like someone wrapped white fabric tight around her and pinned it in place. Two gold bands joined by silver medallions glimmer from her left bicep. That and subtle golden squares on her earlobes are the only jewelry Carson can see on her, far less than what she wears online. Has Viktoriya already taken her Insta photos for tonight?

Viktoriya finally looks into Carson's eyes again, more subdued this time. "Have you a plan? Will you bop me on the head with your baton and take me from here over your shoulder? Is there a business jet waiting at Málaga to take me to Moscow?"

It could go that way. If Viktoriya was what Carson had thought she'd be, she might've done that by now. But no shit-for-brains little girl could've pulled off that scene on the street. That makes Carson want to find out what else Rodievsky didn't tell her. She's well aware of what controlling men are like and the things they'll say when they want something. "All I've heard is your dad's side of the story. Tell me yours."

The waiter reappears with a bottle of J&B and two tumblers

balanced on a shiny black tray. Viktoriya gives him a big smile and shoos him off. She pours two fingers each, hands a glass to Carson, then raises hers as a toast. "To stories." They sip. Viktoriya drapes a hand over Carson's thigh. "Did you know that I've not lived in Moscow for thirteen years?"

Carson resists an urge to snap off Viktoriya's hand at the wrist. "How's that work?"

"The private school in Moscow wasn't up to scratch for Father. Or for me. It didn't challenge me, and I was bored, and as bored children do, I made trouble to entertain myself. Starting year five, he sent me to St. George's International School in Montreux. They were better equipped to deal with a young girl who had no 'slow gear.' Father no longer had any need to be anything but a writer of bank drafts. He was chuffed to pay for my summer boarding so I wouldn't have to return to Moscow. He and Mother would visit when they came to ski at Zermatt. Wonderful skiing, by the way. Do you?"

"No. Hockey and rugby."

Another smile. "I'm not surprised. You and Sebastian should get on. He played rugby in university."

"Sebastian?"

"One of my friends. He'll make an appearance soon." For the first time, Viktoriya looks past Carson. She pops to her feet and holds out her arms. "Celeste! *Mon chéri!*" That part Carson catches; the rest is rapid-fire French.

Iris is back with another woman—or girl, possibly. She'd been with Viktoriya's posse on the street earlier. She has a crystalline face with large eyes, and fine, straight, center-parted hair nearly as light as Viktoriya's dress. She looks almost lost in her drapey, pale-pastel smock top and mid-calf skirt. Her flats make her the shortest of the four women. She reminds Carson of an angel in an old painting.

They have a short conversation in French. Viktoriya turns her to face Carson and introduces her…in French.

Carson says, "Uh, hey."

Viktoriya presses her fingers to her lips. "Oh, dear. You don't speak French. I thought all Canadians do."

"Just the Québécois." Carson stands and holds out her hand. "I'm Lisa. You're Celeste?"

The girl hunches her shoulders. "Um, yes. Hello." Then she

moves in for more kissing. Carson's had her cheeks kissed more tonight than by the past three men she's slept with put together.

They sit with Celeste to Carson's left and Iris to Viktoriya's right. Iris swipes the last mouthful of whisky from Viktoriya's glass. Viktoriya pats Carson's knee. "Where were we?"

"St. George's."

"Of course. When I got my international baccalaureate, I went to Corpus Christi at Cambridge. I had options, but I liked it there. They were happy that Father could pay full tuition, and he was happy that I'd be in England instead of Russia. Once I was finished there, I felt no particular urge to return to Moscow. Father expressed no interest in my doing so."

Carson wasn't sure whether she should be sad that Viktoriya's dad essentially dumped her, or disgusted that a shit-ton of money got spent on her schooling and she's been hanging out in bars for two years. "He changed his mind."

"Clearly."

"Where was your mom in all this?"

"Mother." Viktoriya shakes her head and lets out a private little smile. "Father gives her a very generous allowance and lets her spend it however she wishes. She needs only to have no firm opinions about anything and to never contradict him." She refreshes her glass and Carson's. "Tell me about your parents."

"Why?"

"Well, you know about mine, now. It's only fair. I'd like to know who's stalking me."

Stalking. That's what I've been doing, isn't it? Carson takes a moment to put together the shortest explanation she can. "Well…my folks went to Canada from the USSR in the '70s. Pops worked security for the oil companies. He was gone a lot. Mom's a drunk." She tosses her hand toward the people milling outside the VIP section's invisible bubble. "This is all weird to me. Never had much money. Vacation was going to Calgary for the Stampede, or Edmonton to see the Oilers. Not this."

Viktoriya leans slightly toward Carson, watching her intently. She listens harder than anyone Carson's known lately. "I'm so sorry. It must have been difficult for you. I reckon my problems don't look like problems to you at all, do they?"

"Not so much." Carson sets her empty glass on the table. "Your dad says he wants you to come home and take over his businesses. What's up with that?"

"I'm sure he says that." Viktoriya considers her empty glass, then sets it down. "Father's developed the idea that I owe him money and that I should work off my debt. Can you imagine? As for handing his businesses to me…well, he's not the type to give up control of anything. I've no doubt he'll give me some grand title and a vast office. He'll expect me to do exactly as I'm told and defend it all to the den of thieves in his boardroom. When something goes wrong—and it often does—my face will be on the telly, not his. And when he finally sells the firms, I'll be simply another asset on offer."

"Why would he do that to you?"

"Because I'm expendable. I never learned to behave. I'm far from his favorite child. Do you know that I have a sister?"

"Valeriya. Yeah."

"She's the pretty one."

"Bullshit."

"No, I'm quite serious. All this?" She waves a hand around her face. "It's all paint and hair and nails. You should…no, you *shouldn't* see me in the morning—"

"Oh, Vicki." Iris gives her a playful slap on the arm. "Stop it. You're gorgeous."

Viktoriya squeezes Iris's hand. "Thank you, Iris. What would I do without you?" She leans toward Carson again. "Valeriya's truly beautiful without all this. She's also…" She purses her lips, thinking. "Easily pleased, let's say. She's exactly the daughter Father wanted. He's busy making her into a prize calf to take to auction. I never knew it was possible to envy someone and pity her at the same time." She peers into Carson's eyes again, then pats her knee again. "This all sounds quite petty to you, doesn't it? The problems of a rich girl?"

Carson scoops Viktoriya's hand off her leg and deposits it on Viktoriya's lap. "You got as much right to be happy as anybody." She wants to say something about how they both were neglected by their parents, but can't figure out how without making it sound creepy.

Viktoriya covers her rejected hand with her free one. "I should…apologize. I touch. It's how I connect with people. I should have asked if you minded. Sorry."

Carson can't tell if Viktoriya's tone is embarrassed or resentful and doesn't want to spend time now thinking about it. "I'm not used to it."

"I understand." Viktoriya stands. "The view is lovely from here. Let me show you."

The four women thread through the crowd to the railing overlooking the marina. The back ends of large yachts crowd the closest line of slips. Several have parties underway, their flashing lights and music competing with Pangea's DJ. Dots of light climb the hills behind Puerto Banús and reach all the way to Marbella, which is a blue glow on the northeastern horizon. It's nearly midnight, but the street below is as busy as a normal city street at noon.

Carson points to the yachts. "Is that normal? The boats?"

"Yes, for August and into September." Viktoriya points to their right, past the tower. "See the lights out there? Those are the ships that can't fit in the marina. They moor out there and run their tenders into that landing down there so their passengers can come shop and play."

The yachts in the harbor look like small cruise ships to Carson. "They're bigger than these?"

"Oh, yes. Much larger." Viktoriya tries a small smile on Carson. "How long did it take for you to discover I'm delaying my posts on Insta?"

"A few hours."

"I hope it wasn't a shock. Most influencers stock up snaps and spread them over time."

Now I find that out. "Don't pay much attention to influencers."

Viktoriya's smile slides into rueful. "I don't imagine so. How did you suss it out?"

"You got sloppy with your polo picture."

Viktoriya whips her phone out of her shoulder bag and thumbs through the photos on her Instagram feed. She holds one up for Carson to see. "This one?"

"Yeah. The guys in the background played on Wednesday."

"Good Lord. You noticed that? I'm quite impressed."

"When'd you make me?"

"Sorry?"

"Figure out I was following you."

"Oh. At Tibu."

On Friday. Carson resists the urge to bang her head against the railing. She tried to look for Viktoriya that night, but the place was packed and almost impossible to walk through. "I was that obvious?"

"No, not at all. You remember how it was that night. I like your little trick of using one of my snaps to pose as a friend. You asked our waitress if she'd seen me. She knows us and didn't know you, so she asked if we knew a 'Lisa.' Of course, we didn't. I asked Iris to look into it. She followed you to your hotel and watched for you for the next three days after."

Three days? "Bullshit. I made her Saturday morning. Saw her three more times before Tuesday night, going the other way. If she was there, I'd've seen her."

Iris says, "You stopped looking for me. Saturday? I saw you'd spotted me and bumped into you on purpose to make you think I was some stalker girl so you'd ignore me. After that, I went where Vicki was going to go and watched for you. If you showed up, I waved her off." Iris shrugs.

"I was impressed by how much you knew about my schedule." Viktoriya chuckles. "I believe Iris came to fancy you while—"

"Don't tell her that!" Iris shakes Viktoriya's shoulders with both hands. "You'll blow my image."

"Too late—I already know." Carson kicks herself mentally. Iris is right—Carson had completely written her off until they met again at the club. She'd been so preoccupied searching for Viktoriya that she didn't pay enough attention to what was behind her. Even then, she probably would've looked at the men, not the women. "You followed me to that club? Olivia Valere?"

Iris puts on a Cheshire Cat grin. "I was already there, hon. Vicki and the fam were going there 'til I told them you beat them to it. That's when Vicki told me to hook up with you."

Talk about a blind spot. Carson leans an elbow on the railing, facing Viktoriya. "Here's what I don't get. You're ducking your dad's muscle, but you're all over Instagram. Why? You don't wanna be found, go dark. Stop giving them clues."

Iris says, "Preach it, hon. I've been telling her that for ages."

Viktoriya nods sadly. "Yes, she has done. It's quite simple, really. Father's in charge of Russia's Ministry of Internal Affairs. He has direct access to most of the police agencies in the world. Right now he knows—or thinks he knows—where I am. Let's say he rings up the Guardia Civil headquarters in Madrid and asks them to send me home. They'll ask where I am, and he'll say 'Her Insta says she's in Marbella.' They'll of course look for themselves and see all my snaps. Then they'll tell Father, 'She's an adult and she's not breaking any laws. If you want her, come for her yourself.' But if I 'go dark,' as you put it? Father won't know where I am. I'll be a *missing person*. Then Father can ring up the Guardia and say, 'My daughter is missing. Please find her.' And they'll be obliged to try. I'll have to live like a fugitive, and where's the fun in that?"

She's got a point. Carson tries to pick apart her argument but can't. This isn't at all how she saw this going when she gamed it out today during her workout. "Okay, I get that. But the Vicki on Insta and the Vicki here aren't the same people."

Iris snorts. "That's, like, the Eleventh Commandment: 'Thou shalt be fake on Insta.'"

"Okay, okay, fine. But why be a ditz?"

Viktoriya cocks her head. "Sorry?"

"Your character or whatever on Insta. She's a ditz. She's all about parties and clothes and booze. I hated her when I first saw her. You got thousands and thousands of followers. They're, what, teen girls?"

"Yes. Young women, late teens and twenties."

"Why not give them a role model? A *good* one? Use your money and your schooling to do something to help people. Make things better. Show your fans there's more to being a woman than short skirts and lipstick."

The crowd noise and the music don't change, but silence settles among the four women. Viktoriya studies the hands she's folded at her hips. Iris stares at the Med as she gnaws on her upper lip. Only Celeste—Carson's almost forgotten about her—looks at Carson, with curiosity rather than judgment. *Are they pissed off? Are they ashamed? Did I just step in it?*

Viktoriya finally looks up at Carson and flashes a dimmed smile. She hovers her right hand over Carson's left arm perched on the rail. "May I?" Carson nods. Viktoriya gently lands her fingertips on Carson's wrist. "Thank you for seeing that I'm not my online character. Online Vicki is useful camouflage. It helps the people who wish me ill to underestimate me." She stops to think. "I truly am working to help people, to make the world better. We all are. It's simply best to not call attention to it just now. I reckon I could throw the world as it is at my followers, but…well, I wager they're well-acquainted with it. They follow Online Vicki to get away from it. Does this make sense to you?"

"Don't know. Maybe." There was no Instagram or Facebook or Pinterest when Carson was a teenager. Would she have used them if they'd been around? She had teen magazines and fashion magazines to make her feel inferior, especially before her body had sorted itself out; she didn't need people like Online Vicki to pile on.

"Now you've heard my side of the story." Viktoriya edges a bit closer to Carson, her face tense. "What are you going to do?"

Chapter 11

PANGEA, PUERTO BANÚS

Carson burrows farther into the hallway corner to hear her phone better over the background noise. Not a great place for a conversation, but if Viktoriya tries to bolt, she'll have to go right past Carson. "I said, she doesn't want to go."

Rodievsky makes a guttural sound that's not a word, but says a lot. "This should not be a surprise to you. Would you leave an endless party? Especially when someone else pays for it? Of course not. Was—"

"*Is* Baranov paying for it, or is she using her own money?"

"I have no idea. It matters very little. You have to tell her to go home, not encourage—."

"Not that simple. She told me about her dad. He wants her to be a front for him. Are his businesses in trouble?"

"Oleg Germanovich is an oligarch because he was a talented opportunist in the '90s, not because he is a good businessman. His businesses are always in some sort of trouble. Being a minister helps him keep the wolves away."

"That's what he wants to throw her into. Be a mouthpiece and a flak absorber. That's why she isn't interested." That, and her dad's been ignoring her for years. Rodievsky may not get that the same way Carson does.

"Perhaps he wants the girl to rescue his empire from his own blundering."

"She doesn't believe that. Look, she's not that plug on Insta. She's pretty together. Smart, gutsy, well-spoken, mature. Surprised the hell out of me. This is between them. They need to work this out themselves."

Rodievsky growls, "I thought you might take her part in this. I did not promise Oleg Germanovich family counseling. I promised I would bring his daughter to him. What happens after is their problem, not mine *or yours*. Understand?"

Carson mutes the phone so he doesn't hear her curse. "Okay. One more time: she doesn't want to go. That means I have to…" she looks around for eavesdroppers who might speak Russian, then lowers her voice "…kidnap her. She goes with a group of friends. Don't know how many yet, but it looks like a package deal. I can't do this alone without making noise. Want me to drag her back to Moscow? Then get me backup and a private jet."

The line goes silent. That always makes her nervous; she never knows where the line is between pushing back and going too far, only that it keeps moving.

"How many men do you need?"

Like I've already planned this. She picks a number from thin air. "Five, including two drivers. We'll need gear, too. The jet has to fly nonstop from Málaga to Moscow." She hopes that if she makes this expensive enough, Rodievsky will drop it.

"Hmpf. I will talk with Oleg Germanovich. He still thinks Viktoriya will return willingly. I have no idea if he wants to risk the blowback from using force. I will tell him how the situation stands and find out how far he is willing to go. Until then, keep the girl in sight. Do what you must to stay in contact. Do you understand?"

"Yeah." Carson doesn't know what to do about it yet. She glances to the corridor leading outside and notices Celeste standing at the near end, watching her. "Gotta go."

Celeste's outfit is the palest yellow with lacy hems along the smock and skirt. Her arms are folded across her belly. When Carson stops a couple of paces from her, she notices Celeste's eyes are the color of the Mediterranean on a sunny day. "Hi again."

"Hello."

"Are you cold?"

Celeste's been rubbing her biceps rhythmically. She nods.

"It's funny. These places are usually hot."

"Yes. This place is outside." She has a French accent that's noticeable but not intrusive.

"Yeah, it is." *Something's…off about her.* For one thing, she doesn't seem to blink. For another, she's staring directly and intently into Carson's eyes, but there's no challenge in it. It's a look Carson knows well from Dominik, her youngest brother. She knows why he did it. *Maybe Celeste's the same?*

"Lisa?"

"Yeah?"

"You are unhappy?"

Carson stands there with her mouth half-open. How does she answer that question? "Why do you say that?"

"I hear it."

"From who?"

"No. I hear it."

That doesn't explain anything. Did she overhear Carson's talk with Rodievsky? If she did, it shouldn't mean anything to her—Carson was speaking Russian the whole time. Maybe that's what she's reacting to.

Celeste ducks her head. "Please, will you take me to Vicki?"

"She's right down that way." Carson points down the corridor.

"No. Please take me." Celeste looks up. She's chewing her lower lip. "There are so many people, so much noise. It is so confusing. Please?"

Dom got this way when he was little. Too much sensory input. Celeste's eyes are full of the same fear as Dom's, touching Carson in a way she hasn't been for ages. "Come on."

The corridor's crowded and noisy. Celeste grabs Carson's hand as they pass a hen party—tiaras, sashes, sequins, and a young woman wearing her bra outside her dress, all laughing like hyenas. Celeste's hand is stronger than the rest of her looks.

Once they pass outside, Carson asks, "How long have you been with Viktoriya?"

"Almost one year." Her nose wrinkles as they pass through a bank of shisha smoke.

"Do you like it? Being her friend?"

Celeste's face lights up. "Yes. She is very nice to me. All our friends are very nice."

Well, that's something. "Viktoriya said you're doing things to help people. What are you doing?"

Celeste giggles, then presses the side of her index finger against her lips.

Carson turns Celeste over to Viktoriya when they reach the VIP section. Two new people are with her: a tall, dishy man in a fitted white button-down shirt and dove-gray slacks, and a slender, regal-looking black woman wearing a knee-length wrap dress with an elaborate red-and-gold pattern. Carson remembers seeing her over the weekend. Both had been with Viktoriya outside the restaurant. Their conversation dims when they see Carson.

Viktoriya takes Carson's arm and turns her toward the newcomers. "This is our new friend, Lisa. Lisa, this is Sebastian. I've mentioned him before."

Curly brown hair, deep brown eyes, a square, handsome face, broad shoulders. He'd gone to get the cops earlier. *Hello, Sebastian.* He'd given her an up-and-down scan when she arrived and now didn't hesitate to move in for the *dos besos.* "Grand meeting you." *Scottish? Irish?* Either way, smooth like some of Carson's favorite whiskies.

"And this is Amabelle."

The black woman's at least three inches taller than Carson, though some of that is about the red stilettos that match her dress. She announces "Welcome to our little cabal" after contactless air-kissing. She has a strong French accent overlaid with something else Carson can't figure out.

Carson says, "I'm not used to looking up at another woman."

Amabelle lets out a warm, hearty laugh. "Think of me as the giraffe. Very tall but mostly harmless."

Sebastian says, "Unless you're an acacia."

"That is so." Amabelle waves a finger at Carson. "We will see if this one has thorns."

Viktoriya rescues Carson from having to think of a comeback, pulling her off to the side. She stands very close and maneuvers her lips to Carson's ear. "Did you ring up Father's friend?"

"Yeah. He's gotta talk to your dad. Find out how far he wants to take this."

"You told him I don't wish to go?"

"Yeah." Carson hesitates. "I put in a plug for you. Said you and your dad need to work it out on your own."

Viktoriya nods. "I appreciate that. What will you do now?"

Carson shrugs. She hasn't figured that out yet. "I'm supposed to keep an eye on you." She's sure Viktoriya and her crew already know that.

"Shock horror."

Not the reaction Carson expected. She'd expected the whole bunch to be gone when she got back from her phone call. "Your people know why I'm here, right?"

"Of course. I've asked them to make you feel welcome. We gain nothing by driving you off. Besides, Celeste approves of you."

"She does?"

"Yes. She's quite intuitive about people. When you arrived just now holding her hand and she was smiling? That means you must be at least acceptable. Otherwise, she'd have been like a cat on a lead." Viktoriya lays gentle fingertips on Carson's shoulder. "Drink with us. Learn about us. We're considering going to 11 Banus in a while. It's a spanking-new club and we've not been yet. Come explore with us?"

It's past midnight. Being out until five this morning isn't helping her stay awake. Olympic-level clubbing is a young person's sport, and that's not her anymore. Still, it's better watching from the inside than spying from the outside. "We'll see if I make it that far."

There's not much foot traffic on the street in front of Pangea at just shy of one a.m. when Carson leaves the bar with Viktoriya's posse. Bass backbeats from multiple clubs vibrate the shop windows. The occasional scream of an over-revving V12 engine rips through the night.

Viktoriya's bunch knots up in the middle of the street, checking phones for directions. A sixth member—Tamara—showed up about half an hour ago. Carson stands off, watching. Five gals and a guy. Either Sebastian's gay and he's one of the girls, or the sexual politics get really messy.

While she waits, Carson scopes the scene, looking for threats. Most grown-ups have disappeared. The teens and twenty-somethings who have the endurance to dance 'til dawn are migrating to the entry lines for their favorite clubs. The air's damp and in the upper teens; she wishes her dress had a back, or sleeves, or she'd had the sense to bring a wrap. Her eyes slide over a parked silver Mercedes roadster, a neon-green Bugatti Veyron, a black Ferrari California T, and a white Transit van idling near the stone tower.

Hmm. Weird time to make deliveries.

Viktoriya's laugh grabs her attention. The posse's heading up the street to 11 Banus. Carson falls in, alongside the group but not exactly part of it.

They'd all been nice enough. Viktoriya and Iris were positively warm, including her in conversations, always making sure she had a drink. The others talked with her but ran a few degrees cooler. It doesn't surprise her—after all, she's there to maybe haul their leader off in a straightjacket.

A metallic noise behind Carson makes her spin a 180.

A man is hauling Celeste backward, toward the van. Its side door is open now, and another man stands next to it. The sound Carson heard was the door sliding open.

Carson calls out, "Sebastian, back me up!" as she rushes to help Celeste. The guy has an arm across her chest and a hand covering her mouth. She's squirming, but she can't break the hold.

The guy notices Carson. He doesn't look concerned; he just drags Celeste faster. His buddy moves toward them from Carson's two o'clock.

Carson slings her clutch across her chest, then hikes her skirt to her hips. She doesn't care much who sees her underwear; she can't move and fight with a sausage wrapper around her legs.

The guy with Celeste—now a few steps away—smirks at her. He looks vaguely familiar to Carson, but she can't spare the brainspace to figure out why. His smirk disappears when she deploys her baton.

"Oi!" Sebastian shouts a bit behind her. "What're you doing with her? Let her go!"

"Don't waste your breath!" Carson yells. She points the baton toward the other guy. "Over there." She has no idea if Sebastian can fight—if he played rugby, he must know how—but he's over six feet and solid and maybe can distract these two assholes enough so she can do what she needs to.

First, she has to get Celeste free and out of danger.

She's trotting by the time she reaches the guy with Celeste. He tries to pivot and yells something at her in French. Carson blocks Celeste's legs—the girl's dragging her feet, which helps—then forearms her baton into the guy's exposed left hip. He screams. His left leg collapses under him. He almost takes Celeste down with him until he loses control of her torso. She bolts, shrieking.

Mission accomplished.

The guy's right hand reaches into this windbreaker pocket. Carson backhands the baton into his right elbow. Even with Celeste's wailing and the scuffling behind her, she can hear the bones shatter. If she had real shoes on, she'd roundhouse the guy's head and move on. Instead, she sweeps his right ankle out from under him, flopping him face-down on the street. She mounts him, grabs his hair, and throws her weight into smashing his forehead against the pavement. After the third time, he goes limp.

Sebastian and the second guy—who also looks familiar—are scrabbling at each other like schoolyard fighters, arms and legs all tangled. *Yeah, rugby.* Carson doesn't dare use her baton—it wouldn't do to break Sebastian—so she stows it and circles behind the guy. She punches his kidneys one-two-one-two until he gargles in pain and tries to throw an elbow at her. Exactly what she'd hoped for. She loops her arm under his armpit and locks it around his neck, immobilizing the arm. "Head butt!"

Sebastian's head butt crunches the man's nose.

"Break off!"

When she sees Sebastian stand clear, Carson kicks the back of the man's left knee. His own weight crumples him face-down to the ground with Carson still in control of his right arm. While his face is in the asphalt, she stands sharply and dislocates his shoulder.

His scream is almost as loud as Celeste's.

Carson catches her breath. Pulls down her skirt. Checks her watch. Less than a minute. *Not bad.*

Sebastian's watching her from a couple of paces away, rubbing his chin with the back of his hand. He tries to smile but winces instead. "Have you ever considered rugby?"

"High school. Played lock. You okay?"

"Well enough."

They both glance at the rest of the gang.

Except for Celeste—who's sobbing into Viktoriya's neck—every one of them stares back with their eyes as big as loonies.

The Policía Local drags them to the station in the San Pedro Alcántara district, about ten minutes from Puerto Banús by police van. Questioning, written statements, photos of Carson's scraped knee and Sebastian's bruised jaw. CCTV video from a nearby camera and a mobile-phone video shot from the back of a yacht confirm their stories. Carson's deposited in a linoleum-and-plastic break room with the others. It looks like every other cop break room she's ever been in.

She watches a steady stream of cops file in and out of the room where they're examining the videos. The cops come out, stare at her, then hurry away.

Viktoriya convenes a team meeting in the room's far corner. A murmured conversation starts, involving lots of glances toward Carson. It becomes heated—she can tell from the whispering and the intensity of the body language. This goes on for a surprisingly long time. Eventually, nods all around, some more grudging than others.

Viktoriya plods to Carson's table and sighs into the chrome-wire-and-plastic chair next to her. She wraps her hands around Carson's forearm. Carson doesn't mind; the gentle contact is nice after that scene by the bar. Viktoriya looks deep into Carson's eyes for a few long moments, then murmurs, "Thank you for rescuing Celeste."

"Had to do it. Who were those guys?"

Viktoriya nods toward Tamara, a dark-haired young woman sitting with Amabelle and Sebastian. "Tamara"—Tah-*mahra*—"says a constable told her that one of those men had a French driving license. The plods are still asking questions of Celeste."

"Is she okay?"

"She's terrified." Viktoriya squeezes Carson's arm. "So am I. So is everyone." She peers at Carson. "Where did you learn to fight that way?"

"Hockey." Not true, but the real story would horrify her. "Why'd those guys try to kidnap Celeste?"

Viktoriya stares at the table.

"Viktoriya? I deserve to know."

"Yes, you do." Viktoriya's voice is one click above a whisper. She raises her head like it weighs a lot and plumbs Carson's eyes. "Celeste's parents are quite protective. Celeste says she can't breathe when she's with them. Anyway, they've been increasingly unpleasant about her stay with us. They've threatened us with lawyers and police, though nothing's come of it." She looks over her friends, who look back with various levels of fright and sadness. "People come and go. Someone stays with us for a spell. When he or she decides it's time to move on, we put on a nice party for her and wish her well. Celeste has no interest in leaving. She's happy with us and she's free to do what she pleases. She's safe…well, she was, until now. Her parents don't listen to her, though, which I gather is part of the problem. But I never thought…"

Carson waits for her to finish, but she doesn't. "They'd go this far?"

Viktoriya nods. "Yes. This is a shock to us all. No one's ever tried to kidnap one of our friends before tonight."

"First time for everything." Nobody ever sees it coming, even in places where kidnapping's an industry. "I saw them on Saturday, following Celeste, Amabelle, and Tamara. Took me a while to remember why I recognized them tonight."

"You…*saw* them?" Viktoriya's eyes explode. "How…why didn't you stop them?"

"Two creeps following three pretty girls? Take down all those scenes and half the men in this city would be on ice."

"But you saw they were up to no good."

"I saw them being creeps. There's lots of that here. What happens now?"

Big sigh. "We'd planned to move house tomorrow, ehm, this morning. I reckon this episode proves that's a good idea."

"Where are you going?"

Viktoriya nibbles her lip for a moment. "Come with us."

"What?" Carson had been wondering whether the team meeting was about voting her off the island. Apparently not.

"Come with us. We've been discussing security for some time, but tonight's convinced us we need to do something about it. Come with us. You saw danger where we didn't. Protect us. You're obviously capable of doing that. I'm sure we'd all feel safer."

Carson leans back in her chair and folds her arms. Of all the things she'd expected, this is the last. "Remember why I'm here?"

"Of course. I could hardly forget, could I?"

"Is this a 'keep your enemies close' thing?"

"I'd prefer to not think of you as an enemy." Viktoriya carefully lays her fingertips on Carson's wrist. "You seem to be a person who will help when she sees someone else in trouble. Is that so?"

"I try."

Viktoriya's eyes go distant for a moment, then refocus on Carson. "So I can depend on you if Father decides to do something extreme to me?"

Think before you answer. "Depends."

"I understand. In the meantime, Celeste's parents may try something like this again, and Celeste's very special to us. We sometimes have issues with other petty villains along the way. But more than that…Celeste says you're a good person, and good people always join with us."

There it is. "Join up and help you with your dad?"

Viktoriya smiles. "I'd not object."

They did fine with Gangster Boy—what does she want me for? Unless she wants me to buy in. Carson nods toward the four posse members staking out a table in the back of the room. "It didn't look like they were all on board with this."

"They're not all completely convinced you should come with us. We're a democracy—we don't insist on unanimity. I'm certain the doubters will come around in time. Enough agree that you've earned a place with us."

Weird way to put it. "If I say no?"

"I hope you won't." Viktoriya squeezes Carson's arm. "I'm sure you'll want to think about this. Do you remember the little white building with the tile roof at the end of the road outside Pangea?"

"Yeah."

"That's the Captain of the Port's office. The tenders tie up at the end. If you wish to come with us, be there by nine this morning." She squeezes again, then releases Carson. "Whatever you decide, please know that I'm grateful for what you did tonight." She kisses the top of Carson's head, then walks away.

Chapter 12

MARBELLA

Carson, swaddled in a hotel bathrobe, slumps in the wicker-bottom chair on her balcony, listening to the shushing surf and the racket in her head.

She didn't get back here until three-thirty. Her body's still buzzing from the action. She's been out here ever since, trying to think.

It should be an easy decision. Rodievsky told her to keep an eye on Vicki until he could talk to Baranov. What better way than traveling with her? If Rodievsky calls it off, she's out nothing but some time. If he tells her to grab Vicki and haul her to Russia, she's already in place. A win either way.

But.

It would've been easy six days ago, when Vicki was still some shit-for-brains heiress pissing away more money than Carson will ever make in her life. Someone who Carson could hate without reservation. As usual, hearing the story's flip side muddied things. Seeing her take on Gangster Boy and save Party Girl from a trip to the emergency department blurred that clear picture.

Can I force her back to Moscow?

Can I afford not to?

If Carson had a list of the five stupidest things she's ever done or ever could do, saying *no* to Rodievsky would rank way above marrying Ron, her ex, but below…well, maybe below nothing. Sometimes Rodievsky treats her like some kind of foster daughter. Then again, he murdered his own uncle, so family isn't off the table when the killing starts.

Even if Rodievsky decides to let her live after she refuses to kidnap Vicki, there's Baranov. She means nothing to him. He could swat her like a fly and not feel a twinge. Vicki would still end up under Baranov's thumb, and Carson would be turning into sludge in a barrel of acid someplace.

So do it. Eat her food, drink her booze, then lock her in a cage when you have to. Easy.

Except she can clearly see that moment when she'll have to look Vicki in the eye and stab her in the back. It won't get easier after another week or two.

So don't do it. Don't go to the marina. Lose her on purpose. The western Med's a big place. You'll never find her again.

Rodievsky would figure it out. He didn't become *pakhan* by being stupid. He'd consider the deceit to be worse than defiance. That leads to the barrel of acid.

A glimmer of purple fringes the eastern horizon. Down on the beach walk, someone jogs toward the soon-to-be dawn.

What do I do?

Iris paces nervously from waterside to the Captain of the Port's front door and back, dodging tourists here for the view. She's been at it for almost twenty minutes. She checks her phone for the millionth time: 9:02 a.m. *She's late. She said she's always on time.*

She's done what she can do to stall. She sent the luggage to the ship first. The tender can't fit all the peeps and all their stuff at the same time, but usually the stuff comes after them, not before. The fam's been giving her shit ever since. The tender's back and she's out of ideas.

Amabelle leans back against the Captain of the Port's building in the shade next to a barred window. "Iris!" Her voice cuts through the chattering-tourist noise around her. "We get older every minute!"

Amabelle's screaming-red romper makes Iris's eyes vibrate…in a good way. *That woman looks fab in stuff I could never, ever get away with.* "Vicki told me to wait for Lisa. So we're waiting."

"Is it only because Vicki wants her with us? Or do you want to play with her in bed?"

Gawd, if only… "I'd love to bury my face in Lisa's boobs. But after last night? I'm not making a move on that girl without a written invite. On *good* paper."

The rest of the fam's hanging out on three big, white concrete blocks at the end of this whatever-it's-called. Jetty? Whatevs. Celeste's hovering near Iris with her eyes glued on the road leading here. The boat driver's standing at the top of the stairs to the tender, tapping his watch. *I know! I know!*

Another time check. 9:04. No answer to Iris's texts.

She's not coming. Shit.

Iris sighs. "Okay. Get on the boat."

Tamara mutters something in Spanish. One of the guys grumbles, "*Finally.*"

Iris scuffles along behind Amabelle, craning over her shoulder. She almost trips on a concrete flowerpot. When she recovers, she sees someone down by the car barrier passing through the gap in the chain. She's carrying a duffel and pulling a roller bag. *Is it…?*

It must be: Celeste squeals and runs to hug the woman, who catches her in mid-leap.

"Hey, Celeste. Hey, Iris." Lisa waves at her. "There still room on your cruise ship?"

Chapter 13

ABOARD *ALFARAH*

Carson thought she was being funny by calling this tub a cruise ship. She wasn't. She's never been on a ship this big that wasn't painted Coast Guard red or navy gray. "This thing's fucking insane."

Iris laughs. "You haven't even seen it yet! *Alfarah's* sixty-seven meters of insane. That's two hundred and twenty feet. Do Canadians use feet or meters?"

"Both." Carson follows her up a spiral staircase next to the elevator shaft. (The ship has a glass elevator. *Nuts.*) "How are we on this boat?"

Iris's messy bronze ponytail swings like a metronome as she climbs. The stairwell's translucent back wall throws warm amber light on her. "Oh, Michel's one of Vicki's friends. It's his."

"Michel?"

"Rabbath. He lives in Beirut. He's a businessman." Iris stops on the top step and makes a face. "I guess a really good one."

The only Lebanese businessmen Carson's ever met smuggled weapons, drugs, people, or all three. It must pay well. "Where's Vicki?"

"She's got stuff to do." They step into a marble-lined corridor. Iris heads toward the stern through a glass door into what looks like a huge living room. A rust-colored sectional the size of a not-small car stretches across the back of the room. A bar and a huge-screen TV take up the forward wall. Sebastian and two posse members Carson met on the tender—Karl and Dareh—are busy making themselves comfortable. Iris chirps, "Everything good, guys?"

Sebastian spreads his hands. "It's grand." He's wearing khaki walking shorts and a loose cotton shirt that's half unbuttoned. Carson likes the view. He sweeps a hand from Carson to the TV.

"Do you fancy sport, Lisa?"

"Whaddaya got?"

"Football."

She shrugs. "If you find some hockey, let me know."

Sebastian grins. "I will do."

Iris rolls her eyes. "Don't trash the place, boys. The cabin crew's not here. We have to clean up after ourselves."

Karl says, "Yes, *Mutti*."

Iris leads Carson through enormous sliding doors onto the deck aft of the living room. "That was the Sky Lounge, by the way. You met Sebastian last night, right?"

"Yeah. Other than being Irish, what's his deal?"

"Glad you asked. His dad's a big banker back home. But the really important thing is, he has magic hands. You *have* to get a massage from Sebastian. It's *required*."

He's gorgeous and *he knows massage?* "You're joking."

"I wouldn't, not about something important. He's the only man I let touch my body, and I *never* regret it. Listen to Auntie Iris. Now, the other two are Dareh and Karl. Karl's the tall, blond, German one, and Dareh's the short, dark one with the incredible lashes. Why do guys get such good lashes? It's not fair."

"Where do they fit?"

"They're our tech gurus. It explains their clothes."

"And you need tech gurus…why?"

Iris shrugs. "Doesn't everyone?" She leads Carson up a flight of stairs to another deck. "This is the sun deck. You can see why."

Amabelle and Tamara are stretched out on two of three aft-facing sunbeds. Both are completely naked and glisten in the sun. Tamara's tan, pretty, and curvy, with lots of thick, black hair piled on top of her head; Amabelle's sleek body looks like it's made of shiny, dark walnut. Two pairs of large sunglasses turn toward Carson.

Iris chirps, "Morning, girls! Glad to see you haven't wasted any time. Got everything you need?"

Tamara grumps, "Except quiet."

Iris gives her an obviously fake smile. "What's that brick you're reading, Belle?"

Amabelle holds up a thick hardcover book. "*Capital in the Twenty-First Century*. I read it when it was new. I read it again because I have had time to research what it says."

Tamara says, "Normal people read mysteries or romances when they travel."

Amabelle laughs. She has a great laugh. "I would like to do that, too, but I have a nation to run."

Carson throws a *huh?* look at Iris, who holds up an index finger.

Iris heads toward the glass wall beyond the ten-place dining table forward of the sunbeds. "Well, I need to finish showing Lisa around. Thanks tons for leaving a lounge open for me."

Tamara cranes over her shoulder, shading her eyes with her *Elle España.* "What makes you think it's for you?"

The glass wall is a series of sliding doors. Iris hauls one open and leads Carson into a small gym with a rowing machine, treadmill, compact universal machine, and wall racks of hand weights and free weights. The equipment still has that new-gym smell. Iris says, "Welcome to the happiest place on Earth."

Carson pulls on one of the universal's handgrips. The movement's like silk. "You're into working out?"

"Oh, God, no. *This* is why I love this place." Iris pats a massage table hung near the free weights. "It's where Sebastian does his magic." She slips an arm around Carson's shoulders. "Now, I wouldn't be a good auntie if I didn't warn you about men and their evil ways. Sebastian's gorgeous—yes, even I think so—and his massages are the next best thing to mainlining dark chocolate. *Some women*"—she aims two loaded eyebrows at Carson—"don't mind a bit when he massages parts of them that don't usually get massaged in spas, if you get my drift. Your mileage may vary. Don't say I didn't warn you."

Somehow, that doesn't sound like a warning as much as a prediction. Carson nods out the back windows. "What's with those two?"

Iris slides to the mirror and barre next to the treadmill and strikes a series of ballet positions. "Belle's our resident smarty pants. She reads stuff like that doorstop so we don't have to. Her dad owns, like, half of Rwanda or something. He wants her to be president someday."

"For real?"

"Totes serious. Tamara…well, Tamara's *special.* Her dad's the king's cousin or something. I don't—"

This is nuts. "The King of Spain?"

"That's the one. I don't know if that makes her royal, but she sure thinks it does. She thinks that's why we keep her around. But…" she spins, then settles back against the barre, facing Carson "…the real reason is, she feeds us. And Lordy, she's good. It's almost worth putting up with her complaining about everything, you know? Oh, and Sebastian likes looking down her shirt. C'mon."

Carson follows her past the elevator and through a large, curved sliding-glass door to outside. A raised Jacuzzi pool sits three steps above and in front of them. "This is my second-favorite place. It's away from stinky boys, and *look* at the view."

It's a great view: a hundred-eighty degrees of Mediterranean studded with other boats. The coast fills the area to Carson's left. The breeze from the ship's movement takes the edge off the hot sun. "Wow."

"You said it, hon. Follow me." Iris skirts a semicircular area of gray pads curled around the pool's front edge, then leans her elbows on the rail. The ship's bow seems impossibly far away. A figure in a demure pastel-pink sundress stands at the extreme end, holding out her arms like wings.

Carson takes in a big lungful of fresh sea air. "Is that Celeste?"

"It sure is. And I'll bet…wait for it…"

"Wait for wh—"

A pair of porpoises flanks the ship, skimming the bow wave's outside edges, their dorsal fins slicing fast through the water. They both leap at the same time, then disappear. Celeste claps her hands and bounces up and down. The show repeats a few times.

Carson can't help but smile at the sight. "Celeste's a little…*different*, isn't she."

Iris gives her a cool look, pursing her lips. "Is that bad?"

"No. My youngest brother was different, too. Just wondering."

"Okay." Iris focuses on Celeste. "Tamara *thinks* she's all that, but Celeste's the real thing. You're her hero, you know."

That usually doesn't last long. "Hope I can spend some time with her today. Anything I should know?"

"I'll let you come to your own conclusions. Just be gentle with her. And listen to her music. You've defs *never* heard anything like it."

Carson's to-do list keeps getting longer. After a few moments of watching the world slip by, she says, "I'll ask again. How are we riding this thing?"

Iris rolls her eyes. "Like I said, Vicki knows the owner. He moves the boat sometimes so it's where he wants it to be. We can ride along if Michel's not on it." She glances at Carson. "Don't worry, it's okay. We do this a couple-three times a year."

Nice to have rich friends. "Too bad Vicki's missing it. Where'd you say she is?"

Iris flounces. "I told you, she's busy doing Vicki stuff. It's a lot of work being us. She finds us places to stay and works out food and gets us boat rides and… Don't *worry*. She didn't run away. She'll meet us in Ibiza."

Carson worries. Did Vicki bail on them? This would be the way to do it—take off and leave Carson with a bunch of people who keep telling her "Vicki'll be back soon" while Vicki heads for South America. "You know what happens if she doesn't, right?"

"Yes." Iris crosses her arms and huffs. "You'll go chase her and drag her back to Russia."

"Worse. Guys with no necks or brains chase her down and drag her back by her hair. Want that?"

Iris sighs. "No." She puts on her sad face. "Why does she have to go at all? Things are great here."

"Ask her." Carson watches Celeste laugh at the seagulls for a few moments. "What'd she tell you all about why I'm coming along?"

"She said you'll protect us from stuff like what happened last night."

Celeste's kidnapping or Gangster Boy? "Yeah. She told me not everybody wants me here. Who voted 'no'?"

"I'm not telling you that. You'll throw them off the boat while it's still moving."

"Everybody can swim, right?"

Iris laughs. "Look, I need to go do Iris stuff. That's mostly annoying people, but I'm really good at it. You can stay here and trip on the view, or go to the bar in the Sky Lounge, or go join the girls and get some sun on you. They'll leave tooth marks, but they usually don't break skin. I'll hook you up for a massage date with

Sebastian." She grins and taps the tip of Carson's nose. "You can thank me later."

The massages Carson's had in this part of her life have been therapeutic, anonymous, and clinical. When she was training with Yurik—the ex-FSB *spetsnaz* operator who taught her how to break people like a pro—the workouts were so brutal that he brought in a woman every evening to unkink Carson so she could walk again the next day. The guys she sleeps with aren't into sensual massage, or at least, not giving it.

She wanders the little gym, examining the equipment, trying out the treadmill. The massage table's set up by the tall windows. Beyond it, the ship's wake stretches almost to the horizon. Other than the view and the trace vibration in the floor under her bare feet, she can hardly tell she's moving.

Why am I nervous?

Maybe because this isn't some physical therapist or doctor thing. Maybe because she'd caught Sebastian checking her out, and vice-versa. Maybe because he's handsome. Maybe because she doesn't know what to expect. That always makes her skittish.

The door to the hallway opens. It's Sebastian, right on time for their noon date. "Morning, Lisa. Are you enjoying our little sail?"

Carson leans her butt against the treadmill controls and folds her arms, trying to hide any clues about her butterflies. "So far."

"Grand." He raids a wall locker for towels, then ambles to the massage table. "Would'ja like the windows open?"

"Okay."

Sebastian slides the windows to the right, opening the gym's entire rear wall to the outside deck. Amabelle and Tamara vanished sometime between Iris's tour and now; Carson's alone with Sebastian. The warm air rushes in. He unrolls and spreads a towel on the table.

"How's your jaw?"

He smiles and touches the bruise. "I've had worse. Everything still works and I've lost no teeth. How's the knee?"

"Fine. A scrape. Don't even remember doing it." She pauses, groping for something non-stupid to say. "You did good last night."

He ducks his head. "Cheers. You were fierce."

She hopes that's a compliment. She watches him smooth the towel, thinking about how his hands will be doing that to her in a few minutes.

He pulls a small, dark bottle with a pump top out of his pocket and sets it on the head of the table. "The oil should be warm for you now."

That's her cue. Carson wore her black tank swimsuit under her clothes this morning, figuring there'd be some sitting out on deck. She hadn't counted on this. She slips off her shorts and polo, draping them over the treadmill's safety rail. Not for the first time this job, she wishes she had a nicer swimsuit.

Let yourself live. "It's warm in here."

"It is."

"Need that shirt?"

He shrugs, then takes it off.

Oh. My. He's well put-together without looking like a 'roid monster. The tan must've taken a while to grow. Celtic tattoos crowd the tops of his shoulders.

Carson pushes off from the console, slowly peels off her swimsuit, then hangs it next to her shorts. She's never had a problem with being naked; growing up in a European family in small homes with four brothers and no privacy, she never got the chance to become modest. She stands there for a moment, her hands on her hips, letting him take a good, long look.

He smiles. "Aren't you the fit one, then?"

She steps off the treadmill and ambles to the table. He watches every single move. "Iris says you have magic hands."

"Does she, now?"

Carson holds eye contact with him for what feels like a very long time. "Prove it."

Chapter 14

Carson lolls in the Jacuzzi, watching the Mediterranean skid past. It's like every bone in her body has dissolved. There's no reason to turn on the jets; she can't possibly be warmer or any more relaxed.

"Well, *there* you are." Iris appears off to her right. She smirks. "Look at you. You liked your massage?"

"Yeah."

"And did we fuck?"

"No."

"You dork! Why not? He's hot for you, you know. He likes women with curves."

Carson figured that out a while ago. "I'm easy, but I'm not that easy. He has to buy me a drink first."

Both of Iris's eyebrows arch like Halloween cats. "You know this boat's, like, crammed with booze, right?"

"Not the point. He's gotta *buy* me a drink."

"Gotcha. Skin in the game." Iris drops her green gingham shirt and shiny green bikini, then slides into the water next to Carson. She's slender verging on skinny, with B-cup breasts, sharp hipbones, and the kind of peachy skin redheads get. "If you didn't fuck, what *did* you do?"

"None of your business. Everybody walked away happy."

"Oh, I *love* happy endings!" Iris claps and giggles. "Glad you came?"

"So far. How's Celeste doing?"

"Okay. Happy about the dolphins, but still scared. I don't blame her—I am, too."

"Is it normal for parents to send hired guns to get their kids back from you?"

The question puzzles Iris. "Normal? Not really. The scarier

thing's when they send lawyers. But…well, you've probably figured out we're wading in a lot of money. There's always someone who wants to take some of it away from us. There's the usual stuff, too. Guys who don't understand what 'go away' means. Pickpockets and purse-snatchers. That's what Vicki meant by 'keep us safe.' I'm the closest thing we have to security, and I'm not scary at all except first thing in the morning."

"That's me, now. The hired muscle."

Iris twists and grabs Carson's bicep. "No no no. Don't make it like that. No. You hang with us, you party with us. You're our new friend. But I bet you can see trouble way before we can. So you let us know or keep us out of its way. But I like hanging with you. And it's not all about you being naked." She thinks for a beat. "It's a lot about you being naked, but—"

"Yeah. Keep digging that hole. Where are you from?"

"Newport." Iris must see the lack of clue on Carson's face, because she adds, "Rhode Island? Next to Connecticut and Massachusetts?"

"Got it." Most Canadians have a better grasp of U.S. geography than people from the States do of Canadian geography, though that's a low bar. "So, what's your story?"

"What do you mean?"

"How'd you get here?"

"Oh, God, my *origin* story." Iris settles into her seat and blows out a long breath. "Well, you know, it's the same old story… Daddy sent me to boarding school because the stepmonster told him to. The Deerfield Academy's this obscenely expensive place where I could hang with other kids from rich families who didn't want them around. Remember Vicki's origin story?"

"Yeah."

"Well, Vicki and I are a lot alike—we're smarter than we look and we get bored easy. Deerfield kept me busy. That's also where I discovered I like *femmes* instead of *hommes*. That was a big light-bulb moment. After I graduated, Daddy sent me to Barnard. It's a women's college in New York City. Ivy League for girls. He had *no idea* he was sending me to Disney World. Think about it—every year, a whole new crop of cute little bi-curious freshman girls washed in, just looking for an older, more sophisticated woman to show them the ropes. I had So. Much. Fun." She winks at Carson.

"When I was done there, I decided to see the world. I met a lot of things, did a lot of people, had a lot of fun.

"About two years ago, I was at a café in Cannes when I saw this blond goddess walk by. And I said to myself, 'Self, you gotta get you some of that.'" Iris leans into Carson. "It was Vicki. She's as straight as you are. No fun at all. She'd already hooked up with Sebastian by then. We floated along the coast. Saw a lot, drank a lot, talked a lot. Solved all the world's problems. Then we figured, with the money we could get to, we could actually *do* it. Vicki found Karl and Dareh and we started saving the world, one little piece at a time. And here we are." She nudges Carson again.

That again. "What's 'saving the world' look like?"

Iris waves the question away. "It's boring. I have a much more interesting question—where are your *clothes*?"

"In the gym. You know, I think the whole 'saving the world' thing sounds fucking *fascinating*. Give me a hint."

"Well, if you insist…" Iris sighs and perches on the pool's rim. Carson can't tell if she's cooling off or showing off. "You know how charities are always begging for money? It's because they're always broke. We find civil society groups who're doing good stuff in places that really need it, and dump money on them." She flutters her fingers like falling snow.

That's the big secret? "You said Vicki and Sebastian were 'hooked up.' They a thing?"

"Not anymore. That stopped last year. They're still friends, though. Karl's Vicki's current project."

Karl's the kind of guy Carson would pick up for a weekend: tall, broad-shouldered, and sort of a pug. "She's way out of his league."

"You'd think, but not really. She likes 'em tall and built. He played soccer in college when he wasn't messing around with computers. I guess faces aren't so important—Vicki just hit the jackpot with Sebastian."

"What's Sebastian's story?"

Iris laughs. "Wouldn't *you* like to know. Go ask him. I'm sure he'll be happy to tell you"—she waves a finger at Carson—"especially if you go like that."

Sure thing. Carson checks her watch: almost two. She had breakfast at her normal time and now she's on the edge of starving.

The weird meal times have been the hardest thing so far about being in Spain. She climbs out of the water to towel down.

Iris pays very close attention. "Those *are* real."

Carson ignores her. "Going to lunch. Then maybe I'll hit up Sebastian. With clothes on."

As she walks down the steps, Iris giggles behind her. "Hit *up* or hit *on?*"

Carson wanders the ship after an enormous, buffet-like lunch laid out on the main deck's fourteen-place dining table. She's half being nosy and half figuring out what she's up against.

From the bathtub in the sprawling owner's suite that looks like half a nautilus shell, to the exotic wood and stone veneers on every surface, to the striking black-and-white photos of Islamic architecture on the walls, *Alfarah* looks more like a movie set than a real boat. What this thing cost could feed a small Third World country for months. *Must be nice to be Michel.*

Carson leans on the rail next to the Jacuzzi, sucking on a beer and watching the Med go by as she reviews what she's found.

Unless someone else is missing, Vicki's entourage tops out at seven people—three men, four women. Of those, Sebastian's the only one who fits the picture of a bodyguard. Carson doesn't get that he *is* one, though. Vicki's decision to send him to get the cops instead of facing down Gangster Boy says a lot, as does his lack of proper fighting skills while he backed up Carson at Celeste's attempted kidnapping. Carson doesn't read a threat off the "tech gurus" Karl or Dareh, either.

What about the women? Iris is clearly Vicki's right hand. She can follow people well and camouflage herself effectively. Vicki had Iris deal with Gangster Boy; that implies some level of courage. Does that equal a threat? Carson doesn't see a physical threat from Iris, but she may present a social or political problem. Vicki listens to her.

Amabelle and Tamara are blanks. Carson tried to chat with them at lunch and got nothing back. Did they vote no on Carson joining the group?

Celeste seems entirely inoffensive. If she really is like Dom, she can't lie to save her life and conflict terrifies her. She might accidentally get in the way of a rendition but wouldn't fight.

Carson didn't find any evidence of weapons when she nosed through the stuff the posse had left in the bedrooms. Not that she expected any.

So Vicki has no real protection that Carson can see. How has she dodged the MVD for the past six months?

On her way down from the sun deck, Carson finds Sebastian, Amabelle, and Tamara behind open laptops on the dining table at the bridge deck's after end. Amabelle's across the table from Sebastian, draped in an orange-and-gold beach cover-up; Tamara sits at the end between them, wearing a low-cut, red crop-top. They're having what looks like a serious talk.

Carson stops next to the Sky Lounge sectional to parse the picture. Tamara's aiming some impressive cleavage directly at Sebastian. *Obvious much?* Carson shakes her head—*welcome back to high school*—and watches Karl and Dareh play some kind of noisy space-marine game on the huge-screen TV. Great twitch speed, but no tactical brilliance. She then steps out onto the deck.

The conversation stops dead. Sebastian and the women all turn to stare. She's reminded of walking into a police leadership meeting once when they were talking about super-secret personnel stuff. "Hey." She tries to sound innocent. "Working?"

Sebastian says, "We are, yes." It's not a scolding, simply a statement of fact.

Tamara hisses, "Are you? Is this you being our security guard?"

Back off, bitch. "Don't mind me." She crosses to the stairs leading to the main deck with three pairs of eyes pushing her along. *What was that? Fundraising is top secret?*

Piano music drifts from the grand saloon. She remembers the white grand piano near the dining table.

The grand saloon is a huge, shiny space lined on both sides with big windows looking straight out onto water that seems close enough to touch. Three sofas arranged in a U around a massive, marble-topped round coffee table sit under two seamless concentric rings of light. It looks more like an overgrown jewelry box than a room in a boat.

Celeste's on the piano bench in the back corner, entirely focused on the keyboard. Carson doesn't recognize the music, but it's pretty. She perches on the nearest sofa arm to listen.

Whatever Celeste's playing, it has a lot going on. She gets to a part with a complicated rising-and-falling melody that meshes with an underlying rhythm. It repeats over and over, a bit different each time. Her eyes and mouth are set in a frown. Her lips get tighter with each repetition until she stops abruptly with her hands hovering over the keys. She closes her eyes, then nods in rhythm with what she'd been playing. Her face smooths out. Finally, with a nod, she resumes playing the same motif, this time subtly changed and delicate as hummingbird wings. Celeste smiles.

She stops and opens her eyes again. When she sees Carson, she jumps off the bench and rushes to her. "Lisa!" She crashes into Carson and wraps her in a hug so violent that they nearly tumble to the floor.

It was like this on the quay this morning. All the hugging and touching is starting to bug Carson—she hardly ever has this much physical contact with strangers. She pulls away from Celeste, corralling her hands. "Hey, calm down. How're you doing?"

"Okay." She holds up her left hand and points to the dark bruise on her wrist.

"That'll go away in a few days. What were you playing?"

Celeste shrugs and lays her head on Carson's shoulder. "My music."

Once again, Carson flashes back to her brother Dom. He needed physical contact to feel safe. She sat like this with him for years. "It was pretty. I didn't recognize it, though."

"Oh. I make it."

"You write your own music?"

"No, no. I hear it, and then I play it. Sometimes I do not make it right and I have to try again. It is frustrating. I know how it should sound, but I cannot make the right notes."

"Is that what you were doing just now?"

"Yes."

That explains the frown. "What else do you play?"

Celeste sits straight. "Many things. Let me show you." She trots to the piano, thumps on the bench, then plays a familiar intro.

After a moment, she sings.

> *J'ai toujours besoin de dire*
> *Ce qui se passe en moi…*

It's "Your Song" in French. Her voice is small but clear and nearly as fragile as the cut-glass notes she'd played a few minutes before. She stops at the end of the verse, beaming. "Do you like that?"

"Yeah. The music you make…you said you know what it sounds like. Where's it from?"

"I listen. I listen to everything. Everything that is alive has its own music. I remember it, then I try to make it. If I like it, I keep it."

This is getting too woo-woo for Carson to process. "I don't get it. Everything makes music?"

"Yes, if you know how to listen. People do not know how to listen." She chews on her lower lip. Then she points at the sofa closest to the piano. "Sit there. When it feels good, close your eyes."

Carson does what she's told, more to not make Celeste upset than because she expects anything to come of it. Celeste's good feelings about her seem to figure in whether Vicki's posse lets Carson stick around. Once she's settled, she says, "Now what?"

"I play. Listen. Do not think, only…feel."

It starts simply: a few notes in a high register, almost like birdsong. Then something slow begins down low. More sounds layer in—complicated, freeform melodies that wind around each other. Carson tries to clear her mind and let the music wash over her, but when she does, the movie screen in her head fills with all kinds of strange, unconnected images. Or are they unconnected? There's not time to think; there's not room to think. She grabs onto the notes and follows them wherever they lead her, usually someplace where there's something else happening just beyond the edge of her mental vision.

She doesn't know how long she sits there, wrapped in the sounds and emotions the music brings her. When it ends, she's both exhilarated from the experience and desolate that it's over. She's never heard anything like it. Ever. She's afraid she never will again. "What was that?"

"What did you see?"

"Trees. Birds. Sunlight, rain. Ferns. Is that what a forest sounds like to you?"

Celeste nods solemnly. "That is the music the forest makes. I…I cannot make it all the same. This is a little part only." She hunches her shoulders. "Do you like it?"

"It was amazing. Do you have more like that?"

"Yes, I do."

"Can you…play another one?"

Celeste blushes and glances down at the keyboard. "For you, I will play anything."

Chapter 15

ABOARD *ALFARAH*

The morning sun shoots through the grand saloon's windows to land on Carson's eyelids, waking her. She's draped in a blanket on a plush sofa. Her watch says 7:16.

The ship has seven sleeping cabins. She'd learned last night—too late—that each of Vicki's seven posse members had grabbed a cabin the moment they got on the yacht. Iris offered to let Carson bunk with her in the owner's suite. Carson remembered the room had one bed and knew that if she accepted, she'd be forced to drown Iris in the fancy bathtub sometime during the night. She turned in after midnight and caught up on sleep she'd lost while deciding to come on this cruise.

Iris told her yesterday that they expected to pull into Ibiza around ten in the morning. There's not much equipment in the yacht's gym, but Carson can do a little something to burn off the metric ton of food she ate yesterday. Tamara may be a diva, but damn, the girl can cook.

She throws off the blanket and swings her feet to the floor. Instead of rug, they hit something soft that lets out a little squeak. *Huh?* Carson peeks over the cushion's edge and finds herself face-to-face with a surprised-but-sleepy Celeste. She's rolled up in a blanket like a human burrito and displaying Olympic-caliber bedhead on two fluffy pillows. Little birds dot her pajama top.

Carson says, "What are you doing here?"

Celeste smiles. "I could not sleep in my room. I feel safe with you."

Ibiza is a collection of low-lying hills camouflaged in olive green and dusty tan, surrounded by Mediterranean blue. The

Alfarah slices past the smaller boats—almost all are smaller—like a whale past sardines.

Carson and Iris watch from the rail around the sun deck pool as the island grows on the horizon. Carson glances at her watch. "Not gonna make it by ten."

Iris sucks on the straw sprouting from a screwdriver in a highball glass. "You've got a plane to catch?"

"You said ten."

"Well, we're on Spanish time now. I guess here we're on Spanish *island* time. That's, like, twice as slow." Iris smirks as she gives Carson a sideways look. "Are we messing up your schedule for kidnapping Vicki?"

Carson ignores the dig. "Vicki's here?"

Iris sighs. "Did you notice how bad the cell service is in the middle of the ocean? I don't know where she is. I'm sure I'll hear all about it when we get bars again. Maybe she's at the marina, wondering why we're a whole *half an hour late*."

If Viktoriya wanted time to run off to Tahiti, she'd stick Carson on an island with her friends and tell them to hold tight. "I listened to Celeste's music yesterday."

"And?"

"It's amazing. You're right—I've never heard anything like it before." Carson thinks carefully about what she says next. "She reminds me of Dom, my youngest brother. He didn't start talking 'til he was almost four. Schoolwork was always hard for him. He had ADHD, didn't sleep well, couldn't keep track of time. Doctors figured it was fetal alcohol syndrome. FASD. Mom was drunk when she carried him. So…what should I know so I don't do anything to upset her?"

Iris doesn't answer for longer than normal. "Do you like her?"

"Yeah. She's awfully nice. Sweet."

"Isn't she?" Iris smiles. "I was hoping you weren't gonna make fun of her. We're a little protective of Celeste. We don't know for sure, but Dr. Google makes us think she's on the spectrum somewhere. The one thing that doesn't line up is that she's really friendly once she gets to know you. I guess that's not normal for people with autism."

"Yeah. Dom was real friendly, too. That's what made the doctors lean toward FASD instead of autism."

Iris waves at the half-dozen people waving at the yacht from their dwarfed sailboat. "Celeste's really smart in a couple things and not in most anything else. You know she's got a degree in statistics from some fancy school in Paris?"

"Statistics?"

"Yeah. Music is math, or math is music. The Pythagoreans were saying that way back when. Scales, octaves, harmonies—they're all ratios of frequencies. That's what they told me at Deerfield, at least." She shrugs. "Anyway, she doesn't do well in new places. Clubs are too much for her—too many people, too much noise, too many lights."

"Why'd you take her to Pangea?"

"That was Vicki's idea. She wanted Celeste to meet you. Celeste's *très*…I don't know, *intuitive* about people? Her music-is-everywhere thing goes for people, too. She can tell if someone has 'good music' or 'bad music' after being around them a little while."

"I must've passed."

"You did, or you wouldn't be here. She said your music's 'good but sad,' whatever that means."

Carson remembers Celeste in the hallway at Pangea: *you are unhappy*? "Anything I should watch out for?"

"She gets confused when there's too much going on. Try to keep it simple. And when you talk to her, she concentrates crazy hard on you. It freaks people out."

"Dom did that, too."

Iris empties her drink with a straw-rattle. "What happened with your brother?"

"He's a youth counselor in Calgary. He's great with the kids. Not so much with the adults, but the kids love him."

"Good." Iris starts for the stairs. "We want Celeste to have a happy ending, too." She waves a finger over her shoulder. "Be careful—don't hurt her. You won't be popular if you do."

The ship moors at 10:45 on Marina Ibiza's outer jetty, the only place big enough to handle it. Because it came from another Spanish port, the customs and immigration people stay in their offices.

Carson's first onshore to do her security job, even though she doesn't know what she's securing Vicki's posse from. She feels ridiculous doing this in shorts and a polo, but it's 30° C out here and she'd rather not roast.

The slate-gray, fourteen-passenger bus waiting by the jetty is clean and doesn't have any terrorists hiding behind the seats. The driver's too skinny-looking to be wearing a bomb vest. Carson doesn't see any mercenaries or process servers on the pier, only marina staff helping unload the shit-ton of luggage from the yacht. They'd better help; what Michel's paying for slip fees each week would cover more than a month of her rent.

Iris is waiting for her at the gangway's bottom. "Any boogiemen?"

"No visible ones. The invisible ones…" Carson rocks her hand.

The bus takes them through a scrim of white high-rise apartments, condos, and hotels, across a wetland, and into the hills to the port's northeast. The farther they go, the bigger the houses are and the more lush the backyard plantings. After a crawl along a barely one-lane road, they finally stop at what looks like an ancient wooden door set into a tan-stone wall.

Sebastian strides out of the bus. "I'll just unlock the doors and chain the velociraptors. Won't be a moment."

The house is two floors of honey-colored stone set into a semi-manicured jungle. The more Carson explores the white-plaster interior, the more appalled she is. The kitchen's big enough to hold a sizable party; there's an endless number of bedrooms; and the washrooms are bigger than her apartment. A well-equipped gym fills an outbuilding tucked into the landscaping.

Sebastian catches up with her while she stands on the wooden deck surrounding the fifteen-meter swimming pool behind the main house. A large, seated Buddha sits on a pedestal across the pool from her. She points to it. "What the fuck?"

"It came with the house."

"I saw the pictures on the mantle in the living room. You were a cute kid. How many bedrooms? I count eleven, but…"

"Fourteen. All *en suite*."

Fourteen bedrooms. "There weren't that many people in the pictures."

"There wouldn't be. It's me, Ma and Da, two sisters, and a few cousins we rarely see. My older sister's married and has a new chiseler. Two—"

"Chiseler?"

"A baby. Sorry. Two of my cousins are in America. Sometimes Da brings friends or work friends here."

Fourteen bedrooms. "You guys use it a lot?"

Sebastian shrugs. "Two or three weeks a year, maybe." He gives her an apologetic smile. "It's daft, I know. But like they say, the victor gets the spoils."

Fucking nuts. "Where'd the money come from?"

"My da's a managing director at Allied Irish. It's a bank." He scuffs the wood with the toe of his sandal. "That's nothing to be proud of in Ireland."

"Why not?"

Sebastian settles on a sunbed, then pats the cushion next to him. "Come here 'til I tell you." Carson takes the spot warily, wondering what this is about. "D'ya know what happened with Irish banks in 2008?"

"Not really. Lots of pictures of empty houses on the news."

"That there were. The long and short of it is, Irish banks started taking cheap money from foreigners and lent it on the cheap to developers and builders. They put up houses and offices to sell to Irish people. There were too many buildings and not enough Irish. The bubble broke and all the banks were going bust, and all the developers, and all the builders. The banks got the government to guarantee their losses. So all the daft and bent things the bankers did became property of the Irish taxpayer, and they still are. The four biggest banks, including Da's, the government bought. Of course, the normal working people were the ones who were hurt the most."

Carson remembered seeing all that happen, even some in Canada, though not nearly as bad as in the States. Still, she'd been glad to have a stable job with the police. "Your dad was involved?"

"Oh, yes." He sighs and shakes his head. "A few of the big men—chairmen, managing directors—got the sack, but men just below them, where Da was then, never did. He never believed the bubble would last, no matter what he told the staff or the press. He did some insider deals and sent his money to stable offshore investments. When prices crashed in 2009, he could buy on the cheap. That's how he got this place." He throws his hand over his shoulder, toward the house. "And the one in Cortina. And the penthouse in Manhattan. And the beach house on Grand Cayman."

"Crime pays. Usually in cash."

"It does do, yes."

They sit quietly in the sun. Carson's deeply aware of his nearness, even though they're not touching. She doesn't want to screw it up, but she's been grinding over yesterday afternoon and figures this is as good a time as any to bring it up. "Iris told me what you guys do between club crawls."

"Did she, now? What did she say?" A bit more interest, but no obvious agita.

"Giving money to do-gooders. That right?"

He shrugs. "It's the simple version, but right enough as far as it goes."

"Hmm. Yesterday afternoon, when I came out on deck? You guys looked at me like I caught you planning to knock over a bank. Keep wondering why fundraising seems so sensitive. I'd love to hear the complicated version of what you're doing."

"It's not as interesting as all that." His words are careful, borderline edgy.

"I'm interested in all kinds of weird shit. Try me."

Sebastian's face darkens. "You'll excuse me for not telling you all our business, seeing why you're here and all." His voice is harder than she's heard it until now.

She mentally drops back a step. There's clearly a sore spot here, and she just poked it. But it could be about her mission, or her screwing up some balance of power, or the posse being pissed that somebody crashed the party. She'll leave this alone until she can figure it out better. "Where's Vicki?"

"I've no idea. You should ask Iris."

"She doesn't know, either. Iris says you and Vicki used to be a thing. Figured maybe you talk to her more than Iris does." Carson takes Sebastian's temperature: he's softened a bit. "Is Vicki really coming back?"

"She'll turn up. She always does. She can't stay away—we're her family now." He looks deep into her eyes, which she doesn't mind as much as she probably should. "This is God's honest: I don't know how much she wants you to know. Maybe there are things you haven't told us that we should know."

Carson chuckles. "Got nothing to hide. You saw that yesterday."

"You showed me your body, not your mind."

"That's usually all guys are interested in."

He coughs out a *heh* sound. "Now you're the one who's dodging questions. What haven't you told us about you?"

Where do I start? Carson doesn't know the pecking order well enough to tell whether blowing off Sebastian's questions is a bad idea. It probably is. So what does he want to hear? He already knows the lead story—they all do.

A couple of amplified thumps derail her thoughts. They're followed by a deep-house rhythm track that turns into a loud remix of R.E.M.'s "Losing My Religion." Carson winces.

Sebastian stands and yells, "Turn it down! It's too bleedin' loud!" The volume drops by about half. He sits. "Sorry. We've a sound system through the property. They never remember how loud it is."

Carson hopes the interruption will cover for changing the subject. She takes in the view around them. "Fourteen bedrooms for five people. I didn't get my own room 'til I was almost sixteen."

"You had brothers and sisters?"

"Four brothers."

"How'd that work?"

"Not great. When I stripped for you on the boat? For the massage? Been practicing that my whole life."

Sebastian smiles again. *Nice smile.* "You're good at it."

Glad he noticed. Carson keeps up the eye contact until she notices that they're both drifting toward each other. She stands. "Guess I better find someplace to sleep."

He nods and stands. "Well, then. Let's find you a nice place to lay your head, shall we?"

Chapter 16

MÁLAGA

Grebnev says, "You're sure it's them?"

"Of course, we're certain." Severinov—Grebnev's boss—sounds mildly annoyed that Grebnev would ask. He must be on the secure phone in the Zapadneft emergency command center; his voice sounds hollow and there's a slight hiss in the background, an encryption artifact. "The same signatures, the same profiles, the same collateral activities. The IPs have changed, but that's to be expected. What are your…*helpers* doing now?"

He means Grupo Sabadell. When the hacker group dropped off the scope on Wednesday, Severinov jumped down Grebnev's throat about Sabadell scaring them off. *At least that's over now.*

Grebnev settles at the small kitchen table in his Airbnb flat on a busy street in central Málaga and continues sipping his coffee. "They backed off from shadowing the subjects when the police got involved on Tuesday. They're standing by, waiting for a new location."

"Well, tell them to get their people to Ibiza immediately. I've already chopped the recon team there."

Grebnev thinks, *nice of you to tell me in advance.*

"I expect we'll get a fix on the subjects by this evening. I want your *helpers* in action as soon as possible after that. Understand?"

"Yes, sir. Do you want me there, too?"

"Of course. There'll be an aircraft waiting for you at the airport in two hours. I'll send the details." The line goes dead for a few moments. Just as Grebnev starts wondering if Severinov hung up on him, the hiss reappears. "There's something you should know. That incident in Marbella? The two men belonged to a French private security company. Obviously they weren't hired for their planning brilliance, but they were former French marines." He means the *Troupes de marine*, France's overseas intervention force—

serious people. "We checked the police reports for the incident."

"You have access to those?"

"Of course. Money can buy access to almost anything. As I was about to say, the subjects may have recruited a new member, another woman. The interesting part is, *she* was the one who took down those two men."

A *woman?* That seems incredible, though Grebnev has met women who were highly skilled with weapons. "Who is she?"

"We don't know yet. Our friends at the MVD are running her photo through facial recognition. She goes by 'Lisa Carson,' though that's almost certainly a cover. Anyway, tell your *helpers* to watch themselves. And be on that aircraft when it takes off. Understand?"

Hackers and some ninja woman. It just gets more interesting. "Yes, sir. I'll be there."

Chapter 17

IBIZA

It's after five a.m. when Carson staggers out of Pacha—her ears still half-dead after a full-out techno assault—with the posse minus Celeste and Dareh, who are asleep (separately) at the mansion. Karl tries to flag down two cabs while the others half-yell things like, "The club was *lit*. Did you see…?"

Iris throws an arm around Carson's shoulders and leans her head against Carson's. "We're going shopping later."

"That a threat?"

"Totes serious. It's an emergency." Not all her words come out unslurred. She pats Carson's stomach. "You're better than that outfit."

"There's a dress code for saving the world?" Carson's wearing a plain white tee, her navy shorts, and the dance sandals. Tamara sneered when Carson joined the group to go into town.

Iris giggles. "Of *course* there's a dress code. We gotta get you some decent clothes so you look like you belong with us."

The costumes in the mammoth dance club ranged from tees and cutoffs to cocktail dresses, stilettos, and serious bling. Carson looks at the posse's women—each with her own style—and wonders what *belong* means. "I don't have a lot of money." And she loathes shopping.

"Don't worry about the money, hon. We got that covered." Iris looks straight into Carson's eyes. "Are you totes into the way your hair is?"

Carson groans. "Not this again."

"Yes, this again. Why are you trying to disappear?"

"My hair does what I need it to."

"Talk about a low bar. Listen to me, hon—you could be hot if you tried."

Carson nearly chokes on her tongue. She frowns at Iris and

points at her own face. "Hot? With this? Bullshit."

"Stop that! There's this energy coming off you. I can read it; I'm sure even guys can. Plus you're strong and healthy. That's sexy. As. Fuck. Haven't you heard this whole 'strong is the new sexy' thing? It's true. Do you get laid?"

"No comment."

"A lot?"

"No comment."

Iris hugs Carson with one arm. "Girl! And that's with no makeup and that hair. Imagine if you step it up a notch." She grabs for Carson's hand, but misses. "I'm not gonna bug you about makeup. There's only so much it can do, anyway. But I'm going to Musa today. It's my fave salon on the island. Please please *please* let my girls there fix your hair. You'll love it, I promise." She leans closer and drops her voice to a whisper. "*Sebastian* will love it."

Ah, shit. She had to say that. Early yesterday morning, Carson woke up in the middle of a dream about that massage. The dream was taking things to a…*different* ending.

It's not like Carson hasn't thought about a new 'do. Bri's been on her case about it ever since they both fell out of the Toronto police. She simply hasn't taken the time to do anything about it. It's such a girly thing to worry about. And who'll really care?

Let yourself live.

"Two conditions. It can't go below my collar. And it can't get in my eyes—no bangs or any of that shit. Understand?"

"Yes!" Iris pumps her fists in the air. "Tell that to my girls and they'll hook you up. You're gonna love it."

Grebnev spots the two women as they wander out of the side street that leads to their hair salon. Iris Vernon—the redhead—and the big woman who's traveling under "Lisa Carson." The one who took out the two French ex-marines three nights ago.

Severinov sent the video to him this morning. There was no nonsense in the woman's actions. She was quick, brutal, and efficient. One kidnapper will have to find another career; he won't get far in private security with a crippled arm. Grebnev's never seen a woman fight like that. Biting, scratching, and kicking are more normal.

Once the women get past the café tables at the corner, Grebnev aims his camera's 300mm lens and snaps off a series of shots as they stroll to the curb. The Carson woman's hair is different. She stops to peer into the driver's-side window of a VW Golf parked next to the crosswalk, touching her hair tentatively, as if she's making sure it's real. More photos.

He'd notified Grupo Sabadell right after his call with Severinov, but he has a private jet at his disposal and they don't. They'll have to charter an aircraft. In the meantime, Grebnev thought he should check out the situation and see what the hacker group is up to.

Apparently, shopping and beauty work.

Suddenly, the Carson woman straightens and looks around her. Grebnev stows the camera and starts drumming his fingers on the steering wheel, playing the impatient husband waiting for his wife to reappear.

The Carson woman's eyes skate across his car. *Did she see me? Did she notice? It's like she's sniffing the air for predators.*

Vernon laughs. *At Carson, or with her?* Eventually, Vernon pulls Carson across Carrer Carrasco—the street he's parked on—and around the corner onto Carrer Clapés behind him, where they'd left their little red Mini Countryman.

Grebnev checks his photos to make sure he got a few useful ones. At least there's plenty of sunlight. He enlarges a shot of the Carson woman admiring herself in the car window. The new hairdo does her more favors than the old one did; it's feminine but sporty, fluffed up and a bit spiky on top. It suits her.

The red car squeals onto Carrer Carrasco and charges east down the narrow street. Grebnev follows at a safe distance, doing his best to keep up with Vernon, who's a maniac driver. Between the scooters, motorcycles, and lorries, the follow's more of a thrill ride than anything at an amusement park.

He'll keep an eye on the villa until he can hand off to Grupo Sabadell. If the gang goes out on the town, maybe he'll nose around the grounds to see what he can find. He knows he's supposed to let the locals take care of this, but the soldier in him hates letting someone else do work that he can do better.

If Sabadell can't do it, at least he'll be ready to take over.

Chapter 18

DALT VILA, IBIZA

The view from the Plaça de la Catedral sweeps across the entire harbor and beyond into the hills, a carpet of lights competing with the mass of stars in the transparent night sky. Carson had no idea Eivissa—the Catalan name for Ibiza Town—is this spread out or could be this pretty. "Wow."

Sebastian brushes the back of her hand with the back of his. *Accidental? Hope not.* "Worth the climb?"

"Totally." The posse had come to the walled Dalt Vila—Old Town—for dinner and a pub crawl through the narrow streets packed with tourists, cafés, shops, and taverns. She barely noticed the climb until now, when it's clear they're forty or fifty meters higher than they started. A nice way to work off the huge meal.

The thirteenth-century cathedral's uplit bulk casts a warm glow over the plaza. Somehow, she and Sebastian are separated from the others by several meters and a few parked cars. She's not sure if she caused that or he did, but she doesn't mind. "Always this warm this late here?"

"Yes, in August. It's perfect swimming weather."

"That an invite?" She hopes it is.

Sebastian chuckles. "We'll see when we get back to the house."

They both gaze at the shimmering lights and stars and trade sighs for a few minutes. Carson knows she should just stand here with this gorgeous man and listen to him breathe, but something's been bugging her since their talk by the pool yesterday. She finally asks, "Why are you here? Why aren't you back home, making tons of money?"

Sebastian grunts something between a chuckle and a snort. "That was Da's plan. I'm supposed to follow his footsteps. I got my business degree at Trinners. I—"

"Trinners?"

"Trinity College Dublin. Maybe you've heard of it. I knew the moment I walked off Parliament Square the last time, I could walk into a position I didn't deserve at the bank and do as Da did—make myself rich by cheating other people and pitching the mess on the government to clean up."

"So you came here instead."

"I did."

"And you picked up Vicki in a bar one day and got way more than you expected."

He laughs. "I can't say that I picked her up or she picked me up, but the rest's true."

She examines this for some moments. If this is a sparring session, she's been giving Sebastian light jabs to counter. It's time to hit harder to see what happens. "Iris gave me the lowdown on most of your friends. Sounds like you all have daddy issues or mommy issues, and you ran away from home."

Sebastian scowls. "I reckon everything was sunshine and rainbows at home for you?"

"Not even. Mom's a sloppy drunk and Pops is up to his eyeballs in hock. I had to raise my three younger brothers because Mom was fucking useless. A five-year-old changing a two-year-old's diaper. Big difference is, I couldn't run away. There was no place for me to go and no money to get there. Call me 'jealous' that you had choices."

The next quiet is tense. Sebastian shakes his head and lets out a long breath. After a while, he says, "Sorry. I'd no idea. You're right—we all had choices. It's odd how much alike we all are. We got all the advantages people like you never have. Nannies, tutors, trainers. We all went to first-class universities and got degrees in business or finance or economics. All the things we were supposed to do so we could take over the world from our folks. But something else you didn't have were the expectations. The plans that Ma and Da make for you that you don't get a say in. That silver spoon tarnishes when it's in your mouth too long."

"I'm supposed to feel sorry for you?"

"No. It'd be nice if you'd give us a nod for not doing the easy thing and going along. Iris lost her trust funds because she's here. Same thing happened to Lukas—he was with us last year—and his parents called the guards on him. Serena—she left in April—her granddad wrote her out of his will. That cost her a right pretty sum."

"But what're you doing that's worth…*that*? Why did they stay?"

Sebastian stares off toward a lit-up cruise ship across the harbor. "We give them something to believe in that's not about making money for themselves."

Jesus, that again. "Giving money to charities? They could do that at home. Why's it worth losing their trust funds?"

"It's the scale, and the way we do it. We can make far more of an impact together than we can alone." He gives her a sharp look. "You wouldn't understand unless you'd grown up in our world."

Try me, she wants to say. That nugget about Iris is worth stashing in her back pocket. "Sorry. I don't know where the land mines are."

Now he frowns at her. "Are you always like this? Never satisfied with what you already know? Always digging deeper, trying to turn up dirt?"

If I had a loonie for every time somebody asked that… "It's what I do. Something sticks sideways in my head and I gotta work it out. That's what made me a good detective."

"Detective?" His eyebrows climb his forehead. "You were in the guards?"

"Police. Toronto. Long time ago."

"That's what I meant. We call them 'the guards' in Ireland. The *Garda*." He focuses on her eyes for a while. "You were a proper copper? Uniform and all?"

"Yeah. On patrol, not when I was a detective. And a sidearm." *Wind him up a little? Sure.* "Handcuffs, too. If you're into that."

His chuckle is a bit nervous. "Why'd you stop? Or did you?"

"Long story I don't wanna tell now." She glances up at him. "You have secrets. So do I."

Chapter 19

CAP MARTINET, IBIZA

Carson steps through one of the Moorish arches overlooking the pool and finds Tamara and Sebastian sitting at one end of a massive wood-plank table, each with an open laptop. They'd been talking, but that stops when Carson appears. "Anyone seen Iris?"

Sebastian shakes his head. "She's out."

What were they talking about? And why'd they stop? "She coming back?"

Tamara glares at Carson. "Why do you care?"

"Because I need to talk to her."

Sebastian says, "She always comes back. When, I couldn't say, though."

Figures. "Either of you hear from Vicki?"

Tamara folds her arms and aims a loaded eyebrow at Carson. "Is this when you arrest her, *guardia*?"

Keep it up, girlie. "Right now, it's so I know she's not dead. The rest we'll handle later."

Sebastian makes a calming-down gesture toward Tamara, then pushes out of his chair and guides Carson out to the deck with a firm hand on the small of her back. It's warm through her tee and she doesn't mind the contact. He stands closer than she expects. "When Vicki rings, she usually talks to Iris." His voice is just loud enough to be heard over the R&B track playing on the outdoor speakers. "Sometimes to me."

Carson would be okay simply standing here in the midday sun, watching Sebastian blink. "Okay. I'll chill until Iris comes back. Can I ask a personal question?"

"Are you asking to see if I'm a threat?"

"Just curious. Why'd you and Vicki split up? Can't imagine how gorgeous your babies would've been."

Sebastian chuckles and ducks his head. "Yes, they'd have been a sight. If you must know, I wasn't enough of a challenge for her. Vicki likes her projects. She didn't want to change me enough to keep her interest."

The truth or humblebragging? Hard to tell. "You were one of the originals in this group, same as Iris, right?"

"That's right."

"How'd Iris end up being Vicki's Number Two?"

"Instead of me?" He shoves his hands in the pockets of his walking shorts and stares toward the Med. "Iris is a bossy lass, and she's got no filter. That's perfect for herding this mess of cats that we are. I…I've not got that. I want too much for everyone to get on." He switches his focus to Carson's eyes. "Disappointed?"

"Should I be?"

"I reckon it's down to the sort of man you fancy."

"Guess it is." Carson squeezes his arm, then walks off before she does something stupid.

She's halfway down the path through the almost-jungle when she meets Dareh coming the other way. He's shorter than Carson, with thick, black hair that looks like it's been through a wind tunnel. Skinny, darkish skin that isn't a tan, and big, dark eyes. She says, "Hey."

"Hallo." He slows. His eyes turn wary.

"You're Dareh, right?"

"Yes." He finally stops just out of Carson's reach. "You are…Lisa, yes?"

"Yeah." She's not exactly blocking the path, but he may not notice that. "Haven't had a chance to talk much to you or Karl. You guys disappeared when we got here."

"Yes. We work."

"What kind of work?"

He hesitates. In his board shorts and tank top, Dareh looks like a lot of the young tourist guys she's seen here and in Marbella, except they usually don't look worried. "Ehm…data analytic."

"Is it part of what Sebastian and the others are working on?"

Another hesitation. He licks his lips. "Yes, it is."

Carson can't figure out his accent. Part of the problem is that he hasn't said enough to help her get a handle on it. "What kind of name is Dareh? Where are you from?"

"It is Persian."

"That's where you're from? Iran?"

"Yes."

Is he scared of me, or scared of talking? She tries a different approach. "Celeste's down there?"

His eyes brighten. "Yes, she is. She makes her music."

"What's she working on today?"

"Rain. It is…wonderful."

"Do you like listening to her music?"

"Yes, very much. It is a good, ehm, stop from work. She is very nice."

"Yeah, she is." He's not scared of Carson; he doesn't want to talk about his work. She'd like to know why. "I like it, too. That's where I'm going now."

"Good. I think she like peoples to listen."

"I think you're right. See you around." Carson waves, then continues down the path to the property's far edge.

Data analytics?

Carson arrives at the thatched-roof pavilion to find Amabelle there, sitting cross-legged on an oversized cushion on the wood-plank deck. Amabelle shoots her a closed look. Carson pulls up another cushion and sits about two meters from Celeste and a meter from Amabelle, who scoots her cushion farther away. Carson sighs, closes her eyes, and dives into the music Celeste's playing on an electronic keyboard.

A rainstorm on a city street plays on Carson's mental movie screen. It's long and lovely and lonely. She can't bear for it to go on, but she doesn't want it to stop. When it finally does, Carson opens her eyes and finds Amabelle watching her. Carson says, "Wow."

Amabelle gives her a solemn smile. This is the first time she hasn't ducked Carson. "That is so beautiful, it is terrifying."

Carson rolls that description through her head, wishing she'd thought of it. "Yeah. So, should I call you Madam President?"

Amabelle's eyes widen, then she laughs. "It is only my father's fantasy. Only one woman has ever led a government in East Africa. He wants me to be president so I can pardon him for all the things that he should not have done. If he tells the wrong people his fantasy, I can be in danger." She nods toward Celeste, who sits listening to them. "Do you like the music?"

"I love it. It's…awesome. Like in the old-fashioned way."

"Yes, it is. I take time from working to listen to it. It clears my mind." Amabelle unfolds her legs and rests her forearms on her knees. "Vicki wants you here to protect us, yes?"

"Yeah."

"Who protects us from you?"

Carson had been waiting for someone to ask that. "Why do you think you need to be protected from me?"

Amabelle laughs, but there's no joy in it. "Vicki's father sends you to take her away from us, yes?"

"Yeah. Indirectly."

"If we try to stop you, you will do to us what you did to those men in Banús, yes?"

"I'd rather not. If you force me, I'll do what I gotta do." Carson glances toward Celeste, who's still perched on her stool, listening in her usual intense way. Her face doesn't give away what she's thinking. "Look…Belle? Amabelle? Which do you like?"

Amabelle shrugs broadly.

"Belle, then. I got no beef with you or your friends. I got a job to do. Vicki gave me another job while I'm waiting for her dad to decide what he wants. I know why she did it. You probably do, too. Far as I'm concerned, if I can walk away and leave Vicki here without getting my head taken off, it's a win for everybody."

"Really." Amabelle makes it sound like *bullshit*. She crosses her arms and scowls. "Why would you do that for her?"

Carson had wanted to keep this in her hip pocket until she needed it. But if she can turn Amabelle around, maybe Belle can sort out the others who didn't vote for Carson. "Ten-thirty Tuesday near Pangea. Some asshole was beating the shit out of his girlfriend."

One of Amabelle's eyebrows shoots up. "You saw this?"

"I was gonna stop it when you guys showed. Vicki took charge. She got the girl away from the asshole with no fighting and nobody getting hurt. Whole thing could've turned to shit fast if she screwed up, but she didn't. Lots of people would've walked away, but she didn't. That's when I figured there's more to Vicki than Insta."

A lot starts happening behind Amabelle's dark eyes. Her eyes and mouth shift as she considers what Carson said. She finally says, "Now you do not want to do your job?"

"It's not about 'want.' Her dad tells me to bring her home, I take her home. His decision. But I'll do it as gently and with as much dignity as she'll let me. Anybody else he sends won't give a shit. You don't want me to go away."

Amabelle peers into Carson's eyes. Eventually, she nods. "I think I believe you. You give me things to think about." She leaves her cushion. "If you like Celeste's music, you cannot be a bad person. We should talk more." Amabelle kisses Celeste's cheek, nods at Carson, then disappears into the jungle.

Celeste moves the cushion Amabelle abandoned next to Carson, sits, then wraps her arms around Carson's shoulders. "You and Belle are friends now?"

"Don't know. I don't think we're enemies."

Celeste is busy trying to cheer up Carson with old Billy Joel and Elton John songs when Iris makes her way down the path to the pavilion. She listens until Celeste finishes, smiling at how strange "New York State of Mind" sounds in French. Then Iris says to Carson, "Sebastian says you realized you can't live without me and you wanna have my babies."

Carson tries not to choke. "If he said that, he's smoking some good shit."

"That happens." Iris smiles at Celeste and coos something in French. Celeste coos back; the only word Carson can pick out is *Lisa*. Iris turns to Carson. "I just borrowed you."

Carson struggles off the cushion—she's been sitting too long— then steps to Celeste and one-arm-hugs her to her side. "Thank you for playing for me."

"I like playing for you. You listen."

Carson and Iris are a good dozen meters away from the pavilion when Iris says, "That girl thinks you shit Skittles. *Please* don't let her down, okay?"

"Last thing I want." She waits until they're halfway between Celeste's pavilion and the pool before she stops. They're surrounded by trees and flowering bushes and shadows dappled with sunlight. The air is noticeably cooler than by the pool. "Where's Vicki?"

Iris turns and shrugs. "Her Insta says she's in Málaga."

The answer Carson expected but not the one she wants. She's had enough time since her talk with Sebastian to get good and tired of non-answers. "She lies on her Insta. Where's Vicki?"

"I haven't talked to her for a couple of—"

"She's supposed to be here, right? She isn't. Where. The fuck. Is Vicki?"

Iris's mouth twitches. Her eyes widen, then narrow. "I don't know."

Again, expected but not wanted. Carson stops for a ten-count. "Call her."

Iris throws up her hands. "It's no big deal. She doesn't always—"

"*Now.*"

An edge of fear slides into Iris's voice. "You've heard something, haven't you. From her—"

"Her dad? Not yet. Been expecting it since Tuesday. When it happens—when he asks if I know where she is—I'm gonna have an answer. Call her *now.*"

"What if she's in the middle—"

"Don't care." Carson fills Iris's personal space. She can't loom over Iris—they're the same height—but she can crowd the woman. "Doesn't matter. Fucking *call her.*"

Iris steps back. Her face is scrunched and anxious. "What's with you? Why are you all up in my grille? I thought we were friends."

Carson almost says *we're not friends.* It's not a good tactic and it's also not quite true. She doesn't have a word for what her relationship is with Iris, but *friend* is a possibility. "Vicki told me to protect the group. That means I protect her, too. Two ways I can do that. One is, I put in a good word for her with her dad. Try to change his mind."

"Any of us can do that."

"He won't listen to you." He probably won't listen to Carson, either, but she doesn't need to bring that up. "Second way is, if she's with me, he's got no reason to send more goons after her. When she's out there"—Carson waves vaguely west—"it's open season."

Iris makes a *hmpf* noise. "Or you can just tell him 'no' and leave us alone."

"People I work for? You don't say 'no' to them. It's a—"

"Who are they? These 'people' you work for? Are you *scared* of them?"

Carson can tell Iris means that as a challenge or a barb. "Yeah. I am. You would be, too. Or should be. If you want to know who they are, ask Vicki when you call her." She waits a beat. "*Now.*"

Iris tries to out-stare Carson. Not a great idea: Carson's had staring contests with real pros. Iris eventually breaks off and watches her feet scuff the gravel path. She mumbles, "What do you want to say to her?"

Progress. "Basic stuff. Where she is, what she's doing, when she'll be here. That way I'll have answers when my people call me."

"What if she doesn't want to talk to you?"

"Then I'm coming after her. And just because she lied to me, I'll drag her back to Moscow myself."

"Belle says you don't want to do that."

"I don't. But if Vicki pisses me off…"

"Okay, okay, okay." Iris drags her phone out of her back pocket, fiddles with it, then presses it to her ear. "Hey, Vicki, it's me. Can you call? I totes gotta talk to you. Love ya. Later." She shoots a grumpy look at Carson. "Voicemail."

"Got that." It's time to lower the temperature. She takes a step toward Iris with her hand out. "Look, I don't want to fight. Sorry I barked at you. Some things I need aren't optional. Access to Vicki's one of them. So…are we okay?"

Iris gives her more grumpiness. "I don't know." She folds her arms and makes a pickle face at the ground.

Her phone rings. It startles them both.

Iris checks the number. Her eyebrows jump up. "Vicki?... Hi. How's it going?... Um, not exactly. I'm with Lisa… She wants to talk to you… She's pretty intense about it… Yeah…"

Carson points at the phone and mouths, *Ask her who I work for.*

Iris waves her off. "Um, where are you?... Okay. Okay. Um, here." Iris hands the phone to Carson.

The first thing Carson notices is that the phone isn't some brand-new, brand-name model with the latest everything; it's a cheap Chinese knockoff. The second thing she notices is Vicki's phone number on the call screen. She memorizes it. "Hey, Vicki? It's Lisa."

"Hello! Are you enjoying yourself on Ibiza? It's one of my favorite places."

"Not favorite enough to actually be here. Where are you?"

Pause. "I'm in Málaga just now."

"Really?"

"Well, yes. I'm arranging some things for the group, such as where we'll stay next." Vicki clears her throat softly. "Has Father contacted you?"

"Not yet. Expect that anytime now. No idea what I'll tell him when he does." Carson watches Iris pace in random directions while she chews on her upper lip. "When are you coming here?"

"Soon, I hope. It's August, so most places we'd normally stay are already spoken for and the hotels are full. That's the problem with high season. We may need to stay on Ibiza until something opens up."

"Poor you."

Vicki coughs out the first note of a laugh. "I know, it sounds dire, doesn't it? We should all have such problems." Another pause. "Have you…thought at all…about what you'll do if Father wants you to take me to Russia?"

Carson's been listening for background noise that might hint at where Vicki really is. So far, nothing. "Been thinking about it. You know I won't hear straight from him, right? I won't be able to bargain with him directly."

"Yes, I'm aware. That complicates things."

"No shit. It'd help if I could talk to you in person. Get to know you. All I got is a couple hours at Pangea. Not enough to make a case for you. Like, what are you guys doing to save the world? All I get is hand-waving and 'Talk to Vicki.' Well, Vicki? What are you up to?"

There's no sound on the other end at all. Vicki muted her phone.

"Vicki? I know you're still there."

"Yes. Yes, I am. I'd rather not discuss it on my mobile. I reckon you understand why. When I get there, I'll tell you every—"

"When's that gonna be?"

"Well, as I said, I—"

"Why Málaga? Sounds like a lot of phone work. Why not come here to do it? Your friends miss you."

Iris scowls at Carson.

"It's…easier here." Vicki's voice is slowly hardening.

How far do I push this? Carson can't order Vicki to come back. If anything, that would probably kick her into going to Brazil or whatever. But she can't be a pushover, either. "This isn't going away, Vicki. Your dad decides you belong in Russia, that's where you're going. That's when you're gonna want a friend with you. Otherwise, his people'll stuff you in a crate and you'll ride back in the cargo hold. Don't want that? Stop running away from me."

"I'm not running away!" Her voice is low and urgent. "I swear to you. You're with my family, the family I chose. I'll not abandon them. Just a few more days? I'll come and you can have all the time with me that you wish."

"We may not have a few more days."

"I know. If it comes to that, please have Iris ring me and we'll talk about it." Vicki sighs. "I truly do want us to get to know each other better. Things are…*difficult* just now. Not only because of Father. Please…have a bit of faith in me?"

"We're not done."

"Of course not. Please let me speak with Iris."

Carson gets one last look at Vicki's number as she hands the phone to Iris, who moves out of eavesdropping range. Carson repeats the number to herself while she watches Iris pace, clutching the phone to her ear and gesturing as she speaks.

After a few minutes of intense conversation, Iris shoves her phone in the back pocket of her dangerously short cutoffs and steps close to Carson. "Vicki says I should treat you like one of us. I think I've been doing better than that, but…" She shrugs. "I'm also supposed to make sure none of the fam is mean to you. Are they?"

"Tamara's been snippy."

"There's reasons for that. If you want to talk to Vicki, ask me and I'll hook you up. And don't bother the peeps when they're working. They have to be extra productive because we take time off to play." She moves in a bit closer. "Vicki said you were right to insist on talking to her. I don't even have to be mad at you to save face."

"Good. Pass the word to the rest of your friends."

"Vicki already told me to do that." Iris turns and marches up the path toward the mansion. "Anubis tonight! I expect to see a new outfit."

Carson hustles to her room—off to the side on the ground floor—and pounds Vicki's number into her contacts. Then she calls Olivia.

Olivia says, "I'm not aware you're assigned to a project now."

"I'm not. Mr. R's got me. Um…I need a favor."

"Of what sort?"

"Can you trace a phone number for me?"

"You know I'm not supposed to do that if you're not assigned to a project. Can't Mr. R do it for you?"

Please, not now… "No. Well, maybe. I don't want to explain to him why I need it."

"And why *do* you need it?"

"I'm supposed to find somebody. She's attached to this number, but don't know where she is."

"I reckon you'd like Mr. R to think you solved the problem through alchemy?"

"Um, black magic. It's sexier. But, yeah." With Olivia, Carson's not too proud to beg. "Please? I swear I won't tell Allyson—"

"You most certainly will not, young lady." Olivia sighs. "One day, I'll do you a favor and Allyson will suss us both. Then we'll both get the sack. Tell me the number."

Carson recites it. "Probably in Spain, but maybe not."

"That certainly narrows it. I'll text the answer to you when I get it. Others are involved, so I can't say when that will be. Do be careful."

"Thanks! You're the best." Carson wishes she knew what Olivia drinks and where she lives so Carson can send her the best bottle of whatever every week. All she knows is four years of Olivia myth and legend from other associates. If only half of it is true…

Twenty minutes later, the "incoming text" tone sounds on her phone. It's from Olivia: `Algeciras`.

Across the bay from Gibraltar. One of the biggest ports in Europe.

What in hell is Vicki doing there?

Chapter 20

The general admission line to get into Anubis is roughly fifty meters long at one-thirty Sunday morning—unfashionably early, but before the VIP areas on the mezzanine are all taken.

Carson scans the people in the "plebe line"—Tamara's words—while she waits with the rest of Vicki's posse in the much-shorter VIP line. Nearby is what Sebastian calls a "stag do"—a dozen and a half guys in their twenties in board shorts, tees with raunchy mottos, and sandals—then a few couples and foursomes in variations on denim and leather and lace, then a "hen do" of a dozen women in matching red-sequined minidresses, then an older couple that looks like refugees from Ibiza's long-gone peace-and-love era.

Carson maneuvers her mouth near Sebastian's ear. "This looks like a warehouse."

"It was a warehouse." He peers into her eyes. His white dress shirt reflects the purple uplighting on the club's outside walls, which are painted to look like they're built of huge blocks of stone. It's almost like he's fluorescing. "Have I told you yet that I fancy your outfit?"

"Yeah. You like the shorts." She's wearing the dressy black shorts she bought on Friday, a ribbed black bodysuit, and her black dance sandals. From the looks of it, she's in the middle of the fashion pack. Unlike with the blue dress, she gets to wear a bra.

"I do like the shorts very much. And I like your hair. Is that wrong?"

"No. I don't mind you repeating yourself, either."

Iris swans up to them. Her short, metallic-sequined, purple-and-green one-shoulder sheath reflects every bit of stray light within a hundred meters. "How are you crazy kids doing?"

Carson says "Fine" in a way she hopes sounds like "Go away."

Iris is distracting her from looking at Sebastian.

"Good, good. It'll be another ten minutes or so. I hear Colin Farrell is here with twenty or so of his closest buds. The VIP escorts are busy wrangling that." She slips an arm around Carson's waist. "Hon, you are *en fuego*. Aren't you glad you went shopping with me?"

"Sure." Carson doesn't feel *en fuego*, though she's noticed the guys in the stag checking out her legs more than she expected. And Sebastian's paying attention.

Amabelle and Tamara start yelling "Iris!" and waving her forward.

Iris says, "My audience's calling for me. See you inside." She hurries toward the head of the line with that shuffling gait women use when they try to go fast in heels that are too high.

Carson envies Celeste, safe at the mansion with Karl guarding her and probably long since asleep. She's the posse's only sensible member.

A few minutes later, after an unusually thorough bag check, a hyper-cheerful young blonde with a northern English accent leads them up *faux*-stone steps to the VIP mezzanine.

Stepping from the stairwell into the club space is like walking into a wall that fights back. The thumping house claws into Carson's chest to change her heartbeat.

The club is unspeakably huge. Thousands of people fill the floor under fifteen-meter-tall sculptures of Egyptian gods. An enormous jackal head of Anubis with glowing orange eyes dominates the stage behind the DJ. Lasers slash pyramids in the air. Moving spotlights stab shafts of yellow and red light into the crowd. An ice cannon roars close to her right, blasting a column of frost into the dancers.

The blonde drops the group at their three black-leather sofas arranged in a U facing the stage. Carson ends up pressed between Sebastian on her left and Iris on her right. She has to huddle close to Sebastian—she doesn't mind, and apparently he doesn't either—to yell, "This is crazy!"

He nods. "They opened at one. They're still warming up."

This is "warming up"? Carson checks out the neighbors. They don't look much different from the people in the plebe line. Nearly everybody has a beer bottle or cocktail glass. "How much do we have to drink?"

"What do you mean?"

"The minimum. To sit here."

"There's no minimum. We paid an extra twenty each to be here, and the drinks are more expensive."

"But in Marbella—"

"Marbella likes a caste system. That's why there are dress codes and levels of VIP tables. In Ibiza, everyone can be a VIP. Except they can't, of course."

Dareh heads for the nearest stairwell. He waves at Iris, then points downward. Iris gives him thumbs-up, then scurries to sit with Amabelle and Tamara.

Carson huddles with Sebastian again. "Karl and Dareh don't mix much with the others. Why?"

He shrugs. "They're different animals. They spend all day on their screens. Maybe you've got to be the loner kind to do what they do."

"What is that, exactly?"

"Data analytics."

More I've-got-a-secret. "There's obviously a bar here."

"Sixteen of them."

Sixteen? "So what's with the pre-gaming?" On the way here from the restaurant, they stopped at a little dive bar to load up on alcohol. Good thing the big SUV they rented comes with a driver.

"You'll not be wanting to drink a lot here. It's sixteen euros for a beer and twenty-four for a mixed drink. Even water is twelve. They salt the water in the jakes so you can't drink from the tap."

"Jakes?"

"The loo."

"You're shitting me."

"God's honest. That's why so many people use drugs—they're cheaper than alcohol. You can score a yoke of E for eight or ten euros and it lasts all night."

A dark-haired waitress shows up to take drink orders. She's wearing a white quasi-Egyptian tunic—a belted, hip-length poncho with open sides—over black bikini bottoms. Both Sebastian and Iris pay close attention when the waitress bends to take the women's orders and the top billows away from her smallish breasts. Carson pities the girl. How often do the drunks grope her?

Does she go home bruised? Does the boss hit on her?

Both Carson and Sebastian order whisky neat—no ice to melt as they nurse their drinks. The waitress has exaggerated cat-eye makeup like a Halloween Cleopatra. She flashes a quick smile at Sebastian before she leaves.

Carson says, "Go chase her if you want."

Sebastian shakes his head. "I'm quite satisfied with my current company, thanks."

The crowd below thickens. The mezzanine fills. People try to drink and dance at the same time and don't always succeed. Random guys pass through—shaking hands, patting shoulders—then move on. The noise slowly drills a hole though Carson's skull.

Amabelle, Iris, and Tamara head for the stairs. Iris raises her drink to Carson and Sebastian, mimes diving off the mezzanine into the crowd, then hustles after the other two.

Carson sighs. "How do I keep them safe if I can't see them?"

"You don't. They're adults. They can take care of themselves."

"That's not what Iris was saying."

"Iris's job is to be the ma hen while Vicki's gone." His mouth edges very close to her ear. "You're not on duty."

"I'm always on duty."

They sit and peck at their drinks. Sebastian's hand parks on her thigh. All her nerve endings spark off under his warm palm. She puts her hand over his in case he gets the dumb idea to move it.

To distract herself, she watches the crowd. She has no idea what a threat looks like here. Everybody could belong, or nobody does. *You're useless here. Stand down.*

But she can't. Gulps of booze chase pills all around her. Next door, a young woman pouring sweat in a halter and denim mini dances with movements as big as her blown pupils. The people around Carson get louder as they get less coordinated, but they're not drinking enough to get so drunk so fast. "Sebastian?"

"Yes?"

"Is everybody up here loaded?"

"I'd not be surprised."

"But…the bouncers were pulling dope off people right and left. Where are these people getting it?"

Sebastian scans the crowd to their left, then nudges Carson with his shoulder and nods. "See the one with the white tee and bandana?"

Carson spots him after a few moments: a young, light-haired man wearing a white tee with two cherries on the front—the Pacha logo, last Thursday's club—works his way down the railing toward them, doing the handshake-backpat thing. She watches his hands. "That was a handoff."

"It was."

"So how'd he get in here?"

Once the dealer passes them—he raises his eyebrows at Sebastian, who shakes his head once—Sebastian leans close to Carson. "People here want to get off their head. It's how you dance at the pool parties or beach parties 'til sunset, then dance here 'til sunrise. The clubs know it. Some let their punters bring it—so long as you're not thick, you can carry your own in. Some clubs, the staff sells. I hear that most of the club staff and waitstaff sell on the side because they're paid so little. Some clubs let dealers work the floor. That can be a problem, though—there are so many gangs here, and they can get into it over turf, and you don't want that in your club. Also, if anything happens that brings in the guards—like a punter ODs on his own dope or gets wrecked and does a dive off the mezzanine here—you're stuffed.

"So some clubs put on a show. They screen for dope at the door to keep the guards happy. Then inside, they sell a concession. The club keeps the competition out and gets a cut of the take. The concessionaire runs a clean operation with no hassles. Everybody wins. None of this shite like what happened a couple of weeks ago, when the plods found a stash of E with five times the MDMA as normal."

Carson watches him for a while, thinking. He's matter-of-fact about it all, simply discussing the workings of some obscure commodities market. Which, basically, he is. She can't get a read on how he feels about all this, and she's not sure she should ask. "Which one is that guy?" She points after the dealer in the white shirt.

"He's a concessionaire."

"How do you know?"

Sebastian shrugs. "I talk to people." He captures Carson's hand between his. "I'm no saint. I've been known to take a walk with Molly myself now and then. We all have done. We don't use the harder stuff—it's not worth the risk. Coke's too easy to love, and meth's too mankey. If this bothers you, I understand."

He hasn't asked if she's done drugs. There's no good reason to volunteer the information. "I'm in no position to judge."

They sit together, chatting off and on and watching the crowd get denser and wilder. Dancers put on a show onstage; they're dressed like the cocktail waitress, except without the bikini bottoms. Carson stands at the rail in a half-hearted attempt to spot the rest of the posse, but all she can see is a surging ocean of humanity. Sebastian eventually buys her and himself another drink at two-thirty. He kisses her for the first time at two-forty. She kisses him back.

Sebastian murmurs, "Do y'fancy going downstairs to dance?"

Carson glances at the scrum. "Animals usually stay on their side of the fence at zoos."

"Well said." He looks around. "We can dance up here. There's even room to move."

They push the cocktail table away from the sofa and start to dance. Carson's still rusty even after Tuesday at the club in Marbella, plus the music's different. She feels stiff and fake.

Sebastian stops her with his hands on her shoulders. "You're trying to dance. It's not aerobics, it's not about steps. Just move with the music. Feel the music." He lays his hand on her stomach. "Here. Feel it here. Move here."

She flexes her core with the rhythm. It'll work her abs, if nothing else. It's easier to let her mind loose to feel Celeste's music, though the warmth of Sebastian's palm helps unclench her muscles.

Now Sebastian moves his hand to her hip. "Now here. Move here. Ride the beat. Empty your mind and ride the beat. Let yourself go."

Carson slowly lets herself go. The beat replaces her pulse. She feels the flow. For maybe the first time, she gets electronic dance music. And she finally understands how people can spend hours surrendering to it.

Carson finally gets to bed by five-twenty. Her ears still throb from the seamless, unstoppable music. The shower didn't relax her;

it only sluiced off the sweat. But now she drifts in the milky dark, the sheets cool and soft on her skin, her mind sorting through the last few hours' sensory riot.

A soft rapping on her door breaks her out of her haze. "Lisa?" Sebastian's voice.

Hm. Carson slides out of bed and shuffles to the door. She cracks it enough to see into the darkish hall. He's a couple of steps away, barefoot but still in his club clothes. Not a bad sight to wake up to. "Hey."

"Hi. Did I wake you?"

"Not really."

"Good. I couldn't sleep either."

She nudges open the door a bit more and leans against the doorjamb. "Tonight was fun."

"It was." He scans her up and down, breaking out a little smile. "You're wearing my favorite outfit."

"It's what I sleep in unless it's cold." *Ask if you can come in. Come on, you can do it.*

"Me, too. Em… Do y'like your room?"

Oh, for fuck's sake. "It's fine. Big washroom. Lots of room in the shower." She "accidentally" bumps the door open some more. "Nice big bed." *Take the hint…*

His smile grows wider. "Grand to hear it." An hour-long few seconds go by. "Would you fancy some company?"

Finally.

Chapter 21

Damir Severinov leans over the technician's shoulder to stare at the mess on the man's curved monitor. "You're certain it's the same people?"

"Yes, sir." The young man—all his hackers are young men—hits some keys on his keyboard. Two windows open on the screen, apparently a side-by-side comparison of some code Severinov can't (and doesn't need to) read or understand. "It's almost identical code. The same approach, the same exploit, the same cover."

Severinov—Zapadneft's Chief Security Officer—straightens and rubs the back of his neck. This semi-darkened room on the eighteenth floor of the company's Moscow headquarters is listed as a storage room, which, in a way, it is: it stores six cubicles, racks of electronics, and pallets of energy drinks and ramen. The six young men in those cubicles appear in the company's human resources database as "customer service technicians," though they have no phones and have never spoken to another company employee other than Severinov himself. The Offensive Cyber Operations Section has no box on any organization chart. It's certainly busy, though.

"Which company is this?" he asks.

"DGI. It's a finance company in Frankfurt. They're bad boys—they've been in trouble with every regulator in the EU."

"That makes the sixth one we've found so far."

"Yes, sir." The bearded hacker—Cyril, Severinov recalls—leans back in his pre-production Secretlab Titan chair and takes a slug of Red Bull. "I can use this for a proxy attack on the crackers, if you want."

"What would that involve?"

Cyril launches into the explosion of half-Russian, half-English, all-gibberish that Severinov expects. He's found that it's best to let hackers talk about the technical aspects first before tackling the tactical details. This time, it takes a ten-minute guided tour of network plumbing in the eastern hemisphere before the man gets to the end.

Severinov pretends to ponder this for a few moments. "As far as they're concerned, they're being attacked by DGI?"

"Yes, sir. No comebacks to us."

"How long will they be down?"

"It's hard to say. A few days, maybe. It depends on how up-to-date their backups are."

"Will DGI know anything about it?"

"Not unless we tell them."

"Let's not do that." This is a new world for Severinov. Not for the first time, he imagines what Russian military intelligence could've done with this technology when he was still in the GRU. The cost-benefit analysis is different from what he had to do for kinetic operations. "Can you take control of the exploit after you lock them out?"

"I can try. I'm still trying to find all the components. The worst that happens is, it closes. No skin off our asses."

A no-lose proposition. Not a bad thing. "Plan it out. Let me know when you're ready to execute. Thank you, Cyril."

Back at his desk on the nineteenth floor overlooking the Moskva River, Severinov closes all but the last folder containing the background information for the members of this hacker gang that attacked the company. The company's friends at the MVD did their usual thorough job.

They're young, from rich families, with degrees from top-shelf schools. If they were Russian, they'd be back here now, settling into their hereditary executive positions on their way to taking over the family businesses—or more accurately, the businesses that have been in their families since the Soviet Union destroyed itself. But since they're mostly Western youth, they're wasting their lives partying at beach resorts. At least one fool is selling party drugs, though God alone knows why. The real money's still in powder cocaine and opioids.

One is Russian. He's surprised Oleg Baranov lets his daughter run wild in the West. The analyst helpfully attached key photos from her Instagram account, including one of her lying nude next to a swimming pool, carefully posed to not show anything that would get the picture banned by whomever does such things in social media. Still, he's of a mind to send it to Baranov. A father shouldn't enjoy seeing his daughter display herself that way in public. It could be useful for Baranov to understand that someone's watching her foolishness—and taking notes.

The two hackers—Dareh Abbasi and Karl Greininger—are at least relatively normal for their kind. Their parents are upper-middle-class rather than wealthy, though Abbasi's father could be considered one of Iran's elites. That could open an interesting avenue for *maskirovka*: could he work things so the Iranians or Israelis take the blame? He makes a mental note to pursue that in the next day or so.

The most unexpected and potentially most worrying issue is the new woman. As he'd expected, "Lisa Carson" is an alias. But this Tarasenko woman's involved somehow with a *pakhan* in the Solntsevskaya Bratva. There's no information about *how* she's involved, though. She's certainly not a *boyevik*; the Bratva doesn't use women as soldiers. But there she is, embedded in this group, and she's had enough training to deal with two marines in a few seconds.

Generally, Severinov wouldn't worry much about an organized crime connection. He's happily disposed of members of a dozen different *mafiya* factions when they crossed the company. But the Solntsevo bunch shelters under the FSB's umbrella. The FSB is already upset with Zapadneft for the debacle in Riga; he'd rather not give them more reasons to look at the company as a target rather than an asset.

He'll tell Grebnev about this new wrinkle. It's time he got that local drug gang to work. If they can actually do what they're told, Severinov will be rid of those damned hackers, save the company some money...and perhaps give his old rival the FSB a black eye. He can't decide which of those prospects he enjoys the most.

Chapter 22

CAP MARTINET, IBIZA

Carson's camped out in the thatch-roofed pavilion behind the swimming pool's waterfall. It's about seven meters by five, well-stocked with large pillows and floor mats, a few degrees cooler and shaded from the sun. From the far corner, Carson can see into the garden below and still catch the breeze coming off the Med a hundred meters away. The waterfall's a relatively gentle cascade that rustles pleasantly and feels nice on a hot day. Old-school ska punk plays on the loudspeakers.

It's past five in the afternoon. Tamara's gone off to the market with a crash of glass bottles for recycling. Amabelle and Sebastian work at the big table on the patio. Carson's been pretending to read on her laptop.

Rogozhkin asks in Russian, "Are you having fun in Ibiza?"

Carson had called him, wanting a grownup to talk to. "The usual—non-stop clubbing, booze, drugs, sex." She winces when she says *sex*. Here she is, sleeping with a young hunk and flirting with a man who thinks she's Miss August. She's really got to sort this out…later.

"I'm impressed you have the energy for all that."

"Me, too. Watching these kids makes me remember what I was like at their age. Endless energy, eat anything, snort or smoke anything, burn the candle at both ends and the middle, then haul my sorry ass out of bed and go to work. Sometimes they make me think I can do it again."

Rogozhkin chuckles. "I know what you're feeling. I'd watch the junior officers in my unit—they'd be twenty years younger than I was—and try to convince myself I could keep up. I learned the truth when I woke up the next morning."

"Yeah. The get-off-my-lawn voice in me wants to tell them, 'Wait 'til you hit thirty. You'll get what sleep is for.'"

They both chuckle. Rogozhkin says, "What are you doing when you're not partying with your young friends? Or is that all you do now?"

The sound of churning water grabs Carson's attention. Iris is swimming near the waterfall. *Paddling* is probably a better description. Carson had thought about joining her but wasn't sure she's welcome. Iris has been preoccupied since she returned from another of her multi-hour mystery missions outside the compound.

Carson says, "Trying to stay out of the way and watch. Wanna see what 'normal' is here. The cliques, who gets along with who, that kind of thing. I still don't get the politics."

"At least you have only eight people to deal with. I had to do that with the Chechens, the Abkhaz, the Serbs, the damn Ukrainians—"

"Yeah, yeah. Okay, boomer."

"You young women," he sputters. "No respect for your elders."

As they spar back and forth, Carson notices a hit on her Google News alert for Ibiza. They've been pretty useless since she set them up when she got here, mostly three-paragraph pieces about British kids getting stupid and falling off hotel balconies and the like. But this one—from *The Sun*, a British tabloid—catches her attention:

```
PARTY DRUG WAR Brit drug dealer
killed outside Ibiza pleasure
palace

A 24-year-old Manchester man
who sold ecstasy on the party
island Ibiza was found knifed to
death behind the louche megaclub
Anubis Sunday morning...
```

Carson skims the story, skipping the stock photographs of dancers and ecstasy tablets, until she comes to a grainy photo of the victim. It's the guy in the white tee who Sebastian pointed out in the VIP section. *Shit. Did that happen when we were there?*

Carson taps a link to a related story about Ibiza drug dealers and gets a white can't-find-that-website page. She checks her Wi-Fi; she's lost the network.

That's when she hears running. Dareh sprints along the pool apron toward Iris while Karl bounds up the steps to the patio and skids to a stop at the table. Amabelle's and Sebastian's reactions tell Carson that something bad has happened even though she can't make out what Karl's saying. "Edik? Something just happened. Can I call you back?"

Dareh kneels at the pool's edge. He waits for Iris to reach him and grab the coping before he downloads what sounds like a news bulletin. A bad one. Carson can hear a random word here and there when the breeze is right but can't make any sense of it. *Is this about the dead guy?*

Iris says, "What do you mean, 'hacked'?" Her voice is higher-pitched and carries farther, plus her volume control isn't the best.

Hacked?

Carson shuts down her laptop and concentrates as hard as she can on Dareh and Iris.

Dareh's side of the conversation sounds like "…Global… backdoor… rootkit… Wi-Fi… custom… scanning…"

Iris says, "Did you unplug it in time?"

Dareh's palms-up gesture translates to *no idea*. "Cut… shut down… power… warning…"

Iris closes her eyes and shakes her head. After a few moments, she waves Dareh aside, then levers herself out of the pool and hurries to the sunbed where all her stuff is. As she puts on an iridescent green robe, she says, "Let me know the moment you figure out how bad this is."

Dareh doesn't look when Iris gets out of the water. Carson knows that any normal guy would watch a naked woman walk past him, even a tall, skinny one with a patchy tan. *Hmm.*

Iris slips into a pair of platform mules and slicks back her hair. "Dareh? It's safe."

Dareh stands and turns toward her. "We will need equipment."

"Okay. Make a list. I'll let Vicki know. Are we all down?"

"Yes, until we can find how far it goes."

"Okay." Iris sighs enough to make her shoulders slump. "Let me know."

"Yes, mum." He trots away.

Iris stands facing the pool, dripping, looking lost. She wipes her hands down her face, then takes a deep breath and scoops up the rest of her stuff. She looks straight at the pavilion, turns away, then back again.

Oops. Busted.

Iris steps to the edge of the pavilion's wooden floor, cocks her head, and examines Carson. "How long have you been there?"

"Since four. I was reading."

"How much did you hear?"

"We've been hacked. Didn't get much detail."

Iris nods. "The Wi-Fi's down, so don't freak when you can't get into it. Dareh and Karl will let us know when it's safe." She frowns. "You didn't come swim with me."

"Didn't think you wanted company. I said 'hi' when you came back after lunch. You just blew right by me."

"Oh. Sorry. There's lot's going on. You're always welcome to come buddy up if you see me alone. Um, after dinner—if we have dinner here—us girls get together in the Jacuzzi to drink and talk smack. You can join us if you want. It's fun."

"Thanks." It sounds like a special form of torture. "I'm old. I need more sleep."

"Uh-*huh*." Iris throws a glance toward the patio table, where Sebastian, Amabelle, and Karl are in a huddle over a laptop. "And you've got an incentive to go to bed early."

Chapter 23

IBIZA TOWN

Carson hates shopping for underwear worse than dental work. Finding something comfortable that will last is a constant trial. Tracking down supportive bras that fit properly is like searching for the Holy Grail without Indiana Jones around to uncover the trail. Shopping online is a total non-starter.

She stands in front of Intimissimi and Tezenis, side-by-side lingerie stores in central Ibiza Town on a business street that could be anywhere in Europe. *Go in? Open a vein?*

She needed to get out of the house in daytime. Trying to stay out of the way is getting on her nerves. The Wi-Fi's still down at the mansion, and attitudes are chafing. As usual on a job, she'd packed eight days' worth of her least-ratty, most-comfortable and -functional underwear, figuring she'd wash it in the hotel sink every night like normal. Being with Vicki's posse shot that all to shit: between the costume changes and the heat and humidity, she's going through two or three sets a day.

And…usually nobody sees her underwear. *Comfortable and functional*—her usual requirements for clothes—hardly ever means *sexy*. The guys she picks up for her weekend adventures don't usually care about fashion, and her underwear doesn't stay on long enough to become a problem for them. But now there's Sebastian. While she's trying to minimize the amount of time she spends around him wearing clothes, there are times that he sees her in her undies.

Her reflection in Intimissimi's glass door shows the new manicure on her left hand, which is wrapped around her shoulder bag's strap. Iris had ambushed her this morning at the pool and announced she was staging an intervention. "Your nails are rough, girl. You use a chainsaw on those things? When was your last mani-pedi?" This led to a circular semi-argument that ended with

Carson caving so Iris would shut up.

Carson stares at her fingernails. Short but all shaped more-or-less the same, covered with a pale-pink polish that she can ignore easily. Iris suggested black, then fire-engine red. Shell pink was the best of a bad selection. *A manicure, for fuck's sake. New hair. What's next—makeup? Nose job?*

While she browses through the heart of darkness, she thinks about the SEAT sedan that appeared in her rear-view mirror soon after she pulled away from the mansion. It followed her until she was halfway to town. It could've been a neighbor also going shopping, but there was something about it that got her neck hairs tingling. The guy didn't look like he belonged in that kind of plain-vanilla car. He pulled into a supermarket along the way. If it was a handoff, the driver who picked it up was better at following; she didn't spot him. Maybe the thing with the dealer getting killed has her paranoia looking for something to do.

After almost an hour of pulling things off racks, putting them back, trying on, discarding, cursing, and submitting to a fitting at the hands of a thankfully mature, full-figured sales clerk, Carson walks out with three different styles of reasonably attractive bras in two colors each and two pairs each of two different styles of knickers in colors that match the bras. None are embarrassing, and they may survive long enough to see the inside of her dresser at home. She didn't kill anyone in the process. A good day all around.

The street's relatively un-busy in this pre-lunch time; the tourists may all be sleeping off last night's binges. When Carson pulls the Countryman out of its parking space, it's obvious when the black VW hatchback swings into the street behind her a few moments later. As she concentrates on navigating the one-way roads that all seem to be going the wrong way, she pulls the four-right-turns trick she learned for uncovering a tail.

The VW's still a block behind her.

She's eastbound on a run-down, narrow street that ends at the road circling the port. If this guy's really following her—she's about ninety-five percent certain he is—she needs to get him boxed in someplace so she can get his story.

A red light gives her a chance to get her GPS going. She picks a random dead end, then tells the GPS to get her there.

The boxy Balearia ferry terminal slides by on her right, as do cranes, the upper works of yachts, and the occasional tour bus. To her left are overgrown wetlands. The VW trails behind three other cars.

She makes a full circuit of a big traffic circle, hoping it'll fake out the tail. It doesn't. Passeig Joan Carles I runs past the harbor's north end, including Marina Ibiza—Michel's megayacht is where she left it six days ago—and an unbroken rank of condos and hotels. The VW's still a hundred meters or so behind her, only two cars back now.

She burrows farther into a knot of newer condos, townhouses, duplexes, and small hotels filling a squarish peninsula between the harbor and the achingly blue Cala Talamanca lagoon. Yellow walls and white buildings blur by. The streets get progressively narrower. She speeds up enough to look like she's trying to escape but not enough to lose the VW. Its driver has closed the distance to keep her in sight. There's no question he's after her.

The Carrer de Barbaria shrinks to one lane and turns to gravel. Carson floors the gas, spraying the cars parked way too close on her left. She slews through a serpentine, blows past the last cross-street, then screeches under a cantilevered, white geometric house, ducking behind a contractor's Transit van. *Come on, keep coming, keep coming…*

The VW rockets past her toward Punta Taberna—and a dead end.

Carson turns off the GPS and rolls the twenty or so meters to the end of a large, pink stucco house, then blocks the road. She grabs her baton and Leatherman from her new Bimba y Lola shoulder bag, wishing she had her Glock. She waits in the house's driveway.

The VW noses to within a few meters of the Mini, then stops. The driver's a stocky guy in a faded-green tee and a black baseball cap. They stare at each other for a full minute. She strolls behind the Countryman and out on the VW's driver's side—no way is she getting between the cars—stops three meters from the driver's door, then deploys her baton. She knows she doesn't look so tough in shorts and runners, but she didn't know she'd have to dress for this kind of thing.

The driver rolls down his window halfway and yells something she doesn't understand.

Carson takes a step forward. "English?"

He chews either gum or chaw for a few beats. "Some."

"Who do you work for?"

Chewing. "Fuck you."

Carson sighs and shakes her head. "You French?"

"No."

So it's not Celeste's thugs looking for payback. "Local?"

"Fuck you."

She stares at him for a while. Then she snaps her baton into the windshield, hard. It doesn't feel great in her hand and arm, but it leaves an impact crater and star right in the middle of the driver's field of vision. "Every time you say 'fuck you,' I hurt your car. When I get tired of that, I hurt you. Who do you work for?"

The driver's eyes switch between her face and the soon-to-be-replaced windshield. He's not buying it yet. "Fuck you, bitch."

"Okay." Carson pulls her Leatherman from her pocket, opens the longest knife blade, then jams it into the left front tire's sidewall. When she pulls it out, the hiss is like a large, angry snake.

The driver yells something in whatever his native language is, then flings open the door. Carson kicks the door shut as he tries to get out, bashing his head against the window frame. He falls back, bellowing. She slams the door twice on the leg he managed to get outside. The third time, he stops the door with his good leg and kicks it out of Carson's grip. She stumbles backward, on the brink of falling.

When he gets out of his seat, he leads with a pistol.

His hand's not clear of the interior yet. She has a second or two to even this up, or else she's target practice. She springs off her back foot and plants her front foot under the door handle, throwing all her weight against it. It crashes against both his shins and his left hand. His weapon fires; a hole appears in the door's center.

Carson falls flat on her back. Her head bounces off the gravel, starring her eyes. She doesn't quite lose her breath, but it's hanging on with its fingertips. If the driver's going to take her, now's the time.

He doesn't. He half-collapses in his seat, panting. His small eyes overflow with pain.

She scrambles upright, shakes her head clear. He's still not coming for her, simply watching. Carson edges toward the back door, then peeks through the front. The driver's right hand hangs limp from his arm, covered with blood. His wrist turns at an odd angle. She spots the pistol on the floorboard, close to his seat. When she slammed the door, it must've hit the muzzle, forcing the weapon up and back, maybe broke his wrist. When it reflex-fired, the slide smashed into his forearm at X hundred miles an hour. *Ouch.*

Carson digs a dirty shirt out of a pile of clothes in the back seat, then recovers the weapon. It's a beaten-up Beretta 92, a big weapon to swing around inside a car. She decocks and safes it, wipes it down, checks the magazine (full minus two rounds), then stuffs it into her waistband behind her back. She hands the shirt to the driver to bandage his arm. "Feel like talking now?"

He closes his eyes and lets his head sag against the headrest.

"Who do you work for?"

The driver breathes hard a few times. He rumbles something that sounds like *Grup Sabadey.*

"And that's, what? A gang?"

He nods.

"Why are you following me?"

He squints at her, then shakes his head.

Moron. She points to his wounded arm. "You need a hospital. The way you're bleeding, you need it soon. You won't get there on a flat tire. Tell me what I want to know and I'll fix your flat. Stiff me, and..." She shrugs. "Understand?"

The driver thinks, then nods.

"Deal?"

"No."

"Let me guess—they'll kill you if you talk."

He nods.

"You'll probably bleed out if you don't."

Another nod.

Men can be so fucking stupid. "Good luck."

Chapter 24

Carson finds Iris talking with Sebastian, Amabelle, and Tamara at the patio table. It looks intense. Too bad—this can't wait. "Iris? Need to talk."

Iris throws her a blank smile. "Uh, kinda busy, hon, but—"

"Now."

They meet in the pavilion at the pool's non-waterfall end. Iris folds her arms over her green floral halter and puts on a serious look. "Anyone tell you you're a bossy bitch?"

"All the time. If I was a guy, they'd call me 'assertive' and say I had leadership potential. Somebody followed me from here to downtown and partway back."

"Followed? Who?"

"Know anything about a Grup Sabadey? It's a gang."

The annoyance on Iris's face slowly melts to confusion. "A gang? No. Why would they follow you? What did they want?"

"No idea. Maybe we can ask the guy parked across from the end of this street we're on. White Citroën compact with a weaselly guy behind the wheel."

Iris's face loses some color. "He's there now?"

"Unless they changed shifts in the past ten minutes." Carson's back and head hurt, the gravel scrapes on the backs of her calves are starting to itch, and she's hungry. None of this helps her mood. "Something's going on here you haven't told me about. Some kind of gang's watching you. You got hacked so bad you still can't risk bringing up your Wi-Fi. That's not random. You or one of your buds got somebody's attention. Why?"

For the first time since they met, Iris looks lost. She covers her mouth with her hand and lets her eyes roam randomly around the pool area. Her hand amplifies her ragged breathing. "Uh…these people. Are they, like…dangerous?"

Duh. Carson pulls the Beretta and holds it up. Iris's eyes get huge. "Took this off the guy following me. He was gonna use it on me." She stows the pistol before it freaks out somebody else. "This is way worse than Vicki's problems with her dad. What's going on?"

"You got me." She turns to wave Sebastian over to join them.

Sebastian frowns when he looks in Carson's eyes. "What's wrong?"

Carson tells him what she told Iris. "Know anything about this?"

"No, I don't." He scratches the back of his neck and frowns. "D'you reckon you can do something about the one across the street?"

"Only if I know what's going on. I already fucked up one of their people—don't want to keep doing it 'til I know who they are." She turns to Iris. "Time to lock down. No deliveries inside the gate. Anybody goes out, have them watch for tails. Maybe minimize outside trips."

Iris scowls. "Really? I mean, what are they gonna do?"

"I don't know, Iris," Carson snaps. "Tell me who they are and I can tell you. Remember the last time you guys had shadows? Celeste almost got kidnapped. This bunch's armed. They're serious enough to put together multi-car tails. What's that sound like to you?"

Sebastian puts a gentle hand on both Iris's and Carson's shoulder. "Let's not fight each other. We've a bigger problem to deal with. I've not seen these people. Have you, Iris?"

Iris spreads her hands. "I've never noticed them. Nobody's said anything." She frowns. "Who'd want to spy on us anyway?"

Chapter 25

Another club, another line. Carson stands with the posse—again, minus Celeste, whom Carson seriously envies at this point—in the pipe-railing maze that's the pre-sale tickets line for Space, one of the original Ibiza megaclubs. They're bathed in the red floodlights bouncing off the big black-and-white sign above them reading, "CARL COX THE REVOLUTION." The revolution must've already begun: thumping bass vibrates the sidewalk. The red light is turning her ocean-blue, mid-thigh miniskirt a dingy brown.

Sebastian's holding her hand. She can't remember the last time she was with a guy who voluntarily holds hands. He's in another tailored-dress-shirt-and-slacks variation. She slides her mouth even with his ear. "Do you know what Iris's surprise is?"

"No idea. It must be something grand—she told everyone to come."

They reach a 180-degree bend in the maze. Tamara and Amabelle are even with Carson across the railing, facing the other way. Tamara glances from Carson, to Sebastian, then gives Carson the evil eye. *That's it? She's jealous? Go back to high school, girl.* Tamara folds her arms in ways that squeeze her boobs together, putting significant cleavage into play above her black lace bustier. Sebastian's distracted for a moment, then looks straight ahead.

After twenty minutes, the group nears the phalanx of bouncers at the main gate. Then Amabelle and Tamara squeal, "Vicki! Vicki!"

What?

The women collide in a three-way hug. Carson can see tanned arms but nothing else to confirm that Vicki's here. Then Karl and Dareh join the scrum. Carson and Sebastian exchange puzzled looks.

The group huddle breaks up. Vicki stands there, glowing in a white-lace minidress with a shiny gold belt. She kisses Sebastian's lips. "Hello, darling." She shifts to Carson and gives her *dos besos*. "I told you I'd come back."

Uncountable thousands of people jam the Flight Area, the club's main open-air performance space. Techno screams out of every speaker. Lasers and moving lights light up the crowd like fireworks. Onstage, a stocky black man with a shaved head holds court at the DJ's station. Practically every move he makes causes the audience to try to drown out the music with cheers.

Carson, Vicki, Karl, and Sebastian huddle against a side wall in the VIP area, a mezzanine that provides more convenient drink service and lower odds of being crushed to death. Sebastian has his arm around Carson's waist; Carson stands shoulder-to-shoulder with Vicki, who looks very cozy with Karl. Carson leans into Vicki's ear. "Where the hell have you been?"

Vicki smiles—she's been doing a lot of that tonight—then yells, "Can we listen to the music for now? The club's closing in October. This is the last but one of Carl's 'Music Is Revolution' sets. We won't be back before the end. I couldn't miss it."

For chrissakes... "When can we talk?"

"When we get home. I'll be all yours." She gives Carson a one-armed hug. "You've been quite patient with me. Thank you." Vicki plants a lingering kiss on Carson's cheek.

Carson can't tell if she should feel special or duped. She forces a smile and steels herself to spend another several hours in the middle of a nuclear explosion.

The group returns to the mansion by four-thirty in the morning. Carson grabs two bottles of water from the kitchen fridge on her way to meeting Vicki by the pool. She notices a carrier bag full of cheap blister-packed mobile phones sitting on the teppanyaki grill island.

The pool and deck lights are on, casting a gentle pale-blue

blanket over everything, including the Buddha. Carson perches on the edge of a sunbed, unstraps her sandals, then chugs a water bottle to replace some of what she sweated out at the club. She tries to pull together a coherent list of questions for Vicki, but her mind keeps wandering. She's exhausted, half-deaf, and wants to crawl into bed with Sebastian and fall asleep in his arms. Work first.

"Hello." Vicki strolls barefoot down the two steps from the patio to the deck, carrying a half-full wine glass. She's swapped her lace mini for a white mid-thigh tee that could be a sleep shirt or a beach cover-up. "Sorry for the delay. I wanted to get comfortable. Sit with me?" She pats the back of a double-wide sunbed.

Carson stands and starts to pace. "Thanks, I'm good. Need to keep moving or I'll fall asleep." And she wants to stay away from Vicki's reality-distortion field. "Iris told you I got followed yesterday?"

"Yes, she did."

"She tell you who did it?"

"Yes. A Grup Sabadey. I've no idea who they are, though. Have you?"

"Nothing about them online, if I'm spelling it right. This is what it takes to bring you back to your 'family'?"

Vicki's mouth turns down. "I told you already, I came to see Carl—"

"So if his show was next week, you still wouldn't be here? Is it me?"

Vicki watches Carson pace a full lap past her sunbed before she answers. "If you must know, then yes, I'm still conflicted about your place in all this. I know why you're here and what we agreed to in Marbella. I still don't know whether you'll take my side or Father's when the time comes." She takes a lingering sip of wine. "How much is Father paying you?"

Carson laughs. "Why? So you can double it? Triple it? My deal's with the Bratva, not your dad. Far as I know, he's not paying them anything. It's for goodwill."

"I see." Vicki switches to Russian. "Should I assume you speak Russian?"

"*Konyechno.*" *Of course.*

"Let's do that in case there are big ears about. Have you heard from Father recently? Or from your Bratva person?"

"Yesterday afternoon." Carson called Rodievsky to check in and to tell him his "no violence, no danger" estimate turned to shit. "Your dad's easily distracted, I hear."

"That's a very kind way of putting it. Busy, is he?"

"Business with Putin." Rodievsky's exact words: *Oleg Germanovich is occupied with licking Vladimir Vladimirovich's boots.*

"Do you see?" Vicki flings a hand in Carson's general direction. "He's too busy to decide my future. This is what I'll have to deal with if you send me back to him. Would you wish that on anyone you like?"

That again. "Don't know yet if I like you. I barely know you. Think about this: if I didn't see you rescue that girl from her asshole boyfriend right before we met, you'd be in Moscow right now."

Vicki's eyes get round. "You saw that?"

"Yeah. From the restaurant. That made me think you're not a complete waste of air. That's why I bothered to get your side of things. That's why I took your offer." Carson stops to glare at Vicki. "That and your dad being distracted are the only reasons we're both still here. And that good thing you did? It was a week ago. Time for a refresh."

"Is that so?" Vicki bolts the rest of her wine and sets her goblet on the little round table next to the sunbed. "I'll arrange to save some other poor girl in distress. As I remember, there was another part to our agreement. You arrive, and suddenly gangsters are watching us. Are you keeping my family safe, or are you endangering them?"

That question shouldered its way into Carson's head more than once since yesterday. "If it was some other branch of the Bratva, I'd be worried. The tail was a local. So was the guy staking out the road out there. Spanish pop music on his radio when I slashed his tires." Last night after dark, before the group headed out for Space. "He's gone for now. So yeah, I'm keeping them safe…when they let me."

"What does that mean?"

"It means, I'm tired of this passive-aggressive bullshit they're pulling. Like locking the gates. Simple, right? Don't let any random asshole wander onto the property? I tell them, 'Lock the gates,' and they pitch a fit, then they say they'll do it, and they don't. I think it's Tamara—she's always leaving the side gate open. I tell Iris—because she's supposed to be in charge while you're gone, right?—and she says she'll fix it, and it never gets fixed. Want them safe?" Carson stabs a finger at Vicki. "*You* need to tell them. And you have to be here to do it."

"Noted." Vicki sits up and returns Carson's hard look. "You're not having trouble with Sebastian, though, are you? Iris tells me you've discovered each other."

Been waiting for that to come up. "That's one way to put it. That a problem?"

"No, no, not at all. Quite a catch for you, I should think."

Meow. "Yeah. So, why'd you drop him?"

Vicki's eyebrows pop up. "My, you do cut right to it. We had a…difference in goals, let's say. We were together for nearly a year. He wanted to marry and start having children. It was tempting. He'll be a wonderful father someday. But there are things I want to do first, and domestic life would, well…"

"Get in the way?"

"Yes. I know, it sounds cold. We women have to be strategic about these things if we're to accomplish anything." Vicki slips on a whisper of a smile. "Have you been married?"

"Yeah, once."

"But you're not now. Why?"

"I married an asshole."

"Right. Other than guarding Sebastian *closely*, what have you done recently to keep my family safe?"

Jealous? She shouldn't have dropped him. "Now you know some street gang's interested in your posse. Didn't know that before, right? You've been dodging your dad's thugs for months, but you didn't see the French guys or this new group. Why is that exactly?"

Vicki flops back against the sun bed with a growl. "Father's little helpers are so bloody obvious. They look the same, dress the same, and act the same. They've no imagination. That's why I let you get close—because you're different. You're not some security robot."

"That's why you holed up in Algeciras?"

Vicki's lips purse. She stretches her legs, then crosses her ankles. She watches the breeze riffle the pool's surface. "I reckon the Bratva has the resources to tell you I was there. I assume Father still wants me. I didn't know what you had in mind for me. I'm more vulnerable on the road than if I stay in place. With its reputation, I thought Algeciras would be the last place anyone would look for me." Another thin smile. "Clearly, I was wrong."

"Clearly."

Vicki sighs and lets her head droop. "Lisa…what exactly do you want of me?" It's a plea, not a question.

Carson can't tell if Vicki's defeated, genuinely tired, or playing for sympathy. For now, she'll go with a combination of all three. "Want me to keep them safe? Tell them to listen to me and do what I say. I won't ask them to do anything hard, but what I ask, they better fucking do. All right?"

"Yes. Of course. Their safety is more important than anything."

"Glad to hear it. And you? You stick around. We spend time together. Get to know each other. You wanted me here so I'll throw in with you when your dad calls, right? Put in some effort." Carson doesn't expect money and parties will seduce her into defying Rodievsky, but at least she'll know where Vicki is and how to get to her.

"Understood." Vicki draws her knees to her chest and rests her chin on them. "If Father tells you to take me to Moscow, what will you do?"

"What will *you* do?"

"I've not decided yet. Does it matter?"

"Depends on how bad you piss me off when you do it."

"I see." Vicki's mouth twists. "That certainly gives me something more to think about." She switches to English. "I need to talk to my friends tomor—*today* and catch up. Tell them to listen to you. I've also a sleep deficit I need to cut down to size. Iris tells me that you and Celeste have become friendly?"

"Yeah. I like her a lot. Sit with her every day. Love her music."

"So do I. I've not paid nearly enough attention to her recently and I'd like to make up for it. I thought we'd go sightseeing Thursday. Would you care to join us?"

Besides keeping an eye on Vicki, it would be nice to get out of this place for something other than clubbing brain cells. She'd also like to see how Celeste is with no keyboard distracting her. "Sure."

"Lovely. It should be fun." Vicki swings off the sunbed, stretches, then meets Carson at the foot of the bed. "I'm so glad we had time to talk. I hope we've cleared the air between us?"

"Some." Carson has to decide how much of it she believes.

"Excellent. We'll talk more later today."

"If you're still here."

She can't tell if Vicki's chuckle is amused or an omen.

Chapter 26

CAP MARTINET, IBIZA

It's daylight when Carson finally cracks open her eyes. The clock-radio says it's way past ten. Between the massage Sebastian gave her after she finished with Vicki and the massage after-party, they hadn't turned out the bedroom lights until the eastern sky was turning its lights on.

She's on her side, spooned against Sebastian with his arm around her waist. He's warm. His breathing—soft, slow—is almost enough to put her to sleep again. She'd be happy to stay here for hours and not move an inch. Except her bladder's about to explode.

She manages to get out of bed without waking him. She closes the washroom door so he doesn't have to listen to her piss for seemingly an hour. She throws some water on her face and checks her hair. Not too bad, considering. This style's growing on her.

Go back to your room. Go do your workout. That's the responsible her.

She ignores that voice and slides into bed again. It's still warm. She props her head on her hand and watches Sebastian sleep. So quiet. Her finger traces a line from the notch at the base of his throat down his breastbone and back. He doesn't startle or fuss.

What are you doing here?

Shut up.

The last thing she needs is to argue with her rational self. Being here isn't rational. Being with Sebastian isn't rational. Him wanting her isn't rational. But it's happening. *Is it right?*

Is any of this right?

"Hey." She hadn't meant to say anything out loud, even at a murmur. Now that she has, she knows why. "So much I should tell you. That you should know. Before this goes too far. Maybe it already has."

He makes a *mpf* sound and shifts but doesn't wake.

"You were born when I was in high school. I've seen things…done things…I hope you'll never have to imagine. Had a shitty life. Here I was, pissed at you because your life's been nice. That was wrong. Sorry."

She lets her fingertips trace the bones in the back of his hand near his pillow. "You're *so* not the kind of man I sleep with. They're macho. They wear uniforms. They don't look at my face. They fuck me like it's a workout or a competition. When they're done, they flop over and go to sleep. But you…it's almost like we're making love. You're gentle. You look in my eyes. When we're done, you hold me. I never knew I wanted that. Never thought I'd get it.

"I'm such bad news for you. I can't be what you want. What you need. You need a girl who'll love you with every piece of her. I'm too hard now. There's not enough of my heart left to give some of it to somebody else. I'll hurt you. I won't want to, but I will. And when I do, I'll hurt myself, too."

She pushes her fingertips through his hair. "If you want me, I'll be here. Until you don't, or until I have to go."

Sebastian sniffles and grunts. Eventually, his eyes flutter open. He squints at her and smiles. "Mornin'."

"Morning."

He caresses her cheek. "You alright?"

"Fine." She presses her body against his. "Hold me."

Chapter 27

PORTINATX, IBIZA

Carson takes in a huge slug of sea air and knows this was what she needed.

Vicki's been driving the Countryman north through the island's rolling heart. Little white villages, orchards, jewel-box churches, markets, food stands. An early lunch at a *chiringuito* (an open-air café) on top of a rise with a view of treetops and an ancient watchtower. A traditional dance exhibition in a fortified church's courtyard. A blessed lack of tourists, tee-shirt shops, and EDM blasting from stores. Celeste's found beauty and music nearly everywhere she looks.

After over two hours on high alert, seeing imaginary threats and tails everywhere, Carson's finally managed to relax.

Now they're at Cala Xuclà, a tiny, almost hidden beach on a rocky inlet at the island's north end. The gravelly beach has a *chiringuito*, two abandoned fisherman's huts, and a dozen people on it despite the sunny, warm day. Three white sailboats bob just off the inlet.

Celeste splashes happily in the clear, warm water while Vicki and Carson lie on their towels and drink beer they bought from the café.

Vicki says, "That's a lovely swimsuit. I love the color."

Carson brought the blue one-piece from her shopping expedition with Iris. It has one shoulder, a cutout on her right side, and is a blue as bright as the water at the inlet's mouth. "Thanks. Is she okay out there by herself?" She nods toward Celeste.

"Of course. She's fine. Ibiza has so many lovely beaches, but they're completely overrun during the season. It's too much for her. This is what it's like when the summer's over." Vicki's been wonderful with Celeste today, maternal without being overprotective.

"Have you heard from her parents?"

Vicki's simple white bikini sets off her tan and, because it's on her, looks ridiculously glamorous. "Not directly. Sebastian tells me the Ibicenco police came by the house Friday last to speak with her. I understand you and Iris were out. He says the police were satisfied that she's healthy and happy." She gazes at the trio of sailboats. "Lisa, there's something I should tell you."

Nothing good ever starts that way. "Okay."

"I've thought about this a lot over the few days past. If Father tells you he wants you to take me to Moscow, I won't go."

Goddamnit… "Look, you—"

Vicki gently touches her forearm. "Please let me finish. I want you to know this is entirely between me and my father. It has nothing to do with you and me. I don't want us to be angry with each other. I simply can't give up my life to spend the next God knows how long covering up for him. Do you understand?"

Carson counts to five. Then ten. At twenty, she's pretty certain she can talk without exploding. "You know what kind of bind you're putting me in."

"I do. I'm sorry."

They debate until Celeste comes trotting up to sit next to Carson. *That's why she waited 'til now—so we won't argue in front of Celeste. Damn her.*

The afternoon's drive back to the mansion is longer and quieter than the morning's.

Chapter 28

SANT ANTONI, IBIZA

Another fucking club.

Carson leans against the wall on the mezzanine of Club Leviathan as the backbeat tries to wrestle her heartbeat into its rhythm. She's spent more time in these places in the past week than she has for the ten years before that, and it's getting old. At least this isn't another cavernous megaclub—only a thousand people fill the dance floor at this relatively early hour (one a.m.). There's some kind of steampunk-cruise-ship theme going on: riveted, rusted metal plates on the walls, fake portholes with psychedelic fish painted on the back of the glass, ladders to nowhere, fog, searchlights, and a steamship whistle that's loud enough to cut through the trap and electro house the DJs are spinning.

Karl nudges her. "Do you want a drink?"

"Beer's fine. Thanks."

Dareh, Iris, Amabelle, and Tamara are downstairs already. Carson's up here with Vicki, Karl, and Sebastian, though she has no idea where Sebastian is. But in her brain, she's still on that beach with Vicki.

If Father tells you he wants you to take me to Moscow, I won't go.

That line's been grinding on Carson ever since. *What do I do with that? Tell Rodievsky no? How does she think this is gonna work? That her dad's gonna just let her walk? That I'll sacrifice myself for her?*

Karl nudges her again. "You are alright?"

She drops her thoughts for now and tries on a smile. "Fine. Zoning out. Oh, thanks." She takes the beer glass he holds out to her. "Where are you from?"

"Braunschweig. Ehm…in north-central Germany. East of Hanover." His English is fluent and only lightly accented.

"What's your family like?" *More rich people?*

He gives her a rueful smile. "They are not as grand as Vicki's or Sebastian's. My father designs exhaust systems for Volkswagen."

"That's pretty bor—wait, there's something in the news about that."

"Yes. Can we please not talk about that?"

"Okay. Um…Iris says you were one of the original group around Vicki. How'd that happen?"

He smiles and peers into his beer. "I graduated university two years ago and I wanted to relax before I return to home. I was in Barcelona with Dareh and we met Vicki. She…" He looks toward the DJ's podium, but his expression says he's seeing the past. "She gave us a reason to not go home."

"You were with Dareh?"

"Yes. We are good friends. We met at university when we were both first-years. He was also looking for a place to be."

"I get him wanting to stay here and not go back to Iran."

"It's more than 'want.' He can't."

That knocks Carson back a mental step. "Why not?"

"That's his business. I know, but you will have to ask him."

"Okay." Her beer's watered down, or just crappy. It's hard to tell the difference. "What happened Tuesday?"

Karl raises an eyebrow at her. "Do you know computers?"

"I can use them."

"I won't give you the full details, then. We were attacked. Dareh's machine was…how do you say? *Trashed.* He shut down the Wi-Fi before it could spread to the rest of you. My machine has some damage, but I powered down in time. We're on our own network as well as the Wi-Fi. We replaced the main drive in Dareh's machine and he's still rebuilding."

"Who attacked you?"

"We don't know. We know where it was supposed to come from, but we don't believe it was from there. The people who did it know what they're about. I'm still researching, but it may be a zero-day exploit."

"What's that?"

"New. Not used before. That takes a great deal of work and time. So many exploits are built from standard parts. You could learn to build a simple virus in a few hours if you want to do. This is much more complex and sophisticated."

Karl drifts back to Vicki when Sebastian returns. He kisses Carson and wraps an arm around her waist. "Are you alright?"

"People keep asking me that. It's been a long day. These late nights are kicking my ass."

He gives her a squeeze. "We'll get you home early and put you to bed."

"Promise to tuck me in?"

"Of course. I'll read a bedtime story to you if you'd like." He knocks back whatever's in his already mostly-empty highball glass. "Would you fancy a dance?"

"Can we actually dance to this stuff?"

"Remember what I said before—ride the rhythm. I want to show you off. You look fierce."

Carson knows now that that's a good thing. She's wearing the new white bodysuit, black high-waisted cigarette slacks, and pointy-toed black ankle boots with low Cuban heels. To her own surprise, she likes the look. "Well, if you put it that way…"

The dance floor's crowded but not yet jammed. She slings her purse strap over her neck and shoulder and follows Sebastian to a spot near a neon-orange life ring hanging on the wall. She manages to find a ridable beat that doesn't leave her feeling stiff or dorky. After a few minutes, Vicki and Karl take a place near them. Karl works harder at dancing than Sebastian, but Vicki makes it look effortless, of course. Everything she does seems seamless. Vicki twirls, then gives Carson a sad little smile and waves by pumping her index finger up and down. Carson pumps back. She hates how the day ended with a cold front between them.

Carson spots Tamara and Amabelle dancing with (or at least near) a couple of guys not too far away. Amabelle's half a head taller than most people around her, and her tiny orange minidress with the Latin American-looking embroidery makes the life ring look faded.

Iris is near the back wall about four meters away. She's talking to a decent-looking guy in the same white-dress-shirt-and-light-slacks outfit half the men in the room wear. They're comfortable enough with each other to stand close so they can talk without screaming over the music. If she didn't know Iris, Carson would figure they were making plans to get it on somewhere.

She doesn't exactly watch them, but Carson's aware of how

much time they spend talking. The guy finally breaks away to plunge into the crowd, leaving Iris moving to her own groove.

Carson's eyes follow the guy as he works to a point roughly even with Tamara and Amabelle and a few meters closer to the room's centerline. She can hardly see him through the throng. He disappears.

Then the screaming starts.

The guy staggers back the way he came, clutching his stomach. Dancers reel away from him with large eyes and open mouths. The spotlights show a dark patch on his shirt as they streak by.

Carson grabs Sebastian's arm. "Get everybody upstairs! Now!"

She starts toward the guy, who's stumbling, on the verge of falling. Her left hand's in her bag, clutched around the baton. She shoulders past a few retreating dancers and sees what she's looking for—a guy with a knife in his left hand, trying to bash his way through the crowd to get to the exit near the DJ's podium. He knocks down a guy, then two women. More screams.

The crowd panics. People go everywhere, pinging off each other, falling, getting trampled. Carson takes a moment to help a young woman, her head bloody, get off the floor. Knife Guy's like a salmon trying to swim upstream. He's tall—at least six feet—and big in a beer-and-manual-labor way, in a dark tank top with some kind of writing on the back. Unfortunately, it's the same outfit dozens of other men are wearing.

Carson shifts her baton to her right hand and takes advantage of a small open area to deploy it. She leads with her left shoulder to bust through the stampede, knocking bodies out of her way. A beefy guy runs full-tilt into her, bowling her over, and she's instantly buried in a forest of moving knees and feet that hit and step on her. The familiar taste of animal fear fills her mouth. *Stay calm. Figure it out. Get free.* She struggles onto her knees, then gut-punches a big man about to run over her. He stops and doubles over, creating a break that gives her a chance to stand in the human flash flood.

Knife Guy's five or six meters ahead of her, bogged down in the melee. Carson struggles to close the gap. The music's stopped. The DJ's yelling "Don't panic! Don't panic!" in his mic, which of course makes everyone panic more.

Four meters. Three. Knife Guy's throwing people out of his

way. As they go down, they create breaks in the herd. Carson collapses her baton and clips it to her waistband; there's no room to use the thing. Two meters. One. He swings his right arm backward, maybe winding up for a punch.

She grabs his wrist with her left hand, cranks up his arm, then slams the heel of her right hand into the soft spot between the radius and ulna just ahead of the point of his elbow. Which hurts. Like. Hell. Then she traps his wrist in her bent elbow, grips his bicep, forces him forward, and kicks his right ankle out from under him.

He goes down face-first. It took about four seconds.

The idiots around her don't give her room to work, though. Someone passing knocks her off-balance and she ends up on her side next to Knife Guy. He rolls onto his back and reaches for something on his belt. It shines in the spotlights. His knife.

Fuck. Carson takes down a shrieking woman—she stops shrieking—to create a barricade, then rolls onto her feet and breaks out her baton. He goes into a knife-fighter's crouch, leading with the blade in his left hand. It's a smallish tactical knife, easy to carry and good enough to open up an opponent. She hates knives. Always has. It's too easy for someone to get lucky with a swipe and tear up something important.

Knife Guy thrusts his weapon at her. His timing's off. She sidesteps and swats at his left forearm with the baton but only grazes it. He grunts and backs off, shaking his arm.

The house lights come up. Carson squints in the sudden glare; so does Knife Guy. At least she can see what she's doing now. For some reason, the lights make the crowd scream more, not less.

Knife Guy has a pre-cancerous tan, a dark buzz cut, tats up and down both arms, and ripped jeans that badly need a wash. She expects boots but sees runners. There's a scar on his upper lip.

An area two or three meters wide clears around them. A few guys stop to watch. The other people run screaming to the exits so they can stomp each other to death.

He goes into his crouch again and circles. Carson follows, her baton cranked behind her neck, her left hand low and close so it doesn't get in the knife's way.

"Who the fuck are you?" Knife Guy growls in English.

"Somebody who paid forty euros to get in here, and some

asshole fucked it up for me. Who the fuck are *you*?"

He snorts. Feints with his right hand—which she ignores—and tries to slip the knife into her flank as she pivots. No chance to hit him with the baton. He tries the same move again a few seconds later, like she forgot. This time, she grabs his right wrist, yanks, and slams the baton into his left collarbone.

Knife Guy howls. His weapon clatters on the concrete slab floor. Carson kicks it away. She finishes spinning him, then hooks his trailing left ankle with her right foot. Once again he hits the floor face-first. This time, she has room to drive her knee into his spine between his shoulders. It forces the air out of his lungs as a prolonged cough. He stops struggling to get free so he can concentrate on struggling to breathe.

Carson's right side is burning. She glances down. Her bodysuit gaps near the bottom of her rib cage, and it's wet and red below the cut. "Asshole!" she screams at the shuddering man underneath her. "These were new clothes!"

Chapter 29

By the time the police and the hospital get done with Carson, it's past noon when Sebastian finally escorts her into the mansion.

He'd called ahead. The entire posse is there, waiting. When she walks through the front door, they all cheer and clap.

"Knock it off! Jesus." Carson's cheeks heat up. Applause isn't something she gets often.

Now they press in, touching her hands and arms, asking "Are you okay?" "Does it hurt?" "Why did you do that?" and generally getting between her and the kitchen. It's nice they're worried about her. But she hasn't slept in over a day, she hasn't eaten in fourteen hours, her fasting hypoglycemia is drilling huge holes in her stomach and skull, and the topical anesthetics are wearing off.

She grabs Sebastian's arm and whispers in his ear, "Get me to my room."

"I will." He holds up a hand to the crowd. "Please. Lisa needs some sleep. She's been up since yesterday morning. She'll come talk with you when she's rested."

Carson collapses on the edge of her bed and sighs. Sebastian sits next to her. She lays her head on his shoulder. "Thanks."

"Ah, go way outta that." He takes her hand. "How's your side?"

"Feels like someone's turned a cigarette lighter on it."

He places a small brown bag on her lap. "Here's your pain pills. I'll get you some water."

She's dry-swallowed her two tablets by the time he's back, but she gulps the water anyway. Pulling off the hospital scrub top is as unpleasant as she expected. The cops took what was left of her bodysuit for evidence and shot pictures of her wound. Thank God she wore one of her new bras.

Sebastian asks, "Do you want anything?"

"Food. I gotta eat."

"Sure. I'll get it." He stands, then bends to kiss her forehead. "I'm proud of you."

"Lisa?"

Carson turns toward Celeste's voice. She's standing in the bedroom doorway, biting her upper lip. "What is it?"

"Can I help you?"

"Um, thanks. I'm just gonna eat and go to sleep."

"You should not be alone." Celeste shoots Sebastian a glance that has more ferocity than Carson figured the girl had in her.

Sebastian gets the message. "I'll raid the larder, then let you be."

Celeste helps Carson undress, puts her underwear in the washroom basin to soak out the blood, then takes her trousers out to get cleaned. Carson pulls on a long, sky-blue tee she's been using as a cover-up when she can't be bothered to dress. Sebastian brings back a thick *jamon iberico* sandwich on crusty bread, piled with veg. She wolfs it down with a pitcher of water, then crawls into bed. Celeste curls up in the armchair in the corner.

Moments before she fades to black, Carson's cloudy brain throws up one last thought: *where in hell was Vicki?*

Carson wakes a bit after seven, muzzy and achy. She rubs the gunk out of her eyes, then sits up.

Celeste unwinds from her chair and sits on the bed's edge. "Hello. Do you want anything?"

Dom would do this. When she was seventeen, Carson caught a bad case of flu that kept her in bed for three days. Dom would park on a chair in the corner and keep watch over her. Payback for all the times she sat with him when he was sick.

Carson strokes Celeste's hair. "You're a good watchdog."

Celeste giggles and blushes.

"Hey, when I came back, I didn't see Vicki. Was she here?"

"No."

Asking the next question takes some serious thought. "Is she here now?"

"I will see." Celeste marches out the bedroom door, closing it silently behind her.

Carson throws on some clothes, rinses out her underwear, then hangs it in the shower. There's no sign her wound opened while she was asleep. She brushes her teeth, fluffs her hair, and avoids focusing on the big dark circles under her eyes.

Her door opens and closes. "Celeste? That you?"

Iris appears in the washroom doorway. "It's me. Disappointed?"

"Looking for Vicki."

"Ah…yeah." Iris scrunches her face. "We need to talk about that."

A rock falls into Carson's stomach. "She's gone again."

"Yeah."

"Fuck." Carson shoulders her way past Iris and starts pacing along the end of the bed. She'd kick something if she wasn't barefoot. "Where'd she go?"

"I don't know. Don't look at me like that! I don't. After the cops let us go, we came back here and the next thing I knew, some BlaBlaCar was hauling her off with her stuff."

Carson may kick something, barefoot or not. "She said she'd stay. For once."

"She was totes freaked. Maybe she panicked."

"I don't see Vicki panicking."

"She usually doesn't, but people don't get stabbed in front of her much, either." Iris hugs herself. "I'm sorry, I should've asked. How are you? How's your side?"

"Cut's messy but not deep. They glued me back together again. It aches. I'll survive." Carson stops pacing and takes several deep breaths. This isn't how she'd wanted to wake up. "She coming back?"

Iris throws up her hands. "I don't know! I didn't know she was leaving until she left. That's how much we talked about this." She sighs. "Look. She always comes back. She usually tells me when she's going, but she always comes back. Maybe she just needs to get her head together."

"Yeah. Except she told me on our trip yesterday that she's not going back to Russia."

Iris's lips form an *oh*. Gears turn behind her eyes. "You think she used the confusion to run off before her dad tells you to take her home?"

"I would if I was her." The toothpaste can't cover up the sour taste in Carson's mouth. *We won't solve this now.* "Who was that guy?"

"Which guy?"

"The one you were talking to way a long time. The one who got stabbed."

Iris's eyes narrow. "Were you watching me?"

"I was dancing in front of you. What the fuck else am I gonna look at?"

"I don't know. The gorgeous guy you're dancing with?"

"I know what *he* looks like. That's probably the longest I've ever seen you spend with a guy. Who was he? Why'd somebody want to stab him?"

"I…" Iris's mouth works without any sound coming out. "Okay. His name's Trent. I know him from the clubs. We come here maybe three-four times a year. We get to know people. He's got a thing for me. Like, maybe he can flip me to the hetero side? I like winding him up. And…I don't know why somebody'd want to try to kill him. Somebody doesn't like him?"

"You think?" Carson paces more. "Was he dealing?"

"I don't—"

"Cut the bullshit. Was he dealing?"

"Well…probably. I mean, almost everyone is, one way or another. Why are you attacking me?"

Heavy sigh. "We're being shadowed by a gang. Last Sunday, a drug dealer got stabbed to death at a club we were at. Last night, a drug dealer got stabbed right in front of us. What does this sound like to you?"

"I…" Iris's head droops.

Carson stalks toward her and lifts her chin with the backs of her fingers. "Sounds like you guys got in the middle of somebody's drug war. You wouldn't know how that happened, right?"

Iris shakes her head. She looks like she's about to cry.

"Figure it out. Next time you go to a club, somebody might try to shank you or one of the others." Carson steps back and glares. "That's not happening on my watch."

Chapter 30

CAP MARTINET, IBIZA

Carson wakes from a weird dream that she can't remember the moment she opens her eyes. The pain meds? The past couple days? Whatever. Her sleep rhythm's destroyed, not just because of the six-hour nap yesterday, but also the wild swings in bedtimes and getting-up times from the past two weeks.

And of course, she has about two gallons of water waiting to come out.

She checks whether Sebastian is still asleep—his even breathing says he is—then carefully slides out from under his arm and takes care of her pit stop. The nightlight in the washroom is just strong enough to let her check out the dressing over her wound. Still no seepage, a bonus.

She wanders to the double glass doors that connect the bedroom to the outside. She can go from here across a tiled path to the gym—very convenient. The landscape lights throw a gentle abstract pattern of leaves on the frosted part of the door glass, which reaches from the floor almost to her chin. It's a nice way to get sunlight (and moonlight) into the room without having to deal with curtains.

Go back to bed. Even if you can't sleep.

Sometimes her inner voice says something sensible. She and Sebastian didn't do anything other than snuggle when he came to her room last night, but that was nice. Maybe by the time they're both awake this morning, she might be in the mood for something more. That is, if she can force herself to stop stewing about Vicki bailing out again.

Carson steps away from the window and stretches.

A person-sized shadow sweeps across the glass doors. *What the…?*

She peeks out but can't see anyone. If it was someone, they'll be at the pool soon.

One of the posse? That doesn't make sense. Why go down the side when they can use the front door?

Grup Sabadey. Stabbings. Tails.

The back of her neck starts to tingle.

Carson pulls on her workout tights, sports bras, and runners. She glances at the roller bag in the corner. *The vest? Yeah.* She unzips the suitcase as quietly as she can and drags out her U.S. Armor Enforcer ballistic vest. Luckily, she's had plenty of practice strapping it on in the dark. She grabs her tactical light from the suitcase, her baton off the nightstand, the Beretta from her duffel, and then slips out the bedroom door into the hallway.

She passes the door to Tamara's bedroom, then steps silently to the hallway's end. It joins with a central corridor that runs from the front door and main staircase to the patio doors. The soft, pink light from the neon under the staircase's treads picks out details in the corridor. She stops to listen, breathing through her mouth to cut down the noise her sinuses make in her head. Adrenaline floods Carson's system, making all her senses like raw nerves. Refrigerator hum. Normal house-at-night creaks. Her heart thumping. Blood rushing in her ears.

A gentle rustling toward the back.

Carson heel-and-toes it down the corridor leading with the Beretta, her right hand propped on her left, which holds the light in case she needs it. She stops at the living room door. Listens. Scratching on tile in the living room at her three o'clock, growing closer; a faint clicking in the kitchen at her ten o'clock.

How many more? Is one upstairs already? Am I too late?

Deal with the closer threat first.

She risks a peek into the living room. The dark silhouette of a man passes by the inside of the front window. He's holding a pistol; the shape's long enough to include a suppressor. She squats next to the door, her weapon ready.

He stops at the door, swings his weapon both ways, then heads for the staircase. He doesn't look down—they never do. When he passes, Carson stands and touches the Beretta's muzzle to the back of the hood over his head. He freezes.

Carson whispers, "Nod if you understand English." He nods once. "Not my house. Don't care where the blood goes. Got it?"

Nod. She could club him down, but it would make a lot of noise. Better to do it gentle. "Left hand. Hold your weapon by the frame." Nod. He cradles his pistol in his left palm. His right hand hovers in front of him. *This could work.*

A door clicks open in the hallway. Bare feet slap on the tile. The corridor light snaps on, destroying Carson's night vision.

Tamara appears at the end of the hallway, nearly wearing a flimsy, sheer red kimono with ruffled sleeves. She stops, squints at Carson and the gunman. "*¿Qué...?*"

The gunman pivots and slams his right forearm against Carson's. She holds onto the Beretta but fires a round into the wall. Now she's both almost blind and almost deaf. She drops back a step. The gunman stumbles backward two steps, shaking his head; he must've taken the full brunt of both the muzzle flash and the report.

Tamara starts to shriek.

Carson yells, "Go back to your room!"

The gunman swings his weapon toward Carson. She'd wanted to take him alive but that chance's gone. She puts two rounds into his sternum, knocking him against the wall she'd shot. Then she bolts toward Tamara—still shrieking—to shut her up. The angry-bee *whiz* of a too-close bullet and the shattering of glass make her swivel to her right.

Another gunman stands in the kitchen door, aiming at her. He hesitates.

Carson body-checks Tamara into the wall, noting that her robe had fallen open. *That's why he didn't shoot?* Tamara sprawls on the tile floor and stops screaming. Carson drops to one knee and fires twice at the second gunman. He disappears into the kitchen. *Fuck!*

"Lisa?"

She glances over her shoulder. Sebastian stands naked at the hallway's end, squinting into the sudden bright. Carson snaps, "Get her in her room! Don't come out until I clear!"

There are two doors into the kitchen. The one that empties into the corridor—the one the second gunman ducked into—is empty now. The lightspill glints off the stainless-steel teppanyaki island and the window beyond. A set of French doors lead from the kitchen to the slider onto the patio; that's where Carson heads. She reaches around the open door's jamb to slap the light switch.

Recessed and pendant lights flood the kitchen, reflecting off all the black granite and steel.

Carson's got only a few seconds before the gunman's eyes adjust to the light. He may be in the alcove to her left between the fridge and the cooktop. She slides as carefully as she can into the space between the fridge and the door wall, then kicks open the other door.

The gunman pops out from the other side of the fridge and fires twice into the semi-darkness outside the doors. His weapon's suppressor muffles the sound to *thump thump.*

Carson pushes her Beretta around the fridge and fires twice at waist height. A body crashes onto the tile, followed by groaning and swearing in a language she can't place.

The gunman's curled in a semi-fetal position where he fell, clutching his stomach. Black balaclava, black long-sleeved Under Armour tee, black utility trousers. Much like the dead guy in the corridor.

Hit team. Somebody's serious.

Carson grabs the man's suppressed Glock 17 and hustles out of the kitchen. By the time she gets to the central corridor's front end, Sebastian stands at the end of the hallway (wearing shorts), while Iris, Karl, and Dareh crowd the staircase landing. Carson barks, "Any strangers upstairs?"

Iris says, "Not that I saw."

The three on the landing press into a corner to make room for Carson as she charges up the stairs, leading with the Beretta. She clears the first floor quickly and not gently. In one bedroom, she finds Celeste weeping into Amabelle's shoulder. Carson asks, "She okay?"

Amabelle says, "She is very scared. So am I."

"Good. Don't let her see what's downstairs. Start packing."

Amabelle doesn't ask why; she just nods.

Carson finds a balcony on the mansion's front façade. A black Mercedes SUV idles just outside the gate below: the hit team's ride. She slips back inside and heads for the stairs. "This place is compromised," she says to the knot of people on the landing on her way down. "Get dressed. Pack. Be back here in twenty minutes. We're leaving. No debate."

Karl asks, "Where do we go?"

"Iris, work it."

Iris is focused on the dead man slumped at the bottom of a vivid red stripe down the wall. She looks like she's about to barf. "I need more than twenty—"

"Get transport," Carson snaps. "Need to be gone ASAP. Work a destination when we're away." She swivels toward Sebastian. "Can you get me two sheets?"

"I can do." He jogs away. The others file wordlessly up the stairs.

Carson returns to the kitchen and squats by the man she gutshot. He's curled in a semi-fetal position where he fell, clutching his stomach and whimpering. There's already a small lake's worth of blood under him. She pats him down as best she can, finding an extra magazine for the Glock but no wallet or ID. Then she pulls off his hood. Mid-twenties, maybe. Not much hair. *So young.* "Grup Sabadey?" she asks.

"Not me."

She points toward the corridor. "Him?"

"No."

That surprises her. *Have I been misreading this?* "Who were you here to kill?"

He pants for a few moments. "All of you."

Everybody? "Why?"

He coughs. Blood wets his lips. His eyes flutter, then his head hits the floor. He still has a pulse, but he's not answering questions any time soon.

She checks the dead man in the corridor. Her hand hovers over the top of his hood, but then she thinks, *do I really need to see his face?* Not at all; this is already bad enough. He also has no ID, but she grabs his suppressed Walther P99, two extra magazines, and another tactical light. She stuffs the extra magazines and both tactical lights into the straps on her body armor, scoops up all three pistols, then heads for her room.

Sebastian's fully dressed and pulling the sheets off the bed. He stares at Carson when she enters. "What are you wearing?"

"Body armor. Don't leave home without it." She lays the pistols on the floor next to her suitcase, which she starts emptying.

"Did you have to kill that man?"

"Thought about letting him cap Tamara first, but figured you guys'd be pissed." She hates being this hard with Sebastian, but she has to if she expects to get through the next few hours with any kind of edge. "Cover those two assholes out there. Don't want Celeste seeing that mess."

"Right."

Carson takes off the vest and sports bras. There's some blood on her dressing; she must've torn open the knife wound. Later. She starts wriggling into her Cheata reducing bra. "Gotta go outside and take care of the hit team's driver."

"Are you going to kill him, too?"

She doesn't care for his tone but doesn't have time to deal with it. "Depends on how bad he pisses me off. Need you to keep your friends focused."

"Right." He points to her chest. "What's that thing?"

"Keeps my tits from moving around under my body armor. Why are you still here?"

She finishes changing into black jeans, boots, a black long-sleeved tee, and body armor. Then she grabs her phone and hits the top call-history entry from Vienna.

After four rings, Rodievsky's voice growls in Russian, "This had best be very important."

"Need a cleaner."

Rodievsky sniffs. Linens rustle. "Why?"

"Why do people usually need cleaners? We were attacked. You set that up?"

"Why would I do that? You are already there."

"Did Baranov?"

"Not that I know. How do you think he will react if I ask him, 'Did you try to kill your daughter tonight?' Is Viktoriya safe?"

This isn't a time for radical honesty. "Far as I know. Cleaners?"

"Right. How much damage?"

"One broken, one damaged."

"Where is the worksite?"

She gives him the address. He harrumphs when she says *Ibiza*. "We're clearing the site in the next few minutes. I'll leave the alarms off."

"Right." Rodievsky holds his palm over his phone mic and coughs. "I will contact my colleague in Madrid. Please stay with Viktoriya and wait for orders."

"Remember you promised me 'no danger, no violence'?" She lets a wave of anger pass. "I do. Gotta go."

"We're going to Barcelona."

Carson glances at Iris, sitting next to her in the front passenger's seat of the hit team's black Mercedes SUV as it bores a hole through the Ibizan night. "How so?"

"I got us someplace to stay."

"Where?"

Iris mumbles, "Vicki's dad's place."

Carson stares at her for a few moments. "You gotta be shitting me. While he's looking for her?"

"She says he doesn't go there much. She just texted me the gate and alarm combos."

"Fucking wonderful." Carson concentrates on following the fourteen-passenger bus carrying the rest of the posse and all their stuff. "She gonna be there?"

"She didn't say."

"Did she say where she is?"

"No, and I didn't ask."

Sebastian, in the back seat, says, "How do we get there?"

"I don't know!" Iris throws up her hands. "I just found out where we're going!"

Carson squeezes Iris's shoulder. "Hey. Hold it together."

"That's easy for you to say." Iris jerks away from Carson's hand. "You kill people for a living."

"Not my main gig. It's under 'other duties as assigned.'"

"Oh, *that* makes it better." Iris palms the tear tracks from her cheeks.

"Can we use the yacht?"

"What? No. Michel's here now. He's using it." She twists to look toward the back seat. "Sebastian, hon, do we have enough money to charter an airplane?"

"How much will that cost?"

"I don't know yet. Just asking. Never mind. Let me see if we can even do that here."

Carson calls Olivia to ask if she can borrow Allyson's Cessna

Citation. It's a brief conversation; Olivia can't help because Carson isn't assigned to an agency project. *Figures.*

Sebastian asks, "Do you reckon they've found the driver yet?"

"Not my monkey, not my circus." Carson tunes out Iris and focuses on the bus taillights. They're driving in circles until they know where they're going. *That's appropriate.*

Who wants us all dead?

How'd they find us?

Who'll get to the house first: the cleaners, or whoever hired the hit team?

What'll they do when they see we've declared war on them?

Chapter 31

EN ROUTE TO BARCELONA

Seven bleary, terrified, confused faces stare at Carson as she stands at the forward end of the Dassault Falcon 2000's cabin. The flight time from Ibiza to Barcelona is only forty minutes, and there's a lot of ground to cover before they land.

"Listen up." She takes a gulp from the mini-can of Coke she got from the jet's mini-galley. It's not a good substitute for coffee or a stiff drink, but it'll have to do. "You people asked me a dozen times if I had to shoot those men back there. Those assholes were gonna kill every one of us in our beds. Anybody want to ask that question again?"

A lot of dropped heads and averted eyes answer her.

"Moving on. Somebody wants you dead. I need to know why."

Celeste starts weeping again. Amabelle—sitting next to her on the four-place sofa along the cabin's left side—wraps her arms around Celeste's shoulders and pulls her close. Amabelle says, "Must we say these things in front of her?"

Carson would give anything to not have to do this in front of Celeste. She also knows that's not an option. "She's not a child. She's got a right to know what's happening to her world." She turns to Iris. "Iris, you gave me the sanitized version of what you guys are doing. Need the real story. Now."

Iris studies the beige carpet between her feet. "You should ask Vicki."

"Love to. She wasn't there. She wasn't around to be shot. She's lost the right to decide who gets to know what."

Iris props her elbows on her knees and leans her face into her palms.

"Anybody?"

Karl and Dareh swap anxious glances. Sebastian takes a deep breath and grinds the heels of his hands into his eye sockets.

Goddamnit. Carson counts to ten. "I'll make this easy for you. If I don't find out exactly what's going on—the *full* story—by the time we land in Barcelona, I'm gone. You can deal with these people all by yourselves. My bet? You won't live out the month."

More silence. Finally, Amabelle clears her throat. "We find civil society NGOs who are doing good work in places that need a *lot* of good work. Then we shower them with money with no strings attached."

Almost exactly what Iris said—like a cover story.

Iris says, "We check them out. Make sure they're legit and they can handle Christmas in July."

Carson growls, "Heard this shit already. Where's the money come from?"

One by one, everyone looks to Sebastian. He says, "We find donors to contribute to our funding pool."

"Who're these donors?"

"Corporations, mostly."

Carson notices that Karl and Dareh are looking everyplace except at her. She thinks about what little she knows about them and gets a wild idea. "These corporations—do they know they're donating?"

The only sounds in the cabin are Celeste's crying and the jet-engine hiss.

"Dareh? Karl?"

They look at each other with you-first expressions. They actually do rock-paper-scissors. Karl loses. He thinks for a moment, then sits up straight. "Sebastian and Tamara pick companies that are…evil. They destroy the environment or profit from wars or oppress their workers or harm people in their communities. They give us those companies' names and we…try to get inside them."

Carson feels like slapping her own forehead. It was so obvious. "You hack them."

Karl nods. "We look for certain things. One thing is hidden accounts for their executives. Another is accounts for bribes or, how do you say? Slush funds. Then we find how they transfer money into those accounts. Then we take some of that money and move it into accounts we create in their system that work the same way. Then, ehm…" He shoots Sebastian a *help!* look.

Sebastian picks up the thread. "We skim from their black accounts into ours on their systems. The accounts never show up in external audits, and the internal audits don't ask too many questions. Then we sweep the funds into numbered corporate accounts in jurisdictions with good bank secrecy laws. Then we transfer those funds into other accounts and so on 'til they're clean. We donate those funds to the NGOs we choose."

Carson takes a moment to digest this. "You steal the money, launder it, then donate it."

Sebastian says, "That's right."

"How many companies?"

Karl says, "Thirty-nine."

Jesus Murphy. "What kind?"

Tamara finally says something. "Oil and coal companies. Companies that make weapons. Vulture capital firms. Private prison operators. Payday lenders. Companies that run sweatshops. Companies owned by dictators or their cronies."

"I told them about two of my father's companies." Amabelle sniffs. "Just for fun, don't you know. We call it 'Project Karma.'"

Carson asks Dareh, "That attack on your computer came from one of them?"

Dareh nods. "DGI. Or someone wants us to believe they did it."

"One of the dirtiest financial firms in Europe." Sebastian breaks out a grim smile. "Even worse than my da's bank."

Carson snorts. "Looks like karma cuts both ways. Anybody here surprised somebody shot back at you?" Nobody answers. "Right. How long since the last time?"

Karl says, "We are attacked often. Our firewalls have contained those attacks until now."

"Meaning you finally stole the wrong people's money. Or somebody finally got serious. Like one set of parents got serious enough to hire muscle to kidnap one of you off the street." Carson nods toward Celeste. "How much did you take?"

Sebastian rocks out of his recliner, stretches, then leans his forearms on the empty seatback in front of him. "If I had my laptop, I could tell you exactly. But we're over a hundred sixty-seven million euros for the past two years."

Holy shit. This is way larger than Carson thought. "How much did you keep?"

"Two percent. That's less overhead than any registered charity in Europe or America. It's a fraction of the admin fees that hedge funds charge."

Iris says, "It's expensive being us."

In more ways than one. Carson rubs a throbbing spot between her eyebrows. They've stolen tens of millions from thirty-nine of the worst corporate citizens in the Western world. At least one has already fought back. Or, they pissed off some drug heavies. Or both.

Anybody could've hired that hit team.

We are so fucked.

<h1 style="text-align:center">Chapter 32</h1>

CAP MARTINET, IBIZA

Kallström prowls the mansion's ground floor, looking for something, anything, that will tell him what happened to the hit team that's disappeared from the Earth.

They didn't drive away. That much was clear when his men discovered the driver, bound and gagged in the unfinished house next door. His men are still looking for the Mercedes.

They'd had to wait for over two hours until they could enter this place. Someone was here before them. Kallström had expected to find police, maybe ambulances, crowding the narrow street and the driveway, but there wasn't a single one, only an unmarked, dark-gray Transit van outside the front door.

Anders, his oldest mate from the motorcycle gang, catches up with him in the sprawling kitchen. Like the rest of the downstairs, it looks like it's never been touched. Anders says in Swedish, "Nothing up there. It's like nobody's slept in the beds *ever*. No hair in the drains, nothing."

Kallström nods and sweeps a hand across the nearest counter, shiny in the late-morning light. "Look at this. It's all like this. My house should be so clean." He sighs and leans against the counter's edge. "Anything from the driver?"

"Nothing. He got a couple seconds of black ski mask before someone turned his lights out. That was around two-fifty." Anders checks the fridge, but it's empty. "Too bad we didn't get here earlier."

"They said they'd check in when they were off-island. That was supposed to be by nine." Kallström shakes his head. "You know what this is? Cleaners were here."

"You mean like those rent-a-maid places?"

"No. *Cleaners*. Like, people who make crime scenes disappear. That Russian *mafiya* bitch—she's behind this. Her or her people."

Kallström pushes off from the counter and heads for the patio. "We're never gonna see those men again."

They both stare past the pool at the sliver of the Med visible from up here. Sunny, clear, peaceful. Anders says, "Remember when we were in Mazar-i-Sharif?" He stuffs his hands in his jeans pockets. "We dreamed about being in a place like this."

"I remember Mazar. A total shithole in every possible way."

"You got that right." Anders sighs. "Now we're here, and we're still fighting."

Five years in the army. Over half of it in Afghanistan. When Kallström came home the last time, Sweden didn't have a clue what to do with him. Civilians got quiet and wary when he told them about his time downrange. And the women…they were all about 'supporting the troops' until they met one. He didn't feel like he belonged to anything until he joined the Demons. So many bikers were ex-soldiers, it was like he'd re-enlisted. They understood. And eventually, they brought him and Anders down here.

"This time, we're fighting for ourselves," Kallström finally says. He pulls his phone to ring up Ferran. A text from one of his other men waits on his home screen: `Charter jet left IBZ 0524 w/8 pax dest BCN`. "There were eight of them here last night, right?"

"Yeah. Why?"

"Thanks. I'll be out in a minute." Once Anders takes the hint and leaves, Kallström calls Ferran. While he waits for the man to pick up, he wonders, *what's with the fucking Buddha?*

Ferran says in Spanish, "You're late reporting."

Kallström switches his brain to Spanish, though it's a rough connection. "Hello to you. The team did not report. They are gone. I think dead. The house is clean, no evidence."

Silence. "You told me the gang was a soft target."

They should've been. "I think now, not so soft. Maybe the *mafiya* woman did this. My man here says they left for Barcelona six hours past."

"I'll tell Grebnev—maybe his people can tell us where they are. Brusin's on my ass already. Just wait until he finds out you let a bunch of children get past you. Get yourself to Barcelona and take care of those damned schoolkids immediately. Understand?"

Chapter 33

OUTSIDE MATARÓ, SPAIN

The Baranov vacation mansion is thirty-six kilometers northeast of central Barcelona outside the coastal city of Mataró. Carson didn't expect that; she'd figured on some over-the-top monstrosity in the middle of everything. Another surprise is that the place isn't either a big white box or a medieval castle. The main building looks like it used to belong to a 1960s airport terminal. Its front leans toward the Med, and a sweeping curved outside staircase leads to the first-floor balcony and walkway.

All the modern stuff is inside. The furniture's geometric, with rich-colored upholstery when it's not leather and chrome. It reminds her of the rooms in *Mad Men*. The ground floor has all the common areas, including the kitchen; all the bedrooms are upstairs.

Carson drags her roller bag along the red-tiled walkway outside the bedrooms. Each has a glass door and big windows on the sea side. She plods to the east end, turns, then retraces her steps until she finds Sebastian unpacking in the second bedroom from the west end. "Hey."

He looks up from the dresser drawer he's stuffing. "Hey yourself."

She can't tell if he's being playful or distant. She shrugs the duffel off her shoulder and leans against the doorframe. At least she had time to dump the body armor while they were waiting for their bus to arrive at the airport's executive terminal. "What is it about seven bedrooms?"

Sebastian stops unpacking and raises an eyebrow at her. "I don't reckon I understand what you're saying."

"Michel's yacht had seven bedrooms. This place has seven bedrooms. Is seven the magic number here?"

"Oh, that. I remember Vicki saying there used to be more, but they knocked some together to get bigger rooms."

"Wonderful. Guess I should've run up here with everybody else and claimed a room."

"Why didn't you?"

"I was walking the property to see how secure it is."

"And is it?"

"A bunch of first-graders could break into this place. Vicki's dad must bring his goons with him when he comes down here."

Sebastian nods. "I should've warned you. Sorry."

If this is his cute way of getting her to move in with him, she hopes he gets around to asking soon. She'll say *yes*, but he's got to put himself out there. "Why didn't you?"

He finds something interesting in the dresser drawer.

Really? "Do we have a problem?"

Sebastian slowly paces to within arm's reach. "Lisa. Darlin'. Very early this morning, a woman I like a lot got out of our bed, put on her ninja suit, and killed a man. I know why she did it. What I don't understand is how it's just another day at the office for her."

"What makes you think it is?" Carson snaps. "What do you want? Want me to fall apart? Cry? Get drunk? All three?"

He rocks back a half-step, startled. "I don't know what to expect. This is the first time for me. I reckon I want to know that you're feeling *something*, because you've—"

"I'm too fucking *tired* to feel anything." She doesn't stop her voice from getting louder and harder. "A fight like that? My body dumps adrenaline on me. When it's over, I'm *done*. All I want to do is turn off. I had two of those in a row. And now I don't even have a place to fucking sleep." She drags her duffel's strap onto her shoulder again and steps outside the door. "Never mind. I'm—"

"Wait." He gingerly slides a hand on her open shoulder. "I just want to understand."

This isn't the discussion she'd wanted with him or the others. It means letting them into places she doesn't like to share. He can be inside her body all he wants, but not inside her head.

Push him away now, he won't come back.

She knows it's true even before the thought's finished. He hasn't rejected her yet (she doesn't think). This kind of violence is new to him. She's getting punchy, because she laughs without thinking. "Just got it, didn't you? You just figured out that the woman you're sleeping with can kill you without trying hard. I wouldn't, but still. You men never have to deal with that shit. Us women?" She finger-stabs the top of her breastbone. "We gotta think about it every time we let a new man into our bed."

"But…isn't it hard to kill a man?"

"When you're doing it? No, it's not. You're too busy to think about it. It's what comes after. When you go to sleep, when you have time…*that's* what's hard. When you see his face. When you start asking yourself questions. Did I have to kill him? Could I have done something else? Could I have avoided the whole thing? *That's* hard. The answers aren't the ones you want. They never are."

Sebastian nods until it seems to be momentum rather than a conscious act. He carefully slips the duffel strap off her shoulder and sets the bag on the tiles. Then he folds her into a hug that she resists until the moment their bodies touch. She sags against him. He strokes her hair. "I'm so sorry you had to do that," he whispers.

"Sorry the whole thing happened." Carson didn't know she needed this until this moment. The human contact helps unclench her brain.

She feels eyes on her. To her left, Iris stands outside the next room over. She gives Carson a thumbs-up sign. To her right, Amabelle does the clenched-fist salute.

Sebastian murmurs, "I reckon I can find a bit of room for you if you promise to not take up the whole wardrobe."

She smiles into his neck. "I don't unpack. I can leave faster that way." Carson pulls back enough to see his face. "Sure you can stand to touch me?"

He smiles. "If you'll not murder me in my sleep, I'll be the best-protected man in the city."

Carson finds Celeste in her room, unpacking. Carson stands in the doorway watching her, hoping Celeste won't run screaming from her.

Celeste turns from the closet and jumps when she sees Carson. She slaps her palm on her chest. "Oh! Hello."

"Hi. Um…can I come in?"

Celeste nods.

"Sorry I couldn't come see you before this. Things were moving so fast. I had to get everybody out of that house and safe." Carson stops a couple of steps short of Celeste. "Do you want to talk about…what happened?"

"It was scary."

"Yeah, it was. Wanna know a secret?"

Celeste hugs herself, then nods.

"I was scared, too. Don't look so surprised. I was afraid I'd screw up, that one of them would get past me, that there were more of them." Carson tries to think of something soothing to say, but can't. "Glad you didn't see it. What I did."

Celeste hasn't moved since she went into her self-hug. Her eyes are locked on Carson's. "Amabelle was with me. She made me stay in my room."

"She took good care of you. Glad she was there. I wish I could've, but…"

"She said that you were busy fighting bad men."

"Yeah." Carson's afraid to ask this question, but she needs to. "Do you still feel safe with me?"

Celeste gnaws on her lower lip, then nods.

Carson's surprised by how relieved she is. "Good. That's good. Um…maybe tomorrow you can play more music for me?"

Finally, Celeste ends her clinch and grows a small, bashful smile. "I will like that."

It's not until mid-afternoon that Carson can get Iris's attention long enough to walk the grounds with her and point out the security problems. They sit by the pool while Carson explains what needs to be done so they're not all sitting ducks.

Iris's face scrunches like she's smelling an especially dead skunk. "You really think there's gonna be another one?"

"Wouldn't be surprised. They'll be pissed that the first one's gone missing. They also know we can defend ourselves now."

"Yeesh." Iris stares out at the Med for a while. "Do you think those guys last night are hooked up with that Group Whatever that was following you, or those dealers who got stabbed?"

"Could be. Or it could be somebody you guys hacked getting

back at you. That's the problem—too many possibilities."

When they return to the main house, Iris calls a group meeting in the living room. Like the bedrooms, most of the ground-floor rooms have floor-to-ceiling windows and double glass doors leading to what passes for a front yard. Project Karma filters in, some with beer or snacks, and stakes claims on various chairs or sofas or bits of floor. It's a quiet bunch. Carson sees a lot of dark circles under eyes, just like hers.

Iris sits on a chair next to the fieldstone fireplace with her arms wrapped around her shins. She and Carson had agreed that the group would listen better if Iris did most of the talking. Carson's on a green-upholstered loveseat to Iris's left; Celeste takes the other half and curls up almost like a cat.

Once everyone's settled, Iris sets her feet on the floor. "Thanks for coming." She sips a double vodka that hasn't yet calmed the slight tremor in her hands. "Before we start, I think we should all say 'thank you' to Lisa. She saved our lives last night. It wasn't pretty to look at and I can't imagine having to actually *do* it, but…well, we're still here because she stepped up. So"—Iris gives Carson a bleak smile—"thanks." She claps her hands.

After a few seconds, everyone (except Tamara) is applauding or whistling in Carson's direction. Sebastian calls out "Bravo!" like she sang an aria or something. Carson ducks her head. Twice in two days; she's still not used to it.

Iris lets the applause die out before she continues. "So, that's the good news. The not-so-good news is, it's not over. Lisa thinks those guys' friends are gonna be pissed. We're gonna have to do some things differently." She chugs her drink's dregs, then checks the list she wrote on the back of an envelope. "First thing. Lock the doors at night. That means the ones down here *and* your bedrooms. If you get deliveries, go down to the gate and get them there. Don't let anyone in, especially if they have a van or truck. Yeah, it sucks, but it's summer and it's not gonna get cold or rainy, so, deal." Iris throws a longing glance at her empty glass. Carson brings her the bottle of Grey Goose from the bar in the back of the room. "Thanks. Um, this one's gonna suck, too. If you go someplace, go with someone."

A couple people make *ick* faces. Tamara snaps, "We're not children."

"No, you're not," Carson says, matching her tone. "You're targets. Guess you didn't learn that last night." Tamara's cheeks flush. "If you're alone, you're an easy target. If there's two or more of you, you can back each other up. Help each other hide or get away, or fight off an attacker."

Iris says, "Like I said. Let us know where you're going and when you think you'll be back. Write it on a note and stick it on the fridge. If you're not back by when you say, we can try to call you or find you."

Amabelle says, "This is how I lived in Rwanda. I had bodyguards. I could go to only safe places. I had to tell my father or mother where I would go." She sighs and slumps into her chair. "I thought I would be safe here."

Tamara's expression is about half grumpy and half embarrassed. "How do you know they'll come back?"

Carson growls, "Because they wanted you dead, and you're not. The kind of people who set up ops like last night don't go away when they fail. They get mad. Try again, but bigger. Harder. I hurt their pride. They'll want payback."

Iris puts up her hands. "We don't know for sure they know where we are. Maybe they don't. But I'll feel better if we're a little more careful, even if we don't need to. I mean, think about who we've been taking money from."

The group gets quiet. A few start counting threads in the rugs.

Iris stares at her envelope, then at Carson. "Lisa…you want to talk about the last one?"

Figures. "Okay. We're not on slabs in the Ibiza morgue only because I had to piss around two this morning. That's how I saw those assholes outside. Think about that. We can't count on my bladder as a burglar alarm."

Celeste giggles. The rest stay still.

"We need a night watch. When everybody else turns in, we need a couple people awake. Lights on, TV on mute, whatever. They see or hear anything, they raise the alarm. We run shifts so nobody has to stay up all night."

Karl asks, "Won't they be the first ones to die?"

Carson had hoped nobody would think of that. "Not necessarily. Activity could be enough to abort the op. A minute or two warning may be all we need to hunker down. Give me two or three minutes and I can gear up and start taking care of the problem. Zero warning means people probably die." She sees a lot of frowns and rolled eyes. "Look. On club nights, most of you are up 'til sunrise anyway. This isn't a big ask. Like they say—the life you save may be yours."

Tamara huffs and folds her arms. "This is silly. You're overreacting."

"*I'm* overreacting?" Carson stops to count to five. "You were about to get your fucking head blown off last night. Why are you *under*reacting? You just happen to know you're not on the target list?"

"What? No! How would I… You really think—"

"Don't know what to think. You're fighting all of this. You more than anybody in this room got reasons to want to tighten things up here. Are you immortal? When I was your age, I thought so, too. Learned the hard way that I'm not."

"I—"

"Or maybe your plan is, the next hit team that shows up, you'll flash your tits at 'em like you did last night and they'll skip—"

"I didn't mean to—"

"They won't, you know. They'll rape you, then kill you. Or maybe kill you and *then* rape you. Long as you're still warm—"

"Stop! Stop!" Iris waves her hands frantically. "Ew! Yuck!"

Tamara stumbles out of the room, crying. Everyone else gets extremely quiet.

Carson checks on Celeste—she looks serious but not repulsed—then turns to the rest. "Tamara almost got me killed last night. I was trying to get one of those assholes alive so I could question him, and she fucked it up. Excuse me for not being as hard on her as she deserves." She groans her way off the loveseat. "Iris, you guys figure out how the night watch goes. I'll take the second shift if you want." She turns to the others. "Any of you have military or police training? Let me know. We need more shooters. If I run out of luck, you shouldn't have to."

Chapter 34

After the meeting, Carson drifts onto the patio and melts into a metal lawn chair. The low sun warms her face and paints the contrails pink. She's drained, and the headache from the adrenaline hangover's knocking on her brain. An early supper and an early bedtime loom in her future.

She pulls her phone to see who texted her during the meeting. Rogozhkin pinged her about ten minutes ago: Are you there?

Carson squeezes her eyes closed. *Am I up for talking with him? Yeah. Need a friendly voice.* She calls him. "Now I am."

"Good evening. Is it night yet in Ibiza?"

"I'm not in Ibiza anymore. Barcelona, now."

"Why did you move? Are you still with your young friends?"

"Wasn't planned, but yeah, I'm still with them. What are you up to?"

Rogozhkin sighs. "Vlasenko's coming tomorrow." Denis Vlasenko's the mini-oligarch who owns the mansion in Cyprus with the sunbed and the view. He hired Rogozhkin to be caretaker. "I finished filling the refrigerator. The housekeeper comes in the morning to see that I haven't left a mess."

"Did you?"

"There's no one here to keep me civilized. I live in a state of nature."

"Sounds like your army days."

"Exactly, including the swimming pool. This is his first visit since he hired me. I have to impress the boss."

Carson snickers at Rogozhkin—a former senior officer in one of the best-trained special forces organizations on Earth—worrying about impressing a run-of-the-mill rich guy. "Take him out to do manly things. He'll like that."

"Maybe. When he hired me, the wife was with him and he was

desperate to do manly things. If he brings a mistress, I have no idea what he'll want."

"Poor you."

"Oh, come now. Say it like you mean it."

Carson wraps her voice in sugar. "Oh, you poor, dear man. I feel so sorry for you."

"Hm. I liked it better the first time. What are you doing in Barcelona?"

Carson's not sure how much she wants to tell him. Plus, she hasn't had time to digest it all yet. "It's complicated."

"What's wrong?" His voice is low and gentle.

She sighs. "I'm really tired. It's been a long, nasty couple of days. Not all fun and games out here."

"You're sure you don't want to talk about it? It helps."

"I know. Let me figure it out first. Thanks."

"Anytime. I'll let you go. Get some rest. Ring me."

"Okay. Good luck tomorrow. Be impressive."

"Sleep tight, Lara."

Carson drops her phone in her lap. She needs to decide what she wants to do about Rogozhkin. He obviously likes her and wants her. *And here you are, robbing the cradle…*

"Lisa?" Dareh stands a careful couple of meters from her chair with his hands folded at his hips, like a schoolboy sent to the principal's office.

"Hey, Dareh."

"Ehm. You ask for people who have military experience. I serve twenty-one months in the *Sepāh-e Pâsdârân* for my national service."

"The what?"

"I think you know it as the, ehm, Islamic Revolutionary Guards." He dips his head. "My father is a colonel. He arrange my service."

Holy shit. Carson doesn't know much about them, but she knows the IRGC is camped out in Syria and Iraq—not on the side of the angels—and supposedly owns a big piece of Iran's economy. She also knows that most Western nations have written them off as terrorists. "You trained as a soldier?"

"Yes. If I go back to Iran, I will be an officer."

She can't imagine this skinny kid—he still looks like a

teenager—dressed in utilities and field gear. Then again, she couldn't see her brother Tosha that way before he joined the Forces. "Okay. Come by my room and I'll give you a weapon. Have Iris put you on the first watch, since I'm on the second. Thanks for letting me know. It's good to have backup."

Dareh flashes her a shy smile. "Thank you for having me." He turns to go.

"Dareh?" He stops and turns to Carson. "Karl told me you can't go back home. It's none of my business, but why?"

He stands blinking at her for a long moment. He studies the flagstone for a while. "The mullahs will kill me."

"Because you're political?"

"Because I am gay." Dareh finally looks in Carson's eyes again. "It is forbidden in Iran. People like me are hung, shot, burned. If my father would know, he would kill me himself."

"No wonder you want to stay here." Her brain makes a series of connections. "Wait. Are you and Karl—"

"No no no." He waves away the idea. "We are good friends only. He knows, and he understands. They all do. Here I can be who I am with no fear. I want to help protect this place, these people. This is why I come to you. For you, this is what you do. For me, it is personal. You can rely on me. I will fight."

Chapter 35

After a partial workout, Carson finds a ring of keys in a kitchen cupboard and decides to see what they open.

In yesterday's quick survey, she discovered that the estate is a compound semi-surrounded by a low wall and a lot of land. She didn't have enough time to explore properly then, but she does now that her morning watch has ended and she's too awake to sleep.

The property's oriented on a northeast-southwest axis. She stands under a flat-roofed pavilion at the south edge, looking toward the Med over a two-lane road and a twin-track railroad right-of-way. Three mature trees screen the pavilion from the main house. *Sucks being this close to the water and you can't get to it.*

She walks west through the formal garden beside the house (curving green hedges and knots of bushy, flowering plants) to what looks like a caretaker's house near the western wall. It's cool and quiet inside. A combination living-dining room, smallish kitchen, a bedroom, washroom, a utility room with a washer and dryer, all clean and sparse but potentially comfortable. Dusty sheets cover the major furniture. It's attached to two one-car garages. One holds miscellaneous old furniture and junk; the other hides a little blue Citroën AX hatchback under a dusty car cover.

The one-car garage grafted onto the main house's north side is full of a black BMW 435i four-door sedan. Unlike the Citroën, the key isn't on the dash (*figures*). The tires look relatively fresh and the body doesn't show much wear.

On the other side of another garden north of the house is a concrete tennis court and, to its east, a boxy building with a glass front. It's a gym, maybe twenty meters long by ten meters wide and five or six meters high. The deep beams and prominent box columns make it look more like a place to hide submarines than one for working out. Carson browses the equipment—not the latest, but a lot of it, and in good shape—and wonders if Baranov's seriously into fitness or just wants people to think he is. She aims a few exploratory kicks at a heavy bag hanging from a chain. *A proper gym. I'm spending some time here.*

By the time she returns to the main house, she finds the others gathered in the living room. The four women are crying and hugging, while the three guys hang back a couple of steps, looking uncomfortable. *What the hell?* Carson watches for a few moments before she slips next to Sebastian and asks, "What happened?"

"Amabelle's leaving." His hair is more tousled than usual and he doesn't look entirely awake. This must be a pop-up event.

Carson doesn't ask why Amabelle's bailing out. She already knows. Living under a possible death threat isn't for everybody.

The guys eventually move in one-by-one to hug Amabelle and murmur things that don't carry to Carson's ears. Carson holds back. This is a family thing, and she's not family.

Finally, the crowd filters out except for Celeste and Sebastian. Sebastian has a long, earnest-sounding murmured conversation with Amabelle; she shakes her head a lot, then finally kisses him lightly and squeezes his shoulder. He leaves as Celeste falls into Amabelle's arms, weeping. They have a hushed exchange in French. Carson can hear it, doesn't understand the words, but gets the gist from the tone and their expressions.

Eventually, Carson's alone with Amabelle. They stand eyeing each other for a few moments. Amabelle is still striking first thing in the morning; in her vivid gold camisole top and matching flowing trousers, she looks like the gilded statue of an African queen.

Carson steps forward and holds out her right hand, not knowing how close Amabelle wants her to get. "Hey."

"Hello, Lisa." Amabelle takes Carson's hand in both of hers and holds on.

"Sorry I didn't get to know you better."

"And for me, the same."

"Is it…anything I did?"

"Oh, no, no, no." Amabelle pulls Carson into an embrace. "It is nothing you have done. But the men with guns, and thinking that they may come back…"

"I get it. It's hard to get used to."

Amabelle pulls away. "No, not at all. I am already familiar. When you are the daughter of one of the richest men in Rwanda, there are many people who want to have dealings with you." She wraps her hands around Carson's biceps and holds her far enough away to look in her eyes. "From the time when Papa became wealthy, I have the bodyguards and ride in the special auto with the bulletproof glass. I live in a bubble. I do not want to live in a bubble. If I want this, I would go home."

Not what Carson expected, but she gets it. "What are you gonna do?"

Amabelle wipes a tear track from one of her amazing cheekbones. "I return to Marseille. I have friends there from before. There I am only another very tall *Africaine*. No one knows who I am, and no one cares. Except for the men, of course." She smiles, though it wobbles a bit. "Lisa. These are my friends. I go, but they are still my friends, and will always be so. Keep them safe for me."

"I'm trying."

"I know. You have to be the adult and spoil their playtime. Iris pretends to be the adult, but…" She tosses off a perfect Gallic shrug.

Carson's never been good at farewells and hasn't gotten any better lately. What do you say? "Well, take care. Be careful out there."

Amabelle cups Carson's cheek. Her mouth turns serious. "You too, my friend. You will need to be careful before I will, I think."

<h1 style="text-align:center">Chapter 36</h1>

OUTSIDE MATARÓ

Four a.m. Every curtain in the mansion is shut tight to block anyone outside from seeing inside. All the lights are on throughout the ground floor. The house is quiet.

Carson, sitting at the end of the dining table farthest from the windows, grinds the heels of her hands into her eye sockets. She'd picked this shift, figuring the others would bitch about it more than the eleven-to-three shift. With good reason.

She forces her skittish attention back to her laptop's screen. She's halfway through the latest *EU Drug Markets Report*, a joint effort by Europol and the European Monitoring Centre for Drugs and Drug Addiction. Not exactly the kind of thing she should be trying to read at this hour, but she needs to get smart about the narco scene here.

Carson spent yesterday morning's shift thinking about who might be behind the hit team on Ibiza. Dareh gave her a list of the thirty-nine companies he and Karl had hacked. It held a few familiar names, including the big pharma company Alivian Healthways. She had to smile at that one; its CEO—a prize asshole—had been the client for a DeWitt project she'd done in Portsmouth last Christmas. If anybody deserves to have his "executive discretionary accounts" looted and sent to help orphans in India, it's him. The two most obvious revenge candidates (a pair of private security contractors with especially bad reputations) are the least likely to be behind the hit; they would've sent a full team and done it right.

That led her back to drugs.

Sandals on tile make her look over her shoulder. Sebastian's carrying two steaming mugs of what she hopes is nuclear coffee. He slides one next to her laptop, then bends to kiss the lips she offers him. "Is this lot your schoolwork?"

"Yeah." The coffee's both heart-stopping and scorching. She's glad Sebastian volunteered to share the shift with her, even though they haven't seen much of each other since they came on duty. "Drug market down here's a fucking circus. Everybody's here."

"What do you mean by 'everybody'?" He thumps into the dining chair next to her.

"Everybody. Dutch and Vietnamese control the cannabis trade. Turks, Pakistanis, and Albanians own heroin and opioids. Colombians and Brits do cocaine. Dutch and Belgians cover a lot of the amphetamine market. Gangs from Liverpool and Manchester compete in MDMA. There's somewhere from fifty to a hundred drug gangs on the Costa del Sol alone."

Sebastian's eyebrows climb his forehead. "I'd no idea."

She'd left one player off the list: the Tambovskaya Group, another splinter off the Russian *mafiya* tree that supposedly does money laundering down here. She wants to ask Rodievsky about the state of relations between the Tambov and Solntsevo gangs before she looks too much farther into the Tambovs. "Looks like Cadiz, Algeciras, Valencia, and Barcelona are the main entry points for bulk drugs into Spain. Then the gangs move it onto the market here and into Western Europe and the Nordic countries." *What was Vicki doing in Algeciras two Saturdays ago?* "Ever see any outlaw biker gangs around here?"

Sebastian frowns. "How would I know they're outlaws?"

"They look like they hope you'll walk in front of them so they can run you over. They're not like the old dudes in custom leathers with bikes that cost sixty grand."

"Now that you mention it, I may have done. Why?"

"They apparently move a lot of product for other markets. There's even Swedish and Danish ones that take the drugs to Scandinavia."

"*Swedish* biker gangs?"

"Hey, Swedes are badass. Ever hear of Swedish death metal?"

"I've heard *of* it." Sebastian chuckles. "Never heard it."

"Well, thank God for that. You still have ears." Talking about what she's read helps Carson's brain organize the information and store it someplace she can find it again. She hopes she doesn't need it.

Sebastian takes a long draw from his coffee, then leans back in his chair. "Now that you know this, does it help? Do you know who sent those men after us?"

Do I? Carson stands and stretches, enjoying that Sebastian watches her closely. She does a couple Warrior I poses to give him something more to look at, then sits. "Maybe. I read a news article about the local cops busting Dutch and Swedish hit teams. Gangs hire them from out of town to settle scores. They come here, do their thing, then leave. They're young—between twenty and thirty." She lets herself picture the scene from that last night in Ibiza. "Guy I shot in the kitchen was real young. Could've been Dutch or Swedish. He had an accent, but didn't say enough for me to figure it out."

"So you think it's a drug gang that hired them?"

"Could be. I haven't seen anything that looks like 'Grup Sabadey.' Can't look it up if I don't know how to spell it. But…" She sighs. "If these guys are around, then any of your 'donors' can hire them, too."

"What's your gut tell you?"

Carson takes a lot of time to answer that. Her gut's signals are highly mixed. If someone in Vicki's posse is dealing, she (or he) needs to launder the money to make it usable. She flicks a glance at Sebastian. Any of Vicki's friends could sell drugs; only Sebastian has the skill set to clean and hide the money. And as he proved to her at Anubis, he knows how the retail end of the drug business works here.

That line of thought makes Carson vaguely ill. *If I don't trust him…why am I sleeping with him?*

Finally, she says, "Drugs. Like you said, they're everywhere. We got the whole United Nations jockeying to sell them here. Ties in the stabbed dealers. And Ibiza wasn't the slickest op ever, so I'm thinking whoever's behind the team doesn't do hits for a living." Carson watches Sebastian for a meaningful reaction but doesn't get one. "Beyond that…haven't got a clue."

Chapter 37

PUIG D'EN VALLS, IBIZA

Grebnev sits in the milky sunshine on the tiny first-floor balcony of his Airbnb rental, waiting on hold. The house is nice enough, though he has to share it with Zapadneft's recon team. Beyond the weedy vacant lot across the street, frowzy worker flats, and a powerplant is a hazy view of Ibiza's Dalt Vila, as overpromised in the welcome book.

The other end of the connection goes live. Severinov says, "Are you still there?" He's on the secure phone again. *Doesn't the man ever go home?*

"Yes, sir. The Sabadell people sent two specialists after the subjects Saturday night. Both the specialists and the subjects are now missing."

"The way you say this, it doesn't sound like good news."

"It's not. The Sabadell man says the specialists haven't been in touch for the rest of their payment, and their vehicle was dumped in a supermarket car park." Another wave of disgust sloshes though his gut. "Permission to speak freely, sir?"

Severinov harrumphs. "This isn't the army. Say what you like…if you're not attached to your bonus."

Grebnev can't tell when his boss is joking, if ever. The man's sense of humor may have been surgically removed in a field hospital in Chechnya years ago. "This is what we get for using amateurs in an operation. We should've hired professionals ourselves. These clowns can't take out a bunch of college kids? Pathetic."

"Exactly the word I'd use. At the same time, their intel appears to be good. Our people picked up the gang's Amazon accounts during last week's DGI exploit. Their recent orders put them in Mataró, east of Barcelona. I've already sent the address. Get yourself and the recon team ready to leave this afternoon."

"Yes, sir." Grebnev hesitates. Severinov never likes to be

questioned. "If I may, sir. The Bratva's involvement worries me. Do we know for certain this isn't one of their operations? I mean, that woman's with the group. Why would she be there unless the Bratva has some interest in what the group's doing? Who are we really fighting?"

The line's other end goes silent; Severinov must have muted it. A bad omen? Severinov's been with Zapadneft for ten years and was a career officer in the GRU—Russian military intelligence—before that. Grebnev's been with the company three years, only eight months in this position, and was an airborne captain before he left the army. Should he even be asking questions? His last brigade commander welcomed criticism—he'd say, *it's the only way I know what's broken*—but he was unusual that way. Things were a lot easier to figure out in the army.

Severinov says, "Are you still there?"

"Yes, sir."

"I'm going to tell you something that you'll keep to yourself. Understand?"

"Yes, sir."

"I met with the minister this morning. He told me we're to forget everything we've seen about his daughter and the Bratva woman. It never happened. Do you know what that means?"

"That...we stand down?"

"Of course not. The plan continues. This is why we're using amateurs who aren't connected to us. If they get carried away and accidentally terminate the minister's daughter or some Bratva figure...well, it has nothing to do with us, right? It'll be damned hard for the minister to explain why that brat of his was involved in a drug shooting. That man needs to be taken down a few notches. He takes too many liberties with the president's trust. Remember, though, you say nothing to anyone else about this."

Grebnev wishes he hadn't heard any of that. The last thing he wants is to get tangled up in the back-room maneuvering that's a spectator sport in Moscow. "Yes, sir. Just in case the Sabadell people fail again, can you send a tactical team? We need an insurance policy."

Severinov sighs. "Again, we can't use company employees. But I do know some people. I'll see what I can do quietly. In the meantime, make sure Sabadell knows what will happen if they keep failing. I want them focused. I want *you* focused. Understand?"

Grebnev understands all too well. Severinov wants the Baranov girl dead so he can embarrass her father and score points for the company with President Putin. If it doesn't happen or if anything more goes wrong, Grebnev may end up as the scapegoat.

Chances are good that Grupo Sabadell will fail again. It seems to be part of their DNA.

If Severinov comes through with a tactical unit, Grebnev can steer the situation to where he needs it to go. Grupo Sabadell may be bumblers, but they could be useful cover for when the professionals get involved. The bodies of a few Catalan drug gangsters scattered around a multiple-murder scene would certainly make things easier for the police. Not to mention that there'd be no way to make a connection between them and Grebnev anymore.

Time to double down or lose his career.

He was already committed to killing a couple of hackers who'd attacked the company. Would the world miss another airheaded, spoiled rich girl?

Grebnev certainly wouldn't.

Chapter 38

Carson's into the last few laps of her morning swim in the fifteen-meter pool south of the main house. She's at the point where she no longer has to think about the swimming; her body's on autopilot and her mind can disengage other than occasionally glancing at her watch. She used to run several miles a day, but her hips and knees told her it was time to stop. So now she swims. It's every bit as good a workout and she's less likely to be hit by a truck.

Her mind drifts to her ninety-minute dry workout earlier this morning. She and Sebastian went off-duty at seven, changed into their gym clothes, and walked straight to the gym. It was a standard workout until Sebastian pulled down her tights and underwear while she was using the chin-up bar. She had to retaliate, of course. Soon enough, their clothes were scattered over half the floor and they were using the abs bench for something it hadn't been designed for. They found non-standard uses for some other equipment, too. They hadn't had sex since last Thursday; she was glad to find out he—and she—still wanted to. Luckily, everybody else was still asleep or they'd have gotten a hell of a show.

Her hour finally runs out. She strokes to the deep end, grabs the coping with one hand, and palms the water off her face with the other.

Celeste kneels on the pool's deck a couple of feet away. "Hello."

"Uh…hey." Carson hadn't seen her arrive. "Coming in?"

Celeste smiles. "No. I want to go to the shore. Will you come with me?" She's wearing a powder-blue sleep shirt and a floppy straw hat, not her normal morning-swim outfit.

"How do we get there?"

"I know a way. It is a secret." Celeste holds her index finger across her lips, the universal "shhh" sign.

Carson grabs her pool bag and towel, slips on her deck shoes, and follows Celeste to a pavilion near the pool with a wavy concrete roof and a back screen made of open circles the circumference of a wine bottle. They clomp down a cement spiral staircase into a concrete well about six meters deep. Celeste unlocks a padlock and wrestles open a steel door. When she flips a switch inside the doorway, lights reveal a concrete tunnel sloping downward into the distance.

Carson asks, "What's this?"

"You will see."

The tunnel leads under the road—cars rumble overhead—and train tracks until it ends in another steel door. Celeste unlocks and opens it. The beach and the Mediterranean spread out as far as Carson can see. "You have a private tunnel to the beach."

Celeste grins. "Yes. Vicki says it is the only one between Mataró and Can Sanç. Come." She scampers across the sand, drops her beach bag by the high-water mark, flings off her hat and shirt—she's wearing a pale-yellow bikini with little red flowers—and charges into the water.

Carson joins her after a minute. It's not as warm as at Ibiza, but having an empty beach for a good klick on either side makes up for it. She watches Celeste play in the water and gets sucked into a splash war with her, leaving them both laughing and drenched.

They settle on their towels and start smearing on sunscreen. Celeste says, "You will wear your swimming suit?"

"Yeah. I don't need to scare people on the train." Her new black one-piece is cut lower in front and higher on her hips than she's used to, but it keeps everything strapped down and shows off her back.

Celeste giggles. "You will not scare them. We are in Spain."

Carson thinks back to all the topless women and vanishingly small bikini bottoms she saw at the beaches and beach clubs in Marbella and Ibiza and gets Celeste's point. Still, sunbathing nude on the yacht or at the pool with a limited audience is one thing; showing off to hundreds of commuters is something else. "You doing okay? With Amabelle leaving?"

"Yes. I think." Celeste concentrates in her intense way on making sure every square centimeter of her belly is covered with sunscreen. "I am sad she will not be with us. But I am happy also that she will be in a place that makes her happy."

"Were you good friends?"

"Yes. She is very nice to me. She likes my music."

"That makes her a good person in my book." Carson finishes greasing up her legs. She leans back on her elbows. "How old are you?"

"Twenty-two." Celeste wrinkles her nose at Carson. "How old are *you*?"

No wonder she looks like a kid. "Thirty-seven. Had a birthday three weeks ago."

Celeste's eyes get huge. "No! So old? I think you are younger."

"I get that a lot. Sometimes I feel older." She's been thinking about how to ask this next question. It's none of her business. But she'd had to talk to Dom about it a lot before he finally focused on the answer instead of the question. "What do you want to do in the future?"

Celeste's turned her attention and sunscreen to her legs. "When we go back to the house, I will work on my new music."

"Not that. I mean…the *future*. Five years, ten years out. What do you want to do? Where do you want to go?"

"I want to work for the census."

"The census?"

"Yes." Celeste's thoroughly covering her left foot. When she's done, she says, "The *Institut national de la statistique et des études économiques* makes the census for France. It uses much statistics in its work. I have a diploma in statistics. It is very interesting."

"Iris told me about your degree. I still can't see how math and music go together."

"It is…" She nibbles on her lower lip. "I cannot explain in English. It is hard to explain in French. Ehm…" Celeste puts away her sunscreen bottle, then lies flat. "Do you know *la musique classique*?"

"You mean 'classical music'? Symphonies and stuff? No."

"Hmm. Do you know J.S. Bach?"

"Not really. Heard of him. When I was skating, we got a lot of Tchaikovsky and Bizet and Strauss." Carson automatically starts counting time whenever she hears anything from *Carmen* or *Swan Lake.*

"Oh. J.S. Bach is how maths sound."

"Huh. You'd still work on your music, right?"

"Oh, yes. I cannot stop. It is…it is what makes my heart work." Celeste focuses on Carson for what would be an overlong time if Carson wasn't used to it. "What do you want to do for the future?"

"I don't know." She lies down and closes her eyes. She hates questions like this, but fair's fair. "Something different. Don't know what that is, though. This is what I'm good at." She sighs. "I'm getting too old for it, though. Gets harder to come back every time."

"What work do you do?"

"Fix things that need fixing." It took her a couple of years to figure out how to describe her two jobs. It has the bonus of shutting down most questions.

"Does Vicki need to be fixed?"

"Her dad thinks so. I'm not so sure anymore."

They listen to the wavelets bubble onto the beach. A passenger train moans past, seemingly close enough to touch. Seagulls wheel overhead. Celeste's hand creeps over Carson's, and her fingers wrap into Carson's palm. It's like a newborn kitten is sleeping in Carson's hand.

Carson's phone bleeps with a text. It's from Rogozhkin: `Still not fired.`☺

Carson snickers at Rogozhkin using an emoji. `Good job. Keep it up.` Once again, she wishes she could've blown off Rodievsky and gone to Cyprus. No rich-kid politics or drug-gang tantrums to deal with.

She chews over her next question. It's something else she'd had to talk to Dom about and help him work out. Asking it means having to answer when Celeste turns it back on her. "Want to meet someone special? Fall in love? Maybe have a family?"

Celeste shrugs.

Not the answer Carson expected. "You ever have a boyfriend? Or girlfriend? I don't know which way you go."

"There was a boy at the *Institut*," Celeste says after a long pause. "His name was Thierry. He liked to draw pictures. He was very good. He would draw pictures of me and make me look very pretty."

"That isn't hard."

Celeste giggles. "*Merci.*"

"Were you guys serious? What happened to him?"

"When he had his diploma, he went to Brussels to work for the UE." If it bothers her at all, there's no trace in her voice.

"Um…did you have sex?" Dom didn't have sex until he was twenty-three. He was incredibly shy around girls his own age. They talked on the phone about it over the years. Eventually, he found a girl who made the first move. They're engaged now. A happy ending.

"He put his thing in me. Two times."

"Did you like it?"

Celeste shrugs. "Do you like what you do with Sebastian?"

"You know about that?"

She giggles again. "Everyone knows about it."

Wonderful. "Yeah, I do. A lot."

"Do you love him?"

"No. I like him. Love and sex aren't the same thing. You can have great sex with somebody you can hardly stand when you're not in bed. Like my ex-husband. You can love somebody like crazy even if you don't touch him or even see him. Nice if the two go together, but, um…that doesn't happen a lot. Not for me."

"You were married?"

"Yeah. Three years. Divorced six years ago, almost." Carson turns on her side so she can look at Celeste without screwing up her neck. "Lots of people are gonna try to put schedules on you. 'You should have a boyfriend by now.' 'You should be married by now.' 'You should have a kid by now.' Don't listen to them. Those are their schedules, not yours. You need to do things when they feel right for you."

"Maman and Papa do this. They always have."

"That's because they're trying to protect you. Probably from everything. When I was raising my little brother Dominik, it was real hard to not protect him to death. He was…*different*, like you."

"Does he make the music, also?"

"No. He was real good with animals. It transferred to little kids pretty okay. But I let him take knocks so he'd learn things himself without me telling him everything. Beat it into his brothers— watch out for Dom, but let him learn the way you did. That meant bloody noses and bruised egos, but it worked. Told them, 'Don't you ever call Dom *dumb*, or *stupid*, or *retard*, or I'll beat the shit out of you.' I did, too. They learned." Carson catches a shadow as it passes over Celeste's face. "Did other kids call you that stuff in school?"

Celeste nods. For once, she's not smiling.

Carson squeezes her forearm. "You're not, you know. You got that math brain, way better than me. You make that amazing music. And you're an incredibly nice person. I like you a lot. Hope you'll find all the happiness you deserve."

"You like me?"

"A lot."

Celeste pulls Carson into a sweet-but-awkward sitting hug. "I like you very much, also."

What Carson doesn't say is that it took Dom years to find his place in the world. There was a lot of hurt and sadness along the way. She hopes it's easier for Celeste but knows it probably won't be. That big heart of hers will get broken over and over.

Carson hopes like hell that she won't be the first one who breaks it.

Chapter 39

Carson and Celeste have emerged from the secret tunnel on their way back to the mansion when Carson's phone plays Bowie. She manages to dig it out of her beach bag in time to answer before it rolls to voicemail. A +43 area code. "*Shto?*"

"Where are you?" Rodievsky's voice, not happy.

"Barcelona." She notices Celeste standing on the swimming pool deck, watching her. Carson waves her back to the house.

"Are you enjoying yourself? Are you comfortable? A suntan, perhaps?" His words are marinated in sarcasm.

"What bit you in the ass?"

"My good friend Oleg Germanovich. Some jumped-up former GRU lieutenant colonel who works for one of our esteemed oil companies met with him yesterday. This insect showed the minister photos from Viktoriya's Instagram account. All the worst ones, of course. He also knows about *you*."

"What?" Carson has to mute to keep herself from saying the next five things that barge into her head. *They know about* me*? Is that what Ibiza was about?* "How does that happen?"

"Knowing how the New Russia works, I would not be surprised if the information came from the Interior Ministry itself. Oleg Germanovich is…livid. He dressed me down like a recruit in basic training about how I could let his darling daughter be publicly associated with one of my 'minions.' You are a minion now—should I congratulate you?"

Carson imagines herself as one of those little yellow guys in overalls from the movies. Rodievsky wouldn't get it. "You know what this means, right? Somebody else's watching her. They got a pipeline to this oil company guy. What do you know about him?"

Rodievsky harrumphs. "First, let me say I would never have realized there is someone else watching her until you told me." His voice is like crushing rocks into gravel. He's pissed. Carson needs to back off some. "Of course someone else is watching! I need to know who it is. Do you know?"

She should've told him earlier, but she didn't want to rile him. Another great decision. "Somebody ran a two-car tail on me on Ibiza. I took down one of the drivers. He told me he was with 'Grup Sabadey.' Tried to look it up, but don't know how to spell it. He had an accent I couldn't place. Vicki says she doesn't know anything about it."

"You have been in public with Viktoriya?"

"Yeah. You told me to keep an eye on her, right? She goes out with her friends. Clubs, bars, restaurants. I went with them. Can't lock her in the washroom."

"You should have done." Rodievsky takes in a long breath. "When did you first know you were under surveillance?"

"Last Tuesday, when I was followed. I asked Vicki to tighten up security. Thursday I went on a road trip with her. Didn't see any tails. Saturday, the hit team showed up." She waits for an explosion that doesn't come. "My theory? It's about drugs. There was some drama about drug dealers on Ibiza. Local gangs hire out-of-town talent to settle their scores. One of the guys I shot had another accent I couldn't read."

"Viktoriya is involved with drugs?"

"I asked. She doesn't know what's happening. Her Number Two—girl called Iris—also swears she doesn't know what's up. While we're at it...why didn't you tell me your best friends are operating down here?"

"What are you talking about?" He'd been cooling off, but the gravel crusher's started up again.

"The Tambovskaya Group. They're into money laundering as well as drugs."

Rodievsky sighs. "Those idiots. They are no friends of mine. Have they contacted you?"

"Not yet. They gonna be a problem?"

"Nothing they do would surprise me. I will have a word with their local *pakhan*. This is entirely academic, anyway. Oleg Germanovich wants his daughter in Moscow immediately if not sooner. You will deliver her personally."

Last damn thing I need to hear. Carson mutes and lets the

venom out of her head so she doesn't unload on Rodievsky. "She won't go quietly."

"I assure you that no one is interested in her opinions on this or any other matter. If you have to bind and gag her, feel free to do so. Try not to break anything in a way that cannot be repaired. When you have physical control of her, inform me and I will have Oleg Germanovich dispatch an aircraft to Barcelona to carry you both to Moscow."

"How many of her friends can I shoot to get her out of here?"

"As many as you wish. I will have cleaners standing by."

Shit—he's serious about this. This is definitely not the time to tell Rodievsky she has no idea where Vicki is. "Fine. It won't happen instantly, though. I gotta cut her out of the pack. They're hunkered down because of the hit team. Give me a few days so I can do it quietly and with no casualties, okay? Any of these kids turn up dead, it'll make a lot of noise."

Silence on Rodievsky's end. *Contracting a hit on me? That'd suck.* "I usually trust your judgment, but I think that perhaps you have grown too close to her. I feared this might happen. Yes, please do this as quietly and damage-free as possible. But Viktoriya Olegovna will return home. If you cannot do it, I will send people who will. They will not care about her feelings or comfort or dignity, nor will they care about her friend's lives. Choose, Larochka. But choose wisely and soon."

Chapter 40

Carson waits until she's showered and changed before she tries calling Vicki. The break gives her time to cool off and strategize. If she can figure out where Vicki is, Carson can get to her without having to wade through the posse. Maybe she can sit Vicki down and talk her into going home for the good of her friends.

She hates having to do this, but she won't sacrifice herself for Vicki. No way to square that circle.

Carson stands staring at the Med through her bedroom windows with her phone in her hand, rehearsing her lines. Rewriting her lines. Hating her lines. She finally thumbs the "Vicki" entry in her contacts.

The phone company gives her the three tones of death and a guy telling her in Spanish and English, "The number you have called cannot be located on this network, and there is no forwarding number."

Carson finds Sebastian and Tamara at a round glass table on the south patio, hunched over their laptops. "Where's Iris?"

Tamara gives her a snide look. "Downtown. She took Amabelle to her train. Remember Amabelle?"

Attitude's the last thing Carson needs right now. "Yeah. Her train was at ten. It's almost noon. When's Iris coming back?"

"Why don't—"

Sebastian taps Tamara's forearm and shakes his head. He asks Carson, "Would you like her number?"

"I'd love her number. Thanks." She walks away before she has to pay attention to Tamara's latest experiment with low-cut tops and push-up bras. For the past almost week, every time Carson's seen Tamara around Sebastian, the girl's tits are about to fall into his lap. Carson hopes she's imagining it or that she's turning into a jealous bitch. If Tamara's making a serious play for Sebastian, it'll be hard to resist the temptation to drown her in the pool.

Sebastian's text rolls into Carson's phone. She calls the number and gets Iris's voicemail. *Figures.*

Carson hauls Iris to the west garden as soon as she returns shortly before lunch. Carson's had more than enough time to get spun up. "Where's Vicki?"

Iris rolls her eyes. "I don't know. Remember the last time you asked me that? The answer hasn't changed."

"When'd you talk to her last?"

"Oh, jeez. I don't know. I texted her yesterday. I'd hoped she'd come to say goodbye to Amabelle, but, well, you saw how that turned out."

"Did she text back?"

Iris pulls her phone from the back pocket of her booty shorts. "No. That's weird. She almost always texts back. Last one I got from her was…Saturday night. She wanted to know if we were okay and if we got into the house okay."

While she was waiting for Iris, Carson checked Vicki's Insta feed. She's still posting Ibiza pictures. The last one was from a bar in Sant Antoni—the bar the whole group went to before Leviathan. "When's the last time you heard her voice?"

Iris peers into Carson's eyes. "Her dad called you, didn't he. He's freaked out and he wants her to come home. You're gonna take her away."

There's no point to lying; Iris won't believe it anyway. Carson doesn't have to confirm it, though. "Right now, my problem is, is Vicki still alive? Is she?"

"Oh, ick. Don't even *say* that!" Iris's face collapses. "I don't wanna be in a world that'd kill her. We need more people like her. She's beautiful and she's smart and she's so nice and she put all this together"—she sweeps a hand around the estate—"so we can do all the good things we've done. She can't die. She can't…"

"So call her. It's the only way we'll know for sure."

Iris snuffles and wipes her nose with the back of her hand. Then she taps her phone screen. After a wait, she says, "Vicki, it's me. Hey, um, call me back, okay, hon? We're real worried about you after the other night. I'm scared for you. Please call. I wanna hear your voice. Please. Um." Iris stares at her phone screen for a moment, then hugs herself. "Voicemail."

"Yeah." In the past two minutes, Carson's gone from being mad at Iris to feeling sorry for her. "Does she know you're in love with her?"

"Yes." All the air's gone out of Iris. She flicks a semi-guilty glance at Carson. "God, I wish she was gay. I'd marry her in a hot minute. If she'd have me. She probably wouldn't."

"Why not?"

She snorts. "I'm the tall, skinny, funny-looking one who can't shut up. She can do way better."

No no no. Crying's next. Can't deal with crying. "I don't know. I think you're pretty. Way prettier than me. And…gotta be powerful stuff, having somebody who absolutely adores you. Never had that."

Sniff. "Knock it off. You'll make me cry." Iris knuckles away a tear. "You heard from her dad."

"Yeah. Look, Iris. She's going home."

"Moscow's not her home."

"I know that, you know that, she knows that. Her dad probably knows that. Doesn't matter. I'm in damage-control mode now. She can either come with me and I'll make it as easy on her as I can, or the guy who sent me will send people who don't give a damn about her. Which do you want for her?"

"Well, if she's gotta go…it might as well be with a friend." Her face scrunches. "Ick. I hate even *saying* that."

"Not my favorite either. Keep this quiet, okay? Tamara's already pissed at me for something. Don't need everybody else looking to shank me in the shower."

"We'll see." Iris starts to drift away, then stops to look back. "By the way, Tamara's mad at you because she and Sebastian used to be a thing after he broke up with Vicki. Don't follow her into a dark alley or anything." She waves over her shoulder as she paces to the patio.

Now she tells me.

Chapter 41

Carson swoops off the Ronda Litoral highway, plunging into the fringes of a light-industrial area west of central Barcelona. Iris's black BMW, about fifty meters ahead of her, turns right.

So does the silver Volkswagen Jetta that's been following her since she left the mansion after lunch, handing off now and then with a white Peugeot.

Carson hadn't expected to pick up a tail on Iris. It's a nice bonus. Carson's real goal is following Iris to see where she goes when she disappears.

Iris's unexplained absence on Sunday got Carson's feelers twitching. Iris hadn't left a note on the fridge saying where she was going or when she'd be back. Carson had a word with her that evening—lead by example and all that. Now Iris posts notes saying, "Going out, back soon." Rather than reading her out, Carson's been flogging the little blue Citroën AX for all it's worth, trying to keep up with Iris without getting caught.

Monday night, Carson followed her to La Rosa in Sant Gervasi, a residential area northwest of the city center. She staked out the BMW while she looked up the place: a bar that's considered an institution in Barcelona's lesbian community. Carson waited almost two hours until Iris left with a femme blonde in a white leather skirt and blood-red camisole top. They seemed to be enjoying each other. Carson gave Iris her privacy.

Iris turns left into a warehouse district. So does the Jetta. Carson closes up on the VW just enough to keep from losing them both in the tangle of short streets.

Tuesday morning, Carson followed Iris into the city's eastern fringes until Carson discovered she had a tail. She went automatically into a surveillance detection run and eventually shook the SEAT she thought was following her, but by that time she'd lost Iris as well. Did she have a tail? Was she being paranoid? She remembered Rogozhkin telling her about something he called Stearne's Law: *paranoia is the result of acute situational awareness.* Somebody really is out to get her.

Iris skates through a traffic circle and turns right onto Carrer del Cobalt, a narrow slot between two unbroken lines of warehouses. The ones to her left have seen their day, while the ones on the right are a bit less run-down. Carson lets the VW pull ahead—on a narrow cobbled street, it's ridiculously easy to spot an unwanted shadow.

When the VW swoops into a parking space ahead of a line of dumpsters to her right, Carson can see the BMW turning left into a driveway roughly fifty meters ahead. Carson pulls into the parking lot for a Saab/Opel/Hyundai service garage. Now she has a decision: go see what Iris is up to behind a warehouse, or take care of the guy in the VW?

Take out the threat first.

She checks the gear in her purse, then pulls down her polo's long sleeves, loops the strap across her chest, and leaves the Citroën. She's about fifteen meters from the VW and about thirty from the driveway. She walks normally toward the VW at an angle to the passenger's door so she'll be behind the driver's line-of-sight and out of the side-view mirror until she's too close for the driver to do anything about it. Already the adrenaline is making her heart race. Her eyes turn crystal-sharp, and her ears can pick up on the squirrels munching nuts in the trees above her.

Carson doesn't draw the Walther from her purse until one pace before she wrenches open the passenger's door and thuds into the seat. She has the muzzle screwed into the driver's ear before he can even turn his head. "Hands on the wheel. Now." He complies; he must understand English. "If you move a hand, even to scratch your ass, I paint the window with your brains. Understand?" He nods. "What do I call you?"

He has to work his mouth for a few moments. "Folco."

"Okay, Folco. Easy question. You with Grup Sabadey?"

"Yes."

"Spell it."

Folco's eyes try to swivel far enough to get a good look at her. They don't succeed. "S-A-B-A-D-E-L-L." He uses the usual

European pronunciation, "ah" for "A" and so on.

Never would've guessed. "Why are you following the BMW?"

He takes some time to work up more spit. "I am told to."

"Why?"

"Ehm… Håkan says to do." It sounds like *Hecken.*

"That your boss?"

"Yes."

Less than two minutes in, and she's already way smarter than she had been. She's probably also gotten everything out of Folco that she can. She plucks the phone from the cupholder near her hip. "Left hand. Unlock it. Show me."

Folco carefully moves his left hand under his right arm, then slowly presses 3-7-1-9 on the screen. A photo of a motorcycle appears under a welter of icons.

Carson drops the phone in her purse, then pulls out two zip ties. "Got no beef with you, Folco. You're just doing your job. Here's how this goes. Gonna tie your wrists to the wheel. You're gonna let me. Fight me, I'll kill you. Understand?"

Folco nods slowly.

"Wanna live?"

He nods again.

Smart man. She quickly zip-ties his wrists to the ten-and-two position on the steering wheel, then retrieves the pistol from her lap. "On my way out, I'm gonna slash your back tires. Just in case." She pops open the door.

"Wait. Hit me on head."

She doesn't even have to ask why. "You saw a woman but didn't think about it. Surprised you before you could do anything. Right?"

"Yes. I have girl. She has baby."

"Got it. Gonna hurt." She drops the magazine, jacks the round in the chamber into her palm, then grabs the frame and whacks the back of Folco's head with the pistol butt. His eyes go unfocused as he pitches forward. His forehead bounces off the wheel.

Carson gets to the open gate at the warehouse's driveway in time to see a beefy guy in gray overalls wheel a dolly to the BMW's open trunk. Iris stands by the back fender, talking to a guy in an untucked polo and jeans. At least she left her farmcore-meets-slutty-Mary Ann costume at home; her jeans-and-tank-top outfit is the most covered Carson's ever seen her.

Overalls hefts a large cardboard carton off the dolly into the trunk, then opens it. Iris looks in, nods. She hands Polo Shirt a thick manila envelope. Polo Shirt peeks inside, nods, then walks away. When Iris climbs into the BMW, Carson trots to Folco's VW and jams the largest blade on her Leatherman into the sidewalls of both rear tires. She's in the Citroën by the time the BMW backs onto the street.

What's in the box? Carson keeps gnawing on that thought as she follows Iris up a major street lined with modern offices and apartments. Her GPS says Iris is heading toward the city center. The modern buildings turn into older buildings, then turn into a maze of little one-way streets hemmed in by five- and six-story buildings needing paint. Laundry hangs from balconies. The ground-floor shops that still exist cater to people who aren't tourists and probably aren't natives. The walkers move like they're in a hurry to get where they're going.

Iris has slowed way down, forcing Carson to drop back. Iris turns right. By the time Carson reaches that point, the BMW's parked halfway down a street so narrow, Iris could block it entirely by opening both front doors. Carson can't stop, though; she'd be way too obvious. She has to drive another three short blocks until she reaches a side street by a church, where she creates a parking space out of thin air and a possible violation of the laws of physics. By the time she charges back to the street where Iris turned, all she can see is a glimpse of Iris's jeans cuffs disappearing into a doorway to the BMW's driver side.

Car's still there. She can't be long.

Carson ducks behind a couple of small dumpsters on wheels to keep a watch on the BMW. There's so little visible sky that the glorified alleyway is draped in its very own dusk. Graffiti crusts every roll-up shop door that isn't open, which is most of them. It's not the interesting-pretty-cool kind of graffiti, either.

The fuck is Iris doing here?

What's in that box?

What starts in a warehouse and goes to a slum? Carson knows a few answers to that one. Drugs. Weapons. Bootleg DVDs. Cigarettes with no tax stamps. Endangered animal parts. Maybe that box was full of tiger pricks or pangolin skins. Probably not, though. *If we'd stopped in Chinatown, maybe...*

Carson looks up "Grupo Sabadell" on her phone. Most hits are about a big international Spanish bank. She doesn't recall seeing it on Dareh's list of companies Project Karma hacked, so that's probably not it. The bank's named for Sabadell (pronounced *sabadey* in Catalan—*aha*), an industrial city north of Barcelona. After scrolling through umpteen pages of search results, she finds something: an English-language article in *El País*, a Madrid newspaper, about drug trafficking along the Spanish Mediterranean coast. It was written a year ago about the scrum of drug gangs in the places she'd been in the past couple of weeks. Halfway through, this line jumps out at her:

```
    Long a province of foreign
 mafias and smugglers, the Costa
 del Sol is now seeing the entry of
 indigenous Spanish trafficking
 groups such as Grupo Sabadell, a
 Catalan gang that has been
 ruthlessly consolidating its grip
 on the party destinations visited
 by hundreds of thousands of
 holiday-makers every year...
```

She finds a scattering of other stories like this from different outlets, including *Deutsche Welle* and the British tabloid *The Sun*.

Drugs again. Is that what's in the box?

Is Iris dealing? Is Vicki? Carson still doesn't know why Vicki was in Algeciras two weeks ago. Maybe she was picking up a shipment? Maybe she's there now? Then she ships it to Iris. Iris does what with it?

What would Vicki and Iris sell? She recalls Sebastian talking about "walking with Molly." From what Carson saw in the clubs, ecstasy is like Pez or breath mints. Carson can't see any of Vicki's posse pushing serious drugs, like coke or heroin, but E, she can believe.

So why is Iris here? Maybe to repackage the product. The standard wholesale package for ecstasy is a boat, or a thousand pills, but no street pusher could hide that. The box that Overalls loaded into the BMW could hold tens of thousands of pills. Breaking down the boats into bags of ten or a hundred makes them more portable.

Then like waking up, Carson sees the entire setup clearly. It explains why Vicki's gone so much, why Iris goes on these unexplained outings, why she was so chummy with the dealer at Leviathan, why she paid the warehouse guys cash, why the group spent so much time at clubs in Ibiza and Marbella.

And why a drug gang would be gunning for them. *Another* drug gang.

But why? Vicki's crew made over three million euros off their hacking scheme over the past two years. Yes, VIP tables in Marbella clubs cost a mint, but really?

A boat of E goes for between two and three thousand euros wholesale in Spain. But retail, those same thousand tablets are worth between eight and ten grand. A minimum five grand a boat gross profit. That box could be worth half a million euros or more to the group. Multiply that by how many a year? In a market that can absorb probably tens of thousands of pills a night?

Holy. Fuck.

No wonder Vicki's friends can afford to blow off their inheritances.

Carson's totally over solitaire and news apps by the time Iris reappears. She's carrying the kind of box that receivers or desktop PCs come in. The BMW's trunk lid pops open before she reaches it; the wonders of remotes. A scruffy, overweight guy with more hair than he needs follows her with another, similar carton. They duck through the door, then bring out another two boxes. Iris shakes hands with the scruffy guy, then he disappears.

Carson's had two hours to stew about her theory and work herself into a rage over the betrayal. She marches down the street fast enough to close in on the BMW quickly, but not so fast that she can't control the noise she makes. She reaches the car in time to grab Iris's ponytail before Iris can sit in the driver's seat. Iris, off-balance, squawks and nearly falls against Carson, who pushes her face-first against the BMW's side.

"L-Lisa?"

Iris tries to turn around, but Carson pins her with one hand while she quickly pats Iris down with the other. No weapons, which is a bad choice for someone hauling big stashes of drugs. Of course, she could have something in her purse inside the car. Carson spins Iris around and flattens her against the back door.

"Um, this is kinda hot, but—"

"What's in the boxes?"

Iris's eyes have turned completely round. Her trembling vibrates through the palm Carson has pressed to her sternum. "What are you talking—"

Carson stabs a finger toward the trunk. "The four boxes you and the slob loaded in the trunk. Yeah, I was watching."

"That? That's some stuff I had to get—"

"Stuff? You mean drugs? You got ecstasy in there? How many—"

"What? Drugs? How can you—"

"—boats you got in there? Fifty? A hundred? All ready for distribution now?"

"Why are you so mad? I don't know where you're—"

"I saw the exchange at the warehouse." Carson leans closer, filling Iris's field of vision. The more Iris dances, the angrier Carson gets. "'Stuff' you get from Amazon. They bring it to you. 'Drugs' you buy with an envelope full of cash from some asshole in a shitty part of town."

"Stop! You're scaring me!" Iris's face is melting. Her eyes shimmer in tears waiting to break loose.

Carson carefully removes her hand from Iris's chest and steps back just far enough to let her stand on her own but still be reachable. "How often does Vicki send you shipments? Been trying to figure out how much you're making off this."

"Wait, what?" Iris shakes her head hard. "You think *Vicki's* selling drugs?"

"Are you? That Grupo Sabadell that's after you guys? Catalan drug gang. Guy who was on your tail to the warehouse? One of them. So was the asshole I took down last week. The hitters at the mansion last Saturday? Bet you any money these Sabadell pricks hired them. Which means *you*"—Carson spikes Iris's chest with a forefinger—"almost got me and your friends killed. That pisses me off."

Iris shakes hard enough to knock loose the tears. But her sobs quickly turn into anger. "You…you're *crazy!* You're totes *insane!* I wouldn't do that! Vicki wouldn't do that! Where'd all this come from? Yeah, we all take some Molly now and then, but *sell* it? That's what you think of us? Of me? I thought we were friends! How can you treat me like this? I—"

"Open the trunk." Carson's not hearing anything she didn't expect. It's the same rap street dealers would lay on her back in Toronto when she had them up against a wall.

"No." Iris wipes her eyes clear with her wrists. "You can't treat me like this. Leave me alone."

Carson storms to the open driver's door, grabs Iris's purse, and empties it on the seat. No weapons other than a nail file, but she pockets the phone. The key's on the floormat where Iris dropped it. Carson opens the trunk with the remote and slashes the tape sealing the nearest box.

A black metal plate with vent louvers on top nestles in a cradle of Styrofoam peanuts.

The other three boxes are similar. The metal plates are the same width, but a couple aren't as deep. What little Carson can see of the fronts or backs reveals LEDs and sockets for plugs.

Carson straightens and stares at the open cartons. Her brain's run head-on into a virtual brick wall. It takes a long time to scrape together enough thoughts to say, "What the fuck, Iris? What is this?"

Iris is still leaning against the car, hugging herself. She hasn't wiped the smeared mascara off her cheeks yet. She keeps her eyes locked on the wall in front of her. "It's network security stuff Karl and Dareh asked me to get." Her voice is low and flat. "I guess normal people aren't supposed to have it. Karl called it 'military grade,' whatever that means. They found it on the dark web. I didn't think the 'dark web' was really a thing, but I guess it is. I brought it here so that guy you saw could put more stuff in it. Boards or something, makes it more better. It'll make us safer from the hackers. Other people's hackers." She finally glares at Carson. "You had it all figured out." Now the pain leaks into her voice. "You wouldn't let me explain or defend myself. You attacked me. You *hurt* me. And you were *wrong.*"

Carson can't look into Iris's eyes. There's too much pain in them. She stares again at the boxes. *But it fit. Everything fit. It all made sense. How did I fuck it up?* She stands there for seconds that last hours. Then she slams shut the trunk and stalks to Iris, holding up the phone. "Send me Vicki's number. The one that still works."

Iris gives her kicked-puppy eyes. "Will you beat me up if I don't?"

"No. I'll keep your phone and figure out how to get into it myself. Then I'll own you. All your texts, all your email, your voicemail, your contacts, your photos. Want that?"

Iris's lower lip quivers. She reaches out to punch in her passcode, then stab out a text. Carson's phone chirps in her purse. She checks the text—it looks legit enough—then hands Iris the phone and marches toward the end of the street.

"Am I free to go, officer?" Iris's words drip sarcasm and hurt.

Carson stops but doesn't turn around. She doesn't dare. "You had a tail from, like, five minutes after you left the house. Pay attention." She hurries off as her humiliation chars the skin on her cheeks.

Chapter 42

I am such an asshole.

It becomes a mantra. *Iamsuchanasshole. Iamsuchanasshole.* Carson can barely see past her anger and disgust at her own behavior. After a couple of close calls on the eastbound Ronda Litoral, she pulls into a giant Repsol gas station so she can park and try to reboot her brain by banging her forehead on the steering wheel.

The story fit. No holes, no ragged edges. She'd accounted for every single bit of weirdness she'd seen since she landed at Málaga.

Right idea, wrong day?

Trying to tie together a bunch of random shit that's not related?

She bolts out of the Citroën and paces in tight circles to blow off steam. Eventually she can breathe normally and think more-or-less straight, which doesn't help her mood.

Carson forwards Iris's text to Olivia. `Can u locate this # for me pls pls?`

`More black magic?`

`Yeah. Pls? Ill luv u 4ever.`

`I thought you already do.`

She uses the gas station's surprisingly clean washroom and buys a Pepsi Lite. Then she can't stall anymore.

I fucked up. Time to face it.

The thirty-nine klicks from the gas station to the mansion take an hour and a quarter in the Friday rush-hour traffic.

Carson makes it to her bedroom without anyone seeing her and flops on the bed. She glimpsed Iris and Sebastian in the pavilion overlooking the road, their heads together. *How many people has she told? Will they throw me out?*

Should I leave before they do?

Carson tried to think during the drive about how to salvage the situation. Nothing workable came to her. She'd let her temper get control over her—again—and went off on not only the group leader-in-residence but her direct link to Vicki.

Has she told Vicki?

That would be a disaster. She'd hoped to get Iris to talk Vicki into turning herself in. So much for that.

She's burned her bridges here. The smart move would be to leave, wait for Olivia to locate Vicki's phone, then grab Vicki and finish this mess.

But the threat's still out there. They're still watching. Sometime soon, they'll make their next move. Is she ready to leave the people she cares about—Sebastian, Celeste, even Iris when it comes down to it—vulnerable to whatever Grupo Sabadell has planned?

Will the posse even let her protect them anymore?

Clean break. Go get Vicki. Do your job.

She fights with that until she feels eyes on her. Sebastian's leaning against the doorjamb, hands in his shorts pockets, watching her. She can't read his expression. She grumps, "If you're here to beat me up, get in line. Still doing that myself."

Sebastian nods. "You made a right bags of things, that's sure."

"If that means I fucked up, yeah." Carson sits up and wraps her arms around her knees. "How is she?"

"She's all in bits. You scared the bejesus out of her."

"Now you sound Irish. Guess she's told everybody about it."

"No, she's not. Only me."

Really? "Why not?"

"She's still sorting that." He pushes off the doorframe and slips into the armchair by the window. "She says she thought about what she'd done and understands that it'd look like a drug deal to anyone else. She wishes you'd asked instead of attacking her. Given her a chance to explain."

"I should've. I was pissed. Thought she was the reason the hit team came after us." Carson rests her forehead on her knees. "Is there any fixing this?"

"I don't know. I asked, and she doesn't know, either. The poor

lass cried all the way here. Her eyes are the same color as her hair."
He sighs. "She says you got the word from Vicki's da."

"Yeah." *Who else has she told?*

"What will you do?"

"I should go find Vicki and disappear. Let you guys get back to normal."

"I hope you won't do that."

"Yeah. You'll miss Vicki—"

"I'll miss *you.*"

When's the last time somebody said that to me? They've been a couple for a week and a half. That's the longest she's slept with the same man since she divorced Ron. *It's nice—a familiar face, a familiar body, somebody who seems to actually like me.* "You still want me around after this?"

"I do, but you've fences to mend. Not only with Iris."

"You mean Tamara?" He nods. "I'll own the mess with Iris, but Tamara's gotta work out her own issues. Why aren't you still with her?"

Sebastian gives her a grim smile as he stands. "That's a story I'm not after telling. You decide what you want to do. I'll go back to Iris—she needs an absorbent shoulder just now."

"Tell her I'm sorry."

"Tell her your own self. I'll tell her you asked after her." He drifts out the door, stops to look over his shoulder at her, then walks off.

The tone of his voice, the set of his mouth… *I broke something there. Sebastian's known Iris and Vicki way longer than he's known me. He's loyal to them, not me.*

You fucked up everything. Leave. Do your job.

You leave and something happens to these people, you'll blame yourself.

Stay and something happens, you'll blame yourself. Lose-lose. Ever since you got here, bad shit's been happening to them.

Carson finally slides off the bed. Her duffel's on the low dresser. It'll take her maybe ten minutes to pack. She can call for a BlaBlaCar to take her to the Enterprise Rent-a-Car office in Mataró.

Fucking coward.

My job isn't being a babysitter. It's getting Vicki's ass on a plane.

Carson's hands gather and pack her stuff automatically. It's like she's watching from the ceiling. Her duffel and suitcase fill as if by magic.

What about Celeste? You gonna ghost her? You're her hero. You'll break her heart.

Shit. The inner voice finally found something she'll listen to.

Carson sleepwalks to the bedroom at the end of the walkway. The lights are on to hold off the gathering dusk.

Celeste's sitting cross-legged on her bed, poking at a laptop. He head jerks up when Carson raps on the door. She leaps to open the door. "Lisa! Hello. Come, please." She grabs Carson's hand and pulls her inside. "I have the gift for you. For your birthday."

God, no. Don't make it harder. "My birthday's almost a month ago."

"But I do not know you then. I do now." She pulls something from the laptop case on her dresser and bounces back to Carson. "This is for you."

It's a powder-blue thumb drive. "What's on it?"

Celeste grins. "It is all my music. You like my music, and with this you can listen when you want. I make one for Amabelle, too, before she went away."

Carson takes the thumb drive, then hugs Celeste as hard as she dares. "That's so sweet. Thank you! That's the best gift ever."

"I am happy that you like it."

They hold onto each other for some while before Carson holds Celeste at arm's length. Carson had been trying to turn her insides into rock so she can do this, but it's all melting into a puddle. "I, um…came to say goodbye."

Celeste's face collapses. "No! You can…no…no, you cannot leave! You…"

Get it out now while you still can. "I hurt Iris today. Not physically, but I scared her, upset her. And it was wrong. *I* was wrong. And…well, ever since I met you and your friends, bad things keep happening to you. Don't want any of you to get hurt. Also, I think Vicki's staying away because of me. So I…I need to leave. For everybody's sake."

Celeste's shaking her head so fast that her hair whips around like it's trying to escape. "No! We need you. We all need you. We all feel safer because you are here. If you go, who will protect us?"

This isn't what Carson wanted to hear. It's hard enough to leave without having to deal with being everybody's last hope. "Dareh can. He's had training—"

"No. You. When the bad men come to us in Ibiza, you saved us. Everyone is scared. Everyone knows that Iris cannot keep the bad men away. You can say to Iris that you are sorry and make it better. You—"

"I broke our relationship. Can't put it together again. You guys don't need to live with that kind—"

"No! You have to stay." She throws her arms around Carson and buries her face in Carson's shoulder. "If you cannot stay for Vicki or for Iris, can you stay for me? For my friends?"

Carson doesn't dare try to say anything. Her voice will splinter. She rocks Celeste and murmurs calming sounds and tries to not break this special, fragile girl.

Eventually, Celeste pulls away and palms tears out of her eyes. She grabs Carson's hand with both of hers. "Come."

"Where?"

"I will take you to Iris and I will help you say that you are sorry."

Carson's heart plummets into her stomach. "That's not gonna be nearly enough."

"Come!" Celeste shows the same determination as when she kicked Sebastian out of Carson's room after the stabbing at Leviathan.

Carson follows her down the stairs and across the lawn to the pavilion where Iris still leans her head on Sebastian's shoulder. They both sit up, puzzled.

Celeste says, "Iris? Lisa wants to say that she is sorry."

Sebastian gives Iris a shoulder-hug, swaps a shaded glance with Carson, then melts out of the picture.

Celeste holds out her free hand until Iris takes it. She forces Iris's and Carson's hands together until they clasp. Then she turns to Carson. "You start."

Chapter 43

BARCELONA INTERNATIONAL AIRPORT

Grebnev leans back against the Range Rover's left front fender as he watches the Dassault Falcon taxi onto the hardstand behind the Corporate Terminal. Even this late in the high season, executive jets from around the world crowd the large parking area. The Zapadneft jet—its broad red and blue stripes running the length of its white flanks, combining into a Russian flag on the vertical stabilizer—is on Tiedown 03, as far from the terminal as possible.

Once the ground crew chocks the wheels, Grebnev climbs into the black SUV and drives it to the aircraft's tail, trailed by two more Range Rovers. The front airstair is already open. He trots to the tail and shoos the terminal's baggage handlers away from the rear cargo compartment. They don't need to see what's in there.

Six men lounge in the cabin's plush seats. The litter of coffee cups, beer bottles, and snack wrappers confirm there's no cabin crew on this flight. A craggy, barrel-chested man in the swivel lounger nearest the door peers at him with eyes that look like marbles. "Grebnev?" he growls.

"Yes." Grebnev shakes the man's hand and gets his nearly crushed for his trouble. "You're Karik?"

"Yes." He rolls out of his seat. Karik is at least ten centimeters taller than Grebnev, who's taller than normal for a Russian man. "How soon before we're in action?"

"Hard to tell, as things stand now. Assume you have forty-eight hours to settle in and rest. After that, we may need you on short notice."

"Good." Karik waves behind him at the other hard-looking men stretching out of their seats. "The sooner we're working, the less trouble they'll get into." He bares his teeth in what he probably thinks is a smile. "Where's our bivouac?"

"We bought out the fourth floor of a hotel near the likely target. The housekeeping's lax, to be kind, but you'll have your privacy. The water's clean and the bugs are smaller than your feet."

Karik laughs. "That's better than the last five places we've been. As long as there's restaurants and whores…"

"Restaurants in both directions. As for whores, it's high season still, so there's more than enough amateurs to go around. Let's get you unloaded."

They file out of the plane and join in emptying the cargo bay. One large, black duffel or gear bag after another disappears into the SUVs. A few black road cases are waiting near the tailgates.

Grebnev stands by Karik, his arms folded, watching the well-practiced relay line shift the baggage. "I haven't worked with your organization before. What's the chain of command?"

"I'm section lead. You want something, you tell me. You're the client. We do what you ask unless it's stupid or it'll get my men killed for no reason. You tell me what you want done and I plan how to do it. We're paid by the day no matter what we're doing. Every day under hostile fire is a flat-rate bonus." Karik lights a cigarette, then offers the pack to Grebnev, who shakes his head. "Did you serve?"

"Seven years in the airborne. You?"

"Spetsnaz." Karik's wearing nondescript jeans and a black Under Armour tee shirt, but Grebnev has no trouble seeing the man in his camo and blue beret. Even the haircut and reflector sunglasses are the same.

Grebnev says, "The targets are civilians."

Karik snorts. "Aren't they always?"

Chapter 44

PORT FÒRUM, BARCELONA

Ferran does what he can to stifle his irritation. "This isn't a penis-size contest, Håkan. It's supposed to be business. And right now, it's bad business."

Kallström grimaces into his glass of beer. "I never say it is."

Someday, he'll learn proper Spanish. Ferran wipes down *Campió's* sparkling glass bar top, then takes a big slug of his Tom Collins. He needs the anesthetic to get through this. "Brusin's little chore has cost us a lot of time, effort, and distraction. That disaster with the contractors will cost us money and reputation. Two of our regular contractors told me yesterday they'll raise our rates by twenty percent."

"Pussies. There are more."

"Like those last two? No, thank you. It's time to tell Brusin to get stuffed and take our business elsewhere. I'm told the Nigerians are good—"

"Fucking *Nigerians?*" Kallström palms the spill off his chin and wipes it on his muscle tee. "Not trust *svartings.* They steal. We learn this. Their rates start small, then things happen. Costs more money."

"This group comes highly recommended. My point is, we're not tied to Brusin for getting our money cleaned. I'm ready to fire him so we can move on."

Kallström slaps the bar top. "No! Sonia makes us fools. We stop, we lose reputation. Now is time to hit again. Hit hard. Before the Russian woman makes them too hard. Brusin is Tambov, yes? Tambov and Solntsevo, they enemy, yes? Why Tambov does not attack this Solntsevo bitch?"

Ferran takes another swig of his drink and comes up with ice cubes. *Did I drink that already?* He builds a replacement. "Brusin says the Tambovs' leader put the Tarasenko woman off limits.

She's here on the Solntsevo *pakhan's* personal business. Professional courtesy, or something." He stabs a finger at Kallström. "That means, be careful what you do with her. You kill her, prepare for blowback. That's *another* reason I want this over with."

"We almost have Sonia's people done. They run away now. You want that stopping?"

"Yes." Ferran braces his hands on the counter and leans toward Kallström. "Our friends in the police tell me they're getting too much heat to solve these killings. Drop one more body in the middle of a tourist place and the police can't ignore it anymore. If you have to eliminate someone, take them *out there*"—he waves toward the Mediterranean—"and tie a concrete block to their feet. You've made your point to Sonia. Now stop."

"We are ready to hit back now. I should stop?"

"Ready to do what? All I see from you is failure. You have a plan that'll work?"

For the first time, Kallström looks away. "Almost."

"'Almost.' Of course. Look, tell Grebnev 'thank you' and break it off. I—"

"Listen!" Kallström pulls his phone and thumbs through some pictures. He shows the screen to Ferran. "This one."

Ferran recognizes the woman immediately. "What about her?"

Kallström stows his phone and punctuates his words with hand slices. "We take her. Get Sonia in open. Kill Sonia. Her group breaks. When hackers go alone, we kill them. Trouble over. Brusin and Moscow people are happy."

They should've used a sniper to eliminate Sonia on Ibiza. Maybe pick off the hackers, too. God knows they had enough opportunities. But killing them in their beds promised to be a much cleaner, quieter solution. Of course, it didn't work.

Ferran leans against the bar basin's rim, his arms folded, and sighs. *Goddamn Kallström. Always wants to force-fit everything. There's nothing he can't fix with a hammer. He's the old way of doing this business.*

Ferran had always wanted to go a new direction. He'd fought his way up and out of Sabadell's slums not with his fists or guns, but with his head. What did everyone want? Profits. He showed them a way to do that one street corner at a time. Put an end to those ridiculous turf wars that used up so much energy and talent.

Drug sales were one of Spain's biggest businesses—why not treat it like a business? Of course, sales organizations competing peacefully can be combined more easily; corporations do it all the time. The tactics are nearly the same. It's how he got here, on this yacht, in these clothes, with dozens of front-line employees and many more contractors.

He needs Kallström as the hard power to his own soft power. But he needs the Swede on a leash so he doesn't bite anyone he shouldn't. That's the problem with men like Kallström—they think they're uncontrollable. "When will you be ready to do this?"

Kallström breaks out that godawful smile of his. "We are ready now. We need only for her to leave the house."

"All right. Do it right, and quietly. Get those new GPS beacons on their cars so we don't have to keep tails on them. Be smart for once. No massacres, no public dead bodies. If you can't manage that, then this project is over and we concentrate on business. Do you understand?"

"I understand." Kallström drains half his glass in one go. "We end Sonia"—he claps his hands once, loudly—"then everything is business. As you like, yes? We make believe we are Nestlé and selling chocolates." He stands and leers at Ferran. "Until your next 'merger.' Yes?"

Chapter 45

OUTSIDE MATARÓ

After an agitated sleep next to Sebastian's back, Carson wakes to find a text Olivia sent after midnight: near Arboçar. It's a little village out in the boondocks west of Barcelona. What Vicki's doing there, Carson has no clue. She's feeling clueless about a lot of things.

Carson fixes herself an early breakfast, saddles up the Citroën, and drives the eighty-some klicks to Arboçar. Freeways in Spain work like freeways everywhere else, except here they randomly turn into toll roads. The route takes her along the north edge of the rolling hills between Barcelona and an inland suburban area. It's much more scenic and far less life-threatening than driving the 401 through central Toronto.

Then Olivia loses the phone's location. It may have switched off or lost power, she texts helpfully, like Carson hasn't thought of that already.

She goes to Arboçar anyway, hoping for a miracle. It's a village out in the middle of endless vineyards. The old part doesn't look all that old but has a cute stone church; the newer part is almost all houses, some surprisingly large. Vicki could be anywhere, in any of them. When she gets tired of waiting for Vicki to walk down the street, Carson tries calling her. "The number you have called cannot be located on this network…"

She should've expected Vicki would swap phones or SIMs as soon as Iris could tell her the old number wasn't safe anymore. Maybe Iris helped Vicki avoid her dad's goons, too. His other goons, that is.

Carson lounges in the car in front of a mini-mart two klicks from central Arboçar, sucking on a Pepsi Lite and waiting for Olivia to pull a miracle out of her bag. With nothing better to do, she checks her news alerts. The one for Marbella serves up info she could do without.

<blockquote>
A Leeds man was found brutally stabbed to death last night in the center of Plaza Antonio Banderas in Puerto Banús.

Policia Nacional report that the 24-year-old man, whose identity has not yet been released, was a fixture in Banús dance clubs and is suspected of selling drugs to holiday-makers.

The police spokesman would not speculate whether this is the latest in a series of drug-related stabbings in Marbella, Ibiza, and Palma...
</blockquote>

The sixth one in the past ten days. *Somebody's been busy.* Her cop gut tells her it's related. There's a drug war going down, and someone's getting his ass kicked.

After a hot and boring drive back the way she came, Carson turns across traffic into the main gate to the mansion. She's sour about wasting most of the day on the road and way past ready to get out of the damn car. It's been in the high twenties and humid, and the Citroën's air conditioning doesn't work worth a damn.

The mansion's quiet except for the tinkling of Celeste's keyboard from the dining room. Carson runs into Iris at the foot of the curving stairs to the bedrooms. "Hey."

"Hi." Iris is still a bit tentative from yesterday, but she's trying to mask it with a smile that doesn't go much past her lips. "Um, you wanna have a drink with me? It's past five in Athens."

She's playing nice. So should you. "Love to. Give me a couple minutes? I need to rinse off and change. I feel real grubby." Carson climbs the first step.

Iris grabs her hand. "It's okay. I don't mind. I thought it'd be nice to sit on the grass under the trees and maybe talk some?"

She's trying awful hard… "That sounds great. Gotta piss, too. Swear I'll be down in a couple minutes. Thanks."

The sheers are closed on all the bedroom windows, normal for this time of day to keep the afternoon sun from warming the rooms too much. Carson wonders about Iris's weird burst of friendliness as she pushes through the door to the bedroom she shares with Sebastian.

She stops.

Sebastian's on the bed, naked. His hands are cupped around Tamara's breasts. She's naked, too, on top and riding him hard, grunting and growling. Their clothes carpet the floor.

Carson's insides shrivel into a soggy lump someplace near her liver.

Sebastian notices her first. His eyes and mouth form matching *ohs*. Tamara takes a few moments to catch on. She eventually looks over her shoulder toward the door. She doesn't even slow down. The bitch *grins* at Carson.

Kill her.

Take the Walther out of your bag and blow her fucking head off.

Carson even reaches into her shoulder bag but stops. *That's too fast. Do it slow. Strangulation. Evisceration, maybe.*

Then her rational thought centers kick in. *You'd have to kill him, too, just to be fair.*

Your point is…?

Tamara's almost stopped pumping. Her grin's melting like frost on a warm car hood. *Is that fear? She's afraid? Good.*

Sebastian croaks, "Lisa?"

"Shut. The fuck. Up." The control she has to put into not shrieking at him burns energy like running a 10k. "You got nothing to say that I want to hear." Carson pins Tamara's ears back with her eyes. "Don't stop because of me, bitch. Won't be a minute."

Her bags are still almost completely packed from last night. All she has to do is shove her laptop, bathroom stuff, and this morning's gym clothes and swimsuit into her duffel. Doing that keeps her from exploding. She's got to avoid a screaming fight now. She's not ready. She tries to ignore the rustling sheets and urgent whispering behind her.

It's not until she slings her duffel and turns around, catching Tamara pulling on her underwear, that she loses it. "The fuck are *you* going? You bought this room! Fucking stay in it!"

Sebastian, now sitting up, holds up a stop-sign hand. "Lisa, I can ex—"

"No, you fucking *can't* explain! I already get it. She's younger and prettier and more flexible and doesn't have as many scars. Should've seen this coming. Shame on me." She stalks toward the bed. Tamara yelps and tries to get out of the way, but the panties around her knees hobble her. "I put up with this shit from my husband. When I left him, I swore I wouldn't do that anymore." Sebastian flinches when she flings a loaded finger his direction. "I was happy to fuck you. But you can't fuck me like this."

Carson rounds on Tamara. "You. Listen to me. Don't you fucking turn away from me. Gonna tell you two things. One. He knows what it's like to fuck a woman who's got fifteen years' more experience than you do. Good luck catching up. Two. What he just did to me? He'll do to you, too. Enjoy it while you can."

Carson doesn't slam the door on her way out. She wants to, though. Hard enough to shatter all the windows.

Iris is still at the base of the stairs, memorizing the flagstones. Carson pauses next to her to say, "Going to the caretaker's house. Come over in a few minutes. Bring the bottle."

Carson's got the dust covers off the bed and the simple wood dining table by the time Iris calls out "Knock, knock" at the open front door.

"Come in."

Iris edges into the tiny living room. "I brought you a present." She brings out an unopened bottle of Glenfiddich 21 single-malt whisky from behind her back.

Carson feels herself unclench a little. "Let me rinse out a couple of glasses."

While Carson rinses, Iris pokes around. It doesn't take long. "I love what you've done with the place."

"Anybody live here?"

"Not that I've seen." She strips the seal off the bottle, works the stopper out, and pours two fingers for herself and four for Carson. They clink glasses. "To…what are we drinking to?"

"Five o'clock in Athens." Carson tips back the better part of two fingers of whisky in one slug. The burn down her throat momentarily takes her mind off the burn in her heart. "Good choice. Knew there's a reason I like you." They sit on opposite sides of the table. "You knew."

"Yeah."

"Could've warned me."

"You know, I was thinking about that. It always came out like"—her voice turns perky—"'Hi, Lisa, have a nice trip? Oh, by the way, Sebastian and Tamara are fucking upstairs. I'm sure they'll be down soon.'"

"Good point."

"You're taking this awfully well." Iris is back to her careful voice.

"No, I'm not. Just not showing it." The whisky hasn't put out the hot pit of anger burning in Carson's bowels.

"When this happens to me, I cry for, like, three days." Iris watches Carson warily. "It's okay to do that, you know. Cry."

Carson snorts. "Right. Crying wasn't one of my options growing up."

"That's so sad. So…what *are* you gonna do?"

"Don't know. Avoid killing Tamara, I guess. Unless you want me to."

"That's okay. Thanks for the offer."

Carson's glass is empty too soon. It's a sin to bolt good whisky like this. She pours another two fingers and forces herself to sip rather than chug. "This is a good time for me to go…but Vicki's dropped off the net again."

"I know. I tried to call her at lunchtime and got the 'no such person' thing." Iris's face scrunches. "It's kinda weird. She usually tells me when she's swapping phones."

"Is she running?"

"I don't think so. I don't know." Iris pauses to empty her glass. "Something's wrong. She's never away this long. It's been almost a week. I can't believe she's really *gone* gone, though. We're her family. We love her, and she loves us. I just can't stand the thought of her out there all alone."

"Maybe she's not. Maybe she's got friends you don't know about."

"Maybe." Iris's sad eyes and drooping head tell Carson that the idea depresses Iris more than Vicki simply being alone.

They chat for a spell, but they're not into it for their separate reasons. The bottle's half-empty by the time Iris pushes away from the table, hugs Carson gingerly, then disappears into the early evening.

A text from Rogozhkin is waiting for Carson when she checks her phone. `Vlasenkos mistress spends all day sunbathing nude by the pool. Wish you were here instead.` ☺

Carson slumps in her chair. Rogozhkin—*Edik, his first name is Edik*—is trying so hard. *When's the last time a guy chased me? Sebastian didn't; I stood right in front of him and waited for him to crash into me.* Then again, Sebastian's probably used to having women throw themselves at him…like she did. Edik, not so much. He's more mature. He knows how badly paved the road of life is. He's had to work for what he's got and probably appreciates it more. *Maybe he'll appreciate me more. I should call him or text him. Not the way I feel now, though. Edik deserves better than that.*

She changes into her gym clothes, tapes her hands, then marches to the gym. She throws an experimental punch at the heavy bag. Then another. A kick.

Carson beats the shit out of the heavy bag. Fists, feet, elbows, knees. She hits and hits and hits until her knuckles bleed and her joints seize up and she can hardly catch her breath. She hits until the rest of her body feels the pain her heart does. Then she hits some more until she's on her screaming elbows and knees, pressing her forehead against her forearms, struggling to breathe. She stays that way until the night takes over the gym and the sky.

Chapter 46

MATARÓ

Carson goes to see Celeste in the dining room after lunch on the patio. Her hands and feet still ache from pummeling the heavy bag last night and she's looking forward to letting Celeste's music wrap her brain in a blanket of serenity. She finds Celeste slumped on the floor, cradling some kind of piano pedal in her lap. Carson asks, "Are you okay?"

"Oh!" Celeste sits straight. "Yes. I am okay. But my sustain pedal does not work." She holds up a black housing with a silver lever sticking out the front, like Carson can see the problem.

"What does that do?"

"It is hard to explain in English. It, ehm…it makes the notes sound longer. I cannot make my music without it. It is not right." Celeste sounds like she's lost a favorite pet. She carefully sets the dead pedal on the floor and looks up at Carson. "You are sad, too."

No point denying it. "Yeah. Different reason, though. Can you fix your pedal?"

"No." Celeste thinks for a few moments, then brightens a little. "There is a place in Mataró where I can buy a new one. Can you take me to it?"

Can she? Carson has been making herself even more unpopular since Monday by discouraging nonessential travel. This fits any rational definition of "nonessential." But Celeste without her music will become a crisis for the whole group after a day or two. It's full daylight, nobody's seen a tail or surveillance for a while, and Mataró's less than a klick away. How much of a risk can it be?

"Come on," Carson says. "Let's get you a new pedal."

Auvisa is in the end of a warehouse surrounded by other

concrete tilt-ups in western Mataró. The two-level shop is stuffed with electronic instruments. Carson can't remember the last time she saw so many electric guitars in one place.

Celeste is like a kid in a pet store at Christmas. Watching her beaming ear-to-ear as she zig-zags from one display to the next makes Carson smile. She needs to smile. She needs to laugh. She needs to *feel* something other than yesterday's anger and disgust. She needs to see something other than Tamara grinning at her as she humps Sebastian.

Did Celeste set this up? If she did, she's a genius.

They finally buy a new pedal and head back to the Citroën. Celeste practically bounces on the way. When Carson starts the car, Celeste grabs Carson's hand and asks, "Can we get gelato? There is a very good place in the center. It is very close. Please?"

Carson should say *no*. Being off the reservation makes them vulnerable. Then again, spontaneous changes to their plans make things hard on anyone tracking them. Still… One look in Celeste's pleading eyes turns Carson's better judgment into marshmallows. *You used to bend the sky to get Dom a giant pretzel.* She sighs. "Get us there."

They each get a cup of gelato at Gelateria Verdú, which is stuffed with dangerous-looking sweets of all kinds, and chow down on the block-and-a-half walk back to the parking garage. The sun is warm on Carson's face. Children yell and laugh behind the wall she and Celeste walk along. Celeste chatters happily next to her. It's a good day.

Back at the plaza over the parking garage, Celeste hugs Carson and nestles her head on Carson's shoulder. "You are happy now."

"Yeah." If somebody had told Carson three weeks ago that she'd spend part of a day holding the hand of a grown woman and hugging her in public, she'd have told them to piss off. But it's the most natural thing to do right now.

"You were very sad before."

"I was."

"You are not with Sebastian anymore?"

"No. He's got somebody else now."

Celeste pulls away. Her face is as serious as it ever gets. "I think Sebastian is very silly."

Carson can't help but smile. "So do I."

They're both almost done with their gelato by the time they reach the Citroën in the bowels of one of the cleaner parkades Carson's seen. There's no rate board at the entrance, so she can only imagine how much it's going to cost to get out of here.

She's digging in her shoulder bag for the keys when her brain explodes.

Agony.

She can't move. Her whole body spasms. She's face-down on the concrete, screaming.

Somewhere far away, Celeste shrieks in frantic French. Her voice cuts off. Wheels, doors, men's voices.

The pain stops as suddenly as it started. Carson tries to push herself up on her elbows, but she can only rock back and forth on her stomach.

A man's voice grating in her ear: "This is for Folco and Arnav, bitch."

The agony rips through her body again.

Chapter 47

"Those Sabadell assholes have Celeste."

Carson leans her head against the Citroën's driver's door. Her brain's splitting in half, the front of her blue polo's splattered with blood from her nose hitting the slab, and two spots on her back ache like someone punched her on a second-degree sunburn. She's also panting as if she sprinted here from the mansion. It was all she could do to haul herself into a slump against the car.

Iris—on the phone connection's other end—finally stops sputtering. "What does that *mean*? What happened?"

"Got jumped. Tased me twice. First time was so they could grab Celeste. She's gone. Don't know where."

"But…*gone*? Where are you?"

"Mataró. Celeste needed something for her keyboard."

"How do you know it wasn't her parents?"

"Second time they tased me was for taking down their drivers. The tails. Anybody call?"

Iris is starting to hyperventilate. "Call? What do you mean?"

"Ransom. Threats. Anything?"

"N-no. You sound awful! Are you hurt?"

"I'll live." *Won't enjoy it much.* "Listen. They didn't follow us. Never spotted a tail. But they knew where the car was. BMW there?"

"Yeah. Tamara got back from the market maybe half an hour ago. Why?"

Too bad they didn't grab her instead. "Have the guys go over it. Look for anything that doesn't belong. Anything that could be a GPS bug. They're usually underneath. Rip it out. Get everybody together. Nobody leaves the house. Got it?"

"Yeah, yeah, okay." Iris's voice gets more scared with every word. "Do you need help? I can come—"

"*Don't leave the house.* Tell Dareh to step up. He knows what that means. Iris?"

"Yeah?"

"Gonna call the cops. Need to turn up the heat. Can't let—"

"You can't do that!" Her squawk stabs straight through the parts of Carson's brain that are already coming apart. "You know that! We can't have the cops poking through our shit. We'll all get arrested—including you. Can't you handle this?"

"How? Can barely breathe. Holding the phone's hard. You ever been tased?"

"What? No."

"Try it sometime. Celeste's in danger. Minutes count. They could still be driving around somewhere. This is what cops are for."

"You can't call the cops! Come home. We'll wait for those Sabadell guys to call, then we'll do what they want. We have money. We'll get her back. Promise you won't get the police in this."

"I fucked up. Should've protected her. Can't—"

"They were electrocuting you! Don't blame yourself. Come home. And promise you won't call the cops until you get back here."

"But—"

"*Promise.*"

She shouldn't promise. But Iris has a point—the posse has almost as much to fear from the police as they do from Grupo Sabadell. "Okay. Not 'til I get back there. We'll talk then. Remember—nobody leaves the house. These assholes aren't done yet."

By the time she arrives at the mansion, Carson can breathe semi-normally, and the multiple points of acute pain have settled into a general whole-body ache. The headache's still beating on her skull.

Iris and Sebastian arrive at the cottage's front door while Carson's washing the blood off her face. Her shirt's draped over a ladder-back dining-room chair. Sebastian holds it up and goggles at the twin burn marks on the back. "The Taser did this, then?"

"Yeah." Carson grabs a towel and wipes off on her way to the front room. "That was almost new, too."

Iris shakes her head at the bloodstains on the front. "Do you go through a lot of shirts?"

"Yeah. Any calls?"

"Not from the bad guys. Vicki called around noon. She's local—"

Carson aims a finger between Iris's eyes. "And you haven't sent me her number yet?"

Iris sighs, then starts fiddling with her phone. "You could say 'please.'"

"I could. Let me get another shirt." Carson turns to go to the bedroom.

Iris blurts, "Whoa! Whoa whoa whoa. Have you *seen* your back?"

"Yeah."

Iris fingers the two burned spots. "Tasers do this?"

"The holes or the burns?"

"Yes."

"Both. Fifty thousand volts but low amperage. Fritzes out your neuromuscular system. Pain's a bonus."

Iris grimaces. "Okay. I'm gonna get some antiseptic and some aloe. You and Sebastian can fight if you want. Back in a jif."

Carson and Sebastian stare at each other after Iris scampers off. They're about two paces apart. That used to be enough to keep Carson's attention, but her lack of feeling now makes her sad. *Put on a shirt? Fuck it—remind him what he traded in.* She asks, "Find a GPS bug in the BMW?"

"Yes, we did. It was wired to the battery and tucked out of sight. What do you want to do with it?"

"Stick it in the nearest public garbage bin. Let these assholes follow it to the dump. Can you check the Citroën, too? It's probably in the same place."

"I will do when Iris comes back." His expression softens. "Are you alright? That must've been rough for you."

Now he's playing nice. Buyer's remorse? Hope so. "Ask me in twenty minutes or so when the naproxen kicks in. It's Celeste I'm worried about." She shakes her head. "We had such a nice time before this. Did you hear Iris talking to Vicki?"

"No, but she told me about it soon after, so I assume she did." Sebastian edges closer to Carson. "Lisa, I want to say I'm sorry for yester—"

She shoots up a hand. "Stop. What part are you sorry about—that you did it or that I saw it?" He looks down, frowning. "That's what I thought. You did it. Own it. Gonna put a shirt on. Check the Citroën before it gets dark."

Iris returns to start mother-henning Carson's back. She says, "I don't see any extra blood on the floor."

Carson holds up her shirt hem. "Sebastian's not dumb enough to try to explain away what he did. When you say Vicki's 'local,' what do you mean?"

"That's what she said. She didn't go into details, and I know better than to ask."

"So she could be in Greenland for all you know."

"Iceland's more her style. Greenland's too boring."

"Whatever. Still need to call the cops."

"And we still can't afford to. I know, cognitive dissonance or something, but, this shit don't change. So…how are you gonna find Celeste?"

Carson swivels to glare at Iris. "How am *I* gonna find her? *I'm* not. It's a big city out there, and I don't know the place or the players. The cops do"—Iris starts to say something but Carson waves her down—"and that's why we need them. We're talking Celeste's *life*. Anything you people are doing is fly shit compared to that."

"But…we can't just stand here and wait. This must be *horrible* for her!"

"Yeah. I'm sure it is. I hate that. But as long as she's alive, it can get worse for her if we fuck this up. Time to call in the pros."

Iris swings away and paces around the dining table, hugging herself. "Why'd they do this? What do they want?"

"Leverage. If all they wanted was to kill Celeste, they could've done it in the parkade and popped me, too. No, they want something from you guys. Celeste's a tool to pry it out of you. They're going to a lot of trouble to get it, so it must be important. And we're long past pretending this is all some big mistake." Carson pins Iris with her eyes.

Iris huffs and plants her fists on her hips. "Are we back to that again? You think I'm a drug dealer? Vicki's a drug dealer?"

"Are you?"

"That's crazy! Can you see me selling pills in a club? I'd suck at that!"

"They're going to too much trouble for a two-bit dealer. Are you a distributor? Is Vicki?"

"Really? You think Vicki's doing this?"

Nice sidestep. "Don't know her well enough to say. She's gone a lot for no good reason. She was in Algeciras a couple weeks—"

"How do you know that?"

"Never mind. What's she doing there? It's not a vacation spot." Iris's face starts closing down. There's no point pushing her harder…yet. "Okay, maybe not you or Vicki. What's Tamara do in her spare time, besides Sebastian?"

Iris laughs. "Tamara? For reals? She's too lazy to be a drug lord. It'll get worse now she's got a bed buddy. Amabelle hated drugs. She wouldn't even take aspirin for headaches."

"Sebastian?"

"It's not his style. He's a money guy. He's not El Chapo or whatevs—he'd be El Chapo's banker."

That's too close to what Carson was thinking a few nights ago. It makes perfect sense—someone's gotta dispose of the cash, and Sebastian's already running a laundering operation. He'd know who's handing the money to him even if he doesn't know how they get it.

Iris says, "I see that look. I didn't say he *is* El Chapo's banker, just that—"

Dareh appears in the front doorway, panting. He knocks on the open door. "Iris! Lisa! Someone leaves this on the front gate." He holds up a bundle in his left hand. It's a pale mint-green sack dress—the same kind Celeste wore into town today.

Someone finger-painted a message on the front: Sonia reunirse a las 22:00. *Sonia meet at 10 p.m.*

The rust-red lettering looks like dried blood.

Carson says, "Who the fuck is Sonia?"

Five scared, clueless faces stare at her. They're all gathered in the mansion's living room. All the lights are on. Dareh stands at the windows, peeking through the sheers into the dark, the Beretta tucked into the back waistband of his black jeans. *He's taking this seriously. Good.*

Carson already briefed everyone on the day's events. Simply talking about it stokes the fire in her core. Now she drills into each person's eyes in turn, looking for evasion. Everyone looks away. With a shake of her head, Carson stalks to Iris's phone on the coffee table. "Vicki, you first. Time to come clean."

Vicki's voice scratches out the phone. "I couldn't say. Obviously, no one here has that name."

"Think this is the time for that shit? Thought you cared about Celeste." Carson paces back to the fireplace. "One of you is playing 'I've Got a Secret.' You keep playing, Celeste is gonna die. Think about that. Then think about this: if Celeste gets killed, when I find out who Sonia is, I will *personally* put a bullet in her head. You know I can do that. Fess up now and we can work it out." She stops moving and surveys faces again. Dareh and Karl goggle at her. Tamara gazes at the starburst clock above the fireplace. Iris and Sebastian stare at each other. "Vicki?"

"I'm not Sonia." She clips off every word's edges.

"Okay. Assuming I believe you, that narrows it down. I doubt a guy would use a gal's name—it makes phone calls awkward. So it's either Iris or Tamara. I—"

Iris: "You're crazy! Why would I want to hurt Celeste?"

Tamara: "Oh, you'd love that, wouldn't you, you bit—"

"Shut up *now*." Both women cut off like their switches were flipped. "You wanna confess in private, I'm available after the meeting. Here's the big problem: what if we can't scrape up a Sonia by ten? Sabadell set up this whole act to get a face-to-face with her. Don't know if they want to talk to her, kill her, or sell her to some Saudi prince. But if we show up at the meet with no Sonia, even Tamara can figure out what happens to Celeste."

Tamara blurts, "Hey, wait a min—"

"Save it. Vicki, where are you?"

"I'm...close."

"Not close enough. You need to be here *now*. How long 'til you get here?"

"I...I can't simply leave. I have commit—"

"Vicki. We don't give a fuck about your commitments. They're at eleven on our top-ten priorities. One of your people—your *family*—is in mortal danger. Since we got her dress back, they're probably raping her right now. For all the rest of your family knows, you're pounding Champagne on somebody's yacht. Prove them wrong."

"You have no right to speak to me this way! I told you—"

Carson lunges to the coffee table and leans over the phone. "I'll talk to you this way until you earn something better. If you're the leader of this group—if you really care about them—your ass belongs in a chair in this room. No more stories, no more excuses. Call a BlaBlaCar and start becoming part of the solution instead of part of the problem."

"Lisa!" Iris's eyes are both big and round.

Vicki's huff travels all the way into the room. "Very well. The first thing we do is make certain the rest of the family is safe." Her voice is faster and harder than Carson's ever heard it. "You should leave as soon as possible for Cap d'Antibes. You may need to check into a hotel until I can arrange better accommodations. It's quiet, it's well-guarded, and—"

Carson growls, "What about Celeste?"

"—we have friends there who we can rely on. I'll meet you—"

Carson barks, "What about Celeste?"

"—once you tell me where you've gone. You'll be in France in less than an hour—"

Carson roars, "*What about Celeste?*"

Silence.

Sebastian says, "Vicki, she's right. We can't abandon Celeste. They'll do something awful to her. They may already have done. That looks like blood on her dress."

"Um, Vicki, hon?" Iris's voice wavers. "I'm totes down with getting out of Spain, but Celeste's pretty special to all of us, and…well, we gotta help her."

"Celeste is my friend." Dareh's stepped away from the window. It's the first thing he's said since the meeting began. "She is in trouble. I want to help her." He slaps Karl's shoulder.

Karl, startled, says, "Me, too. We can't throw her away."

After a few moments, Tamara realizes everyone's staring at her. "What? I think Vicki's right. Let's leave here and go someplace safe."

Sebastian says, "What do you propose we do about Celeste?"

Tamara snorts, then waves at Carson. "That's her problem. She lost Celeste, not us."

Carson shakes her head. "Remind me why I saved your worthless ass on Ibiza?"

The others stare at Tamara with a mixture of horror and disgust. Even Sebastian, which gives Carson the only good feeling she's had since Sabadell tased her.

Tamara whips her head around to see all the accusing eyes aimed at her. "What? It's true!" That doesn't win her any supporters. She strangles a scream as she pops out of her chair. "I'm packing!" She flounces out of the room.

Nobody says anything for a while. Sebastian's the object of a lot of side-eye glances. Iris finally breaks the silence. "Anyone think I should go get her?" No volunteers. "Sebastian?"

He hesitates, then shakes his head once.

Iris lofts her eyebrows at Carson, then sighs. "Vicki? It's five to two against. Um…why don't you stay wherever you are. If they're after us, they're after us here, not you. Stay safe. We'll try to get Celeste back. When we're done, I'll call you and we can figure something out. Okay, hon?"

"Right. I understand." Vicki switches to Russian. "Lisa, do you think you can free Celeste?"

Carson answers in Russian. "I'll tell you when I see your face. Until then, you're just another problem for me. Now that nobody can understand us, wanna tell me who Sonia is?"

"Hm. Please remind Iris to inform me how everything turns out. Good luck." The connection cuts off.

Carson kicks Tamara's abandoned chair halfway to the wall.

Iris grabs her phone. "What was that all about?"

"Swapping old Russian sayings. Karl, any luck with the coordinates?"

"Yes." Karl opens his laptop and holds up the piece of yellow notepaper that had been pinned to Celeste's dress. He taps the laptop's touchpad a couple of times, then swivels it so everyone else can see. "The geocoordinates on this note are for a place in El Bon Pastor, a barrio northeast of the center. Right here." He points to the red location pin on the Google Earth satellite shot.

Carson and the others crowd together to get a close-up view of the meeting site: a cluttered gravel lot across the street from a wall of warehouses.

It looks like a kill zone.

Chapter 48

EL BON PASTOR, BARCELONA

Carson and Dareh shelter behind several rows of empty dumpsters at the storage lot's north end. Beyond them lies a jumble of garbage trucks, road barriers, cars covered with dust, steel-framework trailers missing wheels, random junk, and a few scrubby trees trying to eke out a living in what's probably a toxic waste dump. A few sodium-vapor lights cast an orange film over the mess while also creating deep, black shadows. Carson's sure the place looks better at night.

She overlays the map on what she sees to get oriented. The lot's shaped like a trapezoid that's sandwiched between two streets that meet at a forty-five-degree angle. The only vehicle entrance is in the middle of the two-hundred-meter frontage on Carrer de Serra, a divided four-lane road that runs northwest-southeast. The one-lane Carrer dels Cresques runs east-west behind them, forming a hundred-meter leg. A ragged line of ratty three- and four-story apartment blocks lines the other side of that street.

Either Sabadell isn't planning to do much shooting, or the locals won't care if they do.

Dareh whispers, "When will they come, do you think?" He's swaddled in black jeans and a black hoodie with a blood-red stylized bird and "Oranssi Pazuzu" splashed across the chest, whatever that is.

"Anytime. It's after nine." Carson tugs down the bottom edge of her body armor. It's never comfortable to sit in it for long. "Ever killed anybody?"

Dareh stares at the dumpster in front of him, breathing slow. Finally, he says, "In the *Pâsdârân*, I am with my platoon by Zaranj. It is in Afghanistan, by the border. *Takfiri* are there. The West call them 'IS.' You know IS?"

"That like ISIS?"

"Yes. They go across border, attack Milak, in Iran. We find them by road. We shoot them all." He glances down at his hands, pressed between his thighs. "We kill wounded IS. I shoot two. Then we burn their vehicles and go back to Iran."

Shooting the wounded. That's hardcore. Normally she doesn't approve of that—though she did it just three months ago—but Dareh was dealing with ISIS, and those evil bastards deserve it. "Okay. This'll be different. Up close and personal. You okay with that?"

"Yes." He draws a wicked-looking combat knife from the scabbard strapped to his left thigh. "Celeste is my friend. This people hurt her. I will hurt them."

"Be quiet about it. Conserve your ammo. You got twenty-six rounds left." He's carrying the suppressed Walther she took from the hit team on Ibiza. She's got the Glock. "How'd you get through the army being…the way you are?"

"Gay? I pretend. My sister sends to me a picture of her friend. I say she is my girlfriend. The men ask if we have relations. I say no, that is forbidden. Not until we marry. I agree when they say bad things about people like me."

"Must've been hard." Metal rattles to their right. "Shh."

Twenty-five meters to their right, a metal gate next to a derelict gatehouse closes the only hole in the fence behind them. It's crusted with junk, but there's no barbed wire to deal with. It's how Carson and Dareh got inside the lot. As she watches, four men jog past a gutted porta-san and fan out across the yard, taking firing positions behind vehicles or, in one case, a roll-off garbage bin. All have long weapons and tactical gear.

Carson checks her watch: 9:36. She'd expected them earlier. *Maybe they still underestimate us. Too bad for them.* She pushes down on Dareh's shoulder until they're both under cover. "You saw where they went?"

"Yes."

"Take the two over there." She points to his left. "Watch them, keep track of them. I'll take these two." She points to her right. "When Iris and Sebastian are a klick away, we move out. When we do, we move fast and hit hard. Celeste's counting on us."

◎

Grebnev lounges in a hotel armchair while Ilya drives the drone around the subjects' mansion. The drone's night-vision camera is doing what it can with the low level of ambient light—the moon has almost set—but the picture on the video screen is seriously muddy.

Not that there's much to see. The lights are on in the mansion's ground floor, a first-floor bedroom, and the landscaping, but there's not much moving in there. There's been no obvious activity since the two cars left, the first forty-five minutes before the second. The two men he has in the field are probably getting extremely bored.

"Sir?" Ilya leans forward in his chair. "What does that look like to you?"

Grebnev sits up and peers at the collection of dark-gray shapes on the screen. "Where is this?"

"The north end of the property by the back wall."

There's something there, but Grebnev can't tell what. "Can you switch to IR?"

"I can try. It hasn't been working well."

The picture wobbles, then blooms bright green. It finally stabilizes (sort of), showing a dull, dark-green field with slightly brighter clumps of vegetation scattered around. The video rotates as the drone turns. After a few seconds, six bright heat sources appear in a line along the wall. They're shaped like men lying flat on their stomachs. The drone stops, hovering.

"Well, that's interesting." Grebnev rings Kallström.

"Hallo. Yes?" Heavily accented English with road noise in the background.

Grebnev switches to English. "Kallström, this is Grebnev. Do you have a team at the mansion?"

"If I do, what?"

"If you do, I know who owns the six men on the property. If you don't, then we have police there. Answer the question."

"Yes."

"You didn't mention that before. What is their mission?"

"When Sonia is here, my people kill other gang people. Then problem solved. You approve?" The way he says it, it's clear he doesn't care if Grebnev approves.

"Just so I know what's happening. Grebnev out." He taps his

chin with the phone for a few seconds as he considers the situation. So far, none of Kallström's plans have worked especially well. He changes to Russian. "Ilya, keep an eye on these jokers. Let me know when they move." He rings Karik. "Get your men ready. You may get your hostile fire pay tonight."

Ferran glances away from the road toward Kallström as the man stows his phone in his back pocket. "Who was that?"

"Grebnev. He is like old woman."

He has good reason. "Your team at the mansion knows to hold until you tell them to go, yes?"

"Yes, yes."

The street is mostly deserted at this hour. Walking down here at night isn't the smartest move, and the run-down warehouses don't host any official business that would bring car traffic this late. They pass the elevator for the Verneda Metro stop. Four short blocks left to the meet. Ferran says, "Let me do the talking tonight."

"Yes, yes."

There are a lot of moving pieces in play tonight, and most belong to Kallström. That doesn't make Ferran as comfortable as it used to. Kallström's becoming sloppier, less attentive to detail, more likely to improvise rather than plan. Ferran will need to have a talk with him about this soon. Tonight, all the man has to do is tell his people to open fire once Sonia's in the open.

Two minutes later, he turns the Gelandewagen right into the storage lot. It looks deserted. He knows it's not.

It's 21:48. Twelve minutes until Sonia arrives. And with any luck, no more than fifteen minutes before she's dead.

Carson's about five meters away from her first target, a guy crouching behind a garbage truck with a burned-out cab. Like her and Dareh, the guy's wearing a black balaclava. Unlike them, he has a suppressed M4 carbine. She needs to make sure he's out of action from moment one.

Sebastian's voice murmurs in her Bluetooth earpiece. "I passed the metro station."

Four blocks away. The black Mercedes SUV's still parked east of the driveway, facing the entrance, still dark. Carson's in the perfect position to take out the guy with the M4. She hates back-shooting people—if they've got their backs to her, they're not threats, right? So what changed?

Celeste changed things. That strange, innocent young woman Carson's known for less than three weeks and is now ready to run into combat for. But why? The music? That's part of it—if she can do what she does now, what will she be able to do ten years from now? Twenty? But that's the easy, wrong answer.

It's the unconditional trust Celeste gives Carson. Trust, and faith. Trust that Carson will protect her, keep her safe. Faith that Carson will always be there. The same trust and faith Carson's younger brothers gave her. She was so tough on them, rode them so hard, and she can't believe how good they all turned out. That trust was what made her grow up so fast—not her father's absences, not her mother's drunken insults and abuse. She had to be worthy of her brothers' trust, no matter what it cost her. Like she has to be worthy of Celeste's trust now.

I failed her once. Can't do it again.

Sebastian's voice: "I'm at the signal before the petrol station."

One block away. Time to go. "Okay. When you come in, keep your lights on. Be careful, both of you." She has Sebastian and Dareh tied into a conference call on her phone. "Dareh? Go."

"Okay."

I'm coming for you, Celeste. Hang on.

She aims at the guy with the rifle, exhales, then fires.

Chapter 49

EL BON PASTOR

Kallström smiles to himself when Sonia's car pulls into the lot right on the hour. She must be serious about getting her pet freak back; otherwise, she'd play the stupid little power game of making him wait to kill her. It's good to know what your enemy's pain points are.

Ferran flicks on the Mercedes's high beams to blind Sonia's driver. The BMW turns toward them and pulls to within ten meters, then stops. Its high beams pin Kallström and Ferran to their seats. Smart, but irritating.

Kallström hopes the Russian *mafiya* bitch is driving. He'd love to even the score for what she did to his contractors and the men she caught following her. Yes, Brusin told them to not cross her, but what can he do when she just disappears?

The BMW's driver's door opens. A tall figure appears behind it. It's the Irish boy, Sebastian Counihan. Too bad, but at least he's no threat.

It's the passenger's door Kallström's most interested in. He wants to see that bitch Sonia up close. Maybe kill her himself.

He calls the team waiting outside Sonia's latest hideout. "Team Bravo, move in. Clean out the estate." Then he taps the radio headset clamped to his right ear to talk to the men covering him here. "Team Alfa, ready. Wait for my mark."

No response. That's odd; Anders always has something to say.

"Team Alfa? Anders? Do you read me?"

Carson slips between a wrecked box truck and a cluster of rolling plastic garbage cans. The roll-off garbage bin is roughly three meters to her two o'clock. Her second target is in it, probably glued to the forward end for the best view of the action.

She peeks between the bins toward the BMW, trying not to look into the headlights. Sebastian's standing behind the driver's door, like she taught him. She doesn't see Iris yet. Maybe she's going to make a dramatic appearance. Whatever. After Carson finishes off her second gunman, the only threats she'll have to deal with will be whoever's in the G-wagen.

She reaches the roll-off bin. It's about five meters by two and has had a really rough life. She braces her toes on the bottom frame and steps up to see over the top, leading with the Glock.

It's empty. *Shit! Where'd he go?* "Dareh. My second target ghosted. Watch for him."

The next thing she hears is a muffled *thump* and the unmistakable *clang* of a bullet hitting metal near her.

Ferran grumbles, "How long do we wait for the woman to get out of the car?"

Kallström frowns at nothing in particular. "Anders? Do you read?"

The edge to Kallström's voice tells Ferran some part of the plan is unraveling. "Is something wrong?"

"I not know. Anders does not reply. Maybe radio is bad."

Typical. "Do we wait for Sonia, or do we get things going?"

Kallström has that bulldog look he puts on when things aren't going his way. He squints into the headlight glare. "She is afraid maybe. We start."

Ferran sighs. He lowers his bullet-resistant window halfway, then pushes open his door to its outer stop and steps outside. Even with the door as a shield, he's more vulnerable than he likes. He glances toward Kallström, who's doing the same thing. *At least he can't insult me for being careful.* "You, driver," he calls out in English. "Where is Sonia?"

"There is no Sonia," Counihan shouts. "Not with us, at least."

Oh, for God's sake. We're playing this game? "We know that isn't true. We have photos showing you together. We told you to bring her here. You didn't bring her?"

"I told you—we've no Sonia. You've made a mistake. I've come to get Celeste."

Ferran does his best to not lose his temper. That's Kallström's specialty. Even though this errand boy is lying to him, Ferran wants to stick as close to the plan as possible. It minimizes the risk to his own people. "Is she in the car with you? I understand that she may be reluctant to show herself. I have business with her, not you. Ask her to step out of the car so we can talk directly."

An odd noise to his right draws Ferran's attention. A metallic sound of some sort, barely loud enough to be heard above the engine and city noises. Kallström's head turns toward it, too; Ferran's not imagining it. Come to think about it, he's heard it two or three times before this but never thought much about it.

But Kallström's man didn't answer on the radio. *Hmm.*

Counihan says, "Sonia's not in the car because there is no Sonia. I need to see Celeste. Make certain she's okay."

Ferran shakes his head. "That isn't the arrangement we asked for."

"I'm after needing proof of life or we've nothing to talk about."

The Irish boy has bigger balls than Ferran—or Kallström—had given him credit for. Ferran switches to Spanish. "Håkan. Bring the girl up. Let them see her. Maybe that will bring Sonia out to play."

Ilya leans forward in his chair, peering into the video screen. "Sir? They're moving."

Grebnev straightens in his chair. The six men—the glowing green blobs on the screen—have paired up and are quickly moving south. One pair branches toward the cottage on the estate's west edge; another heads straight for the mansion's west end; the third aims for the garage attached to the mansion's northeast side. *Let's see if these clowns can do something right.*

He thumbs Karik's contact. "Sabadell is moving. Stay by the gate and the arbor to the east. Wait for my word."

For the past couple of minutes, Carson's been playing cat-and-mouse with her second target—apparently the only one of Sabadell's soldiers left standing. He's good. He stays under cover, fires only when he has a plausible shot, and moves immediately after taking that shot. She's seen him only as a shadow.

She knows how to play this game. But there are too many places to hide here, too many weird shadows, too many rats and feral cats bumping around to maintain a clear sound picture. Plus, Dareh's out there someplace. She won't risk taking him out accidentally.

Carson takes a moment to check out what's happening onstage. The vehicles haven't moved. The Sabadell guy is still behind the driver's door; she can't see the other one. Sebastian's still behind the BMW's door. She murmurs, "Sebastian. Where's Iris? Get her outside. Gotta keep Sabadell distracted."

"She isn't here." His voice is barely above a whisper.

"What do you mean, she isn't here? Where is she?"

"She didn't come. She was too scared."

Fuck! She checks for lurking shadows while she thinks of something to say that won't burn Sebastian's ears off. They needed Iris to give Sabadell a woman to focus on while Carson tries to grab Celeste. "Great fucking job, guys."

The blond Sabadell guy staggers backward from the rear of the G-wagen toward its nose. Carson aims at his head when he enters the headlight glare. Then he pivots to show why he's moving slow: he has Celeste. His left arm's wrapped around her chest under her arms, holding her off the ground. His right hand's grinding a pistol into her ear. She's naked, bruised, cut. The headlights blast all color from her skin. Dark blood trails run from her crotch down the insides of her thighs. Duct tape shines across her mouth. The rest of her face is deformed with terror.

No. God, no.

Carson can't get a clear shot at the Sabadell guy's head, her only option to kill him without him killing Celeste. The light's bad, and Celeste's head mostly blocks his.

She needs to move behind them…and not get shot by the ghost. "Dareh. Got my guy?"

"Yes."

"Keep him busy. Going for Celeste."

◉

Iris doesn't normally pace, but not even her third martini can keep her in a chair tonight. She roves all over the living room, pinging off random furniture. *I shouldn't even be here. I should be with Sebastian. Lisa's gonna be so pissed...*

She'd meant to go. She didn't want to, but she was going to. Then she looked inside the dark car when Sebastian opened the passenger's door and saw a coffin on wheels. She didn't scream—much—but she couldn't get back in the house fast enough.

Not that the house's much better. All the lights are on. All the drapes are closed. All the doors are locked and deadbolted. There could be zombies out there and she wouldn't know about it. Would she even *want* to know?

Tamara growls in Spanish, "Would you for Christ's sake *stop*? You're driving me crazy just watching you."

Iris stops. She's *so* over Tamara's whining. "Why are you still here?"

"It's not because I want to be." She crosses her arms hard and slumps further into the sofa. "That bitch Lisa said she'd kill me if I left. She thinks I'm Sonia or some shit."

Iris gives in to the bar's gravitational pull. Another martini would be a mistake, but she needs *something*. The longer she doesn't hear anything from Sebastian, the guiltier she feels. She shouldn't have made him go alone.

Her hand's hovering over the gin like one of those claw machines at a carnival when a metallic sound from the window area interrupts her. She listens, cocking her head.

Glass breaks behind the curtain.

Tamara screams and leaps off the sofa.

Oh shit oh shit oh shit... Iris lunges to the chair nearest the bar—the one she'd staked out all evening—and grabs the three iron she'd taken from the golf bag in the rec room closet. Then she snatches a handful of Tamara's hair and pulls hard. "Shut up! C'mon!"

Bullets shred the curtains and the sofa as they sprint from the room.

◉

Carson moves in a combat crouch behind a white SUV with its windows busted out, trying to be as small a target as she can. When she steps out on the driver's side, something tugs at the back of her body armor, then clanks into the back-left door. A near miss. She drops prone.

"…your freak!" The blond guy's yelling, probably at Sebastian. "We do what we say! You do not!" His heavy accent sounds more Germanic or Nordic than Spanish.

Sebastian barks, "What've you done to her, you bloody pox!"

Carson low-crawls across three meters of compacted dirt and crushed glass to get to a wall of rolling garbage bins.

While she moves, the blond guy screams, "Fuck you, pretty boy! Where woman you work for? Why she not here? Why she hide?"

Carson rolls up on her knees. She's to Celeste's three o'clock and still can't see the blond guy's head clearly. Celeste's trembling violently. *Hang on, girl. I'm trying.* Carson flinches when the bin in front of her thumps and slews round. She drops flat just in time to avoid the blond guy seeing her as he looks over his shoulder.

Sebastian says, "I told you, you thick. Sonia's not here and I couldn't tell you where she is even if I wanted. You're wasting your time. Give us the girl and we'll be gone."

Carson crawls past the bins, then rolls to her left to put them between her and the ghost, wherever he is. She's finally behind Celeste and the asshole holding her. Is he the one who raped her? His men? He won't survive this to brag about it. She gets up on one knee and tries to aim. She's staring straight into the BMW's headlights. Squinting blurs the target.

Dareh's voice: "Lisa! Right!"

The blond asshole's screaming, "Sonia not here? She does not come? She—"

Carson swivels to her right. Spots a man-shaped shadow crouching by the busted white SUV. She fires.

"—insults us? No need for freak, then!"

One unsuppressed gunshot. A geyser of blood and bone jets out the left side of Celeste's head. The asshole drops her limp body. Before it hits the ground, Carson puts four rounds into his center of mass. He staggers forward several steps, then trips over his own feet.

In an instant, she's up and running toward Celeste, not thinking or caring about the ghost. Two steps shy, Sebastian yells, "Lisa! To your left!"

The dark-haired Sabadell guy's aiming at her through the G-wagen's two open front doors. She fires twice; he drops.

She reaches Celeste at the same time as Sebastian. They kneel on either side of her.

Sebastian mumbles, "Oh, God, oh God, oh God…"

Carson scoops Celeste into her arms. Still warm, but limp and still. Her head lolls back and to her left. Something warm and wet soaks into Carson's left sleeve. Celeste's blood. "I'm so sorry," Carson whispers. "So sorry. I tried. Tried to save you. I…" Her throat closes. She can't breathe, can't talk, can't think. Doesn't want to think.

Dareh's voice murmurs in a language she can't understand. Not in her earpiece—right next to her.

The BMW lunges backward, spraying them with gravel. Carson's head snaps up. The car wallows through a sharp turn, then leaps down the driveway and slams across the street. Dareh fires round after round at it, but the engine's wail covers any hits he scores.

"Fuck!" Carson shrieks. She lays down Celeste's body and fires once, uselessly, at the escaping car. There's no blood on the scraped trail of dirt from where the blond asshole fell to where the BMW used to be. No blood. He had body armor. He's got to be hurting…but he's still alive. Still alive. *God damn him.*

They stand in a loose knot, staring at the empty space that the BMW filled a moment ago. Carson trembles with rage. Not only did she fail Celeste, she let her murderer go free.

She marches around the G-wagen's nose. The dark-haired Sabadell guy's flat on his back, gasping, holding his right side. His light-colored dress shirt's already dark from his armpit to his belt. She thuds to her knees next to him and pushes the Glock's suppressor into his left hip joint. "Who's the blond asshole?"

He chuckles, but it sounds like gagging. "Håkan. Loyal to the last."

"Where's he going?"

"Who can tell?"

Carson pulls the trigger. His scream threatens to shatter

windows. "Where's he going?"

"I…don't know."

After that much pain, he probably doesn't. "Where'd you keep her?"

"Why?"

"Want me to blow up the other hip?"

"You will…kill me…anyway."

Smart man. "Wanna go fast or slow?"

He chuckle-gags again, then hacks hard enough to bounce his upper body off the ground. Blood splatters out of his mouth. "Who…who are you?"

"The most pissed-off woman you ever saw." She moves the suppressor to his right hip. "Where'd you keep her?"

Sebastian's phone rings behind her. She didn't know how close he was. He crunches a few steps away.

The Sabadell guy wheezes, "Gorg. Badalona."

Whatever that means. "Why? Why all this? What'd these people do to you?"

What he does is either a smile or a grimace. "Someone. Moscow. Wants you dead."

In Moscow? "Who? Why?"

He pants for some while. More coughing, more blood. Finally, he gasps, "Hackers. Hackers. With Sonia."

Before she can even think about that, Sebastian yells, "They're attacking the house!"

Attacking. The. House. There's no way to get there in time to help. They're all gonna die. Carson growls at the Sabadell asshole, "This your doing?"

"Håkan's plan."

"You approved it?"

He pants for a long time. Then he nods.

Carson slowly groans onto her feet. She feels useless and stupid and worthless and slow. Everybody who relied on her is either dead or about to be. She failed them all.

Let yourself feel.

Fuck yourself, Bri.

"Lisa?" Dareh lays a gentle hand on her shoulder. "I can kill him? For Celeste?"

She nods. "Make it last." She stumbles away from the

Mercedes. Tosses the Citroën's key to Sebastian.

Zombie-walks to Celeste.

Slams down on her knees. Hugs Celeste's body to her chest.

I failed you. Shoulda moved faster, tried harder. You didn't deserve this. Shoulda protected you and I didn't and you paid for it sorry I'm sorry forgive me…

Things break inside her. Walls. Doors. Her breath. Her heart.

For only the second time in her adult life, she sobs until her ribs threaten to shatter.

Chapter 50

Grebnev leans forward in his seat, watching Sabadell's assault on the mansion like it's a league championship football match.

One team disappears through doors on the south façade. Another enters the garage on the mansion's north side, then comes out almost immediately and hurries up the curved stairs to the first floor. The third team ducks into the cottage, then re-emerges through a swing-up garage door. They stop in the drive to point and talk.

Idiots. Don't they have a plan? Grebnev rings Balaguer, but it rolls to voicemail. The same for Kallström. *They* both *won't take my call?* He's always been able to get one or the other. They know better than to snub him. Don't they?

Curtains across the first-floor windows glow one room at a time as lights flick on behind them. The hackers, or Kallström's people? No way to tell.

"What's that?" Ilya points to the screen's right-hand side.

Three bright green returns hustle from the mansion toward a pavilion at the estate's southeast corner. Grebnev can't tell if they're the Sabadell shooters or what's left of the gang. They pass under the pavilion's roof, out of sight. "Pull back so we can see what's happening under there."

The picture slews until the pavilion is at the top of the screen and the view is around forty-five degrees. No green blobs to be seen.

"That's odd." Grebnev scowls at the screen. "Where did they go?"

"I don't know, sir, but I think I know who they are." Ilya brings up on his laptop a record of the gang's movements. "Tarasenko and one other person left around 20:10. Counihan left at 21:00. The Aguenier girl never returned after going out this afternoon. That leaves three of the gang onsite when Kallström's tac squad showed up." He holds a hand toward the screen: *there you go.*

And Sabadell let them get away to God only knows where. "Orbit the pavilion. See if you can find them."

Grebnev tries again to reach Balaguer and Kallström but gets nothing. He considers the situation for a moment. Sabadell's thugs failed in their mission here. Their leadership's unreachable. Sabadell's people are just in the way now. If anyone's going to salvage anything from this clown act, it'll have to be Grebnev, and it has to be this minute.

He rings Karik. "Secure the mansion. Find the hackers' equipment. The locals have six men in there. If they surrender, disarm them and send them home."

Karik says, "If they don't?"

"Deal with it."

The sixteen minutes it takes Carson to drive the G-wagen from the junk lot to Carrer de Sant Luc in the warehouse district of Badalona—the SUV's last destination before the meet, according to its GPS—goes by slowly and very quietly. She concentrates hard on driving so she won't keep seeing Celeste. Dareh stares out the passenger's window.

"You okay?" Carson finally says when the quiet gets too heavy.

"No." He doesn't move. "You are okay?"

"No."

"Good. If you are okay, I will have to—"

"Beat the shit out of me?"

They'd left Celeste at the lot. They argued about it—Dareh wanted to "take her home." They finally agreed there was no way they could take a naked dead girl with her head blown open to a hospital and not end up in a Spanish jail. Before they left, Carson called 1-1-2 (the Spanish version of 9-1-1) on the dead, dark-haired Sabadell guy's phone and left it next to what was left of him.

Run-down warehouses line both sides of Carrer de Sant Luc. There's an unusual number of Chinese signs. Streetlights halo the thin mist from the nearby Med.

Carson brakes in front of an open flip-up gate set into a

salmon-colored stucco wall to her left. "We're here. Ready for this?"

Dareh finally moves his head enough to side-eye the gate. "If the man who kills Celeste is here…"

"Yeah."

They yank on their balaclavas. Carson rolls through the gate like she owns the place. The G-wagen's high beams light up the mansion's shot-up BMW, then pin a guy by the front door wearing web gear, jeans, and a slung M4. He doesn't get a chance to unsling it. Carson and Dareh take him down in seconds without a fight; the two M4s they confiscated from dead Sabadell shooters at the lot make a persuasive argument.

"English?" Carson asks him as she zip-ties his wrists together.

"A little."

"Håkan here?"

"He was here. He is gone."

"Where?"

The guy shrugs. "He does not say."

Figures. Their main mission was to hunt down and crucify this Håkan bastard who executed Celeste. Of course he's not here.

Carson and Dareh carefully enter the warehouse. A single industrial scoop light is on over the bay's center, shining off three cars and a big BMW motorcycle. From the dead shooters at the meet? Carson doesn't need to think about that now—she'll have more than enough time later.

It doesn't take long for them to clear the open warehouse bay. There's a herd of gym equipment in one corner, a weapon maintenance workbench in another, a couple picnic benches at the other end, two pallet jacks, a half-dozen gas cans, and some other stuff that's not interesting. Except for the oil barrel overflowing with beer cans, the place is surprisingly clean.

Up the open-riser steel staircase to the offices overlooking the bay floor, it's a different story. The first room they check appears to be the place Sabadell cuts its cocaine. Two long trestle tables surrounded by cases of cornstarch, powdered caffeine, and baking sugar, two large rolls of sheet plastic, and a smell like a steel flower remind Carson of her days in uniform. No nose candy, though.

Next door is the obligatory cache of long weapons and sidearms, crates of ammo, and various accessories in and out of their packaging. Carson swaps her M4 for one set up with an M68 Close Combat Optic and a foregrip, then tosses a black backpack to Dareh. "Pack as many M4 magazines as you can carry. I'll look ahead."

Next is an office that doesn't get much use, then a unisex toilet. The last room stinks of sweat, blood, piss, and fear. Carson almost can't go inside; it's the room she's been looking for and hoped she wouldn't find.

There's a massive wooden chair, a box of tools, and a couple pairs of overused MMA kickboxing gloves. Plastic sheeting crackles under her feet. She breathes through her mouth, which cuts down but doesn't eliminate the stench.

On a beaten-to-hell mattress at the room's far end, she finds the torn remains of a pair of pale-pink underwear. *Here's where it happened. Where they beat her and raped her. Those evil fucks...*

"Lisa?"

She doesn't know how she ended up on her knees, clutching the only thing left of Celeste, trying to breathe. She croaks, "Don't come over here."

"Okay." Dareh doesn't leave the doorway. His eyes bore into Carson's back.

Her phone vibrates in her back pocket. She doesn't recognize the parts of the incoming number she can see through the tears filling her eyes. Carson shudders in a breath, then growls, "What?"

"Lisa. It's Sebastian." He's outside; wind fuzzes his phone's mic. "They burned the house."

"*What?*"

"They burned the house." His voice catches. "The fire brigade's here, and so are the guards. I don't know where Iris or the others are. It's gone. It's all gone."

Chapter 51

The warehouse burns beautifully.

Carson and Dareh start in the torture room, emptying jerry cans of gasoline from downstairs onto the floor. Same with the office. They dump boxes of bullets everywhere; the ammo will still burn, but it won't explode like a bomb. They strew gas over the mess. Stuff cleaning rags into the gas tanks of the three cars on the warehouse floor, then spark up each with a lighter they found in the desk drawer. For good measure, they turn the BMW's carcass into a Molotov cocktail.

The fire's hot and bright. Gas tanks explode; bullets cook off by the hundreds. The flames glare in the G-wagen's rear-view mirror as Carson drives away.

Dareh stays silent until they climb onto the eastbound C-31 highway to Mataró to join up with Sebastian. "It is good you make the guard free."

"Yeah." He'd said he didn't know anything about a girl; he'd been outside all the time. Carson believed him. "If he's got any sense, he'll leave the country." She lets that simmer for a moment. "If we had any sense, we would, too."

They slowly roll past the estate's front gate a bit over twenty minutes later. A police car's blue lights flash just inside. The mansion's surrounded by red-and-white strobes. Floodlights shine off plumes of smoke climbing into the night sky. A thick rope of water streams into a bedroom window, sparkling in the light show.

Carson turns around in a hotel parking lot a few hundred meters east of the estate, then calls Sebastian. "Where are you?"

"Just west of the house, there's a turnoff. You'll see a red 'La Canya' sign. I'm there, off the road."

The Citroën's parked in front of a metal gate that looks like it hasn't been opened in a long time. Sebastian sits slumped on the driver's seat, his feet on the gravel, his head in his hands. Carson squats near his knees and watches him for a few long moments before she squeezes his thigh. "We burned their hideout."

He snorts, then nods his head until it's a tic. "Didja catch the bastard who did it?"

"No. He'd been and gone before we got there." She hesitates. "It's where they kept her."

"Grand." He picks his phone off the car's floor and checks for calls or texts. The screen's light shines in his red, raw eyes. "Nothing from Iris yet. I've called and texted, but nothing."

Dareh says, "I send a text to Karl now."

"Thanks." Carson watches Sebastian's head droop. She still resents his throwing her over for Tamara, of all people, but now's not the time. He may have lost all his friends in a fire he'll probably figure he should've been in, too. "They could be hunkered down. Maybe turned off their phones so the lights or sounds don't give them up. Maybe don't have any bars."

"Karl would tell them to turn off mobiles." Dareh squats on the other side of Sebastian's knees. "No one can track them."

Sebastian nods some more as he sits up. He noses over his right shoulder, toward the mansion. "Or they're in there." He wheezes out an endless sigh. "I reckon I should tell Vicki, but I don't know what to say."

Carson snaps, "Fuck her. We got bigger problems." She stands, then points at the gate. "This drive goes behind the caretaker's house. Gonna get my stuff and see what's happening. By the time I get back, have a plan for finding Iris and the others. Time to try somebody else's bright ideas."

Grebnev and Karik pore over the recorded drone video from the attack on the hackers' estate. Grebnev stops the video when the three IR signatures appear on the property's east side. "Did you see them?"

Karik squints at the screen. "No. There's a lot of cover over there. We were concentrating on the Sabadell shooters."

They certainly did, Grebnev grumps. *All six dead. Nobody left to question.* Karik claims they all resisted, but Grebnev doesn't believe him; prisoners can be an avoidable hassle. He uses a red laser pointer to outline the southeast pavilion on the screen. "What is this?"

"It covers stairs that lead to a tunnel under the road. It probably goes to the beach. The door was unlocked, but we had no time to check for escapees."

"No dead civilians?"

"No, only hostiles. My men will bring up the laptops and networking stuff we salvaged once they unpack their gear."

Karik had said "three machines" on the radio once he and his men had dealt with the Sabadell team. That's at least two short of the full compliment. Severinov will take whatever he can get for analysis, but Grebnev knows what kind of shitstorm will fall on his head if neither of the hackers' laptops are in the overnight shipment to Moscow.

He switches the screen to the live drone video. The area around the mansion is awash with fire engines. Their collected red-and-white lights pulsate like a living thing. The building itself is dark and still, the emergency floodlights revealing smoke stains over every window but no lights or intact glass. Someone will be unhappy.

Karik clears his throat. "I need to debrief—"

"Not yet. Send two of your men to the other end of that tunnel. See if you can find the three escapees. If you do, terminate them. That should take care of the people my company's concerned with." Grebnev flashes Karik an empty smile. "Wherever you find them, don't burn down the place. I'm sure the authorities have had enough of arson today."

Carson's gathering her washroom stuff in the twilit caretaker's cottage when her phone pings in her ear. A text from Dareh: I find Karl.

Finally! She calls him. "Where?"

"There is a swimming center in Mataró. They hide there."

"They?"

"Iris, Tamara, and Karl."

Too bad Tamara survived. "Okay, almost done." She scoops up

Sebastian on the way out—he insisted on coming so he could see what's happening to the mansion—and makes him carry her nearly-empty roller bag just because.

The drive from the estate to the Centre de Natació Mataró—a huge swimming complex on the beach near the city center—takes less than five minutes. Dareh leads Carson to a spot on the facility's west end where they can climb over the blue pipe railing to get to the end of the ten-lane Olympic swimming pool. The chlorine smell overwhelms the ocean's tang.

Carson retrieves her carbine from Dareh, who texts Karl. Dareh points with his whole hand to the two-story building at the pool's east end. "There!"

They quick-walk east flanking the pool, rifles ready, then climb a curved staircase to an observation deck on the east building's first floor. Halfway along a concrete arcade, they find Iris and Tamara huddled behind an advertising banner strapped to the railing. Karl kneels next to them, flanked by two laptop cases. He waves his lit cell phone as a beacon.

Iris squeals, "Ohmigod! You're alive! You made it!" She jumps up to tackle Dareh in a hug. Karl joins in. Tamara tries to add to the pile, but Dareh blocks her with his shoulder. *Nicely done.*

Carson stands off a few meters, scanning the complex's perimeter for…what? Håkan, the asshole who murdered Celeste? The Sabadell squad that attacked the house? Cops? Since nobody seems glad to see her, she keeps watch and slowly simmers in an anger stew that started bubbling the minute Sebastian showed up alone at the meet.

When the sounds of relief start to settle down, she calls out, "Dareh? Get Karl and Tamara down to the parking lot. I need a word with Iris."

As the three file past, Carson grabs Tamara's arm. Tamara struggles until Carson's grip makes her squeak in pain. Carson mutters, "By the way…Celeste's dead. Hope you're happy. Get out of my sight." Carson doesn't bother to watch her scuttle toward the stairs.

Iris watches Carson with saucer eyes. "What did you just do…?"

"Wrecked her day, I hope." Carson covers the distance to Iris in three strides. She grabs a fistful of Iris's peasant blouse and slams her against a nearby concrete column. All the air whooshes out of Iris's mouth. Carson goes nose-to-nose with her. "You fucking *coward!* Where were you? I know where you *weren't*—where you were *supposed* to be."

"I…I…" Iris tries to catch whatever air she can. "I…thought I should…stay at the house…in case—"

"It was *safer?* Great choice, bitch." Carson bears down on Iris until all she can see is the terror in her eyes. "You let Sebastian walk into the meet alone? You hung me and Dareh out to dry? Why? Was your precious ass—"

"You don't understand! I-I couldn't—"

Carson pulls Iris off the column, then slams her against it again. "Why not? Sebastian risked it. Dareh risked it. Why not—"

"They'd've *killed* me if I was there!"

The more the woman talks, the angrier Carson gets. "They could've killed us all. Why're you special? Why'd you get to skip it?" She bashes Iris against the column again.

"Stop that! Stop doing that! It hurts!"

"Glad to hear it. At least you're alive to feel pain. Celeste isn't. You—"

"I couldn't go!" Iris shrieks. "They'd kill me! I'm Sonia!"

Chapter 52

Carson stares at her for an eternity. She hisses, "Say that again."

Whimpers leak out of Iris's mouth. "I'm…I'm Sonia."

Before she knows she's doing it, Carson has Iris by the throat and pinned against the column so hard that Iris can't even tremble anymore. "You lying *fuck!*" Carson gets in Iris's face and growls, "Sebastian tell you what happened?" Iris shakes her head so hard, it looks like a seizure. "They raped Celeste before they dragged her to the meet. When they figured out *you* weren't coming? They blew out her brains. Right in front of me. Couldn't get in position in time to stop it. Sebastian tried to tap-dance through it, but…"

Iris's face scrunches into a wad, then starts to melt.

"If you'd been there? Kept them distracted? Could've bought the extra seconds I needed to take out the asshole who shot her. But *you* weren't there. *You* decided to save your worthless ass. So me and Dareh had to leave Celeste there. Dead. Naked. *Alone.* I'll never forget that picture." She bounces Iris off the column one last time, then lets go. "Hope you never will, either."

Iris crumples into a heap on the walkway, sobbing into her hands.

Carson slings her carbine, draws the Glock, then jams the suppressor's muzzle against the back of Iris's head. She can barely see through the red mist coating her brain. "Remember what I said I'd do to Sonia if Celeste got hurt?" Iris doesn't—or can't—answer. "This is all *your* fault," Carson finally growls past the rock lodged in her throat. "Celeste's dead because of *you.* All those people who worked for you? Dead, because of *you.* All your friends could've been killed because of *you.* *You* could've stopped it. *You* could've come clean. But you didn't. And now…"

"Pleeeeze. Pleeeeze don't."

"Why not?" Carson grinds the suppressor into Iris's scalp. "Give me a good reason."

"I…I didn't…w-want any…any of this." She chokes out the words rather than saying them. "I liked you. You…you liked me. We were…we're friends. I'm still…that person. *Pleeeeze!*"

She's right. The red haze thins a bit. Carson tries to tighten her finger on the trigger but can't. She *liked* Iris. It took a while, but she'd come to enjoy Iris's company. She'd felt like such a shit when she accused Iris of being Sonia and Iris convinced her she wasn't. *Now I know the truth…*

It's just like with Ron, her ex. She thought she loved the man until she found out how many women she was sharing him with, and who some of them were. *Truth kills love. Truth kills friendship. Truth kills…*

Carson tries to pull the trigger again. It moves, but not enough. *Won't bring Celeste back. She'd hate you for killing Iris.*

"Goddamnit!" Carson wheels away into a tight, fast circle, trying to pace off the red haze so she can think instead of just reacting.

Carson waits until Iris's huge, body-shaking sobs turn into choking noises and hiccups. Then she squats, wraps Iris's braid around her hand, and wrenches Iris's head so her face is turned to Carson's. Iris's eyes are bloodshot, her mascara's trailing into the snot running down her upper lip, and her expression says she's being slowly disemboweled. Carson can't scrape up a single gram of sympathy. "You're a fucking coward and a liar and Celeste died because of you. And *you lied to me*. Over and over. Can't forgive that." She yanks her hand free, then barks, "Why?"

Every part of Iris's body quivers. "I…I was broke… Daddy cut me off… I was…was sponging…off the fam… I…I didn't want that. I wanted…wanted to pay my way. I met…someone. Someone who…who hooked me up…with a lab… It was…so easy. I made…so much…so much money…and it worked…so well. Everyone was…happy. Until…until those Sabadell assholes ruined everything." Iris dissolves into more weeping and small animal noises, bending lower and lower until her forehead rests on the concrete.

Carson watches her twitch and moan with a mix of disgust and sorrow. Iris isn't an evil person, just a weak one. She probably thought it was all a game…until it wasn't. Stupidity and carelessness can cause more damage than malevolence.

She finally stands and drags Iris to her feet by her ponytail. "Here's how this is gonna work. You're gonna call Vicki. Find out where she is. Sebastian and the others—minus Tamara—go there. They keep her there. Don't care how they do it—lock her in a closet, whatever—but she doesn't leave the place. You and me, we hang out in Barcelona until morning. When the news breaks about Celeste, we go to the cops and *you're* gonna identify her body."

Iris staggers back against the column. "What? No! I can't. Please don't make me, I can't I—"

"You will. It's how you start to pay her back for letting her down. You get to go face-to-face with what you've done. Think that sucks? Vicki gets to explain it to Celeste's parents. I'll see to it."

"But…can't you—"

"Talk to the cops *again*? No. I spent more time with cops on this trip than with Vicki. No, you step up for a change. When you're done, we go to where Vicki is and I take her off your hands. Your friends get to decide what happens to you. Then they figure out what they wanna be when they grow up. 'Cause it's time."

Iris tries to reach Vicki as Carson leads her to the parking lot north of the swimming complex. Vicki's busy at a club or she isn't answering her phone at this hour; either way, Iris's increasingly hysterical messages are rolling to voicemail.

By the time they reach the G-wagen and the Citroën, the remains of Vicki's posse is clustered around the Mercedes's nose. Tamara and Sebastian are a couple meters away, face-to-face in a puddle of streetlight. Tamara says, "…like Madrid. It's a great city. Come with me."

Sebastian rubs the back of his neck. "I can't. Vicki needs me. I need to see this through."

Tamara stamps her foot. "*Vicki* needs you? *I* need you. I want you. *Come with me.*"

Long pause. "No. You should go. It's not safe here."

Maybe Sebastian's stronger than he thought. Carson steps up to Tamara. "Got your phone?"

Tamara grimaces at her. "Yes. Why? Do you—"

Carson grabs a handful of her hair and drags her, squawking

and flailing, to the center of the parking lot near a driveway. She shoves Tamara a couple of meters farther from the G-wagen, then aims a loaded finger at her. "Call a car, get your worthless ass in it, and disappear. You're not coming with us."

"What? I'm not Sonia anymore?" Tamara's trying to sound tough, but her voice is cracking.

"No. I know who Sonia is. You're free to go. Exercise that freedom."

"But…all my stuff is back at the house!"

"Not anymore. The place burned. *Everybody's* stuff burned. Time's up. Get lost." Carson turns on her heel and paces back to the others. Except for Dareh—standing guard at the SUV's tail— they look sad and slow and don't say much.

Tell them who Iris really is? Not yet. Soon. Carson asks Iris, "Anything from Vicki?"

"Not yet."

"Where was she when we talked to her yesterday?" It seems like a week ago.

"There's a place she goes sometimes in the country outside Barcelona. She said she's there."

"Arboçar?"

Iris squints at her. "How did you know?"

"Doesn't matter." She turns to Sebastian as he arrives, looking glum. "You know how to get there?"

"Where?"

Iris says, "Vicki's favorite vineyard? Remember last year?"

He frowns for a moment, then nods. "Yes, I do."

Carson says, "Good. Take Karl and Dareh and start—"

Dareh barks in pain and slams against the G-wagen's tailgate. Iris screams. Sebastian and Karl duck behind the SUV.

Carson drops prone and turns on her laser sight. The streetlights at the curb create a patchy twilight in the empty parking lot. Near the corner of the swim center's two-story building, Carson spies a dark shape crouching in a slightly lighter shadow. She sweeps the red laser designator down the wall until it disrupts on a not-flat shape, then fires three rounds, *phutphutphut.* The shape tumbles backward. "*Khui!*" echoes off the concrete walkway.

She low-crawls to where Dareh's groaning on the gravel.

"Where are you hit?"

Dareh pants, "He hits…my rifle."

"Can you walk?"

"Yes."

"Get in the truck. Go to Vicki's location. Take her passport and ID and don't give it back. Do what you have to to get it. Understand?"

"Yes."

"Good. Move." She rolls a couple of meters away from the SUV and tries to reacquire the target. The dark shape's gone, either under its own power or with help. She'd rather not find out which. "Iris!"

"Uh…yeah?"

"Get your ass in the car." Carson tags the building's corner with the laser, then slides the red dot to the left just far enough for it to disappear. Anyone who peeks around the corner will reflect the beam. When the Citroën's passenger door clunks shut, the laser dot shimmers on something moving by the building. Carson fires twice more, then backpedals to the open driver's door. Bullets punch two holes in the back window as the car screeches into the street.

Carson ignores them.

Khui is a word she knows well. It means *fuck*. The guy she shot at was Russian.

The Russians really are *after us?*

Chapter 53

MATARÓ

Among the dead was Ferran
Balaguer-Noguera, reputed to be
the leader of the Grupo Sabadell
narcotics syndicate.

Grebnev immediately recognizes Balaguer in the not-very-good surveillance photo that pops up on the screen. The English closed-captioning continues to wash over the Canal 24 Horas newscast.

Sources in the Mossos reveal
that Balaguer was shot several
times and bears evidence of
torture.

Grebnev didn't like the man but didn't wish torture on him. *How in hell did this happen?*

The Mossos continue to
investigate the identity and
circumstances of the young woman
found dead near Balaguer's body.

The Aguenier girl's photo replaces Balaguer's. Her eyes are closed and her hair is wet, probably from the medical examiner's office washing away the blood.

Sources say she appears to have
been abused and may have been the
victim of human trafficking.
Anyone with information about the
woman should please contact the
Mossos d'Esquadra at the number
shown on your screen.

Grebnev mutes the audio and kicks a nearby armchair. "Goddamn idiots! Five dead, including their leader. Plus the girl. On national television!"

Karik snickers around the unlit cigar jammed in the corner of his mouth. "You should've brought us in at the beginning. None of this would've happened."

Grebnev whirls to stab a finger at the mercenary. "Don't start! You've got a man down with a broken collarbone. You're lucky he's not dead. And that mess at the mansion…"

"What were we supposed to do?" Karik finally yanks the cigar free and sweeps it toward the west. "Six dead locals, blood all over the place, the shit the kids left there. If we didn't burn it, the cops would be raking through a crime scene, not the end of a summer cookout. Besides"—he points the cigar at the video screen—"they'll think it's more 'senseless drug violence.' We're clear."

Grebnev's about to rebut when he notices video of a raging fire on the screen. It's the mansion.

```
    Six people died in a fire that
    destroyed a seaside mansion near
    Mataró overnight. The fire, which
    appears to have been deliberately
    set, completely gutted the two-
    floor house designed by noted
    Catalan Modernist architect Jordi
    Capell in 1956. The Mossos
    d'Esquadra has not yet released
    the victims' identities. A joint
    investigation by the Mossos and
    the Bombers de Catalonia is
    underway.
```

Grebnev throttles the back of a nearby chair. "Of course, it had to be by a famous architect."

Karik growls, "Did you hear them mention Russians?"

"No. Thank God." Grebnev's phone vibrates. It's Severinov. *Just what I need.* "I have to take this. Go deal with your wounded man. We're not done yet."

◎

Kallström drifts on the recliner, seeing but not watching Canal 24 Horas on the huge-screen TV. The apartment penthouse in the hills overlooking central Barcelona is large, white, and quiet. He avoids looking out the east windows. He doesn't need the hawk's-eye view of El Bon Pastor to remind him why he's here in the first place.

The doctor who services Grupo Sabadell's casualties told him he was lucky to "only" have two broken ribs. "A few centimeters to either side and you'd be paralyzed," he said, like Kallström needed to hear that shit. Now his chest's wrapped like a mummy, and he's flying on tramadol, no use to anybody.

That fucking Russian bitch. Good thing she was all obsessed with that freak girl or I'd be dead and on the TV now, too. At least the damn vest worked.

The picture on the TV changes to a night shot of a building on fire. He squints through the fuzz coating his eyes at the English subtitles at the bottom.

> A large warehouse blaze in
> Badalona may be connected with the
> El Bon Pastor massacre.

Oh, fuck no.

> The complex on Carrer de Sant
> Luc was completely destroyed last
> night in an inferno that officials
> with the Bombers de Barcelona say
> was deliberately set.

Gotta be the bulldyke. She got Ferran's Benz. It knows where the warehouse is.

> Sources in the Mossos
> d'Esquadra say the warehouse had
> been under investigation for
> months as a possible hideout and
> storage place for Grupo Sabadell,
> the Catalan drug gang involved in
> last night's bloody gun battle in
> eastern Barcelona.

Kallström pounds the recliner's padded arms with both his fists.

> Bombers at the scene describe
> the sound of ammunition exploding
> inside the building. Several said
> they feared that someone was
> shooting at them...

He shuts off the TV with a stab at the remote. *Fuck. The weapons—gone. The safe with the hundred grand—gone.*

Team Bravo went dark before midnight. The news said "six dead" at the mansion. *Coincidence? No way. How'd those college pansies take out six of my men? At least the Russian bulldyke has training.*

Six dead in Mataró. Four at the meet. The guard at Badalona? The news didn't say. The group was stretched thin to start with, but with these losses, they're out of soldiers in this area. On the plus side: Ferran's dead. He didn't have an heir. No more of his corporate bullshit.

An idea hacks its way through the fog in Kallström's head.

Severinov pinches the bridge of his nose. Ever since this snake-bitten operation started, he's been living with a low-grade headache. His only consolation is that the hackers haven't been traipsing around in his computer systems for nearly a week. He unmutes his phone. "You'd best hope there's a coup or airliner crash soon to drive this mess out of the news."

"It's not as bad as it seems." The strain in Grebnev's voice contradicts his words. "All the news is about drug gangs and human trafficking. Nothing about Russians. Nothing that will blow back on us."

"Not yet. Do you have a plan to end this, or will we continue causing one disaster after another?"

After a few moments of audible stewing, Grebnev says, "We have a plan, sir. The lead contractor"—Karik—"found a notepad in his wounded man's pocket. He'd written down the registration plate number for a vehicle the hacker group had. It belonged to the drug gang's leader. If I may, sir, I'd like to email it to you to see if your police contacts can track it for us."

"How do you know where the vehicle came from?"

"Because I wrote down the number when our man here met with him last month."

He means Brusin. Severinov would love to talk openly about names and places on this supposedly secure phone connection, but that would break his own protocols. "You mentioned a plan?"

"Yes, sir. We doubt the locals have enough resources left to finish the operation. We have the surveillance team and the five remaining contractors. The hacker group is down to five surviving members and the Russian woman. If you can locate them, we can eliminate them ourselves."

Severinov sighs. Grebnev's been pushing to do this since the locals' hit team failed on Ibiza. He may think he can actually do this, or he may simply miss the army and wants to be a tactical commander again. The man does have a point, though—the locals have botched the job at every turn.

He fishes a half-full bottle of paracetamol from his desk drawer, chases two capsules with a slug of nearly cold coffee, then unmutes. "One step at a time. We locate them first. Once we have them, we decide what to do with them. Understand?"

Grebnev slumps in the side chair on the patio outside the fifth-floor suite, letting the sun bake the day's frustrations out of his head. Karik's wounded man is off to Moldova, and the three laptops from the hackers' mansion are on their way to Moscow. Other than that, nothing has gone right. They all should be breaking camp to return to base with the mission accomplished and good feelings all around. Instead, one if not both hackers are still alive, Karik's men resent losing one of their own, and the company surveillance team, having been at this for over three weeks, has unilaterally taken a day off without asking Grebnev for permission. Not that he can blame them.

His phone buzzes. The number isn't familiar, but that hardly matters when most people who ring him now have burner phones or cloaked caller ID. "Yes?"

"My dear Grebnev!" The familiar Russian voice is far too cheerful for Grebnev's mood. "It's Brusin, of course. Have you time?"

In one sense, Grebnev has nothing but time right now; he can't move until Severinov finds the hackers again. In a more macro sense, he's out of time and waiting for the firing squad at any minute. "What do you need?"

"I just received the most interesting phone call from Mr. Kallström. You've probably already seen that Mr. Balaguer didn't survive last night's soiree. Anyway, Kallström rang to tell me he's taken over Grupo Sabadell and he wants to make a deal. Are you interested?"

So Kallström's alive. Grebnev had figured him for crawling off into some rathole to die of his wounds. No such luck. "What sort of deal?"

"I think it's one that can benefit us all. You should hear the man. Once you get past his miserable English, he has an interesting story to tell. Should I arrange it?"

Chapter 54

OUTSIDE ARBOÇAR

The two-lane road to Arboçar is lined on both sides by lush vineyards and tawny dirt. Carson passes hardly anyone as she steers the Citroën through meandering curves and a gentle rise. The sky is a hard chrome blue, and the warm air blowing through the windows and vents is heavy with agriculture and summer. The smell reminds her of driving across the prairie when she was still in Alberta.

Iris slumps in the passenger's seat, her arms pinning her knees to her chest. She hasn't said much since they left the *Policia Nacional* office in central Barcelona an hour and fifty klicks ago: directions, mostly, and crying. She was in the cop shop over three hours, including a field trip to the medical examiner's office to identify what was left of Celeste. Carson found a park a few blocks away where she could watch people go by and tried to not think about Celeste, either alive or dead.

As they climb out of the vineyards into a semi-twisty road into the hills, Iris rasps, "Have you ever done that?"

Carson knows what she means. "Yeah."

"How do you do that and not lose it?"

"Tell yourself it's just meat. The person you knew isn't there. It helps that they don't look like real people anymore."

Iris stares out at the forest outside her window. "I kept waiting for her to wake up."

"That's what makes you lose it."

The forest gives way to more vines. Iris says, "Turn here." A couple of minutes later, she points to their two o'clock. "See the place with the tower? That's where we're going."

It's two stories of tan stone, tiled roofs, and a round tower that's another two stories taller than the buildings. "A castle?"

"No. It used to be a big farm, like, eight hundred years ago. It's called a *masia*. Now it's an inn."

They turn right onto a rambling driveway that cuts through huge stretches of vineyards. It twists around the *masia*—stone gives way to white stucco—and ends up at a brick patio with a gnarled tree in a stone planter in the center.

Vicki stands waiting for them by the tree.

Carson shoos Iris into the inn, then grabs Vicki's arm and marches her across the drive to a round wooden table on a deck under a green patio umbrella. She dumps Vicki on a folding wooden chair and thumps onto the one across the table. Just out of punching distance.

Vicki chews on her lip for a few moments. She's as dressed down as Carson's ever seen her: a white sleeveless macramé top, plain white shorts, and white deck shoes. No jewelry and hardly any makeup. The bitch is still gorgeous.

"I understand I owe you my thanks again," she says in Russian.

"For getting Celeste killed?"

"For making sure the others weren't." She glances at the deck, dragging in a shaky breath. "Sebastian told me about it. It sounds…horrible. I'm ever so sorry that she's…she's gone. I know you did the best you could to save her."

"Team effort. Dareh was in it with me. You should pay more attention to him than you do."

Vicki nods. "I know. I shall. He's already taken my purse and passport. I'm afraid he wasn't gentle about it."

Carson checks her for bruises. There aren't any; psychic damage, not physical. "I'll get those from him. Ask him what he did and let him tell you about it."

"Of course." She gazes right into Carson's eyes. "Am I your prisoner?"

"Right now? Yes." Carson pulls the Glock from behind her back and thunks it on the table. "Something you should know: I'm letting you live only because my boss and your dad would be pissed if I cap you. That could change. No more running away. You leave, I follow, and I'll be pissed off. You won't like me pissed off. Got it?"

Vicki tries to keep eye contact, but her hollow eyes keep drifting toward the Glock. "Yes, of course. I don't think I have the energy to run anymore. Losing Celeste…"

"Yeah. I know."

"I'm sure you do. What happens now?"

"Need a family meeting. A whole lotta shit happened in the past couple days. Got some heavy decisions to make about the future. You call the meeting. Consider it your last act as leader of this bunch. You sacrificed your position when you told them to abandon Celeste." Carson lurches out of the chair and sweeps the pistol off the table. "Get me when you're ready. I'll be figuring out if we can defend this place."

Carson walks the compound while she waits for Vicki and Iris to get the family meeting together. It's either four separate buildings with common walls or one single building that mutated and grew over the centuries. The complex is forty meters by twenty. The long axis is set on a northeast/southwest line along the top of a twentyish-meter bluff that overlooks a seemingly infinite sweep of vineyards to the northwest. Vineyards also border the north, northeast, and south sides. Random stacks of lumber, tools, and tarps tell her some kind of renovation's going on, which may be why there are no guests. The tower looms over the complex's north half.

She considers her phone for a few moments, then thumbs in Rodievsky's number.

"Where are you now, Larochka?" is his way of saying *hello*.

"Little town in the hills outside Barcelona." She pauses for effect. "I have Viktoriya. She'll go, but on one con—"

"She is in no position to make demands."

"Hear me out. She wants her dad to come get her himself. I'm sure the MVD has a private jet he can borrow." Carson wants to put off the reunion for a day or two until the other Project Karma members can safely get going on the next parts of their lives.

Rodievsky makes a low-bass-rumbling noise. "Why would he agree to that?"

"Does he really want her back? It's the least he can do. She hasn't lived in Moscow for thirteen years. She hasn't seen him for that long except for random ski trips. Your 'good friend' dumped his daughter in Switzerland and ignored her until six months ago.

He can spend a day in a Lear to get her back."

"Do you think Western ideas about parenting mean anything in Russia?" Not that it sounds like he cares much. "I can ask, but there is no guarantee that he will accept. Will she go home without him?"

"I'll see she does. Still need that business jet. No way I'm dragging her through airports. We'll never get her through security if she doesn't want to go."

"Hmpf. I will discuss this with Oleg Germanovich. How long can you keep her secure?"

"Few days, maybe. She likes it here. I like it here. There's a pool and sun decks. We can do some girl bonding." Carson narrowly avoids gagging on the phrase.

"Try not to enjoy yourself too much. Be ready to move her when I tell you. Is there anything else you should tell me?"

On the drive here, Carson worked out how to ask Rodievsky for some shooters to back her up. Now the time's come, she hesitates. Asking for backup would require her to explain why. The explanation will make him think she let things get out of hand. That can't go anywhere she wants to be. "Good for now. Let me know."

Chapter 55

OUTSIDE ARBOÇAR

Carson sits on the pool deck with her feet dangling in the water. The air is full of birdsong and the scent of mown grass. Stands of trees rustle on the grounds, and a forest rims the property less than a hundred meters to the southeast. She can look over her shoulder at the *masia's* south end, thirty meters away. If she looks west, the sun's on its last dive for the hills on the horizon.

If she looks down, Rogozhkin's latest text stares back at her. He sent it yesterday. `Is it something I said?`

The only good things to happen today were scoring a bedroom in the inn—across the hall from Vicki's, in case she tries to take off again—and getting out of her tactical clothes. They're in the washer; she hopes the blood will come out. *Celeste's blood.* Her survey of the inn and its grounds was damn depressing.

She has to talk to somebody who'll understand. If anyone will, it's Rogozhkin.

He answers on the third ring. "Lara?" The name she told him in Ukraine, another diminutive for her real first name.

She switches to Russian. "Yeah. Um. Saw your text a couple minutes ago. Yesterday was…fucking horrible. Sorry."

Something scrapes across a hard floor on his end of the line. "Do you want to tell me about it?"

What do I say? What she knows about him, she's learned through texts, phone calls, and what she saw over those few days on the run in the Donbass. Their first date was him putting her into a stress position in the back of a Russian Army SUV in the middle of the Ukrainian civil war. It got better from there. He was a *spetsnaz* lieutenant colonel at the time, meaning a senior trained killer, but they seemed to understand each other. They've mostly avoided the stories that would scare each other away. Maybe that's what will happen this time.

She tells him everything. In some ways, it's like spilling her life's secrets to the stranger in the next airliner seat. By the time she gets to Celeste's murder, she's choking on her words. Rogozhkin listens, interrupting only a couple of times to ask questions.

When she's done, he's silent for what feels like a long time. Then he says, "I'm so sorry. I wish I could've been there to help."

Carson wrestles her voice under control and palms a pair of stray tears off her cheeks. She croaks, "Funny you should say that. Would you like some action?"

He chuckles. "What do you have in mind?"

"This place we're at…it's hopeless. The buildings are okay, but the grounds are nuts. If these Sabadell assholes attack again—if they come in heavy—I can't fight them off alone."

"What about the Persian boy?"

"Dareh? He was great at the meet. Don't know how much is left there, though. He did some hard things. I…" She stops to put some words in the right order. "Could use somebody like you to back me up. Somebody with your skills, who I can trust. Can you…?"

Rogozhkin sighs. "Oh, Lara… I am *so* sorry. If it was any other time, I'd come. I'd leave right now. But Vlasenko's still here and it's not going well with the mistress. I guess this is a new one. He's got me taking him out every day sportfishing or diving or touring the Green Line to get away from her."

"Thought that's what wives are for."

"So did I. The woman is…excuse me, she's incredibly hot, and you can hear them having sex all the way across the house, but get two or three drinks in her and she has the personality of a scorpion. Why he didn't figure this out before bringing her down here for two weeks, I have no idea. They're supposed to leave next Friday. I can come then. Is that too late?"

Is it? She hopes she won't still be here a week from now. She also hopes it'll be because she's shipped Vicki home and left this place, not because she's been put down by that Håkan asshole. "Don't know. Sorry, I shouldn't have asked—"

"No, you should. There's no shame in asking for help when you need it. Only fools don't. But…well, I need this job. I walked away from my pension when—"

"You deserted. Yes, I know. I was there, remember?" She

checks her tone and winces. "Sorry. I'm being a bitch now. I hate that. Save your job. I'll figure it out. And, Edik?" *Think first, then talk.* "Thanks for listening. I...I really—"

"Not at all. Anytime. You sound so tired. Please take care of yourself."

As if. "You, too. We'll talk later." *I hope.*

The family meeting is in Villa 1, the one immediately south of the tower. The living room is in the back of the house, overlooking the vineyards below the bluff. The sky outside the arched wooden windows is pink, turning purple.

Project Karma's survivors crowd the two leather sofas grouped around the open-hearth fireplace. Carson sits by the fireplace on a wood-frame chair from the attached dining room. Everyone's face looks some combination of tired, scared, and sad.

Vicki says, "Let's please have a few moments of silence for Celeste." She's just finished leading everyone through a round of let's-each-share-a-good-memory-of-Celeste, the last thing Carson needed to sit through. Quiet time inside her own head could be deadly. So she focuses on the ceiling and thinks about whether it would collapse if they use the exposed beams to barricade the doors. It's better than thinking about Celeste with her head blown open.

After what seems like hours of silence, Carson stands. "Listen up. First, the good news. The guy who ran Grupo Sabadell is dead. He died badly, in a lot of pain."

Iris says, "That's good news?"

"Yeah. It doesn't help Celeste, but it's payback for what his people did to her." Carson wants to add *you'd know if you'd been there*, but skips it for now. Forcing Iris to face the cost of her cowardice and deceit was enough punishment for today. "We burned down one of their warehouses. I shot the fucker who murdered Celeste. He had body armor, so it didn't kill him, unfortunately. But he's gonna hurt like hell for days. Maybe it'll slow him down for when we see him again."

Carson clasps her hands behind her neck and stretches her shoulders and back. She's So. Fucking. Tired. She got no sleep last night and managed only a short catnap this morning while Iris was with the cops. "We cost Grupo Sabadell a lot. If they're smart, they'll say 'fuck it' and walk away. This is still the good news.

"Now the bad news. These assholes don't act so smart. We cost them a *lot*. If they still have fighters, some will wanna fight. They could be coming after us right now. They keep finding us. Vicki, you should think about how that happens.

"Spent the afternoon going over this place. The house is probably defensible for a short while. The grounds aren't. If Sabadell comes after us, I can't guarantee we'll stop them. You're all in danger."

Mutters all around. The people who didn't look scared before now do. Sebastian asks, "What do you reckon we should do?"

"Scatter. Get off this coast and out of Spain. Take different routes, keep a low profile. If you gotta meet, do it a long way from here, like the Adriatic." A storm of grousing interrupts her. She lets them have their few seconds of backtalk, then rumbles, "Shut. The fuck. Up." They do. "Project Karma was maybe a good idea when it started, but it's cost too much now. Too much death. Job One for you now is to disappear. Immediately."

"Wait, wait, wait." Iris has both her hands up, signaling *stop*. "Give up? Look, I'm just as gutted as you all are about Celeste getting killed. I hate that people have died and there's been all this violence. But Project Karma didn't cause that. Project Karma is *righteous*." She unwinds off the sofa and starts talking to the whole group. "I don't believe in a lot. I never had much reason to. But I believe in what we've been doing together more than I've believed in anything *ever*. I mean, look at what we've done, peeps!" She spreads her arms to take in everyone except Carson. "We've taken millions of dollars from the worst companies on Earth and given it to people who've made a *real difference* in the lives of thousands of people. People *depend* on us. We have a responsibility to keep that going." She drops her arms and turns to face Carson. "If we run away, Celeste died for nothing."

Carson's anger started building again as she listened to Iris's self-serving little speech. She shakes her head. "She already died for nothing. She died because Sonia pissed off some drug gang." She turns to the rest of Project Karma. "By the way…I wanna introduce a new member of the group." She thrusts her hand toward Iris.

"Meet Sonia."

Stunned silence. Then they all start talking over each other. "What?" "You're joking!" "Iris, is it true?" "I don't believe it!" Iris stands limp, her head drooping. Sometimes she shoots Carson a wounded look.

What, I was supposed to keep it secret? Carson holds up a "stop" hand. The chatter dies out. "Sonia, introduce yourself."

Props to Iris—she confesses. It's basically what she told Carson at the swim center without the sobs and running mascara, but with extra self-justification. It's not until she takes blame for Celeste that she starts to break down. Dareh and Karl look sick to their stomachs. Sebastian props his elbows on his knees and buries his face in his hands.

Vicki doesn't look as surprised as Carson thinks she should. Carson snaps at her, "Did you know?"

Vicki sighs. Her shoulders droop. "I suspected."

"Did you ask?"

"No."

Of course not. "What were you doing in Algeciras a couple weeks ago?"

Vicki's eyes sweep the floor. "I picked up a package for Iris."

"What was in it?"

"I don't know." She glances into Carson's eyes. "She said it was personal."

"Bet she did. Why didn't you ask?"

Vicki squints at Carson. Carson doesn't want to know what her face looks like right now. "My mind doesn't work the way yours does."

"No shit." Carson turns to the rest of them. "You decide what to do with her. Up to me? I'd feed her to the cops. That's your call. She's dead to me. You people keep her under control. She does one more stupid thing, I'll blow her head off, just like I said I'd do when Celeste was taken. Understood?"

Vicki jumps in. "What are you going to do, Lisa?"

"Real question is, what are we—me and you—gonna do." Carson points between them. "You're coming with me to the airport. I'm putting you on a plane to Moscow. I had a job to do when I came here, remember? Now I'm gonna do it. You can sort things out with your dad on your own time."

Sebastian says, "You're leaving us then, are you?"

"If you're smart, you won't stay here. So you're leaving me and Vicki. It's all about perspective."

Iris jumps up again. "But we've been together for *two years*! Doesn't that count for anything?"

Carson's getting tired of this argument. It's stupid and pointless. She heaves onto her feet and gets into Iris's personal space. "Yeah. It does. Just remember how we got here. If Project Karma dies, it's because you killed it, you stupid bitch."

Vicki says, "Lisa, please—"

"Vicki." Sebastian's growl shuts her off instantly. He gently separates Carson and Iris and squeezes Carson's shoulder. "I hear what you're saying, Lisa. I was there, too. And I know you're right. I think we all do. But we've lost everything—our papers, clothes, laptops, all of it. We can't run like this. We need a few days to get ready, to buy clothes and toothbrushes and get money and temporary IDs. Can you give us that, love? Can you stay, and let Vicki stay, until we're ready?"

"Not up to me." Carson shrugs out of Sebastian's grip. "When I hear the jet's inbound, she's going to the airport. Can't put it off anymore. And if she"—Carson thumbs over her shoulder toward Vicki—"takes off again, I'll be gone sooner. Make sure you tell her to stay put. Whatever you need to do, do it fast."

Sebastian nods. "Vicki? You'll not be leaving again until Lisa says so, will you." It's not a question.

Vicki studies her manicure, looking sour. "She has my purse and my identification. As long as she's here, I will be, too." She stands and smooths the front of her top. "Lisa? If the villains are coming for us, shouldn't you be planning how to protect us?"

Carson knew they'd end up here. "If the villains are coming for you, you all better be gone before they get here. Time to grow up and protect yourselves."

Chapter 56

L'HOSPITALET DE LLOBREGAT, BARCELONA

Grebnev can't help but shake his head when Brusin leads Kallström through the office door. The Swede's face is flushed and shiny, he walks stiffly, and his eyes are bloodshot and puffy. Grebnev doesn't know what happened to the man, but it certainly made an impression.

Brusin says in Russian, "This is Håkan Kallström, sir."

Grebnev and Brusin had worked out a device for Grebnev to talk directly to Kallström without giving away his identity. Grebnev will play the "important man from Moscow" and speak only Russian, while Brusin acts as the interpreter. Kallström's never seen Grebnev and has heard him speaking only English over the phone, a very different sound. It's a silly bit of theater, but the last thing Grebnev wants is for this thug to know what he looks like.

Kallström stops two paces from Brusin's enormous desk. He wavers a bit. "Who are you?" he demands in English.

Time to show him who's the dog and who's the hydrant. Once Brusin translates Kallström's words, Grebnev barks in Russian, "Never mind who I am. What do you want?"

"Ferran is dead." Kallström winces when he tries to stand straighter. "I run Grupo Sabadell now. You are with important people from Moscow?"

Grebnev settles into the huge desk chair and peers at Kallström. By now he's seen the news reports about the debacle in El Bon Pastor. "Did you arrange for this Ferran to die?"

"Maybe I do."

Bullshit. He can hardly stand. He's probably lucky he made it out of that disaster alive. "What do you want?"

Kallström puts away his forced smile. "I want to deal. New fighters come to help me. I can finish job you give to Ferran. Give me weapons and say where hackers are. I will finish them. Russian bulldyke, I also finish. Then, we join with you. Move what you want, anything. Drugs, guns, women. Anything. We make you strong here. No more Ferran business bullshit. This is good for you?"

Incredible. This clown thinks he's talking to the *mafiya.* Did Brusin do that, or did Kallström's little thug brain cook this up by itself? It hardly matters; Zapadneft doesn't need these idiots, not with Karik's squad here and ready to go.

Except... The hackers are still alive. One of them visited Zapadneft's computers early this morning Moscow time. Severinov was quick to inform Grebnev that none of the three laptops they flew overnight to Moscow belonged to the hackers, though one erased itself when the techs tried to break the password. *Finish the job or don't come back,* Severinov told him. *Ordered* him.

This thug in front of him is responsible for the job not being done...and he has the balls to come asking for another chance? Grebnev should shoot the idiot where he stands, except Brusin would object to the bloodstains on his carpet. Instead, he glares at Kallström. "Every time you've gone up against these people, they've handed your ass to you. What's different now? Why will you succeed now?"

Kallström tries to pump himself up, but whatever pain he's dealing with stops him in mid-swell. "Ferran wanted small action. Make no noise. He says, 'only college children, no threat.' I tell him this is war, but he says no. Ferran is dead. I know this is war. I know how to fight war. The men I get, the Demons, they know war. Some fight in Afghanistan with me. We know we kill the Russian bulldyke first, then the rest are helpless. We attack strong, no mercy. We will win, you see."

Grebnev doesn't believe the first part or the last. Blaming the dead commander is an old tradition in and out of the military. The stuff in the middle is minimally plausible. "These 'Demons.' Are they a motorcycle gang?"

"Yes. The best. We sell heroin, cocaine, meth in Sweden. Now we come here to control our supply. I do that now with Grupo Sabadell. We join with you, you have network into Sweden, Denmark. Much money to make..."

But Grebnev's already tuning out Kallström's sales pitch and looking at the possibilities. Motorcycle gangs aren't always the knuckle-draggers they appear to be. Russia has found uses for the Night Wolves in Ukraine, Crimea, and the Balkans. President Putin rides with them. Many of the drug "soldiers" Grebnev's run across since leaving the army are hopped-up street toughs at best. A group of combat veterans with bad attitudes might be what's needed to resolve this situation, even if they're being led by this schoolyard bully.

Does it even matter if they win? If they do, fine; Tarasenko can't keep up her luck forever. Karik's men can watch from the sidelines and talk trash, like at a football match. But if this bunch comes to the same end as the others, Karik's men can finish off any survivors, grab the hacker's equipment, and leave the rest of the mess behind for the police to sort out. More "senseless drug-related violence," as the news reporters like to say. The company wins. Grebnev wins. His position with the company will be secure and he can carry on with the rest of this part of his life—a home, a family, savings, status.

Not a bad outcome.

Grebnev points to one of the oversized armchairs facing the desk. "Sit. Tell me more about your plan."

Chapter 57

Partway through her morning rounds, Carson finds Vicki perched on a ladder, attacking a raggedy tree with loppers half her height. She's wearing what must be her idea of work clothes—a white v-neck tee shirt and white jeans—and somehow isn't dirty yet. Carson snaps, "Step it up. Gotta clear these sightlines if we're gonna defend this place."

"I don't want to destroy the tree."

"Worry more about not getting destroyed yourself."

Vicki wipes some invisible forehead sweat on her forearm. She says in Russian, "Are you here to supervise or to keep me from running into the woods?"

"I'm here because the worker guys are breaking my head with their noise." She sticks with English; she's not in the mood to translate both sides of the conversation. "Is that why nobody else's here?"

"Yes." Vicki took the hint; she's switched to English. "It was impossible to keep the inn open and still work on it. Something about wiring and pipes."

"So how are you here?"

"The owners are my friends. We've come here as a group several times. It's a wonderful place to rest and refresh, especially after a busy time at the clubs." She pauses, watching a hawk circle the nearby field. "To be honest, I needed to keep my distance from you. I asked if I could shelter here, and they said yes."

"Now here I am."

"Yes, here you are." Vicki resumes snipping. She almost punches the tree with the loppers.

"Where's the rest of your posse?"

"They went into town." *Clack, clack, clack.* A little faster and it could be gunfire. "Sebastian took them to do some basic shopping."

"They have money now?"

"Yes. Sebastian and Karl stayed up half the night transferring money between bank accounts so he can use his cashpoint card. I'm sure they'll all be chuffed to have toothpaste and a clean change of clothing tonight."

"They took the Mercedes. You need to get rid of that thing."

Vicki snaps an eyebrow at Carson. "Whatever for? It's the only thing we have that fits everyone, and it's quite nice."

"It belonged to a two-bit drug lord. Don't think the cops know about it? Don't think they're looking for it?" She pulls her phone, unlocks it, then holds it out toward Vicki. "Call him. That thing's trouble. Tell him to dump it in the long-term lot at the airport and rent an SUV there."

"I've my own mobile, thank you. I'll discuss it with him when they return." Vicki climbs off the ladder and glares at Carson. "Are you enjoying this? Ordering me about? Keeping me prisoner?"

"Girl, if I was keeping you prisoner, you'd know it." Carson stabs a finger at the v-neck's point. "What I'm doing with you here? It's because you keep running away. Only reason you're not locked in a car trunk at the airport right now is because I bought you some time. I told my Bratva boss that you won't go unless your dad comes to get you himself."

Vicki lets out a whoop of laughter. "You're mad. He'll never agree to that."

"Maybe not. If he says 'no,' you're out nothing. He says 'yes,' you get maybe another day or two with your friends." She watches Vicki stare off to the side for a few moments. "Your next line should be, 'Thank you, Lisa.'"

Vicki rolls her eyes, then huffs. "Thank you, Lisa."

"You know, if you'd been like this at Pangea, you'd be in Russia by now. Was that version of Vicki another role? Is there a real Vicki? Have I met her?"

"You should know that by now." She finally looks at Carson. Her eyes are blurring. "I lost a member of my family Friday night. And I realize…that…I may have been partly at fault." Her voice starts fuzzing out, too. "Friday was not my finest hour. I was frightened. I wanted…I only wanted to make certain the rest of my family was safe." She knuckles the corners of her eyes. "I hope God can forgive me for what I did…what I said…that night. I certainly can't." She finally breaks eye contact with Carson and stares at the ground.

"Yeah. Sucks, doesn't it? Holding somebody's life in your hands...and dropping it?" Carson catches herself wondering whether this is simply another performance. It's a shitty thing to think, but by now she doesn't know what to believe, or who. "So now you're beating yourself up because it won't hurt so much when everybody else starts beating you. Or maybe they'll feel sorry for you and won't kick you as hard as you deserve. Word of advice? It doesn't work."

Carson punches Sebastian's number on her phone's call history. He answers on the third ring. "Sebastian? Dump the G-wagen. It's radioactive." She walks away from Vicki without waiting for her reaction.

Carson's phone rings as she steps over a pile of busted plaster to get to the staircase in Villa 3. It's Rodievsky. "*Shto?*"

"Larochka. You sound distracted."

"A little busy." She checks her watch. "Working the late shift?"

"Always. Baranov agrees to Viktoriya's condition. He will be at the Barcelona airport on Wednesday."

Carson halts halfway up the stairs. "He went for it?"

"He did. I had to apply surprisingly little pressure to get him to agree. He will send to me his itinerary, and I will send it to you. You and the girl will be there on time, of course."

"Uh, yeah. Of course." Finally, a hard deadline. She's done with this project and done with Rodievsky for now. She wants out of this country. "I don't have to go with them, right?"

"No, I would not force that on you. I must warn you, though—if you do not produce the girl when Oleg Germanovich arrives, you may be going someplace not as pleasant as where you have been."

Grebnev's halfway through his delayed-until-early-afternoon morning workout, running up and down the hotel's fire escape, when his phone begins to buzz.

It's Severinov. "We found your missing Mercedes."

"Where?"

"In the long-stay car park at the Barcelona airport."

"Any sign of the hackers?"

"Yes, before they dumped the ute. They went to a shopping mall west of Barcelona, the Centre Comercial Vilamarina in Viladecans. Then they drove to the airport. The security cameras show them getting on a shuttle bus to the terminal."

Grebnev has his boss on speaker and is scrolling through Yandex Maps on his phone, locating the places Severinov mentioned. "Are they flying out?"

"No. There was a huge amount of activity on their Amazon accounts last night. Someone in that gang must own stock in the company. I've sent the shipping address to your email. Their packages won't arrive until tomorrow or Wednesday. It's time to end this. See to it."

"Yes, sir." Grebnev's already climbing to the fifth floor. "We'll find them."

Chapter 58

Kallström waves another Harley to the curb along the narrow frontage road separating the runways from the warehouse-and-shopping area southwest of Sabadell Airport. He counts as the rider dismounts: ten. Fisk had told him a dozen would come. Well, ten's better than what he had, and Kallström knows over half of them.

His back is throbbing again. The heroin he took some while ago is wearing off. His mouth's still dry despite chugging bottled water almost nonstop, and his arms and legs feel like they've been replaced with iron copies. Still, he has to push on. The man from Moscow wants him to finish the job quickly to make up for Ferran's mistakes.

The morning sky is just now losing the last tinge of sunrise red. He paces stiffly down the line of motorcycles and their milling riders, bumping fists with the ones he knows. Most wear dark-gray leather vests with the Demons logo on the back—a bearded zombie in a medieval helmet.

Fisk stands at the head of the line, his big arms crossed. Kallström was there when Fisk got his nose smashed the third and final time, brawling with some Afghan soldiers who couldn't fight in the bar any better than they could in the field. The time they wasted training those savages…

Kallström says in Swedish, "You said twelve. Are more coming?"

"No, this is it. We had business in Granada." Fisk always sounds like he's chipping wood with his teeth.

Business in Granada. Fuck you. "Well, let's get to it, then." Kallström continues to the white Transit van a few meters ahead of Fisk's hog, doing his best to not move his back or breathe too deeply. His broken ribs are trying to kill him.

There are five battered, wooden olive-drab crates inside the van. He's already pried open the lids. Now he hauls out a stubby carbine and hands it to Fisk. "For you and the boys. Straight from Libya."

Fisk expertly examines the weapon, checks the chamber, dry-fires it. He smiles. "Used to pull these off dead Taliban chiefs. Where'd you get *okuroks?*"

"I have friends in high places now." Kallström flips open another crate and produces a black cylinder that looks like an overgrown shell casing. "PBS-4 suppressors for the lot. Also, four Tishina grenade launchers." He opens another crate, smaller and more square than the others. "Subsonic 5.45mm ammo, thirty-round magazines."

"Nice." Fisk scratches his chin through his black beard, the only hair on his head. "Your friends must want something real bad."

"Oh, they do." Kallström swipes the manila envelope off the stacks of magazines. "You want me to brief the whole crew?"

"Not quite yet." Fisk looks around like he's lost something. "Where's your people?"

"You're my people."

"No, the ones that come with this Sabadell whatever you say you took over. Where are they?"

The one thing Kallström had hoped nobody would ask. "They're up and down the Costa Tropical and Costa del Sol. In the Balearics, also." He's trying to sound strong and positive, but the dregs of the H in his system are fucking with his tongue. "We're a little thin up here because the old chief made some shitty decisions. I hope you and your crew will be the beginning of a new Grupo Sabadell in this area."

Kallström's old combat buddy shakes his head sadly, then moves close enough for his folded forearms to push Kallström back a step. "Haven't fucking changed a bit, have you, Håkan? Look. We're here because you used to be a member—"

Used to be? You shit… "I hope I'm still a member."

"It don't work that way, man. You can't drop in and out whenever you want." Fisk thumbs over his shoulder. "There's guys here, they don't remember you. It's been that long. *I'm* here with these men because *I* remember when you used to be worth a shit.

We'll do this one op with you. The weapons are fair payment. When it's done, we can talk about your big plans and if we sign up. That good for you?"

When I used to be worth a shit? You fat bastard, I oughta... No, take it down a few. We need him. Show him what this could be. "Of course. It's good to be back with my brothers here. You'll see how good this will be for all of us" He slides Grebnev's printed map and photo from the envelope and slaps them on an unopened crate. "The target's here, in Arboçar. Southwest of us, outside Barcelona. They're in this place." He stabs the photo with his index finger.

"The fuck is this? Is that a watchtower?"

"It's an inn. There's maybe a dozen of them in there. My important friends want them all dead. We're—"

"Why?"

"These people stole from my new friends. We're showing what we can do. Once these children are gone, we'll have more business than we can handle, more money, more connections."

"Who are these 'children'?"

"College boys and girls. There's only one real threat: this big Russian bulldyke. She's with one of the Russian *mafiya* clans, but it's not their operation, see? It's just her. When I put her down, the rest are like baby rats. Defenseless vermin. My friends want their computers, that's all. We can be done with this before sunset."

"If it's so easy, why haven't you done it by now?"

"That was Ferran's fault. He didn't want to go all in. He wanted to do it nice and quiet. I want to do it right, the way we should've."

Fisk chews on the inside of his cheek as he pores over the map and photo. "You're saying, one shooter?"

"Yes, yes. One. Maybe two, but no more." *Come on, don't be a pussy. Be part of this. Say yes...*

"Take us there. I'll check it out. If it looks right, we'll do it." Fisk turns to glare at Kallström. "This better be for real, Håkan. Old times get you only so far."

Chapter 59

Carson trots along a walking trail that threads through the woods southeast of the inn. She doesn't usually run cross-country—it's a kind of stress her knees don't need anymore—but she is today because she's become a firm believer in Stearne's Law and the prickling on the back of her neck is warning her that someone really is out to get her.

Sebastian rented a white Audi Q7 SUV at the airport after they dumped the G-wagen in the long-stay lot. Did they get rid of it in time? Hard to tell. The way Sebastian described it when he returned to the inn, it was too easy. Carson's learned that easy isn't always right. Yesterday's shopping expedition gave the opposition (Sabadell, cops, whatever) plenty of time to hang a tail on the G-wagen or trace credit card activity.

So she's going to check out the places she'd pick if she was spying on the inn. Just in case.

She jogs up the gentle slope to the forest's edge, walks a few meters, then quietly steps off the dirt trail into the whorl of trees that embraces a small, amoeba-shaped vineyard southeast of the pool. It's still dim under the canopy and she's wearing her black sweats; as long as she stays quiet, nobody should know she's there.

Carson shuffles through the leaf litter, pushing away the potentially loud bits instead of stepping on them. It's slow, but she doesn't have anything better to do. She pauses often, trying to build a sound picture, but doesn't hear anything other than clicking tree branches, leaves flapping in the rising east breeze, and the occasional bird call.

After half an hour, when she's good and tired of staring at the ground, she almost trips over what she's looking for: crushed leaves, snipped-off bushes, and footprints in a patch of bare dirt. She examines the prints. A man's boots, average size, shallow tread, both going to and coming from the leaf bed. A search for tripwires and booby-traps turns up nothing, so she crawls onto the matted leaves, flattens on her belly, and checks the view.

The hide's in a finger of trees that streams along the edge of a vineyard to end at the inn's parking lot. Carson has a perfect view of the courtyard with the gnarly tree.

So she's not imaging things. Someone's been here. Watching.

And because the bootprints are a few hours old, there must be another observation post around here—one with somebody in it. She's not dressed properly to deal with that, and she doesn't have to.

All she has to do is convince Project Karma it has a serious problem.

"What should we do?"

Finally, progress. Carson's led Vicki through multiple rounds of *are you sure?* and *how can you tell?* and *why are they here?* Asking action questions means she finally believes what Carson's saying. "How much longer until your people can move?"

"I'm not certain." Vicki peeks into Villa 1's dining room, where Sebastian is setting up his new laptop. "Sebastian? Could you join us, please?"

Once he enters the kitchen, he glances at Vicki, then Carson, then raises his eyebrows. "What's gone wrong now?"

Carson quickly downloads the watcher situation on him in a few lines. "When can the others travel?"

Sebastian doesn't ask any of Vicki's questions. "Tomorrow or Thursday, so long as we travel by road. We can't fly without documents, and we can't risk trains in case there's an ID check. We've several thousands of euros in Amazon orders coming today and tomorrow that we'd hate to leave behind."

Fuck. One or two more days. Lots can happen. Carson blows out a long breath. "Okay. They probably found us through the G-wagen." She tosses a sharp glance at Vicki, who bows her head. "Now they're here, they know about our other cars. We could try to sneak out after dark, but they had all last night to plant GPS beacons on the cars. They've done it to us before. Wouldn't be surprised if they have tails waiting on either side of the turnoff for the road to Arboçar."

Sebastian says, "So what you're saying is, we can't leave."

"Probably could on foot, at night. But then what? Normally I'd say, do a fast run for the airport and fly someplace random. Airport security will keep the tails out. But you can't fly without ID, so that won't cut it."

Vicki raises an index finger. "Could we walk to the main road and hire a BlaBlaCar to take us from there?"

Carson games that out, then shrugs. "Maybe. Your people will have to leave everything here. You, too. No dragging suitcases through the forest. That also opens us to an ambush in the trees." She turns to Sebastian. "You and Karl need to search the cars for trackers. They'll know you found the others, so they'll have gotten creative. Go."

Sebastian strides toward the front door without hesitation. Vicki watches him go. "You're very good at giving orders."

"Learn by doing."

"Right. What do we do if he finds nothing, or finds the trackers?"

Carson flashes back to times she's needed to dump ultra-persistent tails. "Leave at sunset. Go to Vilafranca." The next nearest sizable town. "There's a place there that rents minivans—it's open 'til seven. Drive it to the airport, rent something else there. Get lost in the dark. Even if Sabadell has a second set of trackers on the cars we have now and they make the credit card at the place in Vilafranca, we still lose them at the airport."

Vicki crosses her arms and aims a loaded eyebrow at Carson. "Does that work?"

"Usually."

"But not definitely. What if Sabadell comes for us early?"

The question Carson hoped she wouldn't ask. "We fight back. We play the Battle of Batoche and hope we're Middleton and not Riel."

Vicki's face looks like her breakfast is eating her in retaliation. "Whatever that means. You've a plan for that?"

"Yeah. Family meeting, right now. Call it."

◎

Carson explains the situation to Vicki's posse. Karl and Dareh exchange a lot of anxious looks; they both know that Dareh will be in the thick of this. Iris sits in a corner wrapped in her own arms and looks nauseated. Vicki doesn't say a word, and no one looks at her.

"This is just in case," Carson says. "Just because they're here now doesn't mean they're ready to attack. Or, they could come through the front door any minute. We don't know. The goal's to leave tonight. If they come before then, we're gonna make it expensive for them to get to us here. Every time they've come after us and we've pushed back, it took a while before they tried again. Need that to work only one more time."

Karl raises his hand. "Why not go to Vilafranca now and get away?"

"Leaving in broad daylight gives us no head start. We need to give Sebastian and Karl some time to find any trackers Sabadell's planted. If we look like we're hunkering down, Sabadell may take longer to get ready. We hurt them bad the night Celeste…" Carson can't say *died* or *was murdered*. From the looks on the posse's faces, she doesn't need to. "They might need more time to get themselves together." She turns to Vicki. "Gonna need those workmen to bar the doors."

Vicki nods. "Of course. I'll speak to them about it."

Carson turns to the group and claps her hands once, loud. They all jump. "Listen up. Here's what we need to do…"

When she first saw the inn, Carson called it a castle. Now that she's been all around and through it, it's not a bad description. No moat, unfortunately, but the outside stone walls are at least half a meter thick. The main doors to each villa are heavy oak protected by lockable wrought-iron gates. Iron grilles enclose the ground-floor windows facing the driveway, which also have interior wooden shutters. The shutters won't keep out bullets, but they'll contain the broken glass and obscure the view inside. And there's always the tower and its sweeping view of all the countryside surrounding the inn.

But.

The windows and doors on the inn's bluff side have neither shutters nor grilles; if a hostile makes it onto the open patios overlooking the vineyards, nothing can keep them out of the building. With all the existing shutters closed, anyone inside is completely blind. Villa 4, the southernmost building, has a huge, pointed arch in its southern wall that's all window, making that villa indefensible. Each villa is completely separate, with no way to go from one to another except by going outside, a bad idea in a firefight. Little stone outbuildings provide durable cover for any attackers to within three or four meters of the main inn.

"Think outside the box," Carson tells Vicki's posse. "Hell, think outside the fucking *planet*. If they get down here, we gotta slow 'em down so we can hurt 'em."

She's in the stone storage hut across the driveway from the courtyard, sorting through the junk to find anything that can be a weapon, when Iris edges through the door. "Hi."

Carson doesn't even look at her. She can't.

Iris goes into a self-hug and watches Carson for a few beats. "Um…I don't know if I'm really useless or I just feel like it, but I'm feeling pretty useless right now. Anything I can do?"

Carson pulls a rusty pitchfork out of a tangle of stuff, then stops to gives Iris a quick scan. She's in her usual sexy-farm-girl outfit. "Put some clothes on."

Iris sighs. "Anything else?"

The urge to pin Iris to the wall with the pitchfork is getting too strong. Carson adds it to the two shovels and a machete near the door, then turns back to rummaging. "What's our food situation?"

"A day's worth, maybe."

"That's all?"

"It's not like back home. We don't buy a week's worth of food and eat it in three days. The fridges here can't deal with that. You get food one day at a time." Her eyes brighten. "I can go grocery shopping."

"If they're out there, they'll kill you."

Iris scuffs the dust on the flagstones. "Maybe that's better for you guys." She sounds broken.

Carson stops and closes her eyes. She doesn't feel sorry for Iris—the woman made her own problem—but she recognizes the deep despair and hopelessness that comes with making a bad call that kills an innocent. Iris's friends still need to decide what to do with her. Right now, they, like Carson, have a hard time even looking at her. As a practical matter, though, a depressed and possibly suicidal Iris will bum out her friends and may throw a wild card into a situation that has way too many already.

Carson takes a long, deep breath, then turns to face Iris. "Wanna be useful? Get the first-aid kits out of villas three and four and put them in one and two. Any water you find? Do the same. See if you can find fire extinguishers. And sheets—we're gonna need those for bandages."

"Okay." Iris's voice is small and airless. Her face is still collapsed.

"Look, it's not exciting, but it's all real important. I mean, look at what I'm doing—going through all this old shit out here. Dareh's taping windows. It'll help a lot if you can do this stuff for me. Okay?"

Iris nods. "At least I can't screw it up." She points at the garden tools by the door. "What're those for?"

"Weapons, in case somebody gets into the inn. We don't have enough guns or enough people who know how to use them. Anybody can swing a shovel. You play baseball in school?"

"No. Soccer, mostly. I was taller than most of the girls, so I played goalie a lot." Iris slings the two shovels over her shoulder. "Hi ho, hi ho. Off to work I go."

When Iris leaves, Carson resumes scavenging. Something under the cluttered workbench catches her eye. She pulls the wadded-up canvas tarp off it and finds a well-used twenty-liter gas can. It sloshes when she picks it up, but it weighs about right for being nearly full. She unscrews the top and gets a snoutful of unleaded fumes. *Hm.* The recycling box had a bunch of beer bottles in it this morning...

It's not until almost noon that Carson notices the text waiting on her phone. Rogozhkin sent it yesterday morning: `Are you okay?` She replies, `Not so much.` Then she calls. It flips to voicemail after four rings. *Story of my life.*

◉

Dareh flags down Carson during one of her delivery calls to

Villa 1's kitchen. She'd turned over the gasoline and a cache of over twenty-odd beer bottles to him to make Molotov cocktails. She notices only one completed flame weapon on the kitchen counter. "What's the holdup?" she asks.

Dareh waves her to his computer on the counter near the fridge. When she sees what he's typed in the DuckDuckGo search box, she laughs. "You gotta be shitting me."

"No, no. It is serious. Please." Dareh scrolls the screen. "The bottle there? It is a test. Do you want to see?" He holds up the bottle, as if she can't figure out which one.

"You bet."

They troop out to the terrace overlooking the bluff. Dareh uses a plastic cigarette lighter to spark the strip of yellow cloth tied around the bottle's neck. Then he hurls it against the low stone wall separating this terrace from the one next door. The bottle shatters; the whole thing explodes with a *whoosh*. The field-expedient napalm slowly oozes down the wall, leaving a trail of intense white-yellow fire and oily smoke.

Carson laughs and claps her hands. "That's fucking *awesome*! How'd you do it?"

Dareh says, "We have much Styrofoam from Amazon packages. I melt some in the petrol until it is like honey. If we have motor oil, I can slow the burn."

"We don't, but this is perfect. Prep the rest of the bottles." She bumps fists with Dareh. "You rock."

She's about to leave when she hears the unmistakable roar of motorcycles on the road to Arboçar. Two Harleys cruise past the wooded rise northwest of the inn, then along the vineyards on either side of the road. When they reach the inn's driveway, they turn right and park their bikes to block the drive. The riders dismount, shake out their legs, then scope out the inn. One waves at her like the Queen of England.

Carson doesn't wave back.

Chapter 60

Carson scopes the forest's treeline with her mini-binoculars from her first-floor bedroom in Villa 1. Nothing moves out there except wind. It's not comforting; what she can't see can kill her. Every time a bird pops out of the canopy, she wonders if it's bird business or because Sabadell's people are moving in.

Last time she checked, the two bikers at the end of the drive were smoking and chatting. They have Ksyukha assault carbines—the compact, concealable Russian answer to the Uzi—slung across their chests. She carried one in the Donbass for a few days last May. Not standard equipment for outlaw biker gangs as far as Carson knows, but she hasn't kept up with that breed of lowlife since she turned in her badge. If she survives this, she should catch up.

Throat-clearing makes her glance over her shoulder. Vicki's standing quietly just inside the doorway, her face serious. "Do you see anyone?" she asks in Russian.

Carson answers in Russian. "Not out there. Dareh's watching the trees at the foot of the bluff in case they come in that way." Carson turns her binoculars toward the window. "Don't know what they're waiting for. They're burning daylight."

"Are they waiting for nighttime?"

"Maybe. Takes a lot of training to fight at night. From what I saw at the meet Friday night, these guys don't have it."

A squeak breaks the quiet behind her. When Carson glances back again, she finds Vicki perched on the foot of her bed with her hands pressed between her knees. "Lisa, if I ask you a question, will you answer honestly?"

"Depends on the question."

"Fair enough." Vicki holds a deep breath, then lets it go. "Are we all going to die?"

Carson picks through half a dozen answers until she finds one that probably won't send Vicki away to slit her wrists. "Not if I have a say in it."

"There's only one of you—"

"Dareh, too. Don't forget him."

"Yes, I know. But you're the leader now. You've been since you and Iris came here." She cocks her head. "It's easy for you, isn't it? Leadership? You wear it like a bespoke coat. I always have to work at it."

Is it easy? Carson's never thought of herself as a natural leader. She sees something that needs to get done and does it, and people usually let her. "If you have a plan and look like you know what you're doing, you get to be leader. When you fuck it up, somebody else takes over." Carson sits next to Vicki. "You were the leader they needed in peacetime. You gave them something to do, something they believed in. It's wartime now. They need different things."

Vicki nods. "Yes, I know. But what do I do now? I've no skills for—"

"They know you. Some of them still love you. Be their mom. Keep them calm. Help them deal with being scared. When I was raising my brothers? Didn't have a clue how to be a mom. Didn't have any good examples to follow. I used a lot of tough love. It worked with my brothers, but it won't with your people. You need to give them what I can't."

Vicki nods again. "Of course. I'll try." She takes a pinch of Carson's long-sleeved black tee. "You look like a ninja."

Heavy steps pound up the staircase. Karl bursts into the doorway, panting. "Lisa! Someone just drove into the courtyard!"

Carson springs off the bed. "Drove? Who?"

"I don't know. He's outside."

She dashes into Vicki's bedroom at the back of the villa and scopes the driveway's far end. The bikers are gone and their motorcycles are parked on either side of the road. *What the…?* "Get Dareh. Now."

Carson returns to her own room and peers into the courtyard. A silver Toyota crossover is nosed up to the stone tree planter. She can't tell if anyone's inside it and she can't see if anyone's at the door.

Vicki steps next to her. "Who is it? Do you know them?"

"No idea." *How'd he get past the bikers…unless he's in on it?*

Two pairs of feet clatter up the stairs. Dareh appears at the door with Karl hovering behind him. "You ask for me, Lisa?"

"Yeah." Carson grabs the M4 from beside the flat-panel radiator and hands it to Dareh as she charges out the door. "You're up here, on overwatch. Remember the asshole who shot Celeste?"

"I never forget him."

"Good. If it's him, kill him. Don't wait. If it's not, wait for my signal. Got it?"

Dareh's face is set to full grim. "I do. Please be careful."

Carson draws the Glock from her back waistband and screws on the suppressor while she hustles down the dark oak stair treads. All the ground-floor windows on the driveway side are shuttered, so she has no way to see who's out there. She waits by the front door with Karl, who tries to give her a brave smile and mostly doesn't succeed.

Dareh shouts, "Ready!"

"Okay." Carson tells Karl, "Lock the door behind me. Don't open it unless I tell you."

"Yes." Karl grips Carson's bicep. "Please don't die. It would be sad."

"I agree." Carson cracks the door, unlatches the wrought-iron screen, then pushes past it while closing the door behind her. She has the pistol at ready by the time she clears the screen. Nobody visible in the Toyota's windshield. Nobody to her right.

A man aims a Ksyukha at her to her left.

She's about to fire—her index finger is heavy on the Glock's trigger—when she freezes. "*Edik?* The fuck are you doing here?"

Rogozhkin slowly lowers his carbine and breaks out a big smile. "You asked if I wanted some action," he says in Russian. "I never turn down an attractive woman who asks that."

Carson hasn't been this glad to see someone for years. She helps him unload his rental car and introduces him as "a friend" to the Project Karma survivors. They're various degrees of wary, but greet him politely. He doesn't look like an action hero—he's an inch shorter than Carson, fifteen years grayer, and swarthy, with Asian eyes. It's the first time Carson's heard him speak any significant amount of English; it's careful, basic, and heavily accented.

She eventually takes him upstairs to her room so they can talk privately. She asks in Russian, "How are you here? What happened to Vlasenko?"

He carefully stages a black tactical duffel, a padded rifle carrying case, and two suppressed Ksyukhas on her bed. He's dressed for a day on the golf course; his gray pinstripe golf shirt exposes ropy, scarred forearms. "I told him about your situation on Saturday."

"He knows about me?"

"I may have mentioned you once or twice. Have you ever watched the television show *Vikings*?"

"Couple episodes. Didn't do much for me."

"He loves it. Never misses an episode. I may have referred to you at some point as a 'shield maiden.'"

Shield maidens were maybe-mythical female Viking warriors. Carson groans. "So he thinks I'm six feet tall, blond, and—"

"Look like Katheryn Winnick? Maybe. When you didn't answer my text yesterday, I told him you asked for my help. He said, 'You have to go save your shield maiden.' His jet flew me to Barcelona this morning. I hope I'm not too late."

Edik came here for me? Yes, she'd asked, but she never expected him to come. They hardly know each other. He's got a life on Cyprus. But here he is.

Edik lifts an eyebrow. "Am I too late?"

"No. No. It's just... I *really* owe you one. Don't know how I'll—"

"We'll talk about that later." He smiles. For a career special-ops soldier, he has a surprisingly nice smile. "Tell me what needs to be done."

Carson briefs him on the tactical situation, showing him the views from both sides of the villa. She nods toward the driveway's end. "Bikers down there..."

"You won't need to worry about them. They weren't your friends, were they?"

"No. That where the Ksyukhas came from?"

"Yes. They won't ask for them back, if that's what you're worried about. How many combatants do you have?"

"Me. Dareh. I told you about him. And...you."

Edik frowns. "That's all? What about the tall Irishman?"

"Sebastian? Don't know. He hasn't volunteered anything."

"You should ask. If he's Irish and upper-class, he's probably gone shooting for game birds at least." He peers almost sideways out the window. "Is that tower real, or only decoration?"

"It's real. There's a door off the kitchen that opens into it. Opposition probably doesn't know it's usable."

"Let's keep that our little secret for now." He places both his hands gently on her shoulders. "Breathe. You're not alone. We'll take care of this."

Just having Edik here takes about a hundred kilos off Carson's neck. She maybe won't die today. She takes his face in both hands and kisses him. "Thanks."

He gives her an almost-bashful smile. "That makes it all worthwhile. Let me change."

Edik rejoins the group in the kitchen, where Carson's staged all their spare ammunition, the napalm bombs, and the trackers Karl and Sebastian found in the Citroën and the Audi. He's changed into tan-brown-and-green *Partizan*-pattern camouflage utilities and brown roughout boots, and has a gray-camouflaged, bolt-action hunting rifle slung from his right shoulder. He stands behind Vicki's crew and listens as Carson explains what everyone is supposed to do and where they're supposed to be.

When she's done, Carson leads him to the heavy oak-plank door that opens into the tower's base. The open-tread iron staircase winds up the rough-stone tower walls to a platform almost thirty meters above their heads. She says, "You didn't say anything in there."

"I didn't need to. You're doing fine. There's something I'd like to ask you, though."

"Okay."

"Why do you stay? Why risk your life for those people? This Viktoriya, the blonde—what is she to you?"

Carson's been asking herself that same question ever since Sunday. Her answer may not be great, but it's the one she tells Edik. "Not doing it for her. She's been a pain in the ass. But if I leave, the rest of them will die, and they don't deserve that. I still need to kill the asshole who executed Celeste, too." She sets her palm lightly on his chest. "I love that you came here. But this isn't your fight. Go if you want and I won't hold it against you."

Edik smiles and shakes his head. "You helped me get out of a bad situation in Ukraine. I'll never forget that. If you're here and you still need my help, then it is my fight." He nods toward the door. "The kids are scared. You can smell it. Go be brave for them. Show them how a shield maiden goes to war."

Chapter 61

Kallström lets his binoculars dangle from his neck and grinds the heels of his hands into his eye sockets. The oxy he took has stopped his back from spasming but has given him a raging headache. He leans the back of his head against the tree trunk to keep his skull from coming apart.

The inn's been quiet in the hour since the man drove into the courtyard. Who was he? How did he get past the guards at the road? Kallström hoped for some fireworks after the Russian bulldyke came out with her pistol, but she and the man acted like they knew each other. Since then, nothing.

Footsteps crackle through the forest underbrush. Fisk appears out of the gloom. He looks pissed. "The men I put at the entry are dead. Two shots each—heart, forehead." He taps his own breastbone and forehead to demonstrate. "Whoever that guy is, he's trouble."

"Don't worry so much." Kallström tries to sound positive, but it's hard when his stomach's doing backflips. "He's inside with the rest. You know, we don't even have to go inside. We can fire grenades in there and tear them apart."

"We have to get close enough to do that."

Kallström mutters "old woman." He watches some more for action at the inn, but it's dead. "Are all your people in place?"

"Yes. Same as ten minutes ago, and thirty minutes—"

"Well, send them in! What are you waiting for?"

Fisk glares at him. "For you to come off whatever you're on so you can lead this operation."

"Fuck you." Kallström lurches to his feet and immediately has to fight off another wave of nausea. Fisk, damn him, doesn't seem to notice or care. Maybe after this is over, he and Fisk will have a meeting—the kind that only one walks away from. "I'm going in.

Tell your men it's on. Wipe out those fucking brats."

Rogozhkin uses his mobile's camera as a periscope to see over the tower's parapet wall. Just as he'd imagined, it's an incredible three-hundred-sixty-degree view. The main drawback is that once the targets are within a few meters of the inn, he'll have to fire almost straight down on them, meaning he'll be as vulnerable to their counterfire as they are to him. He'll deal with that when the time comes, if it does.

It seems like only days have passed since he last saw Lara. Here they are in the field again, about to go into combat. She's a proud, capable woman, but like in Ukraine, the distance in her eyes and the circles below them hint at how tired she is. She's taking too much onto her shoulders. Commanders who do that get overloaded and miss things. He'll try to help her without being obvious about it.

It would be good if we could wear decent clothes and just have a nice dinner. Talk.

The rifle and his spare magazines are laid out within easy reach next to him. Vlasenko insisted that Rogozhkin take one of his best custom hunting rifles with him. It weighs a bit less than four kilos and lets him shoot Winchester .308 rounds for 7.5-centimeter groups at six hundred meters. Since the nearest treeline is around sixty-five meters away, hitting targets shouldn't be a problem.

Something moves on his phone screen. He zooms with his fingertips. It's a man scuttling from the treeline to a row of grapevines about sixty meters from the tower. A few moments later, he spots another man skimming the side of a line of shrubs at the parking lot's far end, perhaps fifty-five meters away.

Three more targets appear within the next thirty seconds, spread across a sixty-meter front.

Rogozhkin texts Lara. `5 targets incoming SE @ 50m+. Engaging.`

He carefully sets down his phone, picks up his rifle, sets his sandbag barrel rest on top of the parapet wall, and goes to work.

Carson group-texts Incoming southeast of inn to Project Karma as she stalks through Villa 1's kitchen, waiting for bullets to start coming through the window shutters. She hates being blind, but it's either that or turn the villa's inside into a shooting gallery.

She glances out the living-room windows in back. Sebastian's out there, crouched behind the patio wall, looking not-too-confident in the way he's holding the Ksyukha. She'd given him a whole five minutes of training on the thing. "I've shot grouse and pheasants with shotguns," he admitted when she'd asked. "I'm not proud of it." She hates putting him in this situation, but somebody's got to cover their asses.

Karl and Dareh are in Villa 2. Dareh can use the M4's scope and longer accurate range to snipe at Sabadell's goons. Karl has the Beretta. She'd taken the other Ksyukha for herself.

Carson can take care of whatever gets through the front or back doors (she hopes). Vicki and Iris are upstairs, armed with shovels. "Swing for the face," Carson had told them. If they have to do it, it means they're the only two people left alive, and they're better off jumping from the terraces and hoping they hit rock on their way down.

Come on, Edik. Take out those assholes before they get here.

Grebnev watches the line of bikers advance on the inn. They're in good order and moving like they know what they're doing; a nice change for Kallström's people.

He and Karik's men are in a line of trees skirting a field of grapevines about a hundred meters east-southeast of the tower. They'd managed to stay out of sight from both the hacker group and Kallström's bunch for the better part of three hours. If they need to intervene, they can circle around to the drive with cover most of the way.

The back of a biker's head explodes. The man collapses like a popped balloon.

Sniper? Grebnev turns his field glasses to the top of the tower. He sees for the briefest moment a bit of movement at the top, perhaps a rifle barrel sliding over the parapet.

Tarasenko? Nothing Severinov's given him makes him think she's a sniper, but nothing he's seen about her so far makes him doubt she can do the job. He keys his radio. "Ilya. Launch the drone. Cover the tower and rooflines."

A second biker flops into a grapevine. At this rate, they'll never reach the inn. Grebnev radios Karik. "They've got a sniper. I need counterfire, now. Send someone up."

Kallström hits the dirt behind a grapevine after the man to his right goes down. He's panting so hard, he hopes the sniper won't hear him. He hasn't been working out lately. He hasn't needed to—he has men to do the grunt work. Had.

He fumbles for the little walkie-talkie Fisk had passed out before they left the airport. "Fisk! Where are you?"

"Ten meters to your four o'clock." The sound is staticky and hollow, but understandable. "Two men down."

"Work toward the south. The end of the drive. When we get there, the sniper's got no shot."

"Right."

Kallström crawls through the dirt, under the vines, heading steadily toward the inn's south end. The oxy may be making him sick to his stomach, but his ribs are numb—good thing, because he's probably doing real damage in there. A bullet cracks overhead. *Only a crack, not a thump—his rifle's suppressed.* He eventually reaches the field's western edge, two meters from a pair of mature trees at the edge of a slight slope that leads to the drive's end.

Ten meters to his left, one of Fisk's men pokes his head through a vine. Kallström waves him down, then points over the slope. They end up on the drive together. As long as they're on their bellies, they can't see the top of the tower—and the sniper can't see them.

Fisk huffs and puffs over the rise to meet them after a minute. He snarls at Kallström. "You didn't say anything about a fucking sniper."

"Must be that Russian cunt." He points with his entire hand. "That way. To the end of the building. Through that big window in the arch. Then we start cleaning out these snots."

◎

Carson squats next to Sebastian with her hand on his shoulder. "Just breathe. Don't think."

"That's easy for you to say." He's trembling under her hand. "There's a reason I was never a soldier."

"You were too smart?"

"Too scared, more like."

"Only the stupid ones aren't scared." She listens for the sounds of pounding on the front door. The bars the workmen put across the doors are real solid; it'll take Sabadell's clowns some work to get through them.

"Lisa?"

"Yeah?"

"I'm sorry I hurt you. With Tamara. I wasn't thinking—"

Shut up. "Obviously."

"We used to be together." He swallows hard. "After Vicki. Not for long—a month or so, maybe. She was pretty and keen for it and…not complicated."

Sort of like the guys Carson picks up, minus the "pretty" part. "And she has great tits."

He nods sadly. "That she does. But she's a very selfish person. 'Not complicated' started to mean 'boring.' She had nothing to say that didn't involve herself. So I ended it, and she'd been trying her best to make me change my thinking. Then I met you…and 'complicated' started to mean 'scary.'"

"Yeah." Not the first time she's heard this. Carson stands, using Sebastian's shoulder for leverage. "Remember, you're on single-fire. When you shoot, aim at center mass and fire twice. Pop pop. Then if you have time, one in the head to make sure. Imagine they're fucking big pheasants." She walks away before she says anything she'll regret.

The clank of metal against stone gets her attention. Carson peeks over the wall in time to see a grappling hook plummet to the bluff's base. Four bikers are gathered below the Villa 2 terrace, partly obscured by the trees. The shot of adrenaline she'd been missing until now finally kicks in. She rushes to the short wall between the Villa 1 and Villa 2 terraces and stage-whispers, "Karl!"

Karl pops up, startled. Carson holds up four fingers, then

points down. He nods, totes four beer bottles to the outside wall, lights all four wicks, then flings them down the bluff face. They break against the rock face three or four meters off the ground and splash burning napalm all over the area where the men are gathered.

One screams and flails as his shirt and hair burn. Carson fires short bursts at the other three as they try to run away. A second goes face-down. A third disappears under the forest canopy. The fourth one runs north toward a rickety, overgrown stone staircase cut into the cliff. Carson continues to shoot at him until she can't see him anymore.

Two down, two gone. Not bad. "Good job, Karl." She turns toward him…and sees three men shouldering out of Villa 2's back door. She barks at Karl, "Get over here! Move!"

Rogozhkin sweeps the vineyards with his binoculars but doesn't find any more targets. He texts Lara with no success. Is it over? Are there more hostiles?

Gunfire erupts on the other side of the inn.

He scuttles in a crouch to the tower's west side. The noise comes from almost directly below him, but between the roof projections and the angle, he can't see a thing.

Stay here or go down? He's not doing anyone any good up here. The rifle isn't a good weapon for close-in fighting, but he has his Grach pistol and a tactical knife. He can still do damage.

He's about to climb through the open hatch to the spiral stairway below when he hears the unmistakable whine of a giant mosquito overhead. He flips on his back and scans the sky until he sees a squarish black shape south of the tower, perhaps fifty meters away.

A drone. The last thing they need is for the enemy to have eyes in the sky. He brings his rifle across his chest and keeps his eyes locked on the drone burning circles through the cloud-flecked sky. *At least it's not armed,* he muses. *I think.*

Three minutes pass. The drone operator's falling into a predictable pattern: start over the tower, swing west beyond the inn to track the gunfire along the terraces over the bluff, skirt the building's south edge, then go wide again to the east before returning to the tower. It tells Rogozhkin that the operator is confident, perhaps to the edge of recklessness; the attackers are now all close to the inn; and there's not much going on south of the tower.

The drone overflies him. When it passes, he brings his rifle to ready and tracks the small, black machine as it sidles over the terraces. Through his scope, he can see the blue electrical arcs inside the motor nacelles. He sets the crosshairs on the nearest motor, lets out a breath, and squeezes the trigger.

Villa 4 is a waste of time. No rats to kill. The covered terrace out back doesn't connect to the others. Kallström shoots up the windows anyway, just because.

Villa 3 is ripped apart for some kind of construction. Another waste of time.

Fisk has to use his 30mm grenade launcher to blast open the door to Villa 2. It takes two tries. A quick sweep comes up empty—*another* waste of time.

Then Fisk's guy—Kallström still can't remember his name— points out the back window and yells, "Look! Out there!"

The German hacker boy's standing by the terrace's stone railing, looking down the bluff.

"Come on!" Kallström yells. He charges for the arched wood door to the terrace. Just as he gets outside, he hears a woman's voice yell, "Get over here! Move!" and sees the hacker boy run for the short wall between this terrace and the next.

The Russian bitch is on the other side of that wall, leveling an *okurok* at him.

Kallström drops hard enough to feel it even through the oxy haze. He hears the clatter of a short burst, then Fisk's guy screams and falls over Kallström's legs. "Get off me!" Kallström yelps, kicking at the man's chest.

Fisk takes a knee in the deep doorway and returns fire, short bursts that echo off the stone wall like a small jackhammer going after concrete. Suppression goes only so far with the carbine's gas-port venting. The woman shoots back, single-fire. Then a brown beer bottle sails over the wall, trailing flame, and explodes on the patio in front of Fisk. Globs of fire splash everywhere.

Kallström knows what he's seeing—*napalm?*—but knows there's no way. *Where'd they…?*

Fisk jumps up, yelling "Ahhhhhhh!" as he beats on the burning parts of his jeans. He dashes into the fire-free center of the terrace, drops, and rolls until the fire's out.

Kallström finally gets the dead guy off his legs. Movement in an upstairs window catches his eye. Someone's up there—*but how? We cleared the place!* Not enough, apparently. He lets rip with a burst that destroys the glass in the window frames. The guy upstairs disappears.

That feels like a win. Kallström struggles onto his knees. The Irish boy is standing, hunched over, at the next terrace's far end. He fires a single shot; the bullet whizzes past Kallström's head. The woman grabs the Irish boy's arm and starts to drag him inside.

Not so fast. Kallström looses a burst that stiches across the pretty boy's chest and knocks him down. The Russian bitch returns fire before he can switch aim. Something like the biggest, nastiest bumblebee in the world plows across Kallström's ear and knocks him on his side.

The pain burns through his oxy numbness. When he touches his ear, his hand comes away coated with blood. *Shit.* He crawls to the short wall, leaving a spotty blood trail on the flagstone, then sags his back against the wall and tries to work through the pain to make a plan.

Fisk staggers to the wall and slides down beside Kallström. His jeans are charred and ragged, and the skin Kallström can see is like blackened steak. Panting, Fisk growls through gritted teeth, "Last time. I listen. To one. Of your plans."

Kallström grins. "They're all in there." He swipes a hand toward the terrace on the other side of the wall. "Right where we want them. Let's go get them."

Carson yells, "Iris! Vicki! Get down here! Help Sebastian!"

Sebastian's whimpering as loud as he can with three holes in his chest. Carson drags him by his armpits away from the terrace door. He's big and heavy and no help and she can't afford to be tied down with him when that asshole who shot Celeste is right outside, probably on his way in. Karl dashes in to take Sebastian's legs and between them, they wrestle him into the kitchen.

Carson pushes Sebastian's weapon into Karl's hands. "Upstairs. Aim and shoot. Got it?"

Karl nods and bolts for the stairs. Running footsteps on tile announce Vicki's and Iris's arrival. When they turn the corner into the kitchen, still packing their shovels, they both scream and rush to Sebastian.

Carson returns to the dining room, trying to tune out the women's crying and pleas of "Please don't die! Please!" She flips the heavy wood-plank table on its side and sets up a barricade inside the door. She can shelter in the doorway and still have a fallback position if she has to retreat.

A heavyset man with a buzz cut and body armor over his biker's vest flops over the wall between the terraces. He drives Carson inside with gunfire. She drops to her belly, slithers across the polished wood planks to the door, then puts her last three rounds into his chest, knocking him against the wall.

She used to have a spare magazine stuffed into her back pocket, but it's gone. Carson slides her carbine toward the table, pulls the Glock from her back waistband, and when Buzz Cut struggles onto his knees, aims for a headshot.

The side of his head splatters against the railing. Dareh must've got to him first.

Carson moves into the doorway. When she leans out, a body slams her against the opposite jamb. Her pistol skitters across the terrace's flagstones. The man jams a metal rifle stock across her throat, trying to crush her windpipe. It takes all her strength to block the weapon and find the guy's face.

It's Håkan. The asshole who murdered Celeste.

Surprise and rage give her probably her last burst of energy. She lashes out with her right foot, driving her heel into something that makes Håkan bellow in pain. The rifle stock lets up a tiny bit, enough to smash the heel of her right hand into the bridge of his nose. He falls back, screaming through the blood pouring down his face.

Carson untangles herself from the Swede and scrambles

backward into the dining room. Her carbine's empty and her pistol's outside; she'll have to get creative.

Håkan lunges after her. He's almost upright when Carson grabs a dining room chair and swings at his head. He ducks. That's okay. She takes the backswing vertical, crashing the chair across his right shoulder. A chair leg rips off and clatters against the wall.

He rolls away, then up on his feet in a fighter's crouch. His left hand swings a nasty-looking tactical knife.

Carson seizes another chair and turns all four legs toward Håkan.

A dark shape in the doorway distracts her for a moment: Edik, suppressed Grach ready, waiting for a chance to shoot Håkan. She's too close to the Swede to give Rogozhkin a clear shot.

And Håkan knows it. He circles, keeping her between him and Edik, trying to slash at her hands. She manages to keep him far enough away so he can't do her any damage, but she can't do much to him, either.

They both skirt the table. Blood dribbles into Håkan's eyes, his right arm swings useless beside him, and his left holds the knife. Carson tries to make him sidestep to his right to give Edik a clear shot, but the Swede doesn't fall for it.

Edik, now close behind Carson, snaps in Russian, "Lara, drop!"

She barks in Russian, "Chest shots. I want him alive." She shoves Håkan backward with the chair.

As Håkan staggers past the entrance to the kitchen, Iris steps through and swings her shovel as hard as she can into the man's back. He goes down like a collapsing smokestack, sprawling face-first on the dining room floor. His knife spins toward Carson, who stops it with her boot.

"Looking for Sonia, asshole?" Iris shrieks. "Here I am!"

Chapter 62

Grebnev and Karik stand at the treeline's edge, heads cocked, listening.

"It's too damned quiet," Grebnev grumbles.

"Agreed," Karik says. "Too bad about your drone. We could use it right now."

Too bad, indeed. Grebnev steps into the clear. It's a foolish thing to do, but it's the only way they have to tell whether the hacker group has any active combatants outside. No one shoots at him. "Is it quiet because the hackers are all dead," he muses aloud, "or because Kallström's people are all dead?"

Karik joins him. "Maybe they're having a firefight inside and we can't hear them because all their weapons are suppressed."

It could be any of those possibilities. Given their past performance, Grebnev's instincts tells him the silence means Kallström and all his playmates are dead. No great loss. But Grebnev still needs to confirm the minister's spoiled daughter and the hackers are terminated and that the hackers' equipment goes to Moscow as an early birthday present for Severinov. Which means someone has to go inside the inn and see what's happening. Grebnev has to finish the mission. If he doesn't, Severinov might well have Karik kill him and leave his body for the Spanish police. Simply another narco assassin come to a bad end.

"Get your men ready to move in. Let's see what's going on in there…and clean up if we need to."

The dining room gets deathly quiet. Carson and Edik stand a couple of meters apart, staring at Iris. Vicki hovers near the entrance to the kitchen, her cheeks shiny with tears.

Only Håkan makes noise, laid out on his face in front of Carson, moaning and choking and trying to roll over. He manages to flip onto his back. Every panting breath bubbles blood on his lips. He tilts up his head enough to see Iris, then drops it against the tile. He coughs out a chuckle. "Yes. You Sonia."

"Shut the fuck up." Carson kicks him in the nearest kidney. "I'll get to you."

Iris edges toward Håkan, ready to swing the shovel. "Is that him?" she screams. "He's the one who killed Celeste?"

"Yeah." Carson knows Iris is going for redemption by killing him. She doesn't deserve it. "You'd know if you'd gone with Sebastian when you were supposed to." Carson steps behind Iris and rips the shovel out of her hands. "You've done enough damage."

She finds Edik next. He's at the other end of the toppled table, his face serious. "Glad you came?"

He says in Russian, "It's always interesting around you."

Carson notices Dareh hovering near the back door, holding her pistol. Then she steps toward the Swede, crushing the knife handle in her right hand. Every time she looks at the insect, the blood burns and bubbles in her veins. She's about to drive the knife through Håkan's body armor into his heart when Vicki calls out, "Lisa! Please help! I can't stop the bleeding!"

Carson groans. *Not Sebastian too.* She points the knife at Håkan and glances at Edik. "Edik, find out who this piece of shit is." Then she tosses the shovel and follows Vicki into the kitchen.

Sebastian's laid out on the tile floor near the sink. Blood-soaked dishcloths and scraps of his shirt are piled in three mounds on his chest, one for each hole. The spreading pool of blood on the floor tells Carson his wounds are through-and-through. There's nothing they can do.

Carson kneels next to his left shoulder and gently lays a hand on the top of his breastbone. His skin is cool and clammy, and he's shivering. Shock's the least of his problems, though. "Hey. Ever hear of 'duck'?"

He either smiles or grimaces; it's hard to tell. "Sorry...for the mess."

Vicki kneels by his right shoulder and strokes his cheek. "It's no worry, darling," she whispers. "The cleaners will sort it."

Carson bends closer so she can hear him, and so he can save his breath. "You did good. You held them off so me and Karl could get inside. You were brave."

"Or daft?"

Vicki's eyes find Carson's. She mouths *will he die?*

Can't she tell? Do I have to say it? Each of Sebastian's breaths is shallower than the last, and the color's draining from his face and chest as he loses blood. *Maybe Vicki's never seen a man die before. It's not her fault.* Carson sighs and nods once.

Vicki's throat makes a rough choking sound. Tears roll down her cheeks one by one. She lowers her face to Sebastian's and whispers, "I'm…I'm so very sorry I didn't say 'yes' when you asked me to marry you. Everything would be different now."

"I reckon…" Sebastian erupts in a spasm of coughing that pushes bloody froth onto his lips. His eyes stay closed when he finishes. He gasps, "I reckon…you wanted…a better offer."

"No, darling." Vicki strokes his hair. "I needed to be a better person."

Sebastian forces his eyes partly open and rolls his head to find Carson. "Lisa…sorry… I made…a haymes of things."

She assumes that means *a mess.* "At least you didn't ask Tamara to marry you."

He tries to laugh but coughs instead. The coughing gets looser and deeper and harder to listen to, then trails off. When it ends, so does his breathing.

Vicki, sobbing, begins to howl.

Carson braces her hands on her thighs and bends over, trying to keep the tears inside. Pictures flash through her head—the first massage, cuddling with Sebastian in bed, dancing with him at Anubis, holding hands outside Space. Now he's dead, too. The ache wrings her heart like a wet towel. *Such a fucking waste. All of it.*

Her anger spikes again when she closes his eyes. Carson groans to her feet, sweeps up the knife, then stalks to where Edik straddles Håkan's thighs, immobilizing the man. It's all she can do to keep from driving the knife through the Swede's throat. "Got anything?"

Edik says in Russian, "His name is Håkan Kallström. That's as far as we got. He says he'll talk to you."

"Fucking right he will." Carson drives a knee into Kallström's diaphragm as she kneels. She waits until Rogozhkin stands, then pushes the tactical knife's tip into Kallström's body armor directly over his heart. She snarls in English, "Well, go on. Talk."

Kallström tries to give her a rude smile, but it comes off more like constipation. "Important people in Moscow want you dead."

Carson swaps glances with Rogozhkin. "Me specifically?"

"All you. Women, hacker boys. All."

"Who? Why?"

He huffs out a thin cackle. "You see. They find you. Ask then."

Carson holds the knife steady with her left hand and slaps the butt with her right. Kallström jerks when the tip jolts through the Kevlar and bites into the skin over his sternum. "Try again. Why?"

The insolence slips from his eyes, replaced by fear and hate. "You make angry. Hacker boys steal money from them. She"—he jabs his chin toward Iris, who's crying into her knees—"excuse. Important people want us to kill you. Keep hands clean."

That sounds to Carson exactly like something someone in Moscow would try. "Who?"

Kallström shrugs as well as he can with Carson pinning his body to the floor.

She slaps the knife's butt again. The tip sinks, then hits something hard—his breastbone. Kallström gasps; his eyes get huge. Carson barks, "Last chance! Who?"

His jaw is set so tight, his teeth should be turning to powder. He struggles to raise his head off the floor. "Fuck you, Russian bulldyke."

Carson winds up to pound the knife through his sternum into whatever passes for his heart. *No. Too quick. He killed Celeste. He killed Sebastian. He chased off Amabelle.*

Kallström snickers. "Too weak to do it, bitch?"

Her anger detonates like a grenade. She yanks the knife free, twists, and plunges the blade deep into his right thigh. Kallström screams. She takes her time standing, then glares down as the writhing insect at her feet. "Hurts? Think about how much more you hurt Celeste…you murdering piece of shit." Carson yanks the knife loose, then marches away as Kallström's femoral artery drains his life onto the floor.

When she reaches the kitchen, the front door explodes.

Chapter 63

OUTSIDE ARBOÇAR

The first man inside takes a bullet in his face and falls three steps past the door.

Carson shelters behind the counter extension that separates the kitchen from the foyer, shaking her head to clear the ringing in her ears. A mist of smoke and plaster dust blurs the far walls. Sebastian's body lies less than a meter from her foot; she can't look at it. Vicki's huddled two meters away against the wooden island with her arms covering her head.

Carson peeks around the base cabinet at the dead man. Black utilities, black tactical gear, body armor, balaclava, ballistic helmet. His MP5SD is just within reach.

What. The. Actual. Fuck?

Something metal skitters across the uneven terracotta tile. Carson yells "Grenade!" slides the submachine gun to the end of the kitchen, then dives for Vicki. They skid behind the island, Carson on top, squeezing her eyes shut and pressing her forearms against her ears.

The insides of Carson's eyelids light up like strobes. The room fills with the sound of an enormous door slamming. Plaster trickles from the ceiling.

Carson rolls off Vicki. Red blobs float in her eyes and a high-pitched whine fills her ears, but she's still got her balance and partial vision. She retrieves the MP5, then grabs a fistful of Vicki's shirt and hair and launches her through the door into the tower's base. If Vicki objects, Carson can't hear it and doesn't care anyway.

Breaching charges. Flash-bangs. Who are these people?

Grebnev had objected when Karik sent in his first pair of men with no prep after keying the breaching charges—"the element of surprise," Karik claimed—and look how it turned out. One man dead on the floor; the other getting a grazing wound on his calf bandaged by a teammate.

He muscles past the pair of shooters ahead of him to get to Karik. "Satisfied now?" he growls in the man's ear. "Didn't get the message from watching these people chew up Kallström's men? Treat this seriously, or stand down."

Karik turns his head enough for Grebnev to see the sneer on the man's face. "Get out of our way, Grebnev. Don't want any friendly-fire accidents, do we?"

If it didn't mean failing to complete the mission, Grebnev would shut down this action right now for Karik's attitude alone. Instead, he leans into Karik. "Fine. But you're first through the door next time. *Lead* your men, don't just send them off to die." He steps away before Karik can take a swing at him.

Karik pats the top pocket of his pack. The man behind him pulls a flash-bang grenade from the pocket, shows Karik the fuse end. Karik nods. The man pulls the pin, then tosses the grenade through the doorway. The team flattens their backs against the stucco wall. *Wham.*

With a parting glare at Grebnev, Karik enters the building high while the man behind him goes in low.

Grebnev doesn't bother to watch the outcome. He turns on Karik's last two men. "You, you. With me. Move."

Muzzle flashes twinkle in the haze. Carson finds two pairs: one pair coming from the front door, the other from behind the dining-room wall, probably Edik and Dareh. She can't hear the suppressed fire through the static in her ears.

She switches the fire-select lever to burst mode, braces against the kitchen island, and waits for the nearest man to fire again. The muzzle flash is low to the floor. *Prone?* She squeezes the red blobs out of her eyes, aims about a meter behind the flash, and triggers two three-round bursts.

Almost immediately, the farthest man riddles the island. Carson drops on her face, covering her head to protect it from the flying chunks of wood peppering her back and side. *Can he see me?* The grenade smoke, leftover haze from the breaching charge, and random powdered plaster make a swirling fog in the minimal cross-breeze from the two open doors, stinging Carson's already abused eyes. These new attackers have goggles and don't have to contend with the side-effects of a flash-bang.

The haze clears faster in the dining room. After a few moments, Carson can see why: the glass is gone from all the windows. Edik has his back against the wall on the far side of the doorway leading from the dining room to the kitchen. He catches her eye and makes the thumbs-up sign. She returns it. *Glad somebody's looking out for me.*

The air clears in the entry. Other than the gunman who went down in the opening seconds, the area's clear. The two new attackers are gone. Carson raids the dead man for his pack and spare ammo, then rushes to the dining room. Edik and Dareh flank the entrance; Iris is huddled by the fireplace, looking blank. "You guys okay?"

Dareh nods. "Yes." His eyes tell another story: wide, scared, sad.

Edik smiles. "How did you know close-quarters combat is my favorite?" he says in Russian. "You're so thoughtful to put this on for me."

Carson slugs his shoulder. "Wait 'til you see the bill." She grabs Edik's sleeve and drags him to where Dareh stands, then waves Iris to join them. "Can't hold this position," she whispers. "Not with the shit these guys have to play with. They can come at us from two sides."

Edik nods. "What do you suggest?"

"The tower. Vicki's in there already."

Iris breaks out of her trance. "Is Vicki okay?"

"She's fine. Busted up because of Sebastian, but she'll live. Look, if we're gonna move, we need to do it *now*."

Dareh asks, "What do we do for Karl?"

Carson had completely forgotten Karl. "He's gotta stay upstairs. If these new guys are outside, they'll see him come down and take him out. Tell him to lie low."

Dareh reluctantly reaches for his rear pocket, then abruptly raises his M4 and fires three rounds out the shattered back windows. Iris screams.

Carson catches a glimpse of a black-clad gunman leaping over the wall onto the terrace. She shoves Edik and Iris toward the kitchen. "Go! Now!"

Edik hardly moves. He plucks the MP5 out of her hands. "You take them. I'll cover you."

"I can—"

"Go! I used to do this for a living, remember? I'll follow you out. Move, soldier."

Carson balks. It's her job; she should do it. But he's got a point. This is why she asked him to come. She kisses his cheek. "Watch yourself." Then she grabs Iris's arm. "Let's go."

They get as far as the kitchen island when someone opens up on them from near the door. Carson knocks down Iris, then hooks around the island's far end while Dareh sends aimed return fire over its top. She plucks the Glock from Dareh's waistband and checks the magazine. Four rounds left; one in the chamber.

Iris grabs Carson's shirt and tries to huddle behind her. "Don't let me die! Please don't!"

"Get off me." Carson breaks free, low-crawls around the island's base, and flattens at a spot that gives her maximum cover and a clear line at the front door. A stocky older guy kneels at the staircase's mouth, trading fire with Dareh; a younger guy's shooting above him toward the dining room. They're good, effectively using what little cover they have, practicing good fire discipline. *Pros. Fucking wonderful.*

Edik's trapped in the dining room between these two and the guy on the terrace. As good as he is, eventually one of these guys will get lucky. She can't let that happen. She brought Edik into this mess—she can't let him get hurt, or worse.

She sights in on the older guy's right knee, braced on the floor. Lets out a breath. Strokes back the trigger.

He falls backward into the younger guy, slapping both of them into the far wall. A round from Dareh's rifle shreds the man's foot, now sticking out into the open. The younger guy tries to haul his partner into the stairwell but exposes his hip while he does it, a nice big target for Carson. He goes down. The older gunman looses a burst into the island over Carson's head.

She startles when Dareh slaps her pack, then shows her an

olive-drab, capsule-shaped RGD-5 hand grenade. She nods sharply, not wanting anything to do with the damn thing. When she hears a *crack*, she flattens herself behind the island. Something metal clunks across the floor, then *whump*. A hailstorm of steel fragments peppers the island, kitchen cabinets, walls, and ceiling.

No more shooting from the stairwell. She calls out, "Edik?"

"I'm good. Get going." His MP5 spits three times.

Carson gathers up Iris and Dareh, then leads them into the tower's base. It's thirty meters up the spiral steel staircase to the small landing at the top, but they all make it in Olympic time. Carson sends the others up the short ladder to the roof while she covers them.

Come on, Edik. Get your ass out of there. Don't be a hero. More automatic weapons fire echoes through the door. *Come on, don't make me sorry I asked you here. Move it. Move it!*

"Lisa?" Dareh's voice, from above her. "Will you come?"

"In a minute. Vicki up there?"

"Yes. She is very scared."

"Smart girl." Another *wham* cuts her off. *No no no. No more grenades. Stop that shit. Get out here, Edik! Now!*

Karl comes flying through the door, tumbles, rolls until he runs into the far wall. He hugs the Ksyukha against his chest. He's barely on his feet when Edik barrels through the door, then stops to slam it shut. Bullets crash into the other side of the thick oak.

Edik stuffs a wood-frame chair under the latch rail. It won't hold long, but maybe it'll hold long enough. He dashes for the stairs, snagging Karl by the scruff of his neck on the way.

Boots kick at the other side of the door. It rattles against its latch.

The chair starts to slip on the worn flagstone floor.

Chapter 64

Grebnev uses his teeth to tie off the bandage around the grazing wound at the top of his left bicep. Whoever that man in camo is, he knows his business. Grebnev had been prepared for one professional, but two? *Who are these people, anyway?*

Tasha—the sole survivor from Karik's squad—hammers away at the heavy wood door with his boot, raising a racket but not making much progress. Even using the last breaching charge probably won't open the thing; it's acting like it's barred, not locked.

Grebnev glances toward the villa's front door. Karik and another of his men lay in a heap at the foot of the stairs, shredded by one of their own grenades. The first of Karik's men to die is still face-down near the ruined kitchen, not far from the dead Irish boy. Another squad member is crumpled in the courtyard; a fourth lies dead on the terrace.

And Kallström's in what's left of the dining room, surrounded by a lagoon of darkening blood. Grebnev idly wonders who did for him—the Tarasenko woman, or the man in camo? He suspects the woman. Kallström's death would've been slow in coming and unpleasant to experience. It feels like revenge.

At least he doesn't have to worry about the hackers getting away. They're all trapped on top of the tower with no way out except jumping.

The pounding on the door and in his head finally gets the better of Grebnev. "Stop!" He shoulders past Tasha and checks the door. It opens five or six centimeters before whatever's blocking it stops its movement. That's enough. "Have a grenade?"

"Yes, sir." Tasha pulls an RGD from his pack and hands it to Grebnev, who stuffs it into the gap between the door and the jamb right next to the latch.

Grebnev sweeps his MP5 off what little is left of the island and marches for the dining room's relative safety. "Pull the pin, then run like hell. You'll have four seconds."

A *crack* breaks the quiet just as Grebnev settles his back against the dining-room wall. He counts. At "three," Tasha dashes into the room. A *wham* drowns out "four."

The door's open. Scattered pieces of a chair litter the stone floor inside the tower. Grebnev pokes his head inside far enough to see the man in camo climb onto the landing at the top of the spiral staircase. He can't tell if someone's on the landing to take potshots at anyone going up the stairs. Someone probably is.

Search the inn. Find the hackers' gear. Take it home. Severinov surely doesn't want scalps, does he?

Grebnev runs over everything he knows about his immediate superior and decides that yes, after all this trouble, Severinov will want scalps. Or at least photos of dead hackers.

Which means that he and Tasha have to climb up there to get them.

Grebnev sighs. "Tasha, find us another grenade."

Carson squats next to Edik as he empties the water bottle she'd found in her pack. Both their backs are pressed against the parapet wall around the tower's top. She asks in Russian, "You're okay?"

"Yes, I'm still okay." He squeezes her knee. "I'm getting too old for this foolishness, though."

"I know the feeling."

"Right. Try adding fifteen years and a balky leg."

A land mine tore up Edik's left leg in Kosovo. Somehow, Carson doesn't feel the age difference. The only times she's seen him limp were first thing in the morning and late in the evening. Once they stopped fighting each other in Ukraine and joined up to fight other people, he was utterly reliable, treated her like an equal, and never tried to get in her pants. Those things alone are enough to put him in the top five percent of men she's known. Him coming here to do all this just because she asked him to puts him in the top one percent. "Hey, have I said 'thank you' yet?"

"Once or twice, I think." A muffled *whump* echoes out the trap door leading to the stairs. "They just blew the door. Back to work."

"Yeah."

Carson starts to unwind from her crouch, but Edik grabs her wrist. "Please be careful. I'm still hoping to see you wear something other than your ninja costume."

"Only if you promise me a dinner that isn't field rations or cold food from a can."

He sighs and shakes his head. "You young women. No appreciation for the best things in life."

She flips him off, then returns to her post. She, Edik, and the remains of Project Karma are spread out at different points around the tower's roof. The hatch to the stairs is at three o'clock; Edik and Vicki are at five; Carson and Iris are at nine, facing the hatch; and Karl and Dareh are at one o'clock. The people with weapons—Carson, Dareh, and Edik—can catch anyone coming out of the hatch in a crossfire without having to worry about shooting each other.

Iris sits with her arms around her shins and her chin on her knees. "Who's the guy?"

"Name's Edik. Met him on my last project."

"Huh. Not bad, if you're into older guys. Where's he from? He looks Asian."

"Siberia."

"Wow. He must like you, coming all this way to do this for you."

"Yeah." Carson stands. "Nice to be able to trust somebody." She throws a barbed glare at Iris, then scurries in a crouch to the hatch and drops almost silently onto the metal landing a couple of meters below.

Two gunmen in black tactical gear edge their way up the stairs. The one in front is the same model as the others; the one that's three or so meters behind him wears gray urban camo utilities and no helmet. They move like soldiers.

She figures the odds. She'll get one shot; the survivor will try to blow her off the landing after that. Plus, her MP5 has only six rounds left, and she gave her last spare magazine to Edik. She can't afford to get into a firefight.

Make it count.

Carson sights in on a point a dozen steps below the landing.

She tries to slow her breathing despite the residual adrenaline banging around her system. Clears her senses. Opens her ears. Rubber boot soles scrape on the steel stair treads. A D-ring clicks against another.

The helmet and an MP5 muzzle appear above a tread. When the top of the man's ballistic vest fills her aperture sights, Carson pulls the trigger.

Tasha jerks backward like someone yanked on his leash. He yells in pain and surprise as he tumbles down the steps. His helmet and rifle spin into space and clatter onto the tower floor.

Grebnev gets off a single round toward the landing before he has to grab the railing to keep Tasha from bowling him off the staircase. Grebnev drops to the treads, aims at the landing, and waits for the next shot.

There isn't one.

He pushes into a crouch, then waits. Still nothing. He carefully backtracks half a dozen steps until he reaches Tasha sprawled with his head and shoulders hanging off the treads' inside edge. Grebnev hauls him to safety, but the man's head rotates in an unnatural way. His neck's broken. The brass button of an expended bullet shines in the subdued light near the top of Tasha's vest. Whoever shot him deliberately tried to avoid killing him. Interesting decision.

Grebnev's a couple of treads short of halfway up the stairs. He'll be exposed all the way up. The only protection he has is speed.

So be it.

He fishes the grenade out of Tasha's pack, whispers a short prayer, then charges up the stairs.

Carson calls out, "He's coming."

Dareh signals to Karl to lie flat. Edik pushes Vicki prone, then helps her arrange her arms to best protect her head. Carson glances at Iris, who's still hugging her legs. "Lie down. Make a smaller target."

Iris turns a wounded look on Carson. "You still care?"

"If you're gonna get killed, I wanna do it." Carson stretches out flat on the tower's dusty stone roof and aims at the dark hole beneath the upright hatch.

The running steps stop. *How's he gonna play this? Spray and pray? Gopher and take us out one by one? He's gotta know we're ready for him.*

Still silence. No head pops into her sights.

Or is this where he tries to bargain with us? Do I trust Vicki to do that, or handle it myself? What's he gonna want?

Silence.

Wait us out? We got four bottles of water and a granola bar. Won't last long in a siege.

Maybe he's waiting for reinforcements.

Maybe we're supposed to make the first move.

Just do *something, for fuck's sake!*

It's not hot, but sweat drips into Carson's eyes.

Crack.

A grenade arcs out the hatch and bounces next to Carson.

Fuck! She rolls to her left as fast as she can.

Iris is on her feet, bounding toward the grenade.

"No! Don't do it! Get down!"

Iris's right leg sweeps forward. She kicks the grenade with her right instep. It rockets into the metal hatch cover. Karl pops up and slaps the cover closed.

The explosion blasts the cover off the top of the tower.

<h1 style="text-align:center">Chapter 65</h1>

Carson, trembling, tries to shake the ringing out of her ears, but it doesn't work. There's no other pain; she's not bleeding. After panting a few shallow breaths, she sits up.

Iris is flat on her back a meter or so from the hatch. There's no obvious blood, but it takes only one bit of shrapnel to hit just the right place…

Carson scrambles to Iris's side. Breathing, no wounds. Iris grimaces up at her. "Ouch."

"Are you hit? Where does it hurt? What—"

"Rock's a lot harder than grass. I slipped." Iris struggles onto her elbows. "Aren't you glad I played soccer and not, like, archery?" She gazes around, a bit dopey. Then her eyes get big. "Karl?"

Karl's sitting against the parapet, cradling his left arm and muttering in German. Dareh fusses over him. "The cover hits him when it flies. His arm is broken."

Carson blows out a relieved breath. "Lucky it's only that." She turns to Iris. "What the fuck, woman?"

"You may hate me," Iris grumps, "but I'm not gonna let any more of my friends get turned into Swiss cheese."

"You dumbshit." Carson still wants to strangle Iris, but right now, Carson hugs her. "Thanks."

She stands as Edik and Vicki approach. Vicki kneels next to Iris and hauls her into a tight hug. Edik gives Carson a wary smile. "Okay?"

Carson nods. "Scared about ten years out of me. Almost your age now."

"That's a shame." They both glance at the hatch. "I'll check."

"Jesus, Edik. Let me do something." Not that she's anxious to see the mess that may be down there, or face down that last guy. She shrugs off the pack, pulls her Glock, then edges to the hatch and looks down.

She barfs.

Edik grimaces when he sees what Carson saw. "Well, he's done."

Carson, facing away from the hatch, wipes her mouth on her already filthy sleeve. She's not shaking anymore, but baby dragons are eating her stomach. "Yeah," is all she can think of to say.

"Let's see who he was." He climbs onto the ladder.

Carson's stomach heaves again, but nothing comes out. "You're going down into *that?*"

Edik stops halfway down. "Yes. I've seen worse. Have you ever seen what happens to people caught by a thermobaric bomb?"

"No."

"Good." He disappears into the hole. A few moments later, a wallet pops out of the hatch and lands near Iris's outstretched legs. Relieved to have something to do, Carson sweeps it up and rifles through it. She pockets the almost four hundred euros. The pink-and-blue Russian driving license says the man in urban camo was Yuri Grebnev from Moscow. He had credit cards and a gym membership card. No photos of girlfriends, wives, or kids. *Just as well.*

Behind the plastic card holders, she finds a slot for business cards. She pulls the top one. *Yuri I. Grebnev, Director of Physical Security, PJSC Zapadneft.* The name's familiar enough to trigger a thought. "Hey, Dareh—did you guys go after a company called Zapadneft?"

Dareh purses his lips for a moment. "Yes. It is a Russian oil company. Very corrupt. The directors are friends of Putin."

The entire story crashes together in Carson's mind. Kallström and Grupo Sabadell were simply pawns.

Vicki says, "Lisa…does that mean something to you?" Her voice is thin and worn out.

Carson doesn't bother to turn around. "Yeah. This whole disaster started when you guys ripped off that company. They got that…*mess* on the landing to sic the Sabadell people on you. Iris's side hustle gave them the idea to make it look like a drug thing." She paces to where Dareh squats next to Karl and hands him the card. "Burn them down."

Dareh studies the card, then nods grimly. "We will enjoy it."

◉

Carson, Vicki, Dareh, and Edik spend the next two hours in the slaughterhouse, erasing themselves. They pack their bags. They wipe their fingerprints off weapons and put them in the hands of dead men. They wash Carson's vomit off the tower's roof, and Iris's off the staircase. Edik rigs up a field splint and sling for Karl's arm.

Now Carson slumps on the least-damaged sofa in the living room. All her adrenaline is gone. She's exhausted, hungry, morose, and disgusted. She's sick of stepping over dead people. "Comfortable?"

Iris frowns at her from the wooden ladder-back armchair she's duct-taped to. "I saved. Your *life*. Can't you cut me some slack?"

"Because you saved my life, I didn't throw you off the tower. Don't push it. All this?" She waves her hand all around them. "*You* own this. It's all on you."

"I never meant for any of this to happen!" Iris's voice gets louder and wobblier with each word. "Nobody was supposed to get hurt!" She starts to cry again.

"Yeah." Carson can hardly look at her. Part of it is the betrayal; part is that Carson's afraid of looking too long into the face of someone she liked, someone who could've been a friend, and losing her nerve. She drags herself off the sofa. "You're a good storyteller. Think of a story to tell the Spanish cops. Don't even think about blaming anybody else. Remember who Vicki's dad is."

"You…you're just gonna *leave* me here? And Vicki's gonna *let* you?"

"Yeah, and yeah. Not that I care much about Vicki's approval."

"But…but…just take me downtown, dump me at the train station. I'll disappear. Please don't make me go to jail. Please?"

It's so tempting. She's broke; Iris said Sebastian had laundered all her drug money and stashed it, but she doesn't know where. All her stuff burned with the mansion. It would serve her right to end up homeless and on the run from whoever might go looking for her next.

But that means she'd get away with it. Iris is clever. She'd figure out a way to bounce back. Maybe do the same stupid shit she did this time. Maybe get more people killed.

Carson swallows the lump of pity floating up her throat.

"Sorry. You broke it, you bought it." She walks away before Iris says the right words to melt Carson's heart.

Iris shrieks, "Don't go! Please don't go!"

Not the right words.

Carson steps into the courtyard. The Citroën, Edik's silver Toyota RAV4, and the rental Audi Q7 crowd the driveway.

She paces to the Citroën. Dareh stands near the driver's door, trying to look calm, but his hands won't stop moving. Carson says, "You did good."

He nods, but doesn't look up from the gravel.

He'll have nightmares for months. Maybe years. "Don't stop at a hospital until you're in France. Don't ever come back here. Got it?"

"Yes." He finally meets Carson's eyes. "Where will you go?"

"Someplace else. You don't need to know where." She holds out her hand to shake. "You're a good man. I hope you find someplace where you can be happy."

Dareh shakes her hand, then tugs her into a one-armed hug. "Please take care of Vicki."

"Don't worry about her." Carson pulls away and tries to smile. "Worry about yourselves. Get out of here."

When the Citroën disappears down the driveway, Carson drifts to the Toyota. Edik leans against the driver's door, his arms crossed, dressed for golf again. He lofts his eyebrows at her. "You don't look happy."

She snorts. "Look around this place lately?"

"You succeeded. You're still alive. I'm still alive. Miss Baranova's still alive, and you know where she is." He nods toward the Audi.

"People who didn't deserve to die did."

He nods sadly. "That's always unfortunate. And common. And not your fault, unless you've skipped telling me a lot."

Carson stares at the open door to Villa 1. She'd tried to save Celeste and failed. Had she tried hard enough? And Sebastian— what was she thinking, putting a weapon in his hands and risking his life? Was it some weird, subliminal revenge thing? Was it her not thinking? He shouldn't have died, and she put him in the line of fire. She'll be seeing them both in her nightmares for a good, long time.

Edik gently squeezes her shoulder. "Lara?"

"There's a lot I haven't told you." She heaves in a couple of deep breaths, then turns to face him. "Do you have to go home right away?"

"No. I didn't tell Vlasenko how long it would take to rescue you."

"Yeah. Rescue. I forgot. Um…I still owe you a nice dinner. And maybe…a long talk." She thumbs over her shoulder toward the Audi. "I have to babysit her until Wednesday after lunch. She probably won't be very good company. Stick around for a couple days?"

Edik smiles. "Gladly. You'll need someone to talk to, someone who understands what you've just gone through." He raises his right hand. "I volunteer. It's the least I can do for my shield maiden."

"Knock that shit off." She doesn't say it with as much heat as she thought she would. "I never want to see this place again. Let's go."

Chapter 66

BARCELONA INTERNATIONAL AIRPORT

The floor-to-ceiling windows at the end of the VIP lounge reveal a forest of private jet tails stretching for what seems like kilometers toward Barcelona Airport's runways. Even though the hardstand is nearly full, Tiedown 49—less than a hundred feet from the Executive Terminal—is somehow empty except for a ground crew and tanker truck standing by.

Carson stands next to Vicki, half-watching the show outside and half-trying to figure out what's going on inside the woman. Her face is perfectly made up and completely unreadable.

It's been that way since the three of them checked into the BAH Barcelona Airport Hotel on Monday night. Carson booked a two-bedroom suite for herself and Vicki; Carson needed to keep track of Vicki all the time, but didn't need to sleep next to her. Edik got a deluxe king room down the hall.

Vicki has been quiet and withdrawn ever since she climbed down from the tower. She refused to go anywhere near the kitchen in Villa 1; then again, Carson avoided it as much as she could, not needing to keep seeing Sebastian's body. Vicki refused all help packing and sat in the Audi's passenger seat for over an hour until Carson drove them to the airport. Carson hasn't seen Vicki touch her phone—it must be torture for her.

Defeat? Mourning? Guilt? Carson's tried to get her to talk, but Vicki just gives her a grim non-smile and maybe nods. Other than to eat, the only time she left the room before today was to go to the hotel's pool and read a fistful of free business magazines in four different languages. Carson let her go alone. She figured Vicki wouldn't get far in a bikini and mules.

An airport tug tows a white Gulfstream down the aisle toward the empty tiedown. Carson checks her watch: right on time. The aircrew wouldn't dare be late, considering who their passenger is.

Vicki sighs. "I reckon it's time to go." She brushes a bit of imaginary lint from the lapel of her beautiful business suit. It looks like a master tailor sewed it on her. The only surprise is that it's jet black. It's the first time Carson's ever seen Vicki wear anything other than white.

"In a few. After they refuel." She glances at Edik, who's sitting next to the lounge door. Not exactly a guard, but someone to slow Vicki down if she tries to run. "Edik? Can you give us a minute, please?"

"Of course." His eyes flick from her to Vicki and back, then he nods and ducks out the glass door. He's been a great sport these past couple of days. He, too, tried to engage Vicki, and he put up with the silent shadow at the table when they ate out. The more time Carson spends with him, the more she likes the guy.

Carson says in Russian, "If there's anything you want to say, now's a good time."

Vicki tries a smile and almost pulls it off. "I've not been good company for you these past two days. I'm sorry. It's just…you know how it feels when something knocks all the wind out of you? That's me."

"I get it. You saw stuff…some really shitty stuff. I mean, it even got to me, and I got experience. How're you doing?"

"I can't believe it's over. Project Karma, I mean. It's been my life for two years and now it's done in an evening." Vicki makes an exasperated sound and switches to English. "Why in God's name am I speaking Russian? I'll be doing that nonstop for…for the rest of my bloody life." She chews her bottom lip. "Sorry. It's been great fun, you know. What we were doing. Both the Project Karma work and the rest—the clubs, the restaurants, Michel's yacht, staying in one place just long enough, never too long. I don't regret a minute. Well…except not noticing what Iris was about."

"Still can't believe you didn't know."

"I didn't *want* to know." Vicki lets the wave of anger pass across her face and break on shore. "I should have done. About a year past, she was poor as a church mouse when her father cut off her trust fund, but then she recovered and I didn't dare ask how."

"How come your dad never cut you off?"

Vicki flashes a sharp look at Carson. "Wherever did you get that notion? He did, near the same time Iris lost hers. I'd squirreled away a small cushion, but it was…distressing."

"That when you started stealing from him?"

"Whatever do you…?" Vicki's eyes close. "Oh. You know."

"You mentioned it. I looked up the companies you guys hacked. You were right—they're all shitbags. One's a big Russian coal company. Follow the ownership far enough and your dad shows up."

"Yes. It's an especially heinous firm, even for the coal industry. It was our test case, our first 'donor.' I only wish we'd taken more from it."

"How'd he know?"

"He doesn't. He thinks that because I didn't run home immediately to work for him, I've stolen the money he spent on my education. Though I must admit, he gave me a fright when he first mentioned it. I thought he'd sussed what we'd done."

"How'd you get out of your hole?"

"Sebastian was a dear. He skimmed a bit off the top of the Project's fees to keep me whole. After I learned to keep to an allowance, I felt very much more secure. I wasn't beholden to Father anymore." She watches the tug wheel the plain, white Gulfstream onto its tiedown.

"Sebastian was a busy guy."

"Yes, he is." She inspects the white loveseat at her feet. "Was." Vicki's quiet for quite a while, then she sniffles. "The three people I love most in this world are gone. I failed all of them. I'll…I'll have to live with that for the rest of my life."

Carson wishes she knew what to say. She never does when other people realize how bad they've screwed up, and how it's hurt the people around them. It's hard enough to know what to tell herself when she does it.

Vicki searches Carson's face for something she doesn't find. "I reckon you've had just about your fill of poor little rich girls whingeing about how dire their lives are."

"Yeah." A petty dig, but Vicki hasn't suffered enough yet. "You said to Sebastian that you need to be a better person."

Vicki nods. "Father's opinion of me may be more justified than I like to admit."

"Then switch it up. Be better. When you take over his businesses, make them play by the rules. Keep Project Karma going with company donations. Then when Celeste and Sebastian visit you in your dreams, they'll be proud of you. Online Vicki's gotta change things up, too."

"She'll need to."

The lounge door whispers open. The blue-suited VIP host, a dark-haired fashion-model candidate, says in unaccented English, "Ms. Baranova, it's time for your departure."

"Thank you." Vicki turns to Carson. "Walk with me?"

"You kidding? I'm gonna strap you into your seat."

The short walk feels like marching a convict down Death Row to the chair. Vicki stops when she reaches the automatic sliding-glass doors leading to the aircraft. Two guys like cement blocks in black suits flank the door. Vicki turns to Carson. "Would you do one last favor for me?"

"Depends on what it is."

"Of course." Vicki hands Carson her phone. "Please take a snap of me. It will be Online Vicki's last post from her old life. Or perhaps, her first from her new life. Please?"

Carson follows directions to move back far enough to get a full-body shot of Vicki standing before the bright light coming from outside. Vicki turns her back on Carson for a few moments, her head bowed. Then she swivels her body to look back at Carson. Her smile is almost as dazzling as the first one she ever gave Carson, back at Pangea centuries ago.

When Carson hands back her camera, Vicki strokes Carson's bare forearm. "Do you remember that night when you saved Celeste and I asked if you'd help me if Father did something extreme?"

"Yeah."

"I reckon this is as extreme as it can be. Can I rely on you to help me get away from him?"

Carson stares hard into Vicki's blue eyes until Vicki looks away. "You just wait on that. Like Celeste had to wait."

Vicki nods and purses her lips. "Yes. Of course." She sighs. "Please follow my Insta. I'd like to know that you'll see…whatever I become next."

Then she's gone.

"Sad to see her go?" It's Edik, standing next to Carson with another coffee cup clutched in his right hand.

"No." It's a relief. She does want to see what Vicki does with her next great adventure, though. Carson turns to face Edik. "What's next for you?"

Edik nips at his coffee. "Vlasenko's jet will be here in two hours. It was either that, or I'd be here until next week. And honestly…I didn't know how you'd feel about that. What's next for you?"

"Don't know." She tries to corral the stray thoughts roaming through her head. "I came into this feeling old and tired. My best friend told me to let myself live and feel. Did that. It feels great, but it also hurts. I need to figure that out."

He watches her stare out the glass doors toward the airplanes. "Do you need to go home to do that?"

Do I? There's a lot of shit in her head that she needs to process. "Don't know where I need to be. It just needs to be quiet." She finally faces Edik and brushes his cheekbone with her fingertips. "Got any plans?"

Chapter 67

Carson holds up her phone with the photo Edik sent her at the beginning of August—years ago, it seems. The one he captioned, "Your view."

The miniature pool and ocean on the screen blend almost seamlessly with the sparkling blue full-sized infinity pool and full-sized Mediterranean beyond.

She's finally managed to find the right place for this sunbed. According to Edik, Vlasenko and his ill-tempered mistress moved around the pool furniture while they were fighting or screwing (or both). Now Carson's found her view.

She stretches and melts a bit more into the sunbed. A gentle breeze wafts off the ocean and caresses her skin. It's almost time to turn over, but who wants to move?

Carson's been here a month. She's got a routine. She knows how to get to the nearest market; she can say "hello" and "please" and "goodbye" in Greek; and she's got a whole medicine cabinet to herself. She has her Best All-Over Tan Ever and has read almost all the e-books on her phone.

And Edik's spoiling her rotten. No one's ever done that. It's kind of nice.

She checks her news alerts and finds six new ones about Zapadneft since breakfast. Last week, *The Guardian* published highlights from a leak of over five million Zapadneft internal documents an anonymous source tipped them to. New stuff comes out every day. So far, the Danish prime minister has resigned, and two Polish cabinet ministers are under investigation for taking the company's bribes. Turkmenistan's looking into the mass-murder of anti-pipeline protestors by company-paid mercenaries. Five of Putin's cabinet ministers may be getting huge retainers for "strategic consulting." And—this makes Carson chuckle—

Zapadneft's been funneling money through shell corporations to a candidate in America's presidential election. Politicians all across Europe are screaming for sanctions and arrests.

Dareh, Karl—you guys rock.

She reaches for her beer bottle and finds it empty. That's disappointing. Getting another will mean getting up. *Later.*

A news alert on "Arboçar" takes her to the *El País in English*. The Spanish Customs Surveillance Service has joined the investigation into the *"masacre de drogas"* in a rustic inn in Barcelona's wine country. It's official—every Spanish law enforcement agency now has a piece of Iris's mess. The story says an unidentified female foreign national is cooperating with detectives to explain how sixteen people ended up dead in what the *Mossos d'Esquadra*, Catalonia's state police, is calling an "unprecedented explosion of gang-related violence."

Carson closes her phone's browser. Celeste, Sebastian, Iris, Vicki—they've all been busy in her dreams since she came to Cyprus. Now and then when they won't let her sleep, she comes out here and looks up at the endless stars and lets the evening mist chill her skin so she can feel alive.

Let yourself live. Let yourself feel.

Did that, Bri. It was great, and it was shit. I had fun, and it broke my heart. Didn't think that could still happen. Once you start, how do you stop?

Bare feet slap on the deck to her left. She sighs, then flops her head toward the sound. Edik's strolling out of the house (*the mansion, more like*), one hand wrapped around the necks of two beer bottles, the other carrying a fresh squeeze bottle of SPF 50.

He lets her select the bottle she wants, then bends to kiss her. When they break the kiss, his eyebrows bunch. "You look serious."

"Yeah, I guess."

It's amazing he put up with her when she first got here. She didn't want to go anywhere or be around strangers. They talked almost nonstop, telling each other everything about their histories, the people in their pasts, the things they've done that they still regret. They worked out together in Vlasenko's over-equipped gym, held the Fairtex heavy bag for each other, and sparred for hours, sometimes drawing blood. Only after a week of this forced purging of the poison in her system could Carson finally join Edik in the shower after a particularly rough workout, then follow him to his bed.

The sex is nice enough, in large part because of the trust they've built with each other. Edik's sexual history has mostly involved farm women and prostitutes. Carson's been trying to gently break his bad habits. It was a shock when she figured out she's trying to teach him how to make love like Sebastian. She'll never tell him that, though. It's hard enough to admit to herself.

"You are okay?" Edik says in English. They've been working together on his English. He still has a way to go.

"Yeah. Just, ghosts."

"Yes. I know of ghosts."

Carson takes a long draw from her new beer, then sits up to lower the back of her sunbed. She snaps the waistband on his black swim trunks. "You know the score. You wanna see me naked, you gotta be naked, too."

He chuckles, then skims off his swimsuit. If there's more than two percent body fat on the man, she hasn't found it yet. He's lean and wiry, with lots of definition. His tan contrasts with the pink scars scattered all over his body, including the mass of shiny tissue covering his left leg.

Then again, Carson's got her own scars. He doesn't seem to mind them.

Edik perches on the edge of her sunbed. He slaps her hip. "You. Turn over."

She spins around and flips onto her stomach so she can stare at the Mediterranean. He rubs sunscreen onto her shoulders and back. Not nearly Sebastian's technique, but it feels fine.

"You are happy?" he asks.

Am I? With Vlasenko gone, they have the run of the place. She lives in a seaside mansion with a nice man who thinks she's the sexiest woman in the world. The weather's beautiful, the people are kind, and there's plenty to do if she wants to. Or she can simply lounge and read and watch the light change on the water, something she's become very fond of doing.

She's *content*. It's been a long, long time since she's been content. *Could this be my life? Settle down with Edik, love him, make a life with him? Can I give him what he wants, whatever that is?* She'd love to say *yes*, but can't. She can't say *no*, either.

Let yourself live. Let yourself feel.

"I will be until you stop what you're doing." A cop-out, but it's the best she can do now.

He chuckles. "I not stop then." He goes to work on the small of her back.

Carson sighs contentedly. She plugs in her earbuds and starts her phone's music player. Celeste's ocean symphony fills her head, then her heart, with peace and wonder and, finally, love.

THE ADVENTURE CONTINUES...

<u>DOHA 12: An International Thriller</u>

Jake Eldar's and Miriam Schaffer's names may kill them.

An assassination in Qatar thrusts twelve innocents into the crosshairs of a hit team bent on revenge. But two of them refuse to die quietly.

"*Doha 12* is an exciting and hard-to-put-down read of fiction, not to be overlooked." – *Midwest Book Review*

Buy DOHA 12 today at your favorite online bookselling site!

LIKE WHAT YOU READ?

Share your experience with friends! **Leave a review** on your favorite online bookselling site, on a readers' social network (such as Goodreads) or promotion site (such as Bookbub), or just on your blog or Facebook wall. Someone told you about this book; please pass on the favor.

ABOUT THE AUTHOR

Lance Charnes has been an Air Force intelligence officer, information technology manager, computer-game artist, set designer, *Jeopardy!* contestant, and is now an emergency management specialist. He's had training in architectural rendering, terrorist incident response, and maritime archaeology, but not all at the same time. Lance's Facebook author page features spies, archaeology, and art crime.

Official Website
https://www.wombatgroup.com
Sign up for Lance's newsletter! Be the first to find out about new books, special deals, and the occasional giveaway.

Facebook Author Page
https://www.facebook.com/Lance.Charnes.Author

Goodreads
https://www.goodreads.com/lcharnes

THE DEWITT AGENCY ADVENTURES

Carson used to have a life. Then a crooked superior in the Toronto Police Services framed her for corruption, her husband turned out to be a serial cheat, and her father didn't pay back the millions he borrowed from Gennady Rodievsky, a Russian *mafiya* godfather.

Now Carson (that's only one of her names) answers to two masters: the DeWitt Agency, which "fills needs" for not-always-honest people and organizations; and Rodievsky, the criminal she tried to take down as a detective.

Follow Carson as she shuttles around the world, dealing with friends and enemies, victims and tormentors, fighting to do the right thing in places where even the right thing may be wrong. Someday she may pay off her debts, work out her demons, and be free of a life that can kill her in an instant... but will there be anything left of her when she does?

Praise for The DeWitt Agency Adventures

"A breakneck tale where enemies and friends are often indistinguishable and the heroine's life is literally minute-to-minute. Highly recommended." – *DP Lyle, award-winning author of the Jake Longly and Cain/Harper thriller series*

"Charnes, a capable writer, crafts an exciting and alluring storyline...The author provides enough breakneck action and unexpected circumstances to keep readers entertained, while the Ukrainian backdrop is well conceived." – *The Booklife Prize*

To learn more, go to your favorite online bookselling site, or to https://www.wombatgroup.com/dewitt-adventures/.

MORE THRILLS BY LANCE CHARNES

<u>SOUTH: A Near-Future Thriller</u>

***Luis Ojeda owes his life to the Pacifico Norte cartel. Literally.
Now it's time to pay.***

In 2032 America, ex-coyote Luis Ojeda must get FBI agent Nora Khaled into war-torn Mexico with her family – and a secret that will rock the U.S. government.

> "*South* is a riveting work of action/adventure suspense that is a real page-turner… Lance Charnes demonstrates a truly impressive knack for deftly creating a complex and thoroughly engaging story…" – *Midwest Book Review*

Buy SOUTH today at your favorite online bookselling site!

THE DEWITT AGENCY FILES

Matt Friedrich has a very particular set of skills that he learned while working in a crooked L.A. art gallery, and other knowledge that he gained while hanging out in federal prison with Wall Street types who had bad lawyers. He's out on supervised release and working for $10 an hour at Starbucks to pay off over half a million in debts and restitution.

Matt's the DeWitt Agency's newest employee. The Agency "fills needs" for not-always-honest people and organizations. When a client has a need to fill that involves art in whatever form, Matt gets the project.

Follow Matt around the world, where he sees new places, meets new friends, avoids new enemies, and discovers (or pulls off) new scams. If he plays his cards right, he can make a lot of money, pay off his debts, and build a new life. All he has to do is not screw up... which is much harder than it sounds.

<u>Praise for the DeWitt Agency Files</u>

"*The Collection* is a breezy read in the way the very early Leslie Charteris' Saint novels were breezy: entertaining with an underlining of grit below the surface..." – *Criminal Element*

"Interlacing storylines give this series its charm... It's nice to have some modern *It Takes a Thief* escapism to slip away to in this world gone awry. Suffice it to say, I can't wait for The DeWitt Agency Files #3." – *Criminal Element*

"A brilliant heist story filled with fascinating art history reminiscent of Dan Brown or Steve Berry. Only better." – *Seeley James, author of the Sabel Security thriller series*

To learn more, go to your favorite online bookselling site, or to <u>https://www.wombatgroup.com/dewitt-agency-files/</u>.

www.ingramcontent.com/pod-product-compliance
Lightning Source LLC
Chambersburg PA
CBHW072045190726
48294CB00005B/1413